A TERRIBLE LOYALTY

BOOK 2

A World War II Submarine Novel

By William Roskey

ISBN: 979-8-6988-1649-2

To Carol

We are all in the same boat in a stormy sea, and we owe each other a terrible loyalty.

G. K. Chesterton (1874-1936)

Foreword

If you've read the first book in this series, welcome back! This book has been written in response to a number of readers who expressed a desire for a sequel. The first book ends on May 18, 1942. This book begins two days later and ends on January 10, 1943. A third book is underway, and I have plans for a fourth and a fifth in the series. Each book in the series is a completely self-contained novel. It is not necessary to have read any of the other books in the series to understand what's going on. However, if you like this book, you will almost certainly enjoy the others in the series. If you have already read one of the other books, you can skip ahead and begin reading Chapter 1.

If you haven't read the first book in this series, this foreword will provide you with a little background about the submarine war in the Pacific in World War II, which is one of the most important and heroic chapters in the annals of military history. When the Pacific Fleet lay largely destroyed on December 7, 1941, submarines were the only way the United States had to strike back in the desperate early months of the war, as the Japanese won victory after victory. American submariners fought against overwhelming odds far behind enemy lines with unreliable torpedoes. One submarine in five never returned. Theirs is a story of indomitable courage and incredible skill that needs to be told in every generation.

Submariners in the early stages of the war were plagued by repeated torpedo failures. It took a long time to discover that there were three problems. First, the torpedoes were running about ten feet deeper than their settings. Most submariners figured this out fairly quickly, but until August of 1942, the Bureau of Ordinance continued to insist that they *were* running at the set depths. Second, the new Mark VI torpedo exploders, highly touted as a wonder weapon by BUORD, were producing dismal results. Most exploded either prematurely or not at all. Despite submariners' deep lack of faith in the Mark VI exploders, BUORD continued to insist that nothing was wrong with them. Finally, on June 24, 1943, Admiral Nimitz ordered that the Mark VI magnetic influence exploder be deactivated on torpedoes in use by the Pacific Fleet. BUORD remained unconvinced that there was a problem, however, as did Admiral Ralph Christie, who commanded submarine operations out of the Australian ports of Brisbane and Fremantle, where it was in use well into 1944.

Third, while the contact exploders used at the beginning of the war were far more reliable that the Mark VI magnetic influence exploders, there were still some problems with them. When the problem was finally discovered, it proved to be a simple fix—replacing their firing pins with newly designed ones made of a stronger, lighter material, but this solution wasn't discovered until the summer of 1943.

In the definitive two-volume history of American submarines in World War II, *Silent Victory: The U.S. Submarine War Against Japan*, Clay Blair, Jr. wrote, "The torpedo scandal of the U.S. submarine force in World War II was one of the worst in the history of any kind of warfare."

Since this is a novel, I have taken the liberty of making a change in the use of capital letters in acronyms that were in use in WWII. In those years, the Commander-in-Chief of the Pacific Fleet was CinCPac and the Commander of the Submarine Force in the Pacific was ComSubPac. I have used CINCPAC and COMSUBPAC respectively, because those are the acronyms familiar to nearly everyone today. I have done the same with BuPers and BuOrd (thus BUPERS and BUORD). For a while, BUPERS was NAVPERS, but BUPERS lives again. BUORD expired in 1959, its functions and personnel transferred to another organization, which in turn underwent a number of other organizational changes. It should also be noted that, during WWII, and up until the early 1970's, ensigns and lieutenants were often addressed by "Mister" instead of their ranks by enlisted men, particularly if they regularly interacted with those officers. During the war and up until the present day, the commanding officer of a boat appoints an enlisted man as "Chief of the Boat." This is a position unique to submarines. The COB is usually (but not always) the highest-ranking NCO on the boat. This individual serves as the chief enlisted advisor to the captain and assists him with matters regarding the good order and discipline of the crew as well as their readiness, welfare, and morale. The spellings of the place names in this book are those used during WWII. Thus, the Chinese city today known as Nanjing is spelled Nanking.

1

May 20, 1942

Pearl Harbor Naval Base

Territory of Hawaii

Slightly irritated with the interruption, Ralph Bankhead, Deputy Public Information Officer of the Pacific Fleet, picked up the ringing phone on his desk. He'd been deeply immersed in a vivid and pleasurably erotic daydream about a woman he'd been with the night before. "Lieutenant Commander Bankhead."

"Bankhead, this is Admiral Onets. Look, I've got a sub commander who's going to be awarded the Medal of Honor on June 1st by the President in Washington. Put out a press release, make his travel arrangements, and do whatever it is you people do. His name is Dade Bowie. He sank two Japanese carriers." At the word "Admiral," Bankhead had been rudely yanked back into reality. He had sat up straighter and gripped the phone harder. Onets was the Commander of Submarines, Pacific Fleet (COMSUBPAC).

"Yes sir! I'm well acquainted with his exploits! In fact, I'm the one who wrote the press releases we put out back in early March when he returned from that famous patrol. Damn, sinking the *Kaga* on January 27th and the *Soryu* three days later! It doesn't get any better than that! Two of the aircraft carriers that participated in the attack on Pearl Harbor put on the bottom of the sea in the same patrol! I received and replied to a number of Stateside news agencies asking for all the details they could get on the mission and the man. It's a story that electrified the country. There were countless articles and stories about it."

"Yes, of course. I'm well aware of that, Bankhead, but there's something you should know about Commander Bowie. This is not for public dissemination, though. Just between you and me."

"Yes sir."

"When Bowie came back from the patrol after that one—which, by the way was also extremely successful—it was evident that the man was a candidate for a complete physical and mental breakdown. I'd noticed his condition as he returned from each patrol and knew that it was beginning to deteriorate all along, but he kept getting excellent results. In fact, he's my best sub skipper. So, against my better judgment, I continued to let him go out on patrols. But, when he returned late last month from a patrol, I could no longer overlook the fact that he was on the verge of, well, as I said, a complete mental and physical breakdown. I had him examined thoroughly by a team of doctors—including a psychiatrist—and I had to relieve him on the spot as a danger to himself and his crew. The doctors diagnosed him as suffering from chronic insomnia, severe anxiety, malnutrition, extreme fatigue, rapid and unhealthy weight loss, persistent terrifying nightmares, the beginning stages of what promises to be a serious stomach ulcer, a facial tic, and frequent instances of nearly uncontrollable tremors of his hands."

"Malnutrition, sir?"

"Yes, the man got to the point where he couldn't eat or sleep most of the time. He told me he subsisted mostly on caffeine, nicotine, and candy bars. When he was on patrol and a Japanese ship was sighted, he quickly ate four or five candy bars for the sugar he'd need to go into battle. Well, the good news was that the docs said that if he took a month's leave, ate three balanced meals a day, rested and exercised, then spent a few months on shore duty, he should be as good as new. That's why we assigned him to new construction in Groton a week after the White House ceremony. By the time he's back in Pearl Harbor with his new boat, he should be fit and ready to let loose on the Imperial Japanese Navy again."

"I see. His current condition . . . . is he able to grant interviews, give speeches, and so forth? It's what we normally do with returning heroes."

"Yes, well, he's been on leave for the past three weeks, so I would think he's improved quite a bit by now, but I haven't seen him recently. I do have a man on my staff who knows him better than I do and has been in closer touch. They were roommates at the Academy and served two years on the *U.S.S. Arizona* right after graduation. Both went to Sub School together, and have been friends here at Pearl. Lt. Commander John Fillmore. I'll have him give you a call."

"Thank you, sir. I'd appreciate that." Only moments later the phone rang again.

"This is Lt. Commander John Fillmore. Admiral Onets asked me to call you."

"Yes, I'm with the Public Information Office, and I'm making the arrangements for Commander Bowie to return to the States, appear at the White House to receive his Medal of Honor, and so forth, and I'm just trying to obtain as much background about him as possible for the press releases and scheduling interviews and speeches for him. Admiral Onets said Bowie has been . . . . ah, somewhat under the weather, and I was wondering if he might not be up to some of these activities. What's your opinion?"

"Well, he's had a tough time since December 7th. In fact, he was wounded that day on the deck of his sub as he and the Chief of the Boat were firing an antiaircraft gun at the attacking Japanese planes. It was only a minor wound, but he was the first submariner in the fleet to get the Purple Heart. You might want to put that in your press release. He left on his first patrol only 12 hours later and he came very, very close to losing his boat. I saw him when he got back and he looked like a wreck. Nevertheless, it was on his next patrol that he got those carriers and some other ships besides. I read his patrol report and spoke to him about it, and I've got to tell you that it took an incredible amount of courage to do what he did."

"I'm well aware of what he did. In fact, I'm the one who interviewed him and wrote the initial press releases about his remarkable feats. He certainly deserves the Medal of Honor."

"Yes, he does. His third patrol was a triumph too. But, you see, the cumulative effects of those patrols have taken a lot out of him. And that's not all. He was John Henry Hammerhand's protégé and the old man and he were as close as father and son. You're familiar with John Henry?"

"Of course. Captain John Hanrahan wasn't only a legend among submariners, but among the entire Pacific Fleet. Quite the picturesque old sea dog. Was any of the scuttlebutt about him actually true? I mean, most of the stories were clearly myths, exaggerations, and so forth, right?"

"Well, the one about him killing a fellow Midshipman at the Academy was false. I understand that there were a number of people present who pulled him off the guy before John Henry was able to kill him. Besides, I'm told that was really a freak accident. You see, John Henry was on the boxing team. He was a heavyweight and undefeated in every fight he was ever in. That's how he got the nickname. His punches packed the wallop of sledgehammers, they all said, so his classmates named him 'John Henry Hammerhand.' Anyway—and of course this was well before my time, because John Henry was in the class of 1911—reliable sources say that one day in sparring practice, his opponent landed a blow that broke Hanrahan's nose. John Henry had had his nose broken many times before in fights, including all the street fights he was in as a kid. It was no big deal, except for this time. As nearly as they could figure out afterward, the blow sent bone fragments smashing right into a nerve that drove the big guy nearly insane with pain. They say he was like an out-of-control bull elephant and he kept trying to take it out on the sparring partner, even after the guy had hit the canvas, unconscious."

"I see. I never met the man, but the story goes that he had the eyes of a wolf. Surely that wasn't true."

"Actually, it *was* true. John Henry's irises were yellow with a bit of copper and rust tint. Such eyes are extremely rare in human beings and the scientific name for it is *Lipochrome*. He was a big man to begin with, but when he looked at you with those yellow eyes, a chill went down your spine. They weren't the eyes of a man, but of a vicious four-legged predator.

"There was always a lot of scuttlebutt about John Henry Hammerhand. Many said that, when his ship was in foreign ports, Hanrahan would switch into civilian clothes, go to bars that no U.S. Navy sailors ever went to, and pick fights with the most formidable men he could find to satisfy his thirst for violence. Some said he even beat men to death, that he *had* to every so often. That it was a dark and powerful urge that could not be denied. Some say that he killed his wife. The San Diego police suspected him of it, but the body was never found and there was no evidence. To this day, it remains a missing persons case. Who's to say how much was true? The only person Hanrahan was ever close to was Slide Bowie. Slide served under him on three different subs, the last two as XO. The reason I bring this up is that when Slide got back from his third patrol, he found that John Henry had committed suicide. It hit him hard, very hard. Slide's best friend, Ray Petro, another sub skipper, was recently lost too. Bowie's had more than enough sorrow and pressure. Then too, in subs there was a recent, ah, logistical problem that affected submarine operations. Slide was in the thick of it, and that too placed a lot of pressure on him."

"Is Commander Bowie . . . . well, is he *stable*? I have to know, because from the way you're talking, giving interviews and making speeches may not be something I should be thinking about."

"Stable? Yes, well . . . . . . I'm sure he's improving every day. I'd say he's pretty stable. Admiral Onets would never have decided to send him to new construction if he weren't. He's just been under an intense amount of pressure and is tired. Tired and, under certain circumstances, a little irritable and impatient. I'd just caution you not to say anything that might make him angry."

"Is there anything *positive* you can tell me? Anything I can use from a public relations point of view?"

"Well, he just got married on May 3rd, and he and his wife are very much in love."

"Newlyweds!" Bankhead crowed triumphantly, "And married less than three weeks ago! That's always public relations gold. What's their story?"

"Their story?"

"Yes. How did they meet? How long have they known each other? What's her background?"

"They met at a dinner I gave at my beach house about a week before last Christmas. Rachael had been a missionary in Japan for about twenty years or so, but in early 1941, three Japanese naval cadets broke into the home she shared with her husband and hacked him to pieces—a lot of pieces—before her very eyes. It

4

was a gruesome thing. Rachael left Japan and got a job with the Office of Naval Intelligence translating Japanese."

"My God, that's horrible!"

"Yes. Rachael and my girlfriend are best friends and Tracy says the suffering she went through was almost unimaginable. Constant terrible nightmares, the works. But things had been rough for her and her husband long before he was murdered. From the very beginning, the Japanese in the town where they lived had treated them badly."

"Ummmm. Does she have any children from her previous marriage?"

"No. Neither does Slide. He was married for about three years, and he doesn't have any either."

"Too bad. Children always make for good copy. You've been very helpful. Can you think of anything else that might be useful?"

"Just four days ago, they unexpectedly learned that they'd inherited more than $1.5 million when a wealthy man Slide knew back in West Texas died."

"They're now suddenly *millionaires*? The war hero and the missionary? Now we're getting somewhere! Newlyweds too. Yes. Tell me more. Anything else you can think of. What are their hobbies, their interests?"

"Slide doesn't really have much in the way of interests besides submarines. Now that John Henry is dead, no one, no one in the United States Navy, knows more about submarines than Bowie. He's also a very serious Shakespeare scholar and knows the Bard's plays and sonnets inside out, but the only other reading he does is mostly adventure novels about the days of 'wooden ships and iron men.' When she was in Japan, Rachael read voraciously. Books literally by the crate. She read philosophy, history, theology, literature, poetry, essays, everything. But, since she's been working for ONI sixty hours a week, that's curtailed her reading time considerably."

"I see," Bankhead said, making quick notes on a steno pad. "That's very useful too. Anything else?"

"Do you know how Bowie got the nickname 'Slide?'"

"No, I don't."

"It's because he's the only Mid who ever went through the Academy without the use of a slide rule. He's an *idiot savant*, born with an incredible ability to solve complex mathematical problems instantly in his head. Actually, he can solve many different problems all at the same time, and keep running solutions as the variables change. You can imagine how valuable that skill is in submarine combat."

"Yes. Anything else?"

"No, I can't think of a thing."

"Thanks so much for calling. You've been a real help. I already have the details of his sinking of the two carriers from the press releases I wrote back in March and I'll be talking with Bowie and his wife tomorrow, so I've got everything I need."

"I'm happy to have been of service."

Ralph Bankhead looked over his notes and nodded. He began a draft press release immediately.

2

May 21, 1942

Pearl Harbor Naval Base

Lt. Commander Ralph Bankhead looked at his watch and saw that it was 0755. Commander Bowie and his wife would be arriving in five minutes. Although he thought he had a lot of good copy and some good ideas for setting up interviews and outlines for speeches Bowie could give, he was still a little nervous about Bowie's physical and mental state. Especially the latter. If one read between the lines of the vague and unsettling remarks made by Admiral Onets and Lt. Commander Fillmore the day before, one could easily come to the conclusion that Bowie might be a ticking time bomb, and the U.S. Navy certainly couldn't afford to have an overwrought man suffering with combat fatigue go nuts during an interview or a speech back in the States. He frowned, then suddenly, they were there.

"Good morning, Commander Bowie, Mrs. Bowie," Commander Bankhead said warmly, standing and shaking each of their hands in turn and gesturing to the chairs in front of his desk, "Please have a seat." Although he had met Bowie before in early March after his famous patrol, it was only briefly. The man had been unusually reticent, so Bankhead had wound up writing the press releases mostly from the unclassified portion of his patrol report and the text of the citation Onets had written. He remembered thinking at the time that Slide Bowie, the most famous of the submarine commanders in the Pacific Fleet, certainly didn't look like a hero. He had been painfully thin, somewhat anemic looking, and looked like he'd been put through a wringer. And he had. But maybe that's exactly what most heroes looked like in real life, Bankhead had thought at the time. In the movies, heroes always looked strong and handsome and confident with chiseled features, like Cary Grant. But in real life, maybe they all looked like Slide Bowie. Guys you'd never even notice on the street. Average looking guys who looked tired and spent, who looked like they'd been through something they didn't want to talk about and didn't want to go through again. Average guys who had the same look as Bowie had had in his eyes then—what the war correspondents had been starting to call the "Thousand Yard Stare."

Bowie looked only slightly better since the last time Bankhead had seen him. The man stood an inch over six feet but looked like he weighed no more than 145 pounds. When Bankhead had seen him in March, the hero's eyes looked like roadmaps. Now they were fairly clear, but there was something unsettling about them. Something the Deputy PIO couldn't quite understand. Rachael Bowie wasn't at all what he'd expected either. She didn't look like a woman who had spent nearly all of her adult life as a missionary. She was 5 feet 4 inches and weighed about 140 pounds, and, although rather plain looking, there was something intriguing about her, even sexy. Behind her horn-rimmed glasses, her brown eyes flashed with intelligence and something else, something undefinable. She moved with confidence. Not with the confidence of a beautiful woman, who knows she turns heads as she walks down the street, and not with the confidence of a wealthy woman who knows she can buy any damned thing she wants. No, it was with the confidence, the ineffable *serenity*, of a woman who knows exactly who she is and who had seen enough of life to . . . . what? To understand it.

"Well," Bankhead smiled, "I imagine you two are looking forward to all that lies ahead. Meeting the President, the Medal of Honor ceremony in the White House, New London, all the exciting days ahead!"

"Yes," Bowie said simply. Rachael nodded.

"I've drawn up a tentative itinerary for you two, and I'd like to discuss it now. The White House ceremony is at 1000 hours on June 1st and you have to report to the New London Submarine Base on June 8th. "I've done some homework on both of you and I think we've got some great Sunday supplement type material for San Francisco's largest paper and for a speech or two you could deliver there. Say, one to the Rotary Club and one at a war bond rally," Bankhead began enthusiastically, and, while you're en route to Washington by train, you can make stops at—"

"I'm sorry, but I have talent neither for writing speeches nor for delivering them."

"You don't have to worry about that, sir. I'll write an all-purpose speech for you that you can deliver before any group. All you'll have to do is change the part where it says, 'I'm happy to be in . . . . . . As for your public speaking skills, well, people aren't expecting Demosthenes or William Jennings Bryan. They're expecting a regular guy who happens to be a hero. And you, sir, are both."

"Actually, I'm not sure I'm either. I think a regular guy would like all this attention, and I don't. As for the hero business, I only did what I was supposed to do. Look, all I want is for the two of us to enjoy a couple of days by ourselves in San Francisco, travel by train to Washington, via Dallas, stop at the White House,

8

then go up to Groton. Just the two of us, alone, continuing our honeymoon. Both of us need a rest. Rachael's been working 60 hours a week at ONI for over a year. I've been . . . . well, the docs say I need a rest. They were very emphatic about that. So emphatic that Admiral Onets took away my boat, told me to take leave, then report to new construction."

"I understand that, sir."

"I don't want to talk about the action I've been in."

"I understand that too. A number of our highly decorated men don't. But it's not that bad, and it helps the war effort." It was at that point that the Deputy PIO noticed a muscle spasm near Dade's left eye. He sighed and looked down at his notes. Turning to Rachael, he said, "You know, ma'am, you have an interesting story too. You were in Japan for what, twenty years?"

"Yes."

"When were you last in the States? About 1920?"

"Yes. I left for Japan from San Francisco in July of 1920. In the small fishing village where my husband and I lived in Japan, there was no electricity or running water. It was very remote, accessible only by boat. It was quite a shock when I saw Honolulu in 1941. I felt like Rip Van Winkle. The modern shops and clothing, the new cars, the tall buildings, the radio, the talkies, everything was just so wonderful and modern. Best of all, everyone spoke English and was friendly."

Bankhead smiled.

"What?" she asked.

"It's just that I haven't heard the term 'talkies' in a while." We just call them movies now. You'll find the San Francisco of today much different from the San Francisco you remember too."

"Do they still have cable cars?"

"Yes, indeed. They're just the same, but almost everything else has changed since 1920. You'll love it."

"I'm sure I will."

Reluctantly, Bankhead turned back to Dade. "Sir, if you could just give a few speeches and interviews, it would greatly aid the war effort. It's pretty much SOP for returning heroes, particularly those with accomplishments like yours. Everyone does it. In fact, two of your fellow sub commanders are helping with the morale of the home front. Commander Pulaski, winner of two Navy Crosses, is on a national war bond selling tour with Bob Hope, Jack Benny, Rita Hayworth, Betty Grable, and others. Commander Romano is in Hollywood acting as technical advisor for the movie they're making about the real life adventures of Commander Romano and his crew, and John Wayne himself is playing the role of Commander Romano. While in Hollywood, Commander Romano is giving speeches to a number of groups. It's kind of expected."

"I know about Harry Romano and George Pulaski and what they're doing. They're friends of mine. But there's a difference between them and me."

"What's that, sir?"

"I'm not going to give any fucking speeches," Dade said with an air of absolute finality.

"Yes sir, well, under the circumstances, you recovering from . . . . ah, your illnesses, I guess we can dispense with the speeches, but I would appreciate it if you'd consent to a couple of newspaper interviews. Actually, it would be to your benefit. Hotel rooms, especially good ones, are almost impossible to find in both Washington and San Francisco because of the war, but if I can sell the papers there on an interview of you and Mrs. Bowie—and I'm sure I can—they'll put you up in nice places and pick up the tab for your hotel bill and meals. For example, I have a contact with the *San Francisco Gazette*. Given your sinking of two Japanese aircraft carriers and your Medal of Honor, along with your wife's being out of the States since 1920, her life in Japan as a missionary, the murder of her husband, her working for ONI, and your being newlyweds, they'll be begging us for an interview. It would be Sunday supplement stuff with lots of photos. Like the two of you at Fisherman's Wharf, both of you riding the cable cars—"

"Wait," said Rachael, holding up her hand. "Before you get carried away, there are a couple of things *I* refuse to talk about. One is the murder of my first husband."

"I understand that it was very gruesome, but your telling of the story will help whip up public sentiment against the Japs, something that will help with the war effort."

"I would think that if Pearl Harbor, Wake Island, the Bataan Death March, and a hundred other things haven't been enough to stir the people up to fight with a single-minded fury, my little story won't make any difference. Besides, it's very painful for me to think about, let alone talk about."

"I understand, ma'am."

"Second, I guarantee that ONI doesn't like the names of their employees published in newspapers."

"So that would be out too."

"Absolutely."

"OK, ma'am, I understand. We won't mention your work with ONI or your first husband's murder. But it is OK to say that you were a missionary in Japan for twenty years and that you and Commander Bowie are newlyweds, right?"

"Yes, yes, of course."

"And an interview and photos for the *San Francisco Gazette* would be OK with you, sir?" he said, turning to Bowie.

Dade appeared to be considering it.

"Oh, Dade, let's do it," his wife said, "particularly if it means no problem in getting a hotel room."

"A *free* hotel room," Bankhead added, "including all your meals, courtesy of the newspaper."

"OK."

"Good. I'll make the arrangements. For the same reasons, I'd suggest you agree to an interview with a Washington paper when you're there."

"That's alright too," Dade replied.

"Now you said something about wanting to go from San Francisco to Washington via Dallas."

"Yes. We have to see an attorney about an inheritance."

"Oh, yes. Commander Fillmore said you've come into quite a bit of money. In fact, he said you're a millionaire now."

"Yes."

"That's a great human interest angle too."

"I'd prefer you didn't make that known. It really has nothing to do with the war."

"Are you afraid of people trying to hit you up for money if it were widely known?"

"No, it's just that it's no one's business but ours. The only reason that Lance Fillmore knows is that his girlfriend and my wife are best friends, and I guess she must have told him. He really should have known better than to tell other people without asking us first."

"OK. I have to tell you though, sir, that the Navy will only pay for your way from San Francisco to Washington. A side trip to Dallas for personal business is something you have to pay for yourself."

"I understand."

"OK, then. I'll make plane reservations for you and Mrs. Bowie to San Francisco and make arrangements for a newspaper interview there and for another in Washington. You'll arrive in San Francisco on Monday, May 25th. I'll leave it to you to make your train reservations to include the side trip to Dallas. I'll give you your tickets, travel orders, paperwork for admittance to the White House, newspaper contacts and their phone numbers, and final itinerary Saturday morning. Just stop by here anytime between 0800 and 1200 hours. Do you have any questions?"

"No," Dade said, shaking his head. "That does it for us." He and Rachael rose, and so did Bankhead.

"Good luck to both of you and enjoy your time back in the States."

3

May 25, 1942

San Francisco, California

The reporter and photographer from the *Gazette* met them at the airport and Dade and Rachael liked them immediately. The reporter, Harry Bloom, was a slightly overweight red-headed man in his early forties, and Doris Hopkins, the photographer, an attractive blonde in her late twenties. Both were friendly and cheerful, and everyone was on a first name basis in seconds.

"Look," Harry said, raising his voice above the clatter and noise in the terminal, "we know you must be tired. We were planning on taking y ou directly to your hotel, get you checked in and your luggage to your room, at which point you'll probably want a nap and a shower. How's about we pick you up at 6:00 and we have dinner together at the best restaurant on Fisherman's Wharf? The paper will pick up the tab, so don't even look at the prices on the menu."

"That sounds great," Bowie smiled. "Where are we staying?"

"Only the best. The Bayonne on Union Square. Just rest today though. The only thing going on will be dinner tonight. Tomorrow will be a tourist's eye view of the city, and we'll be taking a lot of photographs of you two. You know, riding on the cable cars, having lunch in Chinatown, seeing the Golden Gate Bridge, that kind of stuff, OK?"

"That sounds wonderful," Rachael said. "I'd especially like to see the Golden Gate Bridge. That wasn't here last time I was, and I understand it's an engineering marvel."

"That's right, according to the info I got from Commander Bankhead, the last time you were here was 1920?"

12

"Yes."

"You won't believe the changes."

Rachael looked out the window of their seventh-floor room at the dark streets below. It was almost 10:00 pm. "Dinner was nice."

"Yes," Dade replied. He was lying on the bed reading a sea faring novel set in the 19th century.

"I was so glad they didn't press me for a lot of information about my time in Japan," Rachael said. "I think they could sense that it was an unpleasant topic for me. And, of course, no one outside of submarines knows about the torpedo problem, so that didn't come up."

"And they already had all the details—at least the unclassified details—of my sinking the *Kaga* and *Soryu*, so the interview was easy on me."

Rachael laughed.

"What?"

"Oh, just some of the questions. For example, I couldn't believe it when he asked if you were afraid when you sank those ships."

Dade remembered the question well. He had immediately opened his mouth to say that of course he was, when he stopped and thought the reporter was so sincere that he deserved a more thoughtful answer. Bowie had thought for a long moment before replying, "I'm always afraid when I go out on a combat patrol. For one thing, a submarine is extremely complex, and many things can go wrong. A sub can sink even in peacetime on routine training patrols. So there's that to begin with. But in wartime, you also have very dedicated, brave, and intelligent men on the other side who are doing their level best to seek you out and kill you. This increases my fear. Then, when you actually go into battle, the fear ratchets up even more. As I'm making an approach to fire at an enemy ship, I'm so involved in arriving at accurate firing solution that the fear temporarily subsides. That's not so bad. It's probably worse for the crew than it is for me. There are times in battle when there are so many things happening so fast that I don't have time to be afraid. As the skipper, all information flows to me from all over the boat—sonar reports, damage reports, plotting data, and so on, and I have to constantly keep trying to picture what's going on all over the boat as well as what's going on up on the surface with the enemy ships. But there always comes a time when you've done everything you can do, and you just have to listen to the screws of the enemy destroyers come rushing overhead toward you, knowing their crews are trying to kill you, and you hear the sounds of the depth charges hitting the water and you wait helplessly as they begin to sink. You wait for the charges to go off, hoping that they won't explode near you, hoping that the Japs put the wrong depth setting on them, hoping that your boat can take the punishment, hoping, hoping, hoping. That's the most terrifying part of being in a submarine in combat. There are a lot of other times that scare you, like when you're hoping that the destroyers don't detect you. Those are anxious times, but the depth charging is the worst. Depth charges are what usually sink subs. Sometimes they're sunk with a torpedo or shell fire or even ramming. But almost always it's by depth charges.

"I don't know how it is with other guys, because fear is something we don't usually talk about, but I don't think that the fear ever really goes away completely. Well, once the war is over, it will, but even when you're in port between patrols, the fear stays with you. It stays with you because you know you're going out again. So you try not to think about going out again. Guys drink, chase women, read books, see movies, swim, joke around . . . . . sleep . . . . . anything they can think of to keep their minds off going out again. When it comes, it comes. But you don't want to think about it. Still, you have nightmares sometimes, and sometimes you do think about it, and when you do, you're scared. At least I am. I don't want to die, especially now. Now that I have Rachael."

When Dade had begun his answer, Harry Bloom had been scribbling in his steno pad. Like a lot of reporters in the 1930's and 1940's, Harry had learned shorthand so he could rapidly record his interviews and get people's words verbatim. But he had stopped when Dade was about halfway through. He set down his pencil with a pained expression on his face. When Dade had finished, Harry spoke.

"Well, you're certainly very honest about your feelings, Dade. But surely you realize that I can't print what you just said."

"Why?"

"Look, I don't know a damn thing about how to skipper a submarine, but I do know how to write newspaper and magazine articles and a big part of that is knowing what the public wants and giving it to them. And even though this war is only six months old, I know exactly what the public wants in its heroes. They want their heroes to be fearless, courageous, lionhearted, cool under fire, daring, and bold. They want their heroes to have a 'let me at them Japs' kind of attitude. They sure as hell don't want to have a hero who is afraid."

"Dade *is* courageous," Rachael said angrily. "My God, going out there and risking your life time after time when the odds are against you, even though you're very afraid is the very definition of courage. Can you really believe that men who perform heroic acts aren't afraid?"

"No, Rachael. No, I don't believe that. I've never been in combat and hope I never will face death like our men in uniform, but I understand that most of them have moments of fear. It's just that Dade seems to be saying he's afraid most of the time, and that, well that doesn't sound like a hero talking. I mean," he quickly held up his hand as Rachael opened her mouth, "I mean people don't want to hear that. They want to hear something gutsy, something inspirational. Like . . . . . like a few days before Wake Island fell, when the command in Hawaii asked what they needed, and they radioed back, 'Send us more Japs!' That's the kind of thing I'm talking about."

14

"That," Dade said, shaking his head, "never happened. There was a mistake in decrypting a routine Wake message in Pearl Harbor, a radioman repeated it to a couple of friends, and the bogus story was spread far and wide."

"Are you sure?" Bloom clearly didn't want to believe Bowie's explanation.

"Positive."

"But the whole country knows about the message. It's inspired so many people, made them proud of our fighting men."

"And there's plenty to *be* proud of, Harry. Those Marines were very brave men. My sub put into Wake Island on December 12, the day after they'd successfully fought off a Japanese invasion force with their coastal artillery. My skipper met and talked to their commanding officer at length. He said it was one of the most inspiring moments of his life. He told me afterward that now he knew what it would have been like talking to Colonel Travis at the Alamo or to King Leonidas at Thermopylae just before the final battle. The Marines at Wake knew that no help was coming. They knew they were just as doomed as the men of the Alamo or the 300 Spartans. Yet they were determined to fight until the last. Fighting until their ammunition ran out, then fighting with bayonets, rifle butts, rocks, and their fists. Their commanding officer said to my skipper, 'We'll all go down fighting. The Japs will win, but, when the smoke clears, they'll know that they were in a fight.' Now that's real courage and that actually happened."

"Sure," said Bloom, "I hear what you're saying," spreading his hands. "Sure, that's an inspiring story, but it only goes to prove my point. The Marine commander didn't talk about being afraid."

"Harry, that's understood. It goes without saying, especially from one fighting man to another. The whole point is that the Marines were determined even though they were afraid. That's what made them heroes. Look, when I go to sea, there's always the possibility the crew and I will return to port safe and sound. The Marines on Wake Island didn't have that possibility. They knew they weren't going to make it. Can you even begin to imagine how much more courage it takes to fight when there's no hope of winning?"

"Look, I get what you're saying; I really do. But, believe me, people want heroes that are larger than life. Talking about how you were always afraid—"

"And I'm still afraid. Afraid of going back into combat," Bowie interrupted. "I'll go, of course, but I'm afraid."

"Yeah, that too, let's just tone it down a little bit, OK? I mean, I have no problem saying you were apprehensive as you sailed into battle, but let's not make a big deal about it, OK?"

Dade frowned in frustration and looked at Rachael. She inclined her head almost imperceptibly. Dade sighed in defeat and nodded to Bloom. "OK, Harry, you're the reporter, and like you say, I guess you know what the people want."

"So how did you two meet?" Doris asked brightly, in an attempt to steer the conversation to a less contentious subject.

15

"At a dinner party," Rachael smiled. "Back in December. In fact, it was December 19th. Dade had just come back from his first combat mission. I was taken with him from the very start."

"Love at first sight?" Harry asked lightly.

"No, but love came shortly in the days that followed. I suppose there are some who might say that I'm robbing the cradle because of our *vast* (Rachael playfully emphasized the word) age differences, but I don't care. You see, Dade turned 32 in May and I turned 40."

"Sometimes she kids me about that," Bowie smiled. "It wasn't love at first sight with me either. It wasn't until we talked a lot about our lives and our beliefs that I could see Rachael was someone very special. She was so open and honest. And smart. She's very smart, you know. When she was a missionary, the Japanese in the fishing village she was assigned to had practically no interest in learning about Christianity, except to learn enough to mock it. The village was small and remote and primitive. The villagers had a low opinion of both Christianity and white people, and there was virtually no one to talk to except Rachael's husband, who worked ten hours a day, six days a week, alongside the local fisherman."

"He believed it would win over the men," Rachael explained, "working alongside them. We wore the same clothes as they did, ate the same food they did, and spoke nothing but Japanese," Rachael said. "Then too, he was excited by trying to convert simple fishermen, because Jesus Christ himself recruited most of his apostles from the ranks of poor fishermen. He never gave up, though we never came close to even modest success. But with Tom away most of the day and the women villagers uncommunicative, I had a lot of time on my hands. Fortunately, the churches back home that supported our mission sent us regular shipments of books. One of the most wonderful shipments included 'The Harvard Classics.' It was also known as 'Dr. Eliot's Five Foot Shelf' because all 51 volumes take up only five feet on a shelf. Published in 1909, it contained many of the greatest books, essays, and plays, by Plato, Marcus Aurelius, Chaucer, Homer, Shakespeare, Ralph Waldo Emerson, Robert Burns, Charles Darwin, Dante, Goethe, Locke, Berkeley, Hume, St. Augustine, Edmund Burke, Cervantes, Pascal, Milton, Benvenuto Cellini, Sophocles, Benjamin Franklin, Adam Smith, Machiavelli, and so much more. At my urging, the churches back home kept me well supplied with lots of other books, especially books on history, philosophy, anthropology, and literary classics. I read many of the books two or three times. My husband had, of course, little time to read because he worked on the fishing boats all day, so the Bible was basically all he read. I read a lot in the years I was in Japan."

"Before I met Rachael," Dade said, "I thought that—as a graduate of the Naval Academy—I was well educated. But I quickly began to feel like an ignorant hick."

"Dade *is* well educated in mathematics and engineering," Rachael said, "and he knows a lot more about the humanities than most people."

"Just far less than her," Bowie added.

"Humility is one of his traits," she said. "He'll never mention it to anyone, but he's quite the Shakespeare scholar; he knows everything the Bard wrote, most of it verbatim."

"Fascinating," replied Harry Bloom. "Your first husband, where is he now?"

"He passed away in early 1941, which is when I left Japan for Hawaii. Once there, I got a job as a file clerk in the personnel office at the Pearl Harbor Naval Base."

"So you were in Japan for 20 years?" asked Doris. "It sounds like it was rough."

"It was. If I had known what it was going to be like, I never would have gone."

"But why did you and your husband stay so long if it was so bad?"

"Tom never lost faith, never lost hope. He felt that we were called on a sacred mission from God, and that we just had to keep trying. I was ready to give it up as a lost cause a number of times, but Tom always had faith."

"Wait a minute," Bloom said suddenly. "I just figured something out. You two met for the first time on December 19th, last December?"

Both nodded.

"And you got married in May?"

"May 3rd," Rachael said.

"And during that time, Dade went out on patrols?"

"Yes, two patrols," Dade said.

"And submarine patrols last, what? A month or so?"

"It varies," Dade answered, "depending on how quickly your sub uses up its fuel and torpedoes, how much damage it sustains, and so forth, but the average submarine patrol is about two months."

"So, from December 19th to May 3rd, you were at sea for four months?"

"A little less. My last patrol ended after only about five weeks. I got lucky early and used up all my torpedoes sinking the ships in a convoy, so we returned early to rearm."

"Dade sank the whole convoy," Rachael said proudly.

"Still, during that very short time period between your first meeting Rachael and your getting married, you were at sea for over three months?"

"That's right."

"And even when Dade was in port, I had to work six days a week, so we only had evenings and Sundays to be together," Rachael added.

"That's incredible!" Bloom exclaimed, "how the hell could you have possibly gotten to know each other well enough in that short time to take such a big step?"

"It's the war," Rachael said simply. Then, when Bloom and Doris simply looked confused, she added. "Oh! Evidently they don't say that Stateside. We say it all the time on Hawaii as shorthand for why so many things are the way they are now. Why life isn't as it was before December 7th. I guess it's different here in the States, but the war has touched everyone in Hawaii, military and civilian, in many everyday ways. Once pristine beaches now have barbed wire and foxholes on them. We're under martial law. We have curfews, blackout curtains at night, and there are many shortages and inconveniences. There is still the possibility that the Japanese will attack again, perhaps even invade, although the latter probably won't happen. We see our subs and other warships sail out, and many of them don't come back, so, to us, the war is very, very real. We say, 'It's the war,' to comment on a lot of things, from rationing, to roads being closed, to well, in the case of men and women and love and romance now being very different. You see, Dade and I and so many like us know we don't have much time. In fact, with Dade being at sea most of the time, a traditional, leisurely courtship was out of the question. When Dade is at sea, we can't even write to each other. He's gone for two months at a time and we have no way to communicate. When he's in port, we have only nights and Sundays together because of my job. We have to make use of every available second. In addition, we never know if Dade is coming back at all when he goes out. We've been losing a lot of submarines."

"How many?" said Harry, with interest, as he picked up his pencil.

"That's something the Navy doesn't really want to have publicized, Harry," Dade said. "Not only the exact number, but the fact that we're taking heavy losses. You know, 'detrimental to morale on the home front.'"

"Yeah, that's a phrase the War Department has used before with newspapers. We're used to it."

"Rachael only mentioned that to make a point about the effect of war on love and marriage."

"I understand what you're saying, Rachael," Doris Hopkins said, "but it seems like you could barely have gotten to know each other before deciding to get married."

"Oh, but we did," Rachael responded. "We talked about everything under the sun. We told each other the stories of our lives in great detail. We spoke about our likes, dislikes, hopes, dreams, regrets, and the things we'd done that we were ashamed of. We told each other everything."

"'Everything?'" Bloom said, eyebrows raised.

"Yes. You see, I have a theory. I think that most relationships that fail do so because one of the people finds a flaw in his or her potential lover that is a deal breaker. Something that, had he known it at the outset, he would never have entered into the relationship to begin with. Every human being is flawed, of course, and we all have our secrets. Things we've done or felt or said that we're ashamed of. I believe that, if a couple is absolutely honest at the beginning of a relationship, that if they tell the other person *everything*, that one of two things will happen. First, if one or both, decide that something the other person has done, is something that's beyond the pale, they split up and go their separate ways, and they've wasted no time or heartache. They're free to go out and find people they *are* compatible with. Second, if they find they *can* live with each other's flaws, then there will be no unpleasant surprises ahead and their relationship will be successful."

"'*Everything*,'" Bloom said dubiously. "But surely everyone is entitled to some secrets?"

"Of course, but there should be no secrets between you and someone you want to be your lover for the rest of your life."

"I don't know. That *sounds* like it makes sense, but it doesn't seem to me that could work in real life."

"I felt the same way when Rachael sprung it on me, but it does work. At least it works for us. We did disagree at first on whether to wait to get married. I was reluctant to, because I was afraid of making her a widow so soon after she'd already lost one husband. We also want to have children, and I was especially afraid of leaving Rachael behind with a child there or on the way. The only life insurance I have is the standard $10,000 GI policy. That was before we came into some money. Then too, I didn't want to leave her behind to raise a child on her own. I wanted to wait. To wait until the war was over."

"But I told him that, while that sounded noble, it was stupid. For one thing, some of the top military strategists say this war could last until 1947. For another thing, he could be killed and there would be no future at the end of the war for us. I'm a big believer in the writings of the Stoic philosophers, especially Marcus Aurelius and Seneca. You can't postpone living until some future point. Each of us is born with a certain, finite number of moments to live, and we don't know what that number is. We only know that we can live each moment only once, that the past is unalterable, the future unknowable, and that all we have is the moment we are living in now. Time is the one possession we can't get more of, yet we treat it as if we have an infinite or near infinite supply. If we lose or spend our money, we can earn more. If we lose our clothes or car or other possessions, we can replace them. But we cannot add to the amount of moments we have to live. They are constantly being used up with every tick of the clock, and, once gone, they are gone forever. Seneca said, 'Begin at once to live, and count each separate day as a separate life.'"

"You're a remarkable woman," Bloom said.

"She is that," Dade agreed with a smile.

4

May 26, 1942

San Francisco, California

Dade, Rachael, Harry, and Doris had begun the day with a sumptuous breakfast at the hotel, and the weather cooperated beautifully with their day of sightseeing. It was a sunny 72 degrees as they visited the Golden Gate Bridge, went on a walking tour of Fisherman's Wharf, went on a harbor cruise (during which they sailed closely past the famed maximum-security prison Alcatraz), walked around Chinatown, and shopped a bit in some of the most upscale department stores. They travelled the hilly streets mostly by cable car, and Rachael enjoyed every moment. After walking Lombard Street (the crookedest street in town, which has eight hairpin turns in a one-block stretch), they took a cab to a steakhouse Harry knew off Union Square for dinner. Doris had taken a lot of photographs and it had been a fun day for everyone.

After they'd ordered, Harry took out his notebook and pencil. "I hope you don't mind a few more questions for the article, Dade."

"Not at all."

"I've been wondering since last night. What is it that gets you through combat and the fear? Where do you draw your strength from?"

"That's a tough question because there's no single thing," Dade replied slowly. "One thing, of course, is that I took an oath when I entered the Academy that I would protect and defend the Constitution of the United States. So there's that. I gave my word to do this. Another reason is that my country was viciously attacked and that angers me and I will fight to defend my homeland. I fight because Japan is and has been on an evil course for some time now, murdering many innocent people in many countries. In addition, I want to make sure that the world will be safe for me and for Rachael and for the children we plan to have. I've lost friends in this war. I overcome my fear every time I have to because I have to be able to respect myself as a man who does the right thing, regardless of the cost. Because I have to live with myself. I fight because I want Rachael to be proud of me. I fight to protect Western culture and civilization and law. When I'm actually engaged in combat, I fight because I want to go on living. I fight because I'm very, very angry. I don't know. There are so many things I draw strength from, and I'm not sure I could rank them in order of importance."

Halfway through Dade's exposition, Bloom had put down his pencil, just as he had the night before. "That's a pretty complicated answer. I wonder if you think too much. Hell, most guys would probably say, well, something like, 'I'm fighting to protect the country I love and my home and family.' I mean, that's what most of our returning heroes say. In fact, pretty much word for word. To the average Joe, it's as simple as that."

"I was just trying to give you a complete and honest answer."

"And you did, but, look, to the average person—and, believe me, as a newspaperman, I know the average person—things are a lot simpler than they seem to be to you. Ask an Englishman why he fights, he just says, 'for King and country.' Since we don't have a king, Americans, most of them, just shorten it to, 'for my country' or 'for freedom.' Look, I'm sure you wouldn't mind if I condense some of your remarks. I'll get the gist across, but we don't need to go into a whole soul-searching exercise."

"No, go ahead and condense. I don't mind at all. It's not as if I think my words are the wisdom of the ages. I'm just a guy who's oftentimes not exactly sure of why he does certain things. Maybe I do think too much. Maybe things are as simple as you say."

"Well, most of this article will focus on Rachael anyway. If it was just you, I'd devote maybe five column inches to your story, with maybe one head and shoulders photo of you. But Rachael is the real human interest story here. She hasn't been back to the States in over two decades! Not only that, but she spent most of that time living in extremely primitive conditions in Japan. Isolated in a fishing village. No electricity, no running water, no nothing. Now to return to San Francisco after all that time! Like she says, she's a regular Rip Van Winkle! It's one hell of a human interest story. Most of the story will be written about her reactions to all the changes and modern conveniences and so forth. Oh, I know she got an eyeful when she got to Hawaii, but still, San Francisco of 1942 is one hell of a big change! The photos Doris has been taking will really make the piece too. Both of you riding the cable cars, walking in Chinatown, the works. I think it'll amount to a page and a half in the Sunday supplement."

"She is having a great time. It makes me happy to see her this way. That twenty years she spent in Japan was a really difficult time for her in many ways. She deserves a good time now and for the rest of her life, and I intend to give it to her."

WILLIAM ROSKEY

Rachael smiled warmly at them all. "It's been all so wonderful. I love this city. After the war, when Dade gets out of the Navy, we'll probably settle down in Hawaii, but we'll be visiting San Francisco from time to time, for shopping, plays, and the starting point of motor trips we plan to take around the United States. Both Dade and I have come to really love Hawaii—its history, climate, scenic beauty, its flora and fauna, all of it really. When the war is over, and almost all the military people and their families return to the United States, it'll be a lazy crossroads of the Pacific again. I love the smell of the frangipani, the pineapples, all the tropical plants and flowers, and the constant, the eternal lazy rolling of the surf. I guess I fell in love with Hawaii the first day I got off the boat from Japan."

"I understand the cost of living is pretty high there," Harry said.

"That's because so many things have to be imported from the States or other countries," Bowie said. "Gasoline, for example, is more expensive there, as are cars and trucks because they all have to get there via a long sea voyage. There's really hardly any industry at all in Hawaii—except some light industry—so most manufactured goods are more expensive than they are here in the States."

"Living out my days in a tropical paradise," Bloom said with a wistful smile. "I could go for that. Well, I hope you've enjoyed the tour of the city. Doris and I have certainly had fun."

"It's been wonderful," Dade replied. "Thanks so much."

"It was our pleasure. It was like a holiday for us too, and the paper picked up the tab for everything, which was an added plus. So you leave tomorrow morning by train for Washington?"

"We have to make a quick stop in Dallas to take care of some family business with an attorney, and going there by train and from there to Washington would be cutting it kind of close, so we've decided to fly to Dallas and take the train from there."

"Well, good luck to both of you honeymooners, and it's been a pleasant two days."

"Thanks. If you're ever in Hawaii someday, look us up."

22

5

May 28, 1942

Dallas, Texas

They boarded the afternoon train and found their sleeping compartment, feeling not a little tired and overwhelmed. When Dade had stowed their luggage on the overhead rack, they both sat in silence for a few moments.

"That went well, I thought," Rachael said, with a tired sigh.

"It was an experience I certainly never pictured myself in. I felt like a real VIP. I expected to see Mr. Turner's attorney, of course, but not the senior partner in the brokerage firm he used, and the vice president of his Dallas bank. I didn't expect there to be so much paperwork either."

"Yes, but they were very nice. They explained everything to us in detail and answered all our questions. How does it feel to be a millionaire?"

"Well, I've had some time to get used to the idea since we got the letter. It feels really good."

"I feel the same way. If it weren't for the damned war, you could quit the Navy now, and we could buy a beautiful place on Kauai, and just let the world go by. Dade, do you realize how much money we have now? I mean by comparison. I checked. The average salary in the United States is $1,885 a year. A new car costs $1,100. A brand-new big house costs less than $7,000. And what, your Navy pay as a commander is about $330 a month?"

"Actually, it's $335.42, not counting quarters allowance."

"And now we have $1,542,106.23"

"Yes, and like you said, if it weren't for the war, we could do anything we wanted now."

"At least we'll be able to live very well now, even in the Navy."

23

"Yes, we'll find a nice house to rent in New London or Groton and hire a cook and housekeeper. We can buy a new car and pay cash for it. We'll take trips on the weekends to New York City to see Broadway shows and the museums."

"And, all too soon, we'll be back in Hawaii and you'll be going out on war patrols again," she frowned suddenly.

"Don't think about that until it happens."

"You're right, of course. Seneca said, 'They lose the day in expectation of the night, and the night in fear of the dawn.'"

"Meaning to live in the moment we have?"

"That's right. He said, 'True happiness is to enjoy the present, without anxious dependence upon the future, not to amuse ourselves with either hopes or fears, but to rest satisfied with what we have, which is sufficient, for he that is so, wants nothing.'"

"Let's make a pact to do just that. We have months before I'm back at Pearl on combat patrols. Months. Let's make use of every moment."

They made love twice that night, the vibrations and soft rhythmic bumping of the train as it sped through Texas and northern Louisiana only serving to heighten the experiences. Dade slept late the next morning, finally waking around 8:30 am to find Rachael staring pensively out the window.

"What's up?"

"Oh, I've been staring out this window since sunrise, just watching and thinking. We're almost through Mississippi now and into Alabama. I've been watching so many types of scenery go by, so many small and medium-sized towns. I guess I forgot how truly vast our country is, its beauty, its . . . . . grandeur. And I've been thinking that I've been wrong about the war. All I've wanted all along is just for you and me to be out of it. God knows you've already done more than your share, and I don't want to lose you. Back in Hawaii, when I tried to talk you into taking your inheritance and us going to Argentina, buying a cattle ranch, and just letting the world go by, just let us alone, I wanted that with all my heart."

"Or you thought you did. I don't think you could have respected me if I'd deserted my country in time of war. I couldn't have respected myself."

"Well, you made your choice, and now I believe it was the right one. Traveling across the country from San Francisco has been quite an experience. The mountain ranges, the prairies, the deserts, the farmland, the rivers and valleys and cities and towns, they make me feel that we're a part of something big and wonderful and beautiful and important. You and I have been part of this war, not only from the beginning, but before the beginning. The Japanese militarists murdered my husband ten months before Pearl Harbor and I was translating intercepted Japanese messages in ONI months before Pearl Harbor. You've been with the Pacific Fleet for years, preparing to fight them. We've been in it from before the beginning. But these people," she gestured at a small town they were passing, "the people in all the towns all over the country, they're all in it now too.

24

So many of them have already gone now, and so many more will go. Even if we never had before, now we share a kinship with them. I guess what I'm saying is that I feel more American than I've ever felt in my life. We're all interconnected now, Dade. We all owe a tremendous loyalty to each other, to our country. As I've been looking out this window for the past couple of hours, a phrase came to me, you know, that one from Sir Walter Scott, 'This is my own, my native land.'"

"Back in Hawaii, when you were telling me we'd done our share, that the United States didn't need you or me to win the war against the Japanese, you said that a lot of Americans wouldn't do their share. That, while millions of men m ight serve before the war was over, most wouldn't. They'd neither volunteer nor be drafted, and that a lot of people on the home front wouldn't do their share either. You also said that I was a chump because I didn't realize that, while I loved my country, my country didn't love me back."

"I never said you were a chump. And, while it's true that many millions of American men will never fight in the war, and that millions on the home front will do little more than maybe buy a war bond, that doesn't make t hem bad people. This journey has made me reevaluate the things I said in Hawaii. The overarching thing on my mind was the fear of you being killed in combat. It colored the way I thought about the war and it colored what I said to you. I was wrong. I' m still terrified about losing you in battle, but now I know that we have to fight this war, to see it through to its conclusion, no matter what the cost. And I'm very proud of you."

Dade considered all she said for a moment and marshalled his own thought s before speaking. "America is a vast and beautiful country, but mountains and prairies and valleys are things, and things are not worth dying for. What I'm fighting for is freedom. The oath I took was to protect and defend the Constitution of the United States. To me that's what the war is about. Freedom of Speech, Freedom of Religion, and the rest of the Bill of Rights. As for fighting for the country itself or our countrymen, I don't know. Mr. Turner and I were talking about patriotism one day and he quoted something Mark Twain said. 'Any man worth his salt will fight to defend his home, but only a fool runs out into the street to fight for his boardinghouse.' Yes, I love the country itself, but, as for me, I'm fighting for ideas."

"And to prove to yourself that you're a brave man," Rachael said sadly, "when it's so unnecessary. You've already won the Congressional Medal of Honor, Dade."

"You don't understand. Just because a man conquered his fear yesterday and the day before, doesn't necessarily mean he can do it today or tomorrow."

"So you feel you have to keep proving yourself to yourself." She shook her head. "Well, we've been over this ground a million times, and I've never been able to disabuse you of that strange notion. All I can do is pray that it won't get you killed."

"Like I said last night, let's not even think about what may or may not happen when I go out on combat patrols again until we're back in Hawaii."

"Yes. We agreed to that."

6

June 1, 1942

Washington, D.C.

The Washington newspaper reporter assigned to cover Dade and Rachael was able to secure a room for them in the Plymouth Hotel, despite the wartime shortage of available rooms in D.C. The clout of the reporter and his paper, along with th e fact that Bowie was in town to have FDR hang the Congressional Medal of Honor around his neck in the Oval Office, was all that was needed to secure a modest third-floor room. The hotel was old, famous, and elegant, and the White House was only a short walk away.

At the guardhouse where they'd been told to report, the uniformed Secret Service officer asked for their identification. Rachael smiled, remembering how, when she had reported to the Office of Naval Intelligence at Pearl Harbor on what was to be her first day of work, she'd had no identification except her passport. The Marine guards had given her a tough time about it, but it was all she had. She hadn't been in the States since 1920, so she really had nothing else, no driver's license (she'd never learned to drive), no Social Security card (she'd been in Japan when the Social Security Act had been passed), no membership cards, not even a library card. The Marines had been very disappointed at this state of affairs, even after they checked a list and found that Captain Huxley was expecting her. It almost seemed that they suspected Rachael of being some kind of spy.

"You don't have any other identification, ma'am?" the older salt and pepper -haired Marine asked with a sour look. "Just this here passport?"

"No, as I explained, I've been in Japan," Rachael replied, feeling like she should be apologizing.

"In Japan."

"Yes."

"Mmmmmmm. You know, the picture in this passport don't look like you at all. Looks like some young girl."

"It *is* a young girl; I was 18 years old when that picture was taken. I've been in Japan for the last 20 years. Haven't you been listening to anything I've been saying?"

"Twenty...say, wait a minute. Ma'am, this passport is no longer valid. It expired in 1930!"

"Yes, I know. The people in U.S. Customs and Immigration were quite put out about it when I arrived in Honolulu last week. They said my husband and I should have gone to the American Embassy and renewed our passports in 1930. But we just never thought to do it. We lived in a very remote fishing village on the east coast of Hokkaido, and—"

Finally, the guards had made a phone call to Captain Huxley, who sent his secretary out to meet Rachael and conduct her to his office. Well, today Rachael was prepared. She had a driver's license, a Social Security card, a valid passport, the U.S. Navy Dependent's ID she'd been issued when she'd married Dade, and her Office of Naval Intelligence credentials. The latter is what she showed the Secret Service officer. It looked a lot more official and impressive than Dade's standard U.S. Navy ID card he had just handed the man, and it showed that she was a part of the war effort too. She was secretly pleased that it seemed to impress the officer, since he seemed to involuntarily straighten up when he looked at it and gave her a respectful look as he handed it back.

The officer gave a little half-salute to both. "Welcome Commander, Ma'am." He then made a perfunctory check of the reporter's identification. "Mr. Robertson," he nodded, "haven't seen you here for a week or so. Been out of town?"

"No, this past week I've been mostly covering meetings at the War Department, and mightily uninformative they've been. All the most interesting war news always seems to be classified."

"I guess that's to be expected, sir. Now you folks just follow Officer Posito. He'll escort you to the President's outer office."

It was a glorious day in Washington, still not too hot at this hour, and a gentle breeze blew across the well-manicured, impossibly dark green White House lawn. Dade's heart began to beat faster and he noticed he was taking deeper breaths. Rachael was having the same reactions, and she grabbed his hand and held it tight. It was difficult to believe they'd soon be in the Oval Office and speaking to the President of the United States. So much was difficult to believe, she thought. When she was married to Tom what seemed like centuries ago, she thought she knew how the whole rest of her life would turn out. They'd spend their lives as missionaries in Japan, where they'd make many friends and bring many souls to the Lord. They'd have children, probably four or five, and, God willing, they'd retire and return to the United States when they were in their 60's, after a lifetime of fulfilling service to God and man. They'd live in a modest house in a quiet neighborhood in Feldspar, devoting time to the church and their grandchildren.

Now, 22 years later, her first husband had been brutally murdered, there was a world war on, and she was in it up to her eyeballs. Her second husband was a submarine captain whose chances of surviving the war weren't good, and she worked at a Top Secret job in the Office of Naval Intelligence at Pearl Harbor, where she translated secret decoded Japanese intercepts. And, yes, she was about to meet the President of the United States. Who could have predicted 18-year old Rachael Wyer from Feldspar, Minnesota would have ended up here? It must have been different for Dade, of course. When he went to the Naval Academy at age 18, he had always known the day might come when he would have to fight a war. As the years went by, it became clearer and clearer that it was practically certain to happen, and that the war would be with Japan. No matter. Now they were both in it for the duration.

They walked up the steps, then were in a large foyer. They followed the officer down an extremely large corridor, their footsteps echoing on hardwood floors. Suddenly they were in a large area with eight desks fully manned. Phones rang and typewriters clacked. "This," said the Secret Service officer, "is the President's outer office. Special Agent Binder will take over from here." So saying, the uniformed officer turned and left.

"Thank you, Larry. Good morning, folks. We'll wait here until we're told the President is ready to see us. This will be a small and relatively short ceremony in the Oval Office. The President's Naval Attaché, Captain Tykoti, will assist with the ceremony. Our official White House photographer will be taking the photographs, which he'll supply to the newspapers and, of course, to you, Mr. and Mrs. Bowie. I'll also be in the room. Congratulations, Commander."

"Thank you. Is there anything special that we're to say or do when we're introduced to the President?"

"No," the Secret Service agent smiled, "it's not like being presented to the King of England or anything. There's no special protocol. Just refer to him as, 'Mr. President.' That's it."

Then a woman with a phone to her head nodded at Binder, and he said, "Follow me." He opened a door and announced, "This is the President's Inner Office, and this is Mrs. Millet, his private secretary." An attractive woman in her early 50's, who looked incredibly efficient and confident, smiled and nodded. "Welcome, Mr. and Mrs. Bowie, and congratulations. The President has been so looking forward to seeing you." She had hardly finished speaking when a buzzer on her desk sounded and Special Agent Binder looked at them warmly. "Well, this is it." He opened another door and suddenly they were ushered into the Oval Office. Both Dade and Rachael walked in slowly, wonderingly, taking in its size, its lavish décor, and the legendary man behind the large desk.

"Mr. President," Binder said formally, "may I present Commander and Mrs. Bowie?"

"You may indeed, Zane," replied Franklin Delano Roosevelt, a warm smile on his face. "Welcome, Mr. and Mrs. Bowie. These days my schedule is always full and most of the things I have to deal with are unpleasant or tedious or difficult. Often, all three. And then there are the casualty reports I receive. The numbers are never just numbers to me. Every man killed was a fellow American, a living, breathing human being whose voice will be heard no more. The dead leave behind parents, brothers, sisters, wives, and children. And, as Commander-in-Chief, it is I who send them into battle; it is I who is ultimately responsible for making the decisions about when and where and how our men fight.

"So, when the rare happy occasions like this come along, I enjoy them to their fullest. And here we have newlyweds and I am about to confer our country's highest award for valor," he smiled. It was only when he wheeled himself out from behind the massive desk that Dade saw the President was sitting in a wheelchair. All the news photos he had ever seen of FDR showed him standing at a podium or sitting behind a desk. He had never seen the man walking in newsreels. How long had he been incapacitated? It had been reported long ago that the President had been diagnosed with polio, but there was almost never any mention of it in the press, and so almost no one gave it any thought. Of course, people wanted a strong, vibrant leader, especially in bad economic times or in time of war, and it looked like the press was helping to project that image.

"Alright, Captain Tykoti, will you do the honors, please?"

The naval attaché produced a document and began to read it in a formal, official manner. "Attention to orders. The Congressional Medal of Honor is hereby awarded to Dade Bowie, Commander, United States Navy, serial number O134904. The citation reads as follows:" The citation described Bowie's attack on the naval task force headed to Truk, during which he sank the *Kaga*, and his subsequent incursion into Truk Lagoon, where he sank the *Soryu*. Both carriers had participated in the attack on Pearl Harbor. The citation noted this fact and accurately described Dade's approach, attack, and evasion after firing his torpedoes. It also made use of phrases like "far above and beyond the call of duty. . . . . . demonstrating uncommon valor . . . . . . reflecting great honor and credit on the Submarine Service and the United States Navy." After Tykoti was finished, he and the White House photographer helped the President to his feet. During the process, the President grimaced several times in pain, but, once standing, he stood without help. "OK, son, come on over here and face away from me so I can fasten this behind your neck." Dade moved quickly to comply, and then it was done. "Now face me and allow me to be the first one to salute you."

Dade turned, the President saluted, Dade returned the salute, and the President was helped back into his wheelchair. "My dear," he said to Rachael, "in case you're wondering what that salute was about, allow me to explain. According to military courtesy and customs, all enlisted men must salute all officers, who then return the salutes. All officers must salute all higher-ranking officers, who then return the salutes. However, all people, regardless of rank, even generals and admirals, everyone, including me, the Commander-in-Chief, must salute a Medal of Honor recipient, who then returns the salute. That's how important the Medal of Honor is."

The White House photographer had taken several pictures of the President putting the medal around Dade's neck, his saluting and shaking hands with Dade and Rachael, and Captain Tykoti reading the orders. The President wheeled behind his desk and announced, "Thank you all. I'd like to spend a few moments alone with Commander and Mrs. Bowie. Please tell Mrs. Millet I'm not to be interrupted for twenty minutes unless it is a true emergency."

As the room emptied, the President asked both Dade and Rachael to take a seat in front of his desk. At first, he said nothing as he fitted a cigarette into his cigarette holder and lit it. Finally, he spoke. "The reason I asked you to stay for a while is that this war is not being fought by people my age. Instead it's your generation that's doing the fighting and bleeding and dying. My generation only sends you off to fight, and I get almost no opportunity to talk to people who are doing the brunt of the fighting. I already know a lot about both of you. In fact, I make it my business to know a lot about everyone who walks through that door before they come in. And not just ambassadors or members of Congress or industrialists or labor leaders or what have you. Everyone. I insist on knowing a lot about everyone who walks into the Oval Office and sits where you're sitting now. You'd be surprised at how much I know."

Dade and Rachael smiled and nodded.

"Mrs. Bowie, may I call you Rachael?"

"Of course, Mr. President."

"Rachael, you work in L-2 and are in a position to help me out on something that's been troubling me. I'm told that there's no way anyone could have predicted the attack on Pearl Harbor, despite the fact that we've been reading all the Imperial Navy's most secret radio traffic, as well as Japan's diplomatic messages to their embassies and consulates. Frankly, I find this difficult to believe. What are your thoughts on the matter?"

Rachael had been stunned to hear Roosevelt's mention of L-2, and the question that followed had kicked her pulse into high gear. How much did he know? How much should she tell him? He simply waited patiently, and, as her thoughts raced, his eyes narrowed. Of course, as the Commander-in-Chief, he had the right to know everything about ONI's operations; there was no question of that. But if the brass had told him that there had been no indications in intercepted radio traffic that the attack on Pearl Harbor was in the works, that simply wasn't true. Damn it, she and Tracy had told their supervisor, Paul Duvall, about 1130 hours on December 6th that there were clear indications that the Japanese were going to attack Pearl Harbor at 0730 on December 7th. They could see that he thought they were right, but he was afraid to go to his boss with their assessment because he felt there wasn't enough hard evidence to convince him. Tracy had then called CINCPAC. Admiral Van Husen was an old friend of her father who looked upon her as a favorite niece. She had tried to convince him, but to no avail. Later, at about 0130 hours on December 7th, she had called his quarters, frantically pleading with him to put the fleet on alert. What would be the harm if she was wrong? But he had angrily refused, telling her that she was not a strategist o r analyst, and he did not receive intelligence from her, but from the commanding officer of ONI.

Then Rachael saw it all again. The attack. The terrible attack that had seemed like the end of the world. She heard all the guns and bombs and torpedoes goi ng off, all the sirens and bells, all the screams of the horribly burned and mutilated men. She saw the rolling huge black clouds of smoke, and could smell it again now as clearly as she had then. It smelled of sulfur and burning rubber and burning oil and petroleum and burning flesh. There were constant WHOOSH sounds as the superheated air created winds that seemed to suck the air right out of your lungs. And there was the taste in your mouth, the taste of . . . . . of death and destruction. Rachael sat frozen in fear. She didn't want to get Paul Duvall in trouble. Despite his refusal to take the warning to his superior officer, he had, on December 3rd, gone to his boss to tell him that the Japanese were planning a large-scale military attack against American forces on December 7th. With the information L-2 had at the time, Duvall had thought the attack would be on the Philippines. Captain Huxley was unconvinced and had made a few remarks on Duvall's lack of knowledge of strategy and tactics and how the military operated in general, and told him to return to L-2 until he had some real evidence. He had been humiliated and humbled and reluctant to go upstairs again without positive, incontrovertible evidence. Rachael and Tracy found that evidence on the morning of December 6th, evidence that the Japanese were going to attack Pearl Harbor on December 7th at 0730 hours, but, although they could see that Paul was at least 90 percent certain that they were right, he would not climb those stairs again. N ot without 100 percent proof. And Tracy's frantic phone calls to CINCPAC had been fruitless. The Japanese planes had showed up at 0748 on the 7th, only 18 minutes late.

As far as Rachael and Tracy knew, the only people who knew about their warning of the attack the day before it happened were Paul Duvall and CINCPAC, and when the two women spoke to CINCPAC a week after the attack, he had asked them not to mention to anyone that Tracy had warned him. He apologized to them for ignoring the warning, but said that he was going to have enough politicians back in the States looking for a scapegoat and he was number one on their list. Tracy told her uncle she'd mention the incident to no one, and Rachael assured him of her silence too. He was terribly contrite, and Van Husen's being ignominiously relieved of command would not bring back the dead. She was all too aware that the President was still waiting for an answer. What did the President already know? Was this a test? A trap?

Roosevelt smiled. "Never mind, Rachael. The look on your face and your hesitation have answered my question. I fully intend to look into this matter further. If I may give you a piece of advice, it's this: never get in a poker game. At any rate, I want to personally thank you for the work you're doing for ONI. We're lucky to have you participating in the war effort and in such a vital and important way."

"Thank you, sir," Rachael said, flustered.

"And you, Commander Bowie, Dade, I understand not all has been beer and skittles with you. First, you're fighting a war, second, you had that problem with the Mark VI torpedo exploders. You took it upon yourself to deactivate the magnetic circuits without authorization to make them work, and almost had your ass handed to you as a result."

Now it was Dade who was suddenly feeling a rush of adrenalin as Roosevelt's words created a sudden panic. Damn! The man was right when he said he knew things about everyone who came into the Oval Office. "Ah, yes sir, I did do that and, after I told Admiral Onets that I had been doing it, he painted a bleak picture. Among the likely consequences was a stint in a naval prison and a dishonorable discharge. In my defense, I would never have been able to sink those carriers and other ships with the Mark VI as it was."

"That's true, but you still disobeyed the orders of a superior officer in wartime."

"Yes sir, but—"

FDR held up a hand. "I know, I know. Look, as I see it—and this is just between you and me and Rachael—you had two choices and they were both wrong. Frankly, if I had been in your shoes, I would have probably done the same thing that you did. But I would have been wrong too.

"Look, that's neither here nor there. The reason I wanted to talk to both of you privately is to get a sense of how you feel about the war. As I said before, the actual fighting in this war is being done by your generation, not mine. My generation only sends you off to fight. And, by fighting, I don't mean just literal combat. Women are heavily involved in this war too. Scores of thousands of women are working in defense plants building bombers and tanks and rifles. And, whenever a man goes off to war, neither he nor any of his family knows if they'll ever see him alive again. Then there's the rationing. That may not sound like a big deal to people like you two, with the sacrifices you're making, but this is the first time in history that Americans can't buy a lot of things they want when they want them even when they have the money they need to buy them. A lot of people are unhappy with this. A lot of people are *very* unhappy with the draft, and many men try to get out of it by hook or by crook. Our future as a nation is uncertain now. Oh, we'll win the war, of course, but it's going to take years. What keeps me up some nights is wondering if the American people have the fortitude and courage to carry on for a period of *years* as we spend our blood and treasure. As young American men die in parts of the world neither they nor their families ever heard of before. As many of them come home missing arms and legs and eyes. The Germans have the fortitude and discipline to do it. So do the Japanese. Do we? What do you two think?"

"Well," Dade began slowly, thinking as he spoke, "it's not as if we have a choice, is it, Mr. President? The attack on Pearl Harbor put us instantly at war with the Japanese. As for fighting the Germans, the Germans declared war on us four days later. I don't understand why they did that; I think it was a very stupid move. I mean, they were obligated to do that because of the Tripartite Pact with Japan and Italy, but the Nazis haven't shown much respect for any other treaties they signed. Going to war with us just doesn't make any sense to me. Still, they did it, so we didn't have any choice there either. And, when people declare war on you, you have no choice but to fight it until you beat them. I don't like the war. I don't like fighting the war. I hate the war. I don't want to die or become disabled. But, as I see it, we have no choice and I'm resigned to it lasting for years. I'm not happy about it, but I'll see it through until the end."

"And the men you serve with, do you believe they feel the same way?"

"Yes. Yes sir, I think they do."

"And you, Rachael, how do you feel about the war?"

"Well, of course I'm a noncombatant, so I don't know how useful my views are."

"Very useful. Women are playing a significant role in this war. Look at the job you're doing. I also mentioned the many women working in defense plants. Many women are even joining the military. None of them will be combatants, but they'll play a vital role in the war effort."

"First, I agree with what Dade said. We have no choice and we must fight until we're victorious, no matter how long it takes. The worst aspect of the war for me—and I would expect most women—is the constant worry I have about Dade making it through the war, alive and well in body and mind. But that's been the lot of women since before recorded history when primitive tribes warred against each other. If I may, I would like to tell you that Dade and I and people we know at Pearl Harbor don't agree with your 'Germany First' policy. After all, the Germans pose no immediate threat to the United States. No one can seriously suggest that there'll soon be German bombers over New York and Washington and Chicago and Los Angeles, let alone an actual invasion of the American mainland. On the other hand, the Japs *have* attacked the Hawaiian Islands, and they *have* invaded the Philippines and *have* invaded Guam and *have* invaded Wake. It's the *Japs* who are killing Americans every single day."

"Rachael," the President said with a sad, condescending smile, "it's not that simple. Global war in the mid-20th century is extremely complex. The logistics alone are incredibly difficult. Equipping and training millions of men, manufacturing rifles, tanks, fighters, bombers, ships, ammunition, and so forth to fight on two separate fronts a world apart from each other present staggering problems. We also have allies with whom we must coordinate our efforts, and there we get into the sticky realm of politics and diplomacy. I get enough criticism from members of Congress and the newspapers in the United States, let alone from Churchill, Stalin, and leaders in other countries. Our resources are finite, and we must prioritize.

"German U boats are sinking a lot of American ships in the Atlantic, Rachael. And it's vital that Britain doesn't fall. Sooner or later, we're going to have to invade the continent, and we'll need Britain for a huge staging area. In addition, we'll also need to build many air bases there from which we can conduct massive strategic bombing operations. While we don't have large numbers of our troops on the other side of the Atlantic now, our boys will be in the thick of fighting in a matter of months in North Africa." Franklin Roosevelt paused, looked directly into her eyes, and saw that she wasn't buying it. Hell, he admitted to himself, neither would he if he had a loved one fighting in the Pacific, and had seen one American defeat after another. Had witnessed the attack on Pearl Harbor firsthand and had known what the Japanese had done to the poor starving bastards on Bataan who had surrendered. He gave her an appraising look, then looked at her husband. They were both intelligent, dedicated people. Dade Bowie had shown true heroism and continued to risk his life for his country and his wife also played a vital role in winning the war against the Japanese. He had set aside this time because he truly wanted to know what their views on the war were. Why not?

"I didn't get to be the person sitting behind this desk without the ability to be an extraordinarily accurate judge of character, and, of course, both of you have Top Secret clearances. So I'm going to tell you some things we have had to take into consideration in deciding why Europe must take priority, but you must not speak of what I'm going to reveal to you to anyone. May I have your word on this?"

"Yes sir," Dade replied and Rachael nodded.

"We must defeat Germany before it can perfect and deploy a number of advanced weapons they're working on. For example, they've built working prototypes of an aircraft that uses a jet engine rather than a piston engine. It can do up to 540 miles per hour, more than a hundred miles an hour faster than the top speed of our P-47 Thunderbolts. In addition, they're making enormous strides in rockets that can travel great distances and hit their targets with extreme accuracy. They're working on other weapons as well, weapons which I can't tell you about. The point is that their industrial capacity is still considerable, and once they perfect what they call their 'Wonder Weapons,' and put them into mass production, we'll really be in trouble. You see, their scientists are quite a bit ahead of ours. It will take some time for us to catch up. That's one of the major reasons we have to beat them as soon as possible. Obviously, we can't let the general public know that because it would be devastating for morale."

"I can understand and appreciate that, Mr. President," Rachael replied, "but I have another question. I don't see a dime's worth of difference between Adolph Hitler and Joseph Stalin. Both are evil despots who enslave and murder millions. Why not stand aside and let those two fight it out? They're doing a great job of killing each other now. Why spill any American blood?"

"It's simple, Rachael. While I believe that the Russians could defeat Hitler, then Germany would become part of the U.S.S.R., and all those German scientists and the blueprints for the Wonder Weapons would be in Russian hands. And one day, someday, I believe we will have to fight the Russians. As you said, there's really not much difference between Hitler and Stalin, except perhaps that Hitler is crazy. But that means Russia would become an even greater threat to the United States. As the Red Army fights its way west, every country they go through will become a permanent part of the U.S.S.R., including Poland and Czechoslovakia. The Russians are never going to give up an acre of land they occupy. So there's that too. That's why we have to get our own troops into Germany as fast as possible. Now there are other reasons why we must follow a 'Germany First' policy, a number of them, but, as far as I'm concerned, these are the most important."

"What you say makes sense, Mr. President," Dade said, "but just remember us out in the Pacific."

Roosevelt stubbed out his cigarette in a large brown glass ashtray, and lay his cigarette holder on the tray's edge. "You may be certain of that, Commander Bowie. I think of you people in the Pacific many times throughout the day, wishing I had more resources to send you—more ships and planes and tanks and men. We've been at war for six months now, and our factories are cranking out war materiel at a fantastic pace, many working around the clock every day of the week. Our military training bases are awash in eager young men anxious to get to where the fighting is going on too. I promise I will do everything in my power to help those fighting in the Pacific Theatre, but, as I said, our priority must be Germany. I hope you understand."

"I do, sir."

"I do too," Rachael added. "In intelligence, well, I guess in all of life, you have to trust someone, and you're the man the majority of the American people chose to put their trust in. You're our Commander-in-Chief. We trust you."

"Thank you, Rachael. There's a final thing. When a man wins the Congressional Medal of Honor, it's customary to have him pick his next duty assignment. Dade, where would you like to go?"

The question was completely unexpected, and both Dade and Rachael's minds and emotions kicked into high gear.

"I already have orders to go to new construction, Mr. President."

"Yes, but I'm the Commander-in-Chief, and I can change any orders any damn time I feel like it."

This was their out, Dade thought in the sudden turmoil he found himself in. He was thinking about being an instructor at Sub School, where he'd be out of danger and come home to Rachael every night. He thought of John Henry's last job as squadron commander at Pearl Harbor. The man filling it now was only assigned temporarily. A desk job. A nice, safe desk job, where he could come home every night. There were any number of possibilities. *He could be assured of surviving the war.*

He looked over at Rachael and he could see the same thoughts were going through her mind. He owed it to her. There was no question of that. But what did he owe to his country? He remembered back in Hawaii when Rachael had tried to talk him into deserting and living in South America. "You love your country," she had said, "but your country doesn't love you back; it doesn't care whether you live or die. With the sole exception of Tracy, no person and no organization, including the U.S. Navy, gives a damn about us. To the United States government, we're simply two nobodies who have skills to be exploited. I've often met with CINCPAC, Dade. He doesn't give a damn about anyone under his command. None of them do. I don't care anymore! All I care about is that we live. I'm sick of the war and I don't want you to sacrifice your life. I don't care about anyone or anything else except us. We've done more than our share and I don't care what anyone else thinks. Fuck everybody! I want you to live! I'm tired of the war and talk of duty. I don't even hate the Japanese anymore. Well, no, I still hate them, but I'm no longer in favor of eradicating them from the face of the earth. I don't care about anything anymore except us," she had said in a tired, almost defeated voice. "The United States, will, I believe, take care of crushing Japan and its people. I've decided that they really don't need you or me to do it. I'll be satisfied with just reading about it in the newspapers and hearing about it on the radio. Actually, I don't even need that. All I want is you and me together and no one bothering us or trying to kill us."

But, since they had arrived in San Francisco, he had, he thought, noticed a change in her. She'd been doing a lot of looking and listening and speaking to people, and her home country was becoming real to her once more. She had spoken of feeling a kinship with their fellow Americans, had quoted Sir Walter Scott. "This is my own, my native land." She had said she now felt that they owed tremendous loyalty to America. Coming here had changed her. Still, he couldn't be certain of what she wanted him to do. She seemed to sense this, so spoke first.

"Of course, I don't like to see Dade going into combat. I die each time he goes out on patrol, afraid that I may never see him again, afraid that all the plans we made will be dashed to the ground to lie there broken forever. Frankly, if he dies, I wouldn't want to live. This is how I feel, and I must be honest about it.

However, I know how important this war is. I know what's at stake. Whatever Dade decides—and I think I know what it is—I'll back him completely."

Roosevelt switched his gaze to Bowie, and Bowie met his eyes. "Both Rachael and I are in this for the duration. I'll go to New London and take command of a new submarine, return to Pearl Harbor, and continue the fight."

The President was silent for a long moment before he spoke. "You know, in all wars there are some men who are decorated for valor, not so much because they had noble sentiments when they performed a certain act, but because they were so tired or hungry or cold or angry enough that they didn't care or think about the danger for a few minutes. You, sir, and men like you, are the real thing. A real hero. You know all too well that you can die out there, especially using the aggressive tactics that you do, but you go ahead anyway because of your core beliefs. You go ahead and fight hard, taking risks that few others would take. You go ahead even though I just gave you an out. My hat is off to you. You know, even though I'm a politician, I pray daily. I will say a special prayer tonight for you and Rachael."

"Thank you, sir."

7

On a Train Bound for
Groton, Connecticut

Once again, Rachael spent most of her time looking out the window as the train made its way from Washington to Groton. (Although the submarine base was physically located adjacent to the Electric Boat shipyards in Groton across the river from the town of New London, it was named the New London Submarine Base.) She seemed happy and at peace, Dade thought as he watched her from time to time from the top berth. She was, he knew, continuing to bond with her fellow Americans after having been away for more than two decades. She wore a serene smile as she watched the passing scenery, which consisted of some of the major cities on the East Coast, farms, small towns, factories, highways and roads, bridges and rivers, and forests. This was her own, her native land, and she seemed to want to gather it in with her arms and hold it tight.

Dade spent most of the time reading one of his sea adventure novels. He'd had a nightmare the night before, but he hadn't told her about it. It had been a common one for a submariner. The sub had taken too much damage, was on her way to crush depth, and there was nothing he nor anyone else could do about it. That dream had always scared the hell out of him, and he wondered how long he'd continue to have it. Until the war was over, he thought moodily. Maybe even for years after that. Well, bad dreams had never killed a man, and maybe being in New England and being busy getting a new submarine ready for combat would reduce the frequency of the dreams.

He glanced at Rachael again, happy that she was happy. She felt his gaze on the back of her neck and tuned to face him. "Is this what it's like to be aboard a submarine? The small compartment, upper and lower berths, the tiny sink and toilet compartment?"

39

"Kind of, except there are no windows, of course, there are only two toilets on a sub, and the skipper has a stateroom all to himself, although it's pretty small."

"And you live this way for two months at a time."

"Yes, but you get used to it. You can get used to just about anything, I guess. Then too, when you decide to volunteer for submarine duty, one of the first things they do is to make sure you don't have any claustrophobic tendencies and that your personality is a good fit for spending two months at a time at sea without ever seeing land, except through a periscope. You also have to be able to handle the stress of combat and be able to get along with the same small group of men, 24 hours a day, week after week. There's no going home at the end of the work day. Then too, there's always the realization that the highly trained and motivated men of the Imperial Japanese Navy are trying to find and kill you."

"And you volunteered for submarine duty."

"Everyone in the Submarine Service is a volunteer. They don't force anybody to go to sea in submarines. Not only that, but you can get out of submarine duty anytime. All you have to do is fill out a form, and they'll put you on a surface ship or another job. Their choice though. You don't get to choose what your new job is or where."

"Being on a surface ship is much less dangerous, isn't it?"

"Yes."

"Have you ever thought of transferring to a surface ship?"

"Not until my first combat patrol, when we almost went to crush depth. After that, yes, I've thought of it a few times."

"What keeps you from doing it?"

"I don't know. A combination of things, I suppose. Being a submarine officer is what I've been trained to do. I've worked hard at it for years, and I'm very good at it. I have special talents that make me a good sub skipper."

"Yes, like your ability to solve multiple math problems in your head simultaneously, but——"

"I love submarines. I love their complexity, the special challenges they present . . . . . I don't know. I just belong there."

"Just be careful. Everyone says you take too many risks. In fact, isn't that exactly what they gave you the Medal of Honor for? For going 'above and beyond'?"

"I'll be careful."

"You don't have to prove anything to anyone, especially now. Not even to yourself."

"I know," Dade said, knowing that she didn't understand and that there was no way he could make her understand.

8

June 8, 1942

Naval Submarine Base New London

Dade checked his watch as he approached the large two-story red brick administration building. He and Rachael were living in a hotel while they looked for a suitable house to rent in either Groton or New London. It was 0815 hour s. He and John Henry had been here only a year ago and the change was remarkable. Now the base bustled with thousands of men, new buildings were being constructed at a manic pace, and the base itself was being expanded from its peacetime size of 112 aces to 497 acres. Everyone moved quickly and purposefully. The original acreage had been given to the Navy by the State of Connecticut in 1868, but it hadn't become the Navy's first submarine base until 1912, and was still the nation's largest sub base, home to not only operational submarines but to Sub School. The commanding officer of the base was Captain Rory Campbell, a red-headed rawboned Kentuckian who stood 5 feet 6 inches tall.

When Bowie entered Campbell's office, he was momentarily surprised to se e the man immediately rise to his feet, come to attention, and salute him. Then Dade realized it was because of the Medal of Honor. Bowie returned the salute, Campbell reached across his desk, then the two men shook hands.

"I've always wanted to do that," the commanding officer smiled. "Salute a Medal of Honor recipient. And this was the first chance I ever had in my naval career to do it. Please," he gestured, "have a seat."

"Thank you, sir."

"So," Campbell said, as he sat, "you're here to take command of the *Sea Otter*."

"That's her name?"

"It is. She's a *Gato* Class boat. As you know, normally we'd take a third of the crew from your old boat and assign them to your new boat, but, with the war on, we've had to change that practice. Virtually all your crew will be new."

Dade frowned.

"I know, I know. But there's a war on. I did the best I could by getting *some* of your old crew assigned." Campbell picked up a list. "You'll have Armond Robhar as your Chief of the Boat. You'll also have Ensign Thomas Detrick, who, I see, is about to be promoted to lieutenant junior grade. I also got you Lieutenant Edward Milmer. As for the enlisted men, you'll have Brian Quigley, Chief Logan, Christopher Frost, and Jack Kaplan."

"Well, at least that's a good start, sir. Robhar is terrific. I couldn't ask for a better COB. Detrick is excellent too. Milmer's very capable. Quigley is the best sonar man I've come across, and Kaplan is a good radar operator. Chief Logan ran our forward torpedo room. All of them have proven themselves in combat."

"Good. Now nearly all the rest of your crew, perhaps even all of them, will not have seen combat, even the CPO's. Most of the lower ranks will not have been to sea in submarines either. They'll have just graduated from Sub School. You and your officers and COB will have to work them hard to prepare them for combat conditions. Once you finish the sea trials with your new boat and are ready to leave, if I were you, I'd run them through drill after drill all the way back to Pearl Harbor."

"Yes, sir. I plan to."

"After you leave here, go immediately to Personnel to process in. Unfortunately, there are no quarters available on base, so you'll have to find your own quarters nearby. A lot of guys do, so places are scarce and rents are high. I wish you good luck with that. Your immediate supervisor will be Captain Miles Uzbeck. His office is over on the grounds of the shipyards. Report to him this afternoon."

"Aye aye, sir."

Captain Campbell seemed to hesitate for a moment. "About John Henry. When we heard about his suicide, we were thunderstruck. You were closer to him than anyone else. Did you see it coming? Was there any indication at all?"

"I was at sea when it happened, in the middle of a two-month combat patrol. When I left, there had been no indication. When I got back to port, and Admiral Onets broke the news to me, I was as surprised as anyone else. He was unhappy with his new job as squadron commander. Everyone knew that, but unhappy enough to commit suicide? No, no one suspected that. I was with John Henry when Admiral Onets told him he was being promoted to captain and being assigned the job. John Henry was shocked and enraged. He said he didn't want the promotion or the job, that he wanted nothing more than deck plates beneath his feet. When the admiral said he had no choice, John Henry said that he was immediately going to Personnel to put in his retirement papers. The skipper had thirty years in. I remember the date, November 26th, because it was our first day back in port. Onets asked him to at least try the job for a month, and, if he didn't like it, to put in his retirement papers then. John Henry agreed, and 11 days later the Japanese attacked Pearl Harbor. When that happened, John Henry told Onets that he was in for the duration and would serve in any capacity he could contribute to the war effort, including the squadron commander position.

"After that, he made no complaints that I know of, except a few mild ones about missing sea duty. I had taken over his job as skipper of the *Elver* on December 1st, but John Henry wanted to take my place for the *Elver's* first mission, and he did. When we got back, he resumed his squadron commander job. I didn't see his suicide coming. No one did."

"There's some scuttlebutt going around that John Henry . . . . how can I put this . . . . didn't do well on that mission. That his performance was impaired by fear when the boat came under attack. Is there any truth to that?"

"I heard that rumor was going around. There's no truth to it whatsoever. I was there beside him in the conning tower the whole time. What did happen was that John Henry sustained a concussion during the depth charging and that he was a little disoriented for a while, but fear? The skipper never knew the meaning of the word."

"I thought as much. They don't make men like him anymore."

"No sir, they don't."

9

June 9, 1942

Groton, Connecticut

Dade and Rachael decided to have dinner in the hotel restaurant, and were not disappointed. The food and the service were excellent. Both had decided to have the steak, baked potatoes, and mixed vegetables.

"You know, Dade, if you'd like to have something besides water to drink, that's OK. It won't bother me. Seeing other people drink doesn't make me want to."

"You're really sure about that? We're going to be going to social functions where people are going to be drinking."

"Absolutely. There's no way I want to have to go through drying out again. It was the toughest thing I ever had to do. There are no temptations."

"Good. Speaking of social functions, there are customarily some unofficial functions for a skipper's wife. I guess now is as good a time as any to talk about that aspect of your new life. You see, when a sub is at sea, the skipper's wife is kind of the focal point for the wives of the officers who serve under him. She plans social functions and takes action if any emergencies come up. Things like injuries or illnesses or deaths, as well as personal problems like loneliness, depression, financial difficulties, drinking problems, or marital problems. The wife of the Chief of the Boat does the same for the wives of the enlisted men. The women have to know that, when their husbands are at sea, there's someone they can go to and depend on for help or advice. By the same token, the men have to know that there's someone their wives can go to."

"You said that the skipper's wife 'takes action' if a problem arises, but surely you don't mean I'd butt into peoples' personal lives. I'm a great believer in people minding their own business."

"As a general rule, I feel the same way, but sometimes you have to do that. Crews of submarines are small and everyone gets to know everyone very well. Everyone's job is important and we depend on each other for our very lives. We become kind of like a family. Just use your best judgement. Your primary focus will be on the officers' wives, and we'll be having them and their husbands over for dinner, a couple at a time, to get to know each other better. Just before the sub goes to sea, we'll have the customary big dinner party and dance for the whole crew and their wives to celebrate. That'll be in a restaurant. You and the COB's wife will make the arrangements for it and he and I will help too."

"OK. It sounds interesting. I'd like to get to know the men and their wives. I have to warn you though, I've never been a hostess. I'll have to brush up on my Emily Post. Are there any specific Navy rules I should be aware of?"

"Not really. Just be yourself, friendly and gracious. I finished all the in-processing today and have to start work tomorrow. The next thing to do is to find a house or apartment we can rent for a few months. Of course, we now don't have to worry about how much it costs. We could get a big place. Hell, we could even hire a cook and housekeeper."

"Oh, Dade, we don't need a big place for just the two of us. And I can cook and clean. I won't be working sixty hours a week like I do back in Hawaii, so it'll be a vacation. I'll have plenty of time for reading, walks, and I may even decide to do some volunteer work."

"But a rich woman shouldn't have to clean. Let's have a housekeeper come in once a week."

"There's no way I'm going to argue with that," Rachael smiled. "OK. As for finding a place to rent, I'll start tomorrow. Any preferences?"

"No, not really. Except I'd prefer a house to an apartment. A nice house with front and back yards. I've been wanting to live in a house now for years and years. Put a glider on the porch to sit on in the early evenings and watch people stroll by. Maybe put a hammock between two trees in the backyard for a nap on a nice day," Bowie said wistfully.

"I'll see what I can do. As long as you plan on setting aside enough time to work on starting our family. And that would be difficult in a hammock. Less difficult in a glider, but we should probably plan on those activities to take place inside the house."

"You're right."

10

June 19, 1942

Groton, Connecticut

Rachael had been able to find a nice house in the west side of Groton, built during the Colonial Revival in architecture in 1935, so it was practically new. It was a Cape Cod with three bedrooms, clapboard siding, a steep pitched gabled roof, and wooden shutters. Unfortunately, there was no porch on the single-story house for the glider that Dade wanted, but there was a large, beautiful fireplace in the living room. The house was close to the shipyards and on a large lot in a very quiet neighborhood. It was so unlike Hawaii, thought Rachael. Not just the trees and plants and the architecture and the climate. The people were different too. They seemed to move at a faster pace and were less friendly. Dade had explained that New Englanders were somewhat reserved and usually didn't reach out to newcomers, as they did in the South and the Midwest. Nevertheless, she was excited and happy.

The Groton Public Library, despite its size, had an excellent collection of books, and she had already checked out seven books on philosophy, history, and anthropology. Back in Hawaii, she'd had little time to feed her voracious reading habit, so she looked forward to the rest of their time in Groton. Finding a furnished house that rented by the month had not been as difficult as she had feared. The place was neat and clean and new, so they had no real work to do in moving in, aside from unpacking their clothes. Dade made arrangements for a cleaning woman to come in every other Friday, so Rachael had more than enough time to explore the town and learn about its interesting history. There had been European settlers in the area as early as 1614, but the town itself wasn't incorporated until 1705, when it separated from New London. It had a rich history, including trading, shipbuilding, whaling, and, of course, being the primary submarine base of the

46

United States Navy. Rachael had been lying on the couch reading about it when the doorbell rang.

She answered the door to find a well-dressed, young, beautiful blonde woman with a somewhat combative expression on her face. "Yes?"

"Are you Mrs. Bowie?"

"I am."

"My fiancé, Thomas Detrick, told me I had to pay you a courtesy visit. He's assigned to be an officer on your husband's submarine. He said it was a naval custom. So here I am," she said defiantly.

"I see. What's your name?"

"Alice Carney."

"Well, Alice, please come in."

"Thank you."

"Would you like something to drink? Coffee, tea, water?"

"No thank you. I won't be here long."

"Please have a seat."

"Thank you," was the stiff reply.

Rachael sat on the couch and Alice on an easy chair facing her.

"Mrs. Bowie, I want to make it clear from the outset that I am very much a free thinker, a very modern woman."

"I'm a free thinker myself, so we should get along well."

"I'm also an egalitarian."

"As am I."

"I don't think you understand. I don't approve of the Navy. Tom is in it because of the war, and I understand that. I understand that the war has to be fought, but neither one of us comes from a family with a military tradition, and, as soon as this war is over, Tom is going back into civilian life, where he belongs."

"My husband is also getting out of the Navy as soon as the war is over." Rachael said mildly, "as will many millions of men. But I'm afraid that won't be for several years. Until then, you and I and many other people will just have to make the best of it."

"One of the things I don't like about the Navy is its rigid caste system," Alice said argumentatively.

"Are you referring to the system of ranks?"

"Yes, well, not just that but the whole structure of the military subculture. The fact that officers and enlisted men are treated differently. For example, they don't have meals with each other, or sleep in the same parts of the ships. The officers have privileges that the enlisted men don't. The officers are forbidden from fraternizing with the enlisted men, as if the men were lepers or something. And I've already seen on invitations and announcements that it's 'officers and their ladies' but it's 'enlisted men and their wives.' The egalitarian in me just wants to scream. It's as bad or even worse than India and its castes. You know, where they even have a caste that's known as 'the untouchables.' I will try to fit into this military society for Tom's sake, but I sure as hell don't approve of it. But you've been in it for what? Your whole life? So you probably don't even know or understand what I'm talking about."

"There's a lot about the Navy that I don't know, but then I've only been a Navy wife for a little over six weeks," Rachael said with a smile. "I see your point about the use of 'ladies' and 'wives.' It is a bit of an irritati on, but a minor one. After all, the term 'wife' is hardly pejorative. I would imagine that, as both of us learn more about Navy customs, there'll be other things we would do differently if it were up to us."

For the first time since Rachael had opened th e door, Alice Carney was clearly at a loss for words. "But I thought you military people carried on the tradition for years. That you were born into military families, had military careers, and that your children went into the military—that it went on for generation after generation ad infinitum."

"I'm sure that that is the case with some military families, but not with most. My husband, for example, was the first in his family to enter the Navy. He didn't grow up in a military family and neither did I. As for our children, well, we don't have any yet, but what they want to do in life will be their decisions to make. As for some of the naval customs and traditions you mentioned, I may be able to help you out a little on that. Military officers aren't permitted to fraternize with the enlisted men because they may have to give certain orders in combat that can mean the deaths of some of the men under their command. If an officer had certain friends among the men, some of the other men might feel that hi s decisions would not be made impartially. Sometimes in battle an officer has to make life or death decisions, like sacrificing some men to save others or—and this example is more common in the Army than the Navy—deciding which men will go out on especially dangerous missions. Even if an officer *is* truly impartial despite certain friendships, that's not good enough. There can't even be the *perception* that he is not impartial. Both the Army and the Navy decided long ago that it's best just not to permit any fraternization at all. Now this doesn't mean that the officers can't be friendly to the men. Because of the small number of men in submarine cre ws, the officers often have some friendly dialog with the crew members, like asking how the family is or what a man's hometown is, but it's always clear that the officer favors no man over another. It has to be that way. There *are* special occasions when officers and men have a party together, in fact, there will be one just before the *Sea Otter* goes to sea.

"Dade explained to me that there are a lot of U.S. Navy customs and traditions that we got from the Royal Navy. So many are even centuries old. I'm only learning many of them now, and have found that there are certain things I have to do by virtue of my being the wife of a submarine captain. You see, wartime submarine patrols last about two months, and, during that time, when all the husbands are gone and there's no way we can communicate with them, if any emergencies come up among the officers' families, it's my duty to know about it and to step in and do everything I can to help. It could be injuries or illnesses or financial problems, or, well, just about any problem that arises. The wife of the Chief of the Boat has the same responsibility when it comes to the families of the enlisted men."

"The men are gone for two months at a time?" Alice asked plaintively.

"Yes."

"Oh, my. I didn't know that."

"And, after two weeks of rest and relaxation, they're off for another two months."

Alice Carney frowned deeply. "Why, Tom and I will hardly see each other at all!"

"That's true. But we wives have each other to talk to, and do things with. Some, like me, have jobs or do volunteer work. Of course, women with children have them to take care of. Dade and I hope to have children."

"You do? At your age? I mean is that even possible?" Then Alice quickly realized that she had just committed a faux pas and her right hand flew up to cover her mouth.

"Oh, yes, so the doctors tell me, and Dade and I are working very hard at it," Rachael smiled.

Alice blushed, but recovered enough to speak after a few mortifying seconds. "Tom wants us to have children, but I'm against it. How could we possibly bring children into a world like this? The whole world is at war and it looks like it will be for years to come. Then there are other things too. Crime, economic uncertainty, bigotry, shortages, hatred, discrimination, a steady erosion of our rights and of society itself. I just couldn't bring children into this world the way it is."

"Alice, I've lived a lot longer than you and seen and experienced a lot of things. I spent more than twenty years as a missionary. I've seen how cruel people can be. In fact, Japanese naval cadets broke into our home one night and murdered my husband before my very eyes. They hacked him into many pieces with their samurai swords. The walls, the ceiling, and the floor were all practically painted red with his blood, and pieces of his body, bits of his entrails, brains, and other organs covered me and the cadets as well. They killed him because he was an American and because he was a missionary. I've seen a lot of things, and frankly, there are times I doubt very much that there's a God. Do you practice any religion?"

"I was raised as an Episcopalian, but, as I said, I'm a free thinker."

"Which means that you don't believe in God?"

"No. I'm an agnostic. I'm open to believing in God if someone can logically prove his existence to me."

"I see. Look, there have always been wars, economic depressions and recessions, murders, rapes, theft, civil disturbances, natural disasters, diseases, and evil. There always have and there always will be. If you wait for a perfect world you'll be waiting for the rest of your life. In vain. You can't wait to live. Most people are unhappy because they regret their past or fear for the future, or because they plan to be happy in the future so they don't live in the present, which is all any of us have. The present. This moment. The past is gone forever and we can never know what the future will hold. Two years ago, as a missionary in Japan, I could never have foreseen my husband's murder, my doing Top Secret work for the Office of Naval Intelligence in Hawaii, being married to a submarine captain, and sitting here in Groton, Connecticut speaking to you. A person doesn't even know if he *has* a future; he could die later on today. This is always true, but especially in time of war. You have your own life to live and your decisions are, of course, yours and yours alone. I'm just offering a bit of heartfelt advice, and I hope you take it in the spirit in which I offer it."

"Thank you. I do accept it in that spirit." Alice's hard expression that she'd been wearing since she'd knocked on the door softened. "Does that offer of coffee or tea still hold? That is, if you have the time now."

"Of course, but I thought you said you wouldn't be here long."

"I changed my mind. You're not the kind of person I'd thought you, pictured you, to be."

"Is that good or bad?"

"Good. Very good."

"Let's go into the kitchen. Will it be coffee or tea?"

"Tea, please," Alice said as she sat at the kitchen table, which was covered with a red-checkered oil cloth. You said you were a missionary in Japan?"

"Yes, for over twenty years," Rachael said as she put a copper pot filled with water on the stove and turned on the gas burner. "That's where I learned to speak, read, and write Japanese fluently, and why I was offered a job with the Office of Naval Intelligence at Pearl Harbor. It was and is a grueling job, but an important one, because it saves American lives."

"What do you do for them?"

"I translate Japanese into English. I can't say any more than that, because the work is highly classified. In fact, the only reason I'm telling you this much is because you're part of the *Sea Otter* family now. Whenever any outsider asks, I just say I'm a clerk in Personnel. When are you and Tom going to be married?"

"In two weeks. In fact, you'll be receiving an invitation by mail."

"Thank you. I'll be looking forward to the ceremony. You know, Dade has mentioned your fiancé's name to me several times. He has a very high opinion of him. I understand he was recently promoted to lieutenant, junior grade."

"Yes. He was very happy about that. He says he also plans to qualify for his gold dolphins before the submarine leaves to go to the Pacific. From the way he talks, that's even a bigger deal than his being promoted."

"To submariners, it's a very big deal. To get his dolphins, he has to make detailed drawings of all the systems in the submarine, completely explain them, and demonstrate that he knows how to do every job on the submarine. It's a very big milestone for a submarine officer. A rite of passage."

"I see. As a former missionary. do you have any reservations or qualms about your role in the war? I mean you're helping the Navy to kill people."

"I have absolutely no reservations. As I said, I'm helping to save America lives. I don't know how closely you've been following what the Japanese have been doing for the last several years. The Rape of Nanking in 1937, for example, when the Japanese troops murdered, *murdered*, as many as 250,000 civilians *after* the city surrendered. And that's just one example; I could go on. Then, more recently, there was the Bataan Death March, during which they murdered thousands of starving American and Filipino soldiers who had surrendered. When you want to bring despotism to the entire Far East, you will eventually get exactly what you richly deserve. I'll be just fine with the total destruction of Japan."

"I guess their murdering your first husband in such a gruesome way contributed to your hatred of them."

"Yes, but I had long before begun to hate them. It's a long story and I don't want to tell it. I haven't lost my belief in God, but there are *times* I don't believe. Right now, I suppose I believe about 75 percent of the time. Sometimes it's hard to believe in God. Especially during a world war. But, if Dade survives the war, and after some years go by, I may even start to begin to forgive the Japanese. But that day—if it ever comes—lies far in the future."

"I don't know that I hate the Japanese. I want to see them defeated, of course, but I don't hate them. Were you at Pearl Harbor when it was attacked?"

"Yes."

"What was it like?"

"I felt horrified, angry, close to hysteria and helpless, all at the same time. It was what I imagine the end of the world would look like. Death, violent death, and destruction, both on a massive scale. Ships were being sunk or heavily damaged, men were being burned alive and screaming like souls in hell. Heavy, dark smoke was everywhere, along with the loud sounds of explosions and machine guns and when I saw some of the explosions, I saw men and parts of men blown skyward. It sickened me and I'll carry those vivid memories with me for the rest of my life. About 2,400 Americans were killed that day and about 1,200 wounded, and I saw it all from a hill on base overlooking the harbor."

"Tom was there, aboard the *Elver*, along with your husband."

"I know."

"He tried to describe it, but he said he just couldn't find the right words. He spoke of confusion, pandemonium, wholesale death, and fear."

"Yes. That's the way it was. When the first planes began the attack, Dade had been just reading a novel on a quiet, sunny morning in port. Then, in a moment, the world turned upside down. He and other crew members immediately manned their antiaircraft guns and tried to shoot the Japanese planes down. As you probably know, Dade was wounded during the fight."

"Yes, Tom told me that. I'm so happy that the wound was minor."

"On December 7th, I had yet to meet him. There he was, blasting away beneath the hill I was on, never even knowing him, and now I'm married to him. There are a lot of surprises in life. Some good, some bad. Some very good and some very bad. How old are you, Alice?"

"Twenty-two."

"You're just starting out. There are many surprises in store for you. For that matter, there are many in store for me too. The future is truly unknowable."

"I know, and that bothers me. I guess my biggest worry right now is hoping that Tom survives this war, with body and soul intact."

"But worrying does no good. There's nothing you can do, except pray. But you're an agnostic, so that's out."

"If that's all I can do, I may take up prayer. It can't do any harm."

Rachael smiled softly.

"What's it like? Living in Hawaii, I mean."

"It's very different from here. The plants, the climate, the life style. You'll like it. We're still under martial law there, though. That means some inconveniences. There's rationing. There's a curfew. Everyone must be off the streets between 2100 to 0600 hours every day. Some of the beaches are strung with barbed wire and are manned with armed soldiers."

"That's another thing. I guess I'll have to learn military time."

"Nothing could be simpler. Midnight is 2400 hours, 0100 is 1 am and so on until you get to noon, which is 1200 hours. Then you just keep adding. So 1 pm is 1300 hours, 2 pm is 1400 hours and so on."

"Oh, OK, that's easy enough."

"And you'll need to know what the insignia the men wear mean, especially what insignia denote which ranks, but you'll learn that very quickly. There are other things, but you'll pick them up in no time. I believe the family housing on the base is full up, so you'll have to find a place off base. Just remember, if there's anything I can do to help you, just ask. I just turned 40, so I'm old enough to be your mother. I don't want that kind of relationship with you though. I'd prefer us to be just two friends who can speak to each other about anything. How does that sound to you?"

"I'd like that too."

11

June 22, 1942

Groton, Connecticut

"Dade, I have someone in mind for your new XO," Captain Campbell said with a smile.

"I was wondering when BUPERS was going to get around to that, sir. We should have received one by now."

"This doesn't come from BUPERS, but from me. I have, I think, the perfect man for you, Lieutenant Oliver Wirtz. He's been XO on one of our school subs and a fine officer."

"What kind of experience does he have, Captain?"

"He was first in his class at Sub School, so as we always do, we snapped him up immediately for assignment to our school subs. He's been an engineering officer, torpedo and gunnery officer, diving officer, and XO, and received outstanding ratings in all of his positions. What's more, he's been really itching to get in the fight ever since December 7th."

"You don't mean he's never been to sea before. Surely you don't mean that. I was hoping for someone with combat experience, but a man with no experience?"

"He's had plenty of experience, Dade."

"Down the river and just far enough out into the Atlantic to conduct training?"

"Yes. Yes, but he's excellent. What I really want to do is keep him here and give him command of the sub he's assigned to right now, but he's been on me constantly to send him out to the Pacific so he can really get into this war. He's an outstanding submarine officer in every way and I don't want to stand in his way anymore."

"Sir, I can understand and appreciate that, but—"

"Yes, yes, I know. You'd rather have an XO who's had combat experience."

"Or, at the very least, a man who's been at sea before. As XO of one of your school boats, he's home every night, right?"

"Yes, but I'm telling you he's an outstanding officer. Besides, Dade, you yourself had never been in combat until six months ago. It's hard to find submariners with combat experience. Most are either assigned to other subs or now reside in Davy Jones' Locker. You should count yourself lucky to get the few experienced men who have seen combat in your old sub."

"I am grateful for that, Captain. But you know how important the XO's job is. The men and the other officers have to be able to look up to him. He's second only to the captain. How are the men supposed to look up to him if—"

Campbell held up a restraining hand. "I know, I know, but that's the way it is. Lieutenant Wirtz is your new XO. Period. End of sentence." The captain's voice had taken on an edge, and Bowie knew the matter was closed. "He'll report to you at the boat at 0800 tomorrow morning. You'll have time to teach him what he needs to know about submarine combat before you get back to the Pacific. You'll find that he's a quick study and, after your first combat patrol with him, you'll be thanking me for this."

"I hope so, sir."

"Don't be such a damned pessimist. Even John Henry hadn't seen combat until six months ago, and he was one of the saltiest men who ever put to sea. Wirtz'll do alright. Now, is there anything else I can help you with? Are you getting everything you need?"

"Yes sir."

"I imagine you're eager to get back into the fray, yourself."

The easiest thing to do would have been to lie, but Bowie just didn't have it in him for some reason. Instead, he told the truth. "I'm never eager to go into combat, sir. I do it because it's my duty, and I do my very best at it because a submarine full of men is counting on me to fulfill the mission, to do them proud, and to bring them back to port alive. So I do it, but I don't like it. Every morning when I get up, I hope that the war will end that day, even though I know it's unrealistic. I'd rather never go back into combat."

Captain Campbell had a look of shock on his face. Shock and distaste. "You're a Medal of Honor winner, man! How can you talk that way? You sound like a damned conscientious objector or something."

"Sir, with all due respect, you've never been in combat, have you?"

"No. I regret to say no."

"I don't think you'd like it. I don't know of anybody who's been in combat who wants to do it again. I think it's just human nature. No one wants to die or to be disabled for life. Everyone who's been in combat has no desire to go back. I and others go back because it's our job; we're fighting for something that's bigger than ourselves. But we're all afraid. We don't usually talk about the fear, because that only makes it worse. But, in a normal human being, fear is only natural,"

Bowie said in a soft voice. "Conquering fear is what a man has to do, and some do it better than others."

Campbell was silent for a very long moment. "I understand what you're saying. Furthermore, I suppose you're right; fear is a normal reaction when a man goes into combat. I guess I just didn't expect to hear those words from a Medal of Honor recipient. The fear doesn't diminish at all with the passage of time? With experience?"

"No sir, you never get used to it. You're afraid every time you go out. You're afraid every time the destroyers are searching with their sonar, waiting to find you and rain depth charges down on you. Then when they find you and the depth charges are going off, shaking the boat from stem to stern, you become more afraid still. In fact, terror is the more appropriate word."

"Well, I certainly can't fault you for your honesty, Commander. And certainly you've proven that you're a man who can conquer fear."

"With difficulty, sir. With difficulty."

"But you're confident you can continue to get out there and sink Japanese ships?"

"Yes sir. It's just not easy. And I'm confident that the men they let me have from the *Elver* will continue to do well. They didn't give me all the men I requested, but they're enough to form a nucleus of a fine crew. They'll help to train the new men."

"I myself would like to skipper a submarine going in harm's way. You're not the only one who's trained for it for years. I know I'd be afraid too, but I know it's a job for younger men and nobody with my rank and seniority is given a sub to command. I'll probably spend the whole war at this desk."

"But it's a job that needs to be done and it's important."

"Yes, well, at least that's what I keep telling myself."

12

June 23, 1942

Groton, Connecticut

Bowie stood on the bridge of the sub while men swarmed all over her and inside her, working to make her ready for war as soon as possible. There were welders, riveters, electricians, electronics technicians, and a whole host of serious men laboring mightily, noisily, and diligently to get the job done. Only a few crew members had reported in so far, the rest were still on leave. Chief Robhar was below, making sure that everything was being done correctly and asking questions about some of the newest equipment being installed. Detrick and Milmer were below too. Dade looked at his watch, and saw that it was 0755. A minute went by, then he saw what he was looking for. A lieutenant clutching an envelope which undoubtedly contained his orders assigning him to the *Sea Otter* and his personnel records was walking up to the boat, giving her an apprehensive look that Dade knew well. The look that every sailor gives to his new boat the first time he sees her. A few minutes later, the man stood before him and saluted.

"Sir, Lt. Oliver Wirtz, reporting for duty."

"Welcome aboard, Mr. Wirtz," Dade responded, returning the salute and then shaking his hand. "I understand you're a Naval Academy man."

"Yes sir, Class of '37."

"These days we're seeing more and more reservists. Some of them are excellent officers, like my diving officer, Tom Detrick, but most, frankly, have a lot to learn."

Wirtz wasn't quite sure how to respond, so he just smiled and nodded. This was Dade Bowie himself, already a legend in the submarine service. He was a

Medal of Honor recipient and protégé of John Henry Hammerhand, the big, brooding man with the yellow eyes of a wolf and the subject of many disturbing sea stories concerning his penchant for violence and rage. Oliver wanted to make this first impression a good one.

"Sir, you don't know how hard I've been trying to get into this war."

"I do know. Captain Campbell told me," Dade said with a frank, appraising stare that made Wirtz more nervous still.

"Since December 7th, I've been dying to get into combat. I'm looking forward to it. I want to make the Japs pay for Pearl Harbor." When he saw the expression on Bowie's face, he knew he had said the wrong thing. He swallowed hard, his throat became dry instantly, and he had no idea of what to say or do next.

Bowie looked out toward the Thames River and frowned. He let a moment go by before speaking to get control of his temper. When he finally spoke, it was with a calm, even voice. "I was at Pearl Harbor that morning. Those of us aboard manned the guns and did our best to shoot down Japanese planes. I had a front row seat for the whole thing. In fact, I was wounded by machinegun fire from a Japanese Zero. Only a slight would, the bullet just grazed my arm, but the *Arizona* died, taking 1100 men with her, men still aboard her at the bottom of the harbor to this day. I saw the *Oklahoma* capsize. She hasn't been righted yet, and God knows how many bodies they'll find when they try to salvage her. There were men trapped inside when she rolled, and some began tapping against the hull to indicate they were still alive and to show where they were. There were several groups of men in different locations, and rescue crews were able to cut through the hull and bulkheads and get 32 men out alive, but all tapping ceased after three days. Work on her stopped because she's a total loss and they had to use their resources to repair the ships that could be saved and get them into the fight as soon as possible. She's still there, capsized. At least she still was when I left Pearl in the last week of May. The *Arizona* is still underwater. When we get to Pearl, you'll be able to see both of them where they went down that day. Don't worry, the Japanese will pay for Pearl Harbor. Our first real victory didn't come until the Battle of Midway, which happened after I had come back to the States. The government and the press are saying it marks the turning point in the war in the Pacific, and maybe that's true. I hope so. But there's still a whole lot of fighting to do. A whole lot of killing and dying to do. I wouldn't worry about the war ending before you can get into it. I also wouldn't say you're 'looking forward to going into combat.' At least not in front of the men I brought here from the *Elver*. They've already seen combat. And, if they hear you say how much you want to go into combat, one of two things will happen. One, they'll think you're only saying that to impress them, which makes you a liar, or two, they'll think you mean it, which makes you a fool. I can't have them think either thing. You're second in command. The whole crew, officers and men, have to respect you, have to trust you. For that matter, I have to trust you. Did you really mean what you said or were you just saying something you thought I'd like to hear? Level with me."

Oliver swallowed hard. Had he really just gotten himself on the skipper's shit list within minutes of his coming aboard? Evidently. "Yes sir, I meant it. It's what I've been trained for and I think I'll do very well in combat. I won't let you down."

Dade could see the earnestness in Wirtz's face and hear it in his voice. "Well, good. Very good. You'll see plenty of combat under my command. But, after you experience it, you'll find that it's nothing like you thought it would be. In the *Elver's* very first mission, we came within a hair of reaching crush depth. I thought we'd had it several times. In fact, it was a miracle that we survived. You start out a war patrol with anxiety, and, of course, that's normal and even desirable because it keeps you alert and on your toes. Then, just as you head into battle, the anxiety level starts to climb up and up and up. Your hands start to shake a little and you try to make sure that no one notices it. Your heart starts to pound fast and hard, and the adrenalin is dumped into your bloodstream readying you to fight or flee. But all that blood diverted to your major muscle groups doesn't help because you're not in a physical fight. And, since you're in a submarine, there's no place to run to. But there's a third reaction that some men have in combat; they freeze. You worry about that, because a sub under attack needs every man on his toes with a clear head, ready to respond instantly to dealing with any damage caused by depth charges. Or, if you're fighting on the surface, to pour out accurate gun fire to sink the enemy before he gets your range. You worry about freezing, because a single man freezing could mean the difference between life and death for the entire crew, and you don't want to let the rest of the men down.

"Remember this: You have to be brave. You have to come through, to do what you have to despite your fear. In battle, you can't get rid of your fear; it will be with you every minute, screaming to you inside your skull. You have to control it though. You have to conquer it, and the best way to do that is to think of two things. First, that if you fail to conquer it, if you fail to do your job, it might mean that we all die. Second, that if you fail to be brave and do your duty under fire, you'll be ashamed of yourself for the rest of your life. And that might be for another fifty years."

"I understand, sir."

"Good. Are you married?"

"Yes sir."

"Do you have any kids?"

"Yes sir, a son."

"OK. The way I'm working things now, we'll be here five days a week. As I guess you know, the shipbuilders are working two shifts a day, six days a week to get the *Sea Otter* completed, and, as the time grows closer and the full crew has reported, we'll probably go to six days a week too. Right now, it's a matter of our making sure that everything is done right and that we understand any new gear they're installing and educating ourselves in its use. So that means, that you and I and the other officers and men who have our families in the area will be able to spend as much time as possible with them. Once we head out to sea, it may be a long, long time before most of the crew will see them again. If ever.

"We begin work every weekday at 0800 and knock off at 1700. Some days we may need to stay a little later, but hopefully not many. You'll be able to be with your family every night and weekends for the time being. My wife came back from Hawaii with me, and we'll be inviting you and your wife over for dinner sometime soon."

"I'll be looking forward to that, skipper. I was wondering about taking my wife and son to Hawaii. Is that a possibility?"

"Well, family housing on the base is full up. You'd have to find a place to live off base, and it costs more to rent quarters there than here. You have to understand that Hawaii is still under martial law and all that that entails. Then too, you'll only get to see them for two weeks between two-month long patrols. What a number of couples have decided to do is to have the wives and kids stay back here in the States, where they're closer to other family members and friends and familiar surroundings. Some men sent their families back to the States after December 7th because there was the possibility of a full-scale attack and invasion of Hawaii. Especially now, after Midway, there's very little chance of that though. There are good arguments both for and against taking your family to Hawaii. It's really up to you and your wife."

"I'd appreciate it if you and your wife could give us the pros and cons over dinner."

"Of course, we'll be happy to do that. Now let's go below and I'll show you just how far along the workmen are on the job, and point you to a high stack of paperwork you can get started on right now."

13

July 1, 1942

Groton, Connecticut

"I thought that went well," Rachael said as they were getting ready for bed. Earlier they'd had the Milmers over for dinner.

"I thought so too," Dade replied. He smiled. "You always think things go well."

"Is he a good engineering officer?"

"Yes, he's good. Solid. But not exceptional. He's a strictly by-the-book man, which isn't always what you want, especially in a war. He's very competent, but, not, I think, a man I can ever see as a sub skipper. I don't think he has the leadership skills for that. At least he's an Academy man."

"Which means he's superior to any reserve officers," Rachael said teasingly.

"No, no, of course not. There are some fine reserve officers. Tom Detrick, for example. Damn, but he's great! He's as smart as a whip and he's cool under fire. On the Wake Island mission, he quickly and calmly got us our propulsion back when we lost it and were sinking helplessly. On the way back home, he was the one who figured out that the torpedoes were running deeper than their settings and why. The rest of us in the wardroom would have eventually figured it out, but he was the first. That impressed the hell out of even John Henry. No, even though he was commissioned via ROTC, he's a better officer than many Academy graduates."

"That reminds me; don't forget he's getting married on Saturday."

"How could I forget? The Fourth of July. You said you liked his fiancée."

"Well, she's very young," Rachael smiled. "Young enough to think that there are answers to all of civilization's problems and that she knows many of them. And the ones she doesn't know yet, are ones she'll figure out presently."

"So you're saying Tom's going to have a few headaches."

"Yes, but nothing the two of them can't handle. She's very smart too. She also really loves him. They'll make out fine. I do like her. We've met each other for lunch a few times and have gone shopping a few times together. Both of their families come from old money, you know."

"As opposed to those of us who have new money."

"Exactly! We are *nouveau riche*. But she doesn't hold that against us."

"That's nice of her."

"No, Dade, she's not like that. She's OK. You'll see when we have them over for dinner. You know, she's more than OK. I like her a lot. Just as I look upon Tracy as a kid sister, I'm beginning to look upon Alice as a daughter. We've talked a lot about many different things. She's very well read."

"That's high praise coming from you. I've never come across anymore as well read as you are and on so many different subjects. At any rate, I've decided to make Tom the diving officer on the *Sea Otter*. It's one of the most critical jobs aboard a sub, and he's only just made lieutenant j.g., but I'm confident that he's the best man. By the way, how do you like being a Navy wife? So far, I mean."

"I have no complaints, and I especially like this time back in the States. We get to see each other every night, and being away from the ONI job for a while gives me a rest I really needed. Sixty hours a week with no vacations is a hell of a grind. I'm really enjoying myself here, just walking and reading and getting to know some of the wives of the other officers assigned to the *Sea Otter*. I've enjoyed the weekends when we're together the whole time to explore some of New England and see some shows. As you know, I've been kind of rediscovering my identity as an American. Living on Oahu is nice, very nice, but, while it's an American territory, it's not the same as living in the States. After I'd been in Japan for a few years, with no news of what was happening back in the United States and no exposure to its customs and traditions, I kind of felt like a woman without a country. When I was offered the ONI job and living in Hawaii, I felt the faint stirrings of patriotism again, but didn't feel a full bonding with the United States until we arrived in San Francisco in May. It began then and has continued to grow every day since. I feel like an American again and it feels good. The only thing I want now is for this war to be over."

"That may take a while."

"I know. One of the things I want to do is begin going to church again."

"Do you have any particular denomination in mind?"

"Not really, as long as it's a Christian church. That would be good for me, I think. I'd also get to meet more people. How do you feel about it? You don't have to go if you don't want to."

"It's been so many years for me, and I'm not sure it would do me any good. I mean, I went to a church service every Sunday and to Sunday school until I left home. Then I went to church every Sunday all four years at the Academy because it was required. I attended services every Sunday for two years when I was on the *U.S.S. Arizona*. While it wasn't actually *required* there, every officer was expected to go. Anyway, in all those years, I think I got pretty much all there is to get out of going to church. I know what the Bible says and I've listened to thousands of sermons. I don't think I'm going to hear anything I haven't already heard."

"I can understand that, but people don't just go to church to learn things. They go there to worship God, to show respect, and to thank God."

"If you'd like me to attend with you, I'll do it and I promise not to grouse about it. I just wanted to let you know how I felt. Sometimes I believe in God and sometimes I don't."

"I know. Sometimes I don't believe either."

14

July 6, 1942

Groton, Connecticut

Dade had called a meeting for the men who had served with him on the *Elver*, and, as he sat in the wardroom with them, a number of scenes played through his mind. Flashes of how they had handled themselves from December 7th through the first three war patrols of their old boat. He took a moment to collect his thoughts and spoke.

"As you know, Lt. Detrick is on a one-week honeymoon now, but the rest of you who served together on the *Elver* are here. None of the other men who have reported or are scheduled to report have been on war patrols. Some have, of course, served on subs before, even for years, but not in combat. Some have no prior experience in subs, but have recently graduated from Sub School. We will also get a couple of men who have neither been in subs nor graduated from Sub School. One is our new yeoman, the other a cook.

"Now we all have been tested under fire and know we can trust and depend on each other because we have proven ourselves to each other. As for the rest of the crew, they haven't yet had an opportunity to prove themselves. We have to resist the natural inclination to form our own clique and treat them as somewhat lesser mortals. Yes, they have to prove themselves, but give them a chance, help them along. This is not the time to act like arrogant old salts who know it all. We're going back into battle and we all have to depend on each other. These men will have a lot of questions to ask. Answer their questions. They may ask you what it's like when being depth charged or what gun action topside is like when it's for real and a matter of life or death. Be honest. That's not the opportunity to tell tall tales about how brave you were and unafraid. Tell them the truth—that everyone's afraid in combat—that that's why it's so important to have your job down pat. So you can do it automatically even when you're scared. That that's why it's vital that we train hard.

"This being a submarine, I've overheard a lot of stuff, and one thing in particular bothers me. I've heard that some men have doubts about the ability of Lt. Wirtz because he's only served on Sub School boats. I want to be as clear as I can on this; he has an outstanding record and is a first-class officer. If he weren't, I would have refused to take him. I shouldn't have to say this, but I will: Treat any order he gives you as if I gave it. In many cases, I will have. On the rest, trust his judgement without reservation.

"I personally requested each of you six men by name and also Lt. Detrick because I know what kind of stuff you're made of. When we go into battle again, I want you with me. I know I can count on you. Help me train the rest of the crew so we can all count on them when the chips are down. We all need each other."

15

July 8, 1942

Groton, Connecticut

Dade had invited the Wirtzs for dinner at his house, but he frowned now as he looked at his watch and saw that they were already twenty minutes late.

Seeing the look on his face, Rachael said, "Maybe they had a flat tire or something. Things happen."

"When things happen, you phone your host and hostess to tell them you're running late and why."

"I'm sure they'll be here any minute. Can you tell me anything about them besides the fact that Oliver is your XO and that he's only had experience with Sub School boats?"

"Not really. According to his personnel jacket and Captain Campbell, he's smart, capable, and a fine all around naval officer who knows submarines inside out. So far, in the interactions I've had with him, that seems to be true. He's doing fine so far, but so far most of his duties have entailed a lot of paperwork, so I can't yet get a handle on his leadership qualities and how he will react under emergencies. He's never mentioned anything about his family. He's an Academy man, Class of '37. He's 26 years old. He has a son. That's about it." The doorbell rang and both Dade and Rachael greeted the couple at the open door.

"I'm sorry we're late, sir," Oliver Wirtz said, looking both contrite and flustered at the same time.

"Come in," Dade smiled.

"Thank you. Skipper, this is my wife, Madeline."

Dade shifted his gaze to a blonde about the same age as Oliver. She wore her hair shoulder length, and was extremely attractive, except for her boozy bloodshot eyes, flushed face, and slightly clumsy entrance into the living room. She was obviously drunk.

"How do you do, Madeline?" Dade said. "This is my wife, Rachael."

"Nice to meet you," she said, a perceptible slur in her words. "Nice to meet you both."

Rachael murmured something appropriate, while Dade continued to study Wirtz's wife. She was drunk, but there was something else about her. Something was off. It was her smile, the smile of a person who was looking for trouble and confident of causing it. It was the smile a male bully displayed when he was walking up to another man to pick a fight. A fight he knew he'd win. The smile of someone confident of his superiority.

Rachael exchanged a quick look with Dade and invited the Wirtzs to have a seat in the living room. "Well, Lt. Wirtz," Rachael began cheerfully, "Dade tells me that you've been assigned to the Sub School since you graduated. How have you liked it here?"

"Aren't you going to offer us a drink?" Madeline asked petulantly.

"No," Rachael smiled. "We were expecting you at six, and dinner will be ready in just a few minutes, so there's no time for a drink right now. After dinner, we can have a drink if you like."

"I get it. Ollie told me you were a missionary. I guess you Bible thumper types don't want to have anything to do with 'demon rum,' huh? I get it. You don't drink or smoke or cuss or screw."

"I was a missionary," Rachael replied, still smiling. "And of the four things you mentioned, the only thing I don't do is drink. Nevertheless, I don't mind other people drinking and we keep several types of drinks in the house for guests. There's just no time right now."

Madeline was clearly confused, sensing that somehow this woman had said something clever, something that had made her look stupid. She blinked her glassy eyes as she sat trying to figure out what had happened and what she could say to put that bitch in her place. Ollie was clearly mortified, but fuck him, she thought. When he came home and saw how drunk she had been, he had told her he was just going to call the Bowies and say that she was sick or that their babysitter had backed out at the last minute or something and apologize for not being able to come over. They had fought about it, and she had insisted that they go. She had two reasons. First, she wanted to humiliate Ollie in front of his boss and his bitch wife. She liked humiliating Ollie. Second, she wanted to demonstrate to his boss and bitch just what she thought of the United States Navy. She had decided a year ago that the Navy, including Ollie, could kiss her ass. Ollie had been a cute young naval officer and a lot of laughs a couple of years ago. Her father had told her to give him up—that she was marrying beneath her station, that his daughter consorting with a sailor was stupid, that the whole thing was embarrassing him and that she would regret it. She had married Ollie, in great part, for that very reason—

to humiliate her father. As it turned out, her old man had been right about Ollie. She had married beneath her station, and while that felt like a delicious act of rebellion against her father, she was now reaping the whirlwind. Groton was an OK place to live, but not in the military housing on base that had been supplied them. And Oliver could not afford to support her in the style to which she had become accustomed. He could not afford proper clothes for her, nor travel, nor front row center tickets to Broadway plays, nor any damned thing. Ollie was a loser. He also let her walk all over him, and she could not respect him for that. Having a child only compounded her suffering. In the social strata she came from, when a woman had a child, she hired a fulltime live-in nurse to take care of the damned thing. To feed it, to change its diapers, to do all that stuff. And, when the kid got older, a governess was hired to take care of the kid when he was not in school. Ollie expected *her* to take care of the kid. *Her*, Madeline Osborn Wentworth of Newport, Rhode Island.

Well, fuck Ollie and the United States Navy and everybody in it. Even though Ollie was being sent to fight in the Pacific and she wouldn't have to put up with him every day, she still would have no money to pay for the things she needed and deserved. Well, on the bright side, there was always the possibility that he would be killed in combat. True, the GI insurance policy was only ten grand, but that might be enough to keep her until she could latch onto a man with means. And that wouldn't take long. She was well aware that she was a beautiful woman. Many men said she was built like Betty Grable, only with better legs. She'd only been out of college a few years and still kept in touch with a couple of her sorority sisters at Bryn Mawr and some friends from the country club her family belonged to. She had contacts. Suddenly, she realized that a conversation was going on around her.

" . . . which is why I decided to go into submarines," Ollie was explaining earnestly.

"I've never regretted it," Dade replied. "I think it's the most challenging assignment in the Navy."

"Dinner's ready," Rachael announced, returning to the living room. Madeline hadn't even noticed her leave. "Let's all take a seat at the table." Madeline was feeling a little wobbly as they went into the dining room and sat. Through her alcoholic haze, she noticed how carefully Ollie was watching her and how ill at ease he was. She was close to passing out and they both knew it.

During the early part of the meal, Madeline spoke little and the conversation going on about her was just a background sound of murmuring. She could only catch a word here and there as she struggled to stay awake. Then, at mid-meal, she felt a burst of awareness and announced, "I hate the fucking Navy." She loved the shocked and embarrassed look on her husband's face, but could read no expression on Dade's or Rachael's faces.

67

"Dade always wanted to be a naval officer," Rachael said, "and he's spent his entire adult life as one. I myself am new to it. I only began working as a Department of the Navy civilian a little over a year ago and I've only been a Navy wife for two months. My impression so far is that the Navy is a flawed organization, just as any large organization is, civilian or military. Its flaws, I think, are caused by the fact that it's composed of and run by human beings, and all human beings are flawed. Overall, though, I think it's very effective and capably run. It makes mistakes, some big and some small, but it strives to be fair and efficient and mostly succeeds. At any rate, now that we have a war to fight, I believe it's time for us to close ranks and give it our best," Rachael finished in a soft-spoken way.

Damn missionary bitch, thought Madeline, lecturing her like that after making that smartassed remark—whatever it was about drinking. "Well, I hate it," she said truculently. I can hate it if I want to, and I hate it. I hate the war too. Franklin Roosevelt got us into this war."

"I thought it was the attack on Pearl Harbor that got us into this war," Dade said evenly, his eyes narrowing.

Clearly startled, Oliver Wirtz sought to avert a scene. "What Madeline means is—"

"I said what I meant, Ollie! Yes, Japan attacked us, but only because of the embargoes that Roosevelt imposed. It was greedy capitalism that caused the war. Roosevelt, it's he who wanted war so all the arms merchants could profit and all his other industrialist robber baron buddies."

Abruptly, Wirtz stood. "Sir," he nodded, "Mrs. Bowie, I'm afraid Madeline isn't quite herself tonight. If you'll excuse me, we'll be leaving now." His face was flushed.

"That's not necessary, Oliver. But if you want to leave, that's all right too," Bowie replied.

Madeline had a strange smile on her face, as if this was the outcome she had planned all along. The couple left hurriedly, Oliver's embarrassment evident in his every gesture and word.

16

July 9, 1942

Groton, Connecticut

Bowie stood on the bridge of his submarine as the workmen and crew toiled to finish its construction and install all the gear that was required. He saw Wirtz grimly striding up to the boat, a worried frown on his face, and felt sorry for the man. Then he looked toward the hatch to the forward torpedo room, where a group of men labored to lower some wooden crates through the opening. So far, all was going according to plan and on schedule. Going home every night to Rachael was wonderful. The gas rationing didn't allow them to take all the weekend motor trips through New England that he had hoped for. Four gallons a week amounted to about 60 miles with his car. Well, that was a small thing. The important thing was that they were together every night and every weekend. He didn't relish two-month long war patrols again. Given the American submarine losses to date, his odds of surviving the war weren't great. This time they had together, here in Connecticut, might be all the time they had.

"Sir," he heard the voice behind his back and turned to see Wirtz, "may we speak privately for a few moments?"

"Of course, let's go down to my stateroom. There's no one working in there right now."

Once Dade was seated on the only chair in the room and Wirtz on his bunk, Wirtz began. "Skipper, I apologize profusely for what happened last night. I arrived home to find her drunk, and knew we shouldn't have gone to your place, but—"

Dade raised a hand. "Apology accepted, Oliver."

"Yes, well, thank you, sir. That's very gracious of you. Please convey my deepest apology to your wife too."

"I will."

"Thank you. It's just that the babysitter had already arrived at my quarters, I didn't want to cancel out at the last minute after all the preparations Mrs. Bowie had undoubtedly made, I didn't want us to fight in front of the sitter, and Madeline promised me she'd be OK." He quickly ran his hand through his hair and continued, his voice troubled. "I'm truly sorry. I . . . . I'll be frank with you, sir. For the past year or so, ours has not been a very happy marriage."

"Frankly, your private life is none of my business, unless it interferes with your duties as XO of this boat, and, to the best of my knowledge, it hasn't. Look, there are a lot of unhappy marriages in the Navy. John Henry's marriage ended when his wife suddenly left him for another man. My first marriage ended in divorce after only three years. A Navy life is hard on families. And, speaking from personal experience, even if your marriage goes on the rocks, it's not the end of the world. Sure, your heart is broken for a time, even for a few years, but then life goes on. You adjust. This is just a friendly suggestion, but talking to one of the chaplains might help."

"Actually, sir, I already tried that. I went to see the Protestant chaplain a couple of weeks ago, but it didn't do much good. Oh, he listened to me sympathetically, and said he'd pray for me, but that was about it."

"Did you try the Catholic chaplain?"

"No. No Catholic priest is married—they're not allowed to—and I figured how could a man that's never been married himself give me any advice about it?"

"How about a rabbi?"

"I'm not Jewish."

"You don't have to be to talk to a rabbi. And rabbis know a hell of a lot about life. They marry and not only study the Torah, but the Talmud, which is an amazing collection of wisdom. Parts of the written Talmud go back as far as 200 AD. I haven't read it, but my wife has, and she says it's an incredible work of theology that has served as a kind of blueprint for Jews to determine how they should live their daily lives."

"According to scuttlebutt, your wife has read thousands of books," Oliver said with a tired smile."

"That's true. She spent twenty years as a missionary in a small fishing village in Japan in primitive conditions and a population that didn't want to have anything to do with her so she read five or six books a week, everything from theology to philosophy to essays, plays, college textbooks in every conceivable subject, to poetry, novels, medical books, you name it. Let's see, five books a week for twenty years amounts to 5,200 books in all. What's more, she remembers almost everything she reads, well, not all of it. More like 90 percent of it. For example, say one of Ralph Waldo Emerson's essays. Even years later, she'd be able to tell you exactly every point he made in it and give you a lot of verbatim quotes from it, but she wouldn't be able to quote the entire essay verbatim."

"That's amazing."

"I know. Sometimes I feel like an illiterate next to her. Look, your business is your business. As long as whatever troubles you may have don't interfere with your job, it stays that way. But, if you should want to talk with me about them confidentially and ask for help or advice, that's OK."

"Thanks skipper, I appreciate it."

17

July 12, 1942

Groton, Connecticut

Bowie and Rachael sat side by side in two lounge chairs in the back yard on a lazy Sunday afternoon. Although the temperature was 95, a large tree shaded them and a refreshing breeze blew. "I don't know when I've been happier," Rachael said. "Having all this time, in this setting, with you. And, at last, we're winning the war in the Pacific. The Battle of Midway last month, was a tremendous blow to the Japanese. I'll bet that L-2 played a major role in that action because our boys knew when and where the carrier task force would be. That was no coincidence."

"You'll find out the details when you go back to work."

"Yes, you know I've been thinking about that. I've been thinking of going back to L-2 only if they meet one condition: I don't work when you're in port."

"They won't like that at all. In fact, they'll probably refuse."

"Let them. If they refuse, I'll simply refuse to go back at all. We're millionaires now. We certainly don't need the money and I hated only spending the evenings with you when you were in port after working a 10-hour day six days a week. And only the one day a week off. I don't want to go back to that. It was horrible."

"While it's true that we don't need the money, there is the matter of their needing you for critical war work. I thought that you had become a born again patriot since we got back to the States. 'This is my own, my native land.'"

"I *have* felt a resurgence of patriotism, and believe that we need to do our part to defend our country, but I don't think that taking two weeks off every two months is going to cripple the war effort. I don't think it's asking too much. Do you?"

"You'd know better than I. And maybe they've been able to hire more Japanese translators since we left. I just don't know. I'm just thinking of how, when we found that I'd had inherited the money, you formulated a different plan. When we got to Dallas, collect the money, buy a car, drive across the border to Mexico, and then fly into Argentina and live out our days there. I said that there were bigger things, more important things, than just you and me, and you said not to you."

"Yes. I remember very well how I felt back then. I can't adequately express how I feel, or why I feel differently now. I still love you more than I can say. But you were right back then. There *are* bigger things than you and me. The war against fascism has me thinking of what Edmund Burke said."

"'The only thing necessary for the triumph of evil is for good men to do nothing.'"

"Yes, and in kind of a corollary to that axiom, he wrote, 'When bad men combine, the good must associate; else they will fall one by one, an unpitied sacrifice in a contemptible struggle.' You were right. We can't walk away from this war. We'd never forgive ourselves in later years. We do owe a loyalty to our country."

"Even though our country doesn't love us back?" Dade smiled, using the words she'd used to try to get him to leave the country and let others fight the war.

"Yes. There's too much at stake."

"You know, Hitler had to be insane to declare war on us. It's crazy. There's was no advantage, no reason."

"Well, he *does* seem to be insane. Maybe it's as simple as that."

"Maybe, but I still don't like the President's 'Germany First' strategy, despite what he said. We don't have any troops in Europe fighting Germany. Sure, the Navy is seeing combat in the Atlantic as they escort convoys carrying war supplies to England, but that effort is insignificant when you compare it to the full all out war we've been fighting in the Pacific since December 7th. We've lost men, a lot of men in that attack and many more still in the doomed fight for the Philippines and Guam and Wake Island and in naval engagements. The Japanese also captured 12,000 Americans when Bataan fell and 11,500 when Corregidor fell."

"I agree. So does Douglas MacArthur, so do a lot of people. I keep thinking of what Manuel Quezon, the President of the Philippines, said too. He said America's putting Europe first is like a man rushing across town to be with a sick cousin while his daughter is being raped in his back yard."

"And now that Hitler has the war with Russia on his hands, I think that England is fairly safe from an actual invasion. At least for the foreseeable future. Anyway, to get back to my original point, if Hitler hadn't declared war on the

73

United States on December 11th, most of the people in this country wouldn't have backed our declaring war on Germany. Especially since they hadn't attacked us and we had our hands full with a large war in the Pacific."

"And there would be no 'Germany First' policy. Our entire war effort would be in the Pacific, against people who *had* attacked us."

"Exactly."

"I agree with you completely, but, unfortunately neither one of us sits behind the big desk in the White House. The only thing we can do is win this war and try our best to have you come home alive and well. I pray every day for those two things. It wouldn't hurt for you to pray too."

"Every time I go into action, I pray. Oh, it's not a formal prayer, and it's not eloquent, but it's really sincere."

"Something along the lines of, *Please God, get me through this alive. If you do, I promise that I'll be a good man and I'll go to church and I'll* . . . that kind of prayer?"

"That's not verbatim, but, yeah, that's pretty much it," Dade said, smiling in embarrassment.

"That's not a very good prayer. It's better than nothing, I suppose, but you can do better than that."

"How?"

"Get into the habit of praying every day. Even if only for a few minutes. Thank God for all your blessings, tell him you're sorry for wrongs you've done, and ask that he watch over and protect us."

"I can do that. I will do that."

18

July 15, 1942

Groton, Connecticut

Oliver Wirtz sat on a barstool in the Officers Club and morosely stared into his third rum and Coke. The place was very crowded as it always was these days since the war began. So he'd be going home late. Big deal. It wasn't as if Madeline wanted him home, and, for supper, he'd eat a burger here. He'd called to let her know that he had to work overtime today and would be a few hours late, to tell her to go ahead and eat. It was a lie; he hadn't wanted to go home. She was always critical these days. Critical of him, of the Navy, of the people they knew, of the country, and his political and religious beliefs. And there was the constant complaining. Complaining about her having to take care of Timmy, their 18-month old son. Complaining about their quarters on base, the amount of money he made, of how terribly bored she was, about how they never went anywhere.

There hadn't been any problems until her fourth month of pregnancy, when she began to whine and bitch about everything. At the time, he had just chalked it up to the hormones related to pregnancy, figuring that everything would be OK after their baby was born. But things just got worse when Timmy came along.

Damn it, he'd had a good life, a happy life, until Madeline had become the wife from hell. He'd always wanted to become a naval officer and he had. He had gotten an appointment to the Naval Academy and had excelled there, finishing first in his class. While going to Sub School, he'd met a woman so breathtakingly beautiful that she could have been a movie star. She was also smart, witty, and fun loving. What's more, to his great joy, she loved him back and they were married. The first year, their marriage was idyllic. Then, with the pregnancy, they were no longer carefree. They had less money and less time, which was OK with Oliver, but not with Madeline. And lately, she had been drinking too much. She had turned into a bitter woman.

He thought back to months before, when he realized that there was only one way out—sea duty. He had been happy to be assigned a school boat. He had started as its engineering officer, then become its diving officer, then its XO. He had been told he'd be its skipper in three months, when the current skipper left. It was wonderful to go home every night to Madeline. Hell, given his choice, he'd would have stayed on indefinitely. Then two unrelated things happened. The first was the change in his wife, the second, the attack on Pearl Harbor. Being around Madeline anymore was unpleasant. She seemed to have lost all feeling for him and blamed him for her every complaint, and there were many. At the same time, he'd begun to feel a sense of guilt that other submariners were going in harm's way every day, fighting and dying, for the country they loved. They were brave and honorable men and he faced neither danger nor hardship himself. Besides, lobbying for combat duty in the Pacific was one way to get away from Madeline for months. Maybe for years. The problem was that he'd be away from Timmy too. And could he really trust her to take good care of Timmy? Especially with her drinking?

Four months ago, he had made a long-distance call to his parents in Indiana. He'd told them that he could be sent to the Pacific at any time, for a long time, and asked if they would be willing to take in Timmy and Madeline while he was away. They'd instantly and enthusiastically assented, as Oliver had figured they would. After all, they loved their grandson, and they'd only met Madeline a few times, times when she was still an easy person to like. When he got home, he'd put the idea to Madeline.

"With the war going on, I could get orders to report for duty in the Pacific. We need to make plans now for what to do if that happens. I called my folks earlier today and asked if they'd take you and Timmy in while I'm gone, and they said they'd be happy to."

"I don't think *I'd* be happy to live on a farm in Indiana. Couldn't I go with you to Hawaii?"

"Well, you could, but you'd hardly ever see me. War patrols last two months. Then too, Hawaii is still under martial law with a curfew every night from 9 pm to 6 am. No one is allowed out on the street during those hours. Bars and restaurants can only serve beer and wine. There are blackout restrictions, and many of the beaches are strung with barbed wire now. It's no longer the Hawaii of the travel posters."

"Oh, great. I get to choose between living under martial law in a war zone and living on a farm with my fucking in-laws. Is that what you're saying?"

"Mom and Dad could help you with Timmy," Oliver said, trying to ignore the language she used and her whole spoiled attitude.

"Well, that's one good point. I wouldn't have to be constantly changing diapers and wiping his ass and feeding him and listening to him cry and whine all the time."

Oliver suddenly, painfully, became aware that he was grinding his teeth. He stopped.

"Or," she continued thoughtfully, "I could take him and we could move in with *my* parents. They could hire a nurse to take care of him. I could spend time playing tennis at the country club, swim, sunbathe, and see movies and shows. Get back in touch with a lot of my old friends."

"A person hired to take care of Timmy is . . . . . well, is by her very nature, going to go about her duties impersonally. To her it would be just a job. But my mom and dad love him. I think he'd be much better off with them. Besides, a farm is a good, healthy place to raise a kid. I grew up on that farm."

"Yeah, and look at you," she sneered. "OK, I have a solution that'll please everyone. If you get orders for the Pacific, we'll send Timmy off to your parents, and I'll go to live with my parents."

Some mother. Oliver was torn between wanting to slap her and walking out the door. He chose to do neither. Instead, he tried to keep a neutral expression as he said, "That might be best for everyone concerned." From that day forward, he'd tried everything possible to get assigned to a sub bound for war patrols in the Pacific. Everything. Both the Commandant of Sub School and Captain Campbell had tried to talk him out of it, saying that he was doing something very important, very critical, to the war effort by turning out quality submariners. He countered by saying that he wanted to get into the fighting war, that he personally wanted to get some payback for Pearl Harbor and Guam and Wake Island and the gallant men of Bataan and Corregidor. He *needed* to get in the fight, he told them, to do his part. He had laid it on pretty thick. In reality, he loved being an integral part of Sub School. *He* knew his job was an essential one. Before his marriage had been flushed down the crapper by Madeline, he wouldn't have minded staying with the school for his entire career. He knew that, in the unlikely event they'd allow him to do that, he wouldn't have gone very far, but he didn't have any ambition to ever make flag rank. Hell, it wouldn't have bothered him if he didn't even become a four striper. It took little to make him happy. He loved Groton and the rest of New England too. Of course, he would have gone to war if sent, and done his best, but he had no driving ambition to do so. Just a vague discomfort that other men in other submarines were in desperate battle in the vastness of the Pacific. Men who wore the same uniform and same insignia, and who were fighting and dying every day. It wasn't really fair that he was safe and sound in the United States.

But going to war now seemed the only way to handle the situation, so he impersonated a man who *must* go to war, who was champing at the bit to do his part. It wasn't hard to impersonate such a man, because he had seen some of them and such men were lionized in all the war movies that Hollywood was churning out to make the American populace eager to fight the Axis menace.

Well, he had succeeded and here he sat in the Officers Club staring into his third rum and Coke. When it was time for the *Sea Otter* to sail for the Pacific in October, Madeline would take Timmy to Indiana, drop him off, then head for her parents' home in Rhode Island. Until then, he had to put up with daily interactions with her, and each day it was getting harder. In addition, he knew that Dade Bowie and the rest of the crew had reservations about his ability to perform the duties of an XO. Bowie was an unusual man. It was hard to read the protégé of the legendary John Henry Hammerhand. A man who had just been awarded the Congressional Medal of Honor. A man, who according to fairly reliable scuttlebutt, was a Texas millionaire. Oliver's phony 'can't wait to kill Japs' bravado hadn't fooled Bowie at all. And the seven other crewmembers that Bowie had brought with him from his last boat probably couldn't be bullshitted either, at least that's what Bowie had told him when he said that Oliver's gung ho lust for combat would, in their eyes, mark him as either a liar or a fool. Maybe he had laid the act on a little thick, but he felt he had to in order to get to sea. Oliver *was* afraid, as any sane man would be who was about to go to war. Bowie had seen right through him. Did men who had been in combat acquire some kind of special insight which enabled them to recognize dishonesty in men who hadn't? Maybe, he thought as he finished his drink and ordered another. He would make this his last drink before going home.

There was so much to do. He'd have to brush up on his navigation skills, since he hadn't held a sextant in a couple of years now and he'd be hard pressed to recognize even the north star in the night sky. He'd have to brush up on mapwork and plotting courses. He'd have to learn about the capabilities of the new electronics being put in the new fleet boats. The school boats didn't have the newest radar and sonar equipment. He'd have to learn or relearn a lot of things. He'd have to prove to Bowie and the rest of the crew that he was smart, capable, and brave. And he was confident he could successfully demonstrate all three qualities to the officers and men of the *Sea Otter* if they just gave him half a chance. He would be brave. If millions of other fighting men throughout history had done it, he could too. A man with all three qualities could still get himself killed in battle though, since you also had to be lucky. Which is why he was afraid. A man who wound up being married to Madeline Osborne Wentworth was obviously not a lucky man.

19

July 22, 1942

Groton, Connecticut

Dade and Rachael were driving home from a double feature at the Paramount. The movies had been *The Maltese Falcon* and *The Road to Zanzibar*, preceded by a newsreel giving the latest news on the war, along with two cartoons. "A penny for your thoughts," asked Rachael because Dade had said little since they had left the theater.

"Oh, I thought the movies were good. I was just thinking about the newsreel. The fight for North Africa. I was thinking that, if I were an Australian or a New Zealander fighting in North Africa now, I'd be pretty angry. They ran off to fight alongside the British in World War I, and for what? *Their* countries weren't being threatened by what was going on in Europe. And they took extremely large losses, totally unnecessary losses at Gallipoli, because of very poor decisions made by the British high command. The Aussies took 26,000 casualties there, and the Kiwis over 7,500. Overall, for the entire war, the Aussies had 218,000 casualties of which 62,000 were killed in action. The New Zealanders had 58,000 casualties, of which 18,000 were killed in action or as a result of wounds received in action. That's one *hell* of a sacrifice for 'Old Blighty,' especially considering that the population of Australia was only 54 million at the time and the population of New Zealand was only one million. That's one *hell* of a sacrifice, when your own country is in no danger and half a world away.

"Nevertheless, along comes Hitler twenty years later and, without hesitation, the Aussies and Kiwis run off to save England's ass again. They send their troops to fight alongside the British in Europe and North Africa, only to find after they left that their own countries were suddenly in extreme jeopardy by a powerful Japan running amok. Fortunately, when that happened, the Australians brought two of their infantry divisions home, but the Australian 9th Infantry Division is still fighting in North Africa. *All* of those guys should be back. Any debt they figured they owed the British was already paid by the fighting they've already done for them, both in this war and the last war. If I were one of the Aussies still fighting in North Africa, I'd start to wonder what the hell I was doing risking my life for the Brits when my home and family back in the Pacific were in dire danger. The Japs could well decide to launch a major invasion of Australia at any time. They've already bombed it, although not yet on a large scale."

"Don't you think that the chance of that is lessened by our victory at Midway?"

"Lessened, yes, the loss of four carriers was quite a blow for them to take, but it's still a very real possibility. And we can't afford to lose Australia."

"I know. Both CINCPAC and MacArthur would have to reassess their entire strategy."

"And MacArthur would have to flee Australia the same way he had to leave the Philippines—one jump ahead of the invading Japanese. It would be devastating to morale too, both civilian and military. And think of the suffering of the Australian civilians in an invasion."

"Well, at least we're out of the war until the *Sea Otter* sails. Which is when?"

"We're still looking at the first or second week of October. Unfortunately, there's no way in the world we could get you on a flight to Hawaii from the West Coast. Not in your status as a dependent. I'm afraid you'll have to go by passenger liner. I'm thinking that you take a train to San Francisco and sail from there. It's probably not too early to make reservations."

"Do you think it's safe?"

"So far, the Japs haven't attacked any passenger liners. At least not that I'm aware of. Still, anything can happen. Make sure you're always close to a life jacket and find out how they go about lowering the lifeboats. Don't panic, if there is an attack. Remember that all ships are required to have enough lifeboats to accommodate all their passengers. A hell of a lot of people—in fact, perhaps nearly all of them aboard the *Titanic*—would have been saved if that had been the case in 1912."

"You know, I think I'd have felt a lot better about my impending sea voyage if you hadn't brought up the *Titanic*," Rachael smiled.

20

July 30, 1942

Groton, Connecticut

Rachael had known from the start that something was bothering Alice, but decided to let the young woman she'd come to like so much talk about it when and how she chose to. *If* she chose to do so. They'd met each other for lunch and a movie in the early afternoon downtown and were just finishing lunch. It was a hot, humid day outside, but the large fans in the diner and the shade indoors made it bearable. After some small talk, Alice came to the point.

"I'm having reservations about going to Hawaii. The idea of not seeing Tom or even being able to correspond with him for stretches of two months at a time — and then seeing him for only two weeks before he's off on another patrol—well, it hardly seems worth it. And frankly, before the war started, my plans were to start teaching high school math. Our plan was that I'd start teaching after we were married, while Tom did his two years of active duty that he agreed to when he got his commission. Neither of us foresaw the war starting, and we kind of assumed he'd spend the two years at a naval base in the United States. We'd both work for a few years while we saved up enough money to have kids and make a down payment on a small house. The thing is, I can't really count on getting a job in Honolulu as a math teacher, could I? There can't be too many high schools there."

"I don't really know. I do know there's a large public high school in Honolulu, a smaller Catholic school taught by nuns, and a still smaller, very exclusive, very expensive prep school that the rich people on Oahu send their kids to. There might be another one or two high schools, but you're right. You can't count on finding a job with a high school there."

"Whereas, in New England, there are many high schools, both public and private, and I can relocate anywhere I find a job. I'd miss Tom terribly, but we wouldn't be seeing much of each other even if I moved to Hawaii to be with him. And then, even when he was in port, if school were in session, I'd still have to work during the day. All we'd have would be evenings and weekends. What do you think?"

"We're different people, Alice, and it wouldn't be right for me to tell you what to do. There are pros and cons for both courses of action, and only you are qualified to make the decision."

"Yes, well, I've come to respect your judgement and experience, and, well, your wisdom. You must have made some difficult decisions in your life. What do you think?"

"Alright. First, you can live a lot in two-week periods, even when you have to work during the day. In fact, Dade and I met and fell in love during the two weeks between his first and second war patrols. And we packed a whole lot of living and loving into the next one."

"During the first two weeks?"

"Actually, during his first week in port."

"But you definitely don't seem like the type to be swept off your feet! I mean, that's for younger women, I mean," she added hastily, "for less mature women."

Rachael smiled. "That's OK, I know I'm not a young or even younger woman. But, yes, I was 'swept off my feet.' It was at a dinner party given by an enormously wealthy young man who was a classmate of Dade's at Annapolis. I hadn't wanted to go, but my best friend, Tracy, talked me into it. I felt strongly that I was too old for a blind date, and I was tired from the 10-hour days of work we were putting in, but Tracy can be very persuasive. Dade had just returned from his first war patrol, and his submarine had almost been lost. It was clear to me that he had been under terrible stress. He was grinding his teeth and he would have moments when his hands began to shake. When that happened, he gripped both of his hands tightly together to hide the tremors, hoping no one would notice. At first, he hardly spoke at all, and when I tried to draw him out by asking what it was like to serve on a submarine, he awkwardly launched into a detailed explanation of why submariners smell so bad."

Alice laughed, and so did Rachael, who continued. "It got better though, between the drinks he was having and us asking him how a submarine went about sinking a ship, and his answering that in great, and I thought, fascinating detail, he began to relax a little. It was at that dinner table that first night, that I began to fall in love with him. Later that night, at my apartment, my feelings for him continued to grow. I told him that I was attracted to him, and perhaps we were right for each other, but, with the limited amount of time we could see each other, we'd never find out if we courted in the traditional way. To speed things up, I suggested we tell each other *everything* about each other, including all our flaws and things we had done and thought that we were ashamed of. If, after that, one or both of us decided that we had no future together, then we'd go on our ways wishing each other luck and having saved a lot of time. If we both decided to stay together, after that, then we'd probably stay together for the rest of our lives."

"And he agreed?"

"Reluctantly," Rachael nodded. "We were both reluctant, but went ahead anyway. And, as they say, the rest is history."

"But you had spent your life as a missionary, and, well, given the kind of person you are, I can't imagine anything that you could possibly have in your past that you would be ashamed of."

Rachael smiled sadly. "Everyone has said or done or thought things they're ashamed of. Everyone. I did and so did Dade. But we accepted those flaws. Actually, some of Dade's secrets—things that he was ashamed of—I didn't think were as serious as he thought they were."

"I can understand your reasoning in an exchange of secrets, but still can't imagine you having anything dark in your past."

"I'll illustrate then. Just between you and me?"

"Of course. I won't even tell Tom."

"Alright. First, I'm an alcoholic. A high functioning alcoholic, but an alcoholic nonetheless. I stopped drinking in March and will never drink again. The withdrawal was hellish, but I made it through, thanks to Dade, Tracy, and two friends of Dade. But when I told Dade, I was still on the bottle. I also told him how I came to resent my husband for taking me to that horrid little Japanese fishing village where the people hated us and were very open about it. I was miserable and told my husband about it. He was miserable too, but was intractable that this village was to be our lives' work. What kind of man, I kept asking myself, would insist on his wife spending her life in primitive conditions, surrounded by people who despised both him and her? What kind of man would do that? In my more forgiving moments, I answered my question with: a man who put what he saw as his duty to God before anything else. A misguided man, who year after year, failed to establish any Christian community in the town at all, but who never stopped trying. Nevertheless, I resented him. I respected him but resented his stubbornness, his choosing to make both of us martyrs for the glory of God. I had taken vows to stand by him for better or worse until we were parted by death, but thought of leaving him constantly. The only thing that prevented me from doing so was practicality. I had married him at age 18. I had no trade or skill as a means of supporting myself if I left him. I had no way of even purchasing a ticket home. And, even if I had, how would I be received back home? A woman who had deserted her fine Christian husband?"

"Yes, well, I think I can understand that."

"Not completely, I think. A woman abandoning her husband, getting a divorce, things like that were scandals years ago. Today people are more . . . . oh, I guess tolerant."

"Yes, and your alcoholism. That afflicts a lot of people."

"True, and most alcoholics lose the battle. When I told Dade I was an alcoholic, he couldn't be certain at all that I'd ever be able to quit. But h e stood by me anyway. And then there was the fact that I killed a man and felt no remorse for it." Rachael noticed the sudden shock on the young woman's face and continued, "I did it in self-defense. A man from the village came at me with a knife and tried to rape me. Sometime perhaps I'll tell you the whole story. It's unimportant. The main thing is not that I killed him nor that I concealed the fact that I had done it. What I'm ashamed of is that I took a human life and felt no remorse. Don't you think that's terrible?"

"I . . . . . . well . . . . under the circumstances, I'm sure that your lack of remorse is, ah, only natural," Alice answered, clearly uncomfortable.

"Then there was my hedonism when I went to work for ONI in Hawaii. They're paying me a lot of money by anyone's standards. I had been so poor for so long, and suddenly I was back in the 20th century, on a magnificent tropical island, and I could afford the finest clothes, a new automobile, eating out in the best restaurants, in short, could have just about anything I wanted. I love that. I've become a materialist, I suppose. I also took up smoking, fairly frequent salty language I picked up from my best friend, who also works at ONI, and, oh, yes, I had frequent and enthusiastic premarital sex with Dade. I also, years before my husband was murdered by Japanese naval cadets, and years before the attack on Pearl Harbor, developed a hatred of the Japanese people. I realize that isn't Christian or even rational. And it's not ent irely due to the way the Japanese treated me and my husband. I've done an enormous amount of reading since 1920, including books written by and about the Japanese about their history, culture, religious beliefs, and world view, and they do have a strong . . . . . bigotry against Westerners. They have an unswerving, a supreme belief in their superiority over all non-Japanese. That's why they want to conquer all of Asia. They see it as their right. They torture, beat, starve, and even murder Americans wh om they've captured. They see that as their right too. And the atrocities they've committed in China are truly bestial, unworthy of any civilized human beings.

"Dade says hating people makes it easier to kill them and that's why people hate in wartime. He says that's why he hates them, but, that, after the war is over, and after there have been a few years of peaceful healing, the hatred on both sides will fade. At least for most people, and I think he's right. If I were a better person, more virtuous or wiser, or a better Christian, I wouldn't hate them even now. But I can't help it." Rachael stared off into the distance, seeing things, unspeakable things. Finally, she spoke again. "So you see, I have plenty to be ashamed of, but Dade decided to love me anyway. Everyone has secrets, things that they're ashamed of. At any rate, we decided to tell each other all of those things before making a commitment, and I think our marriage is far and away better for it."

"Tom and I have been very honest and open with each other, although it never occurred to us to go through the exercise that you and Commander Bowie did.

Still, I'm sure that we're on solid ground. We love each other very much. I'm sure that our love would be undiminished by a long separation if I stayed back in the States until he came home from the war. But we wouldn't have to be apart that long, would we? I mean, the Navy gives him 30 days of leave a year. He'd be able to come home on leave now and again, wouldn't he?"

"He can only apply to take leave and his leave can be rejected if they can't spare him. Remember too that he'd have to cross the Pacific, then cross the country as well to get back here to you, and that takes time. Frankly Alice, if you stay here, you may well not see him for years."

"My God! Years?"

"Yes. Look, you've asked for my advice and I'm going to give it to you. As I said, a lot of living can be packed into two-week periods between submarine patrols. I know that for a fact, because Dade and I have done it. Secondly, if you decided to wait until the end of the war, you might never see Tom again. Many submarines are being lost in combat, far more than the government wants people to know about. Every time I see Dade off on a patrol, I know there's a very real possibility I'll never see him again. That, I think, is one of the reasons the two-week periods are so intense. If Tom does survive the war while you lived in Hawaii, why there could be as many as five two-week periods a year you'd be able to see him. That's 70 days a year."

"As opposed to probably none if I stayed here. Maybe not until the end of the war. *If* he lived to see the end of the war," Alice said, frowning deeply.

Rachael nodded. "Yes. Then too, if you lived in Hawaii, you might wind up having a child or two by the end of the war. Look, if you love each other, and I can see that you do, go to Hawaii. You won't regret it. At least that's my advice.

"I don't know what the job market in Honolulu is for high school math teachers, but even if there isn't one of those jobs immediately available for you, there are other jobs. Hawaii is just like the States now; there are a lot of jobs doing war work. In fact, I'll ask at ONI when I get back about whether there's a job opening for a mathematician."

"ONI employs mathematicians?"

"Yes."

"Doing what exactly?"

"That's something I can't talk to you about. It's classified. The only downside is that they expect you to work 60 hours a week. But the pay is very, very good and so is the job satisfaction. ONI is playing a very big part in winning the war in the Pacific."

"It sounds intriguing, but first I'd like to check out the job market for teaching jobs."

"And, of course, talk it over with Tom, but I think he'll be delighted if you decide to go. In fact, I'm sure of it."

21

August 3, 1942

Groton, Connecticut

"Ollie," Dade said, "let's take a walk." They left the boat and walked along past other submarines under construction, and, for a few moments, Dade said nothing. The noise was almost deafening. Dade turned down a street between two large warehouses and kept walking until most of the noise was far behind them. Then he stopped, lit a cigarette, and offered one to Oliver, who declined.

"You know, you haven't quite been hitting on all cylinders lately, Ollie, and frankly, I'm surprised. All your previous fitness ratings are outstanding. You've proven to me that you know submarines inside out. Furthermore, you volunteered for war patrols in the Pacific and stood your ground when they tried to keep you at Sub School, where you had a very cushy gig."

Knowing full well what was coming, Wirtz tried to look properly penitent, which was easy; he *was* sorry for his performance of late.

"You've been fucking up and you know I can't stand to have a single man aboard who fucks up, no matter who it is. One man fucking up at the wrong time can mean the death of all of us."

"I know sir."

"Look, it's easy to see that something is bothering you. As a rule, I stay out of my men's personal lives unless it endangers the boat and her crew. You can talk to me or not. That's up to you. I assume it's your marriage. Is that right?"

"Yes sir. That's exactly what it is." He sighed deeply. "You know, I love my wife. Well, the feeling isn't reciprocated. Next week, she's going to take our son to my folks in Indiana, then she's going to move back in with her parents."

"She's not even waiting until it's time for us to sail?"

"No sir. The fact is that she wants out of our marriage. Oh, she hasn't brought up divorce yet, but it's clear that this is where things are headed. We used to have a good marriage. A really good marriage."

"Damn! I feel for you, Ollie. I really do. My first marriage ended in divorce because my wife just stopped loving me. But you have a duty to your country, to the Navy, and, most of all, to your shipmates. You've got to be at your best when we set sail for the Pacific. What can I do to help you?"

"If you don't mind skipper, I know it's personal, but how did you get back on the beam when this happened to you?"

"Well, I was lucky. It was in peacetime and I guess I just threw myself completely into my job. I knew that the marriage couldn't be saved and just accepted it. I don't know, I just cast the whole thing into the back of my mind and accepted reality. The only day you can live is today. That's all you have, and, you'll learn that that's enough. You can never think of what might have been, that maybe you should have done this or you should have done that. It's over. It's gone. There are no do overs in life. All the days you spent with your wife are as remote as the days of the Roman Empire. Nothing in the past can be changed. Accept that and move on. You'll find the pain won't go away for a while, maybe for a long time. But you don't have to let it own you."

"I'll do my best, skipper."

"You have to do more than that, Ollie. You need to guarantee that you can pull yourself together in a week. If you can't, I won't be taking you out to sea with me. I have a responsibility to the crew. For the next week, I'll probably tolerate a few screwups, as long as I know you're going to put this behind you, that you're back on your way to being an outstanding XO."

"Yes sir. Thanks, skipper."

"How was work today?" Rachael asked as Dade entered the kitchen.

"OK, except that Ollie needs to get his head screwed on tightly pretty damn quick." Dade filled her in on the problem.

"Do you think he'll be OK?"

"Yeah. Yeah, I do. How was your day?"

Rachael looked at him sadly. "I got a letter from Tracy today. I'm sorry, but the *Lungfish* was overdue from patrol for two weeks, and there's been no radio contact. It's presumed lost."

Dade sat down heavily on one of the kitchen chairs. "George Pulaski." He sat silently for a few moments, remembering his friend, the skipper of the *Lungfish*. He had been a hardy, strong, and confident man with a ready smile. Now he was nothing, for, after his boat had gone to crush depth, there would be nothing left that resembled a human being. He could hear the kitchen clock on the wall. It seemed to be ticking a lot louder than normal, but Bowie knew that had to be just his imagination. George had come back from that War Bond tour, had resumed command of the *Lungfish*, and had taken her out on her last patrol. And that was the end of his life. How very final. And it might well happen to him, when he took the *Sea Otter* out to the Pacific. Now Dade was aware of the beating of his heart and felt an overpowering yearning to live. To live through this war and spend decades to come with Rachael and hopefully their children and grandchildren. Not to end up in the flattened hull of a submarine at the bottom of the vast Pacific some months hence.

"I didn't know you were that close to him," Rachael said gently, walking over and putting her hand on his right shoulder.

"Neither did I until just now. It's sad to see the end of a human being you liked, but it's especially hard when he was very much like yourself. I think that's it. A reminder of my own mortality just as I'm gearing up to go back there. It could happen to me."

"No it can't," she replied. "All the newspapers say that 'Slide Bowie' is a naval hero, that he's invincible, and the newspapers can't be wrong, can they?" A tear trickled down from her left eye, then another from her right eye. Keeping her one hand on Dade's shoulder, she rubbed them away briskly with her other hand.

"That's right," he said. "I forgot all about that. Scuttlebutt calls me, 'the Terror of the Pacific,' and the 'Great Japanese Widow Maker.' I forgot that I'm invincible. Immortal." He heard her sob softly behind him, stood up and took her in his arms. They simply held each other tightly for a long moment.

22

August 11, 1942

Groton, Connecticut

Both Rachael and Alice established a ritual. Every Tuesday and Friday mornings, they'd take the streetcar to the large public library downtown and browse, finally check out two or three books, then have lunch together in the diner across the street. Their topics of conversation were wide ranging, and they also exchanged information on each other's lives. Day by day, they grew closer. They also exchanged confidences and their hopes for the future.

Alice was a most unusual young woman, Rachael discovered early. Her reading ran to mostly abstruse papers and journal articles on advanced mathematics on one hand and detective novels on the other. As they sat in a booth in the diner on this hot, humid, sunny day, Rachael was saying, "It seems to me that your grasp of mathematics and your research into it is at a level far above what you need to teach at the high school level."

"That's true, but you see, I plan to not only teach high school, but to do ground breaking research of my own into the field. That's the beauty of mathematical research; you don't need a lot of test tubes and chemicals and lab equipment. All you need is a lot of paper and pencils, a slide rule, and your own mind. And you can do it anywhere."

"You really love the field, don't you?"

"Oh yes, I've been fascinated by it since high school. Besides, mathematics is the only place on earth where there's true purity."

"That's an interesting observation. I'm surprised that someone of your age came to that realization."

"Oh," Alice laughed, "I can't take credit for that. My favorite professor in college said that once. I thought a lot about it, and came to the conclusion that it's absolutely true. I minored in physics, a field where you'd expect to find unity of thought, hard and fast answers that will stand the test of time, but you don't. Newtonian physics is an example. When Isaac Newton published *Principia* in 1687, everyone thought that the secrets of the universe had been completely discovered and finally defined. His physical theories described a beautiful clockwork universe and were accepted as inviolate for two centuries. His three basic building blocks were the law of inertia, the law stating that the acceleration of an object is equal to the force acting on it divided by its mass, and third, the venerable law of action and reaction. Every school kid still learns Newtonian physics because in any fixed inertial frame of reference, Newton's laws hold true.

"However, once you get into the late 1880's and 1890's, you run into some phenomena that just don't square with Newtonian physics. The first big indication that it was flawed was the Michelson-Morley experiment in 1887. It was designed to detect the motion of the earth through the ether by measuring the difference in velocity of two perpendicular beams of light. The experiment concluded that the ether that Newton had insisted permeated the universe didn't exist. Neither could Newtonian physics explain some of the questions raised by the discovery of other phenomena in the 1890's—Henri Becquerel's discovery of radioactivity in uranium, William Roentgen's discovery of x-rays, or J.J. Thomson's proof of the existence of the electron. It took Einstein to begin to answer these questions with his Special Theory of Relativity in 1905."

"You've read Einstein's papers?"

"Oh, yes, and I think he's brilliant."

"I think you're pretty brilliant yourself."

"Oh, I don't know about that. I'm smart, but I don't know about brilliant," Alice said with a blush.

"Does your husband know how incredibly intelligent you are? I'm serious."

"He's very intelligent himself, and when we first started to date, he told me that a lot of men want to marry women who are less intelligent than they are, and he didn't understand it at all. He said he wanted to marry a woman who was *at least* as intelligent as he so he could be assured of interesting discussions over the decades of a marriage."

"He *is* smart. And wise. You both are."

"Thank you. But you know, I'm still basically a schoolgirl. Until a year ago, that's all I had done in life—go to school for 16 years. I don't have any of the kind of life experiences that you do. I've never traveled or held a job. I only speak one language. You've experienced a lot more than I have, some of them horrible experiences. I feel like a kid next to you."

"I don't think of you that way, Alice. Not at all. You're a good friend and I treasure that friendship. Now let's get off the mutual admiration track. There's something that I want to share with you. I saw a doctor yesterday, and, well, I'm pregnant. You're the first to know. I haven't told Dade yet."

"That's wonderful news! Dade will be so happy! Why haven't you told him yet?"

"I know this sounds silly, but I've been trying to think of just the right words to tell him. You know, some way that's tender and special, the words actors might use in a good romantic movie, but so far I haven't thought of any."

"Something sweet and sappy."

"Exactly."

"One way I saw it done in a movie was for the woman to say nothing, just to start knitting baby booties. Eventually her husband notices, and says, 'Darling, what? Why, are we going to have a blessed event?' Then she smiles a special smile, and he knows."

Both women laughed. "That won't work. I don't know how to knit."

"Well, don't worry. The right words will come. How far along are you?"

"Only four weeks.

"So your due date is in April?"

"Yes, roughly about April 12."

"This is exciting. You've got to tell Dade today."

Dade came through the front door and headed straight for the kitchen, propelled forward by the seductive smell of a pot roast. "Hi, honey, how was your day?"

"Dade, I'm pregnant," Rachael blurted out, as she turned from the stove to face him.

"Do you have any idea of who the father is?"

"I've narrowed it down to 25 or 30 guys, and I don't remember all their names, but one of them is you."

"Are you sure? I don't recall ever having sex with you."

"I'm not positive, but if it wasn't you, he sure looked a lot like you. Anyway, since you already live with me, I was thinking that you should be the kid's father."

"OK. I guess I can do that." Then he smiled warmly and held her. "Really? You're not kidding around? We're going to have a baby?"

"Not exactly. *I'm* the one who actually has the baby. You're just kind of a bystander who hands out cigars. You do get to help me chose the baby's name though.

"But I don't smoke cigars or know anyone who does except Chief Robhar. Can I hand out cigarettes instead?"

"I don't think so. I'm pretty sure it has to be cigars. Handing out cigarettes would make you look like a real cheapskate."

"Cigars. I guess I can do that."

"Let's go into the living room and talk. I know you're as happy as I am about this, but the doctor said something I need to talk to you about."

Dade sat down on the couch first, then Rachael sat next to him and he put his arm around her, drawing her into his side. "You look pretty serious. Is this bad news?"

"The doctor said things look fine, and, if I'd already had children before, he wouldn't be especially concerned, but since I'm 40 and this is my first baby, there are some risks. Women my age have a higher incidence of losing the baby when it's their first."

"Oh."

"He said we should take precautions. For example, from now on, I'm only to do light housework, not to lift anything heavy, and be doing light exercise every day. He said walking is ideal. I told him that I'll be going back to Honolulu soon, where I have a desk job and work 60 hours a week. He said there are two problems with that. I'm not supposed to get fatigued, and he said 60 hours a week is just too long. He thinks that I shouldn't work any more than 24 hours a week."

"Well, that's easy enough. ONI won't like that, of course, but if they refuse to agree to it, you can just quit. We don't need the money. I know you like the contribution you make to the war effort, but our baby is more important."

"I agree. But he also said that traveling halfway around the world might be quite a strain on me, particularly in the latter stages of my pregnancy. He said that after he asked me to describe the trip and I told him it meant traveling across the country by train to San Francisco and taking a passenger liner from there. He said that, the sooner I make the trip, the better."

"You and the other wives who are going planned to leave here on October 15."

"Right, the day after the *Sea Otter* is scheduled to sail."

"How many months will you be pregnant by then?"

"Three."

"Mmmmmm. Maybe you should leave as soon as possible, just to be safe."

"That's what I was thinking. I'll miss you, but we've been apart before."

"Yes, but I don't like the idea of you making that trip alone. I mean, who's going to help you with your luggage and so forth? What if something happens? It would be impossible for me to get leave to take you there now. Furthermore, I couldn't ask anyone in the crew to do it. It would be a personal favor, and it just wouldn't be right. And we don't have any family members, at least none that we could ask. Of course, we have a lot of money now, and could pay for someone to escort you there."

"Like who?"

"Well, there are executive protection services in the big cities like Boston and New York."

"You mean bodyguards?"

"Yes, but they're also trained in first aid for emergencies, could handle your luggage, and deal with any problems that come up."

"Frankly, I'd prefer to travel with a woman—you know, someone I could share my ship cabin with and someone to talk to."

"Maybe they have women who are trained in executive protection."

"That would be good."

"OK, I'll make some calls tomorrow morning and see what I can do."

"OK. Things'll be fine, Dade. Don't worry. Now, how about your news? How was work today?"

"OK, things are moving along on schedule. In fact, we might wind up finishing the sea trials and everything and be ready to sail early. Maybe even a week early. Ollie seems to be shaping up too. Look, I wish we had someone we knew who could go with you, but—"

"I know. Things'll be alright. Now let's see about supper."

23

August 12, 1942

Groton, Connecticut

"Skipper," Kaplan said, "phone call for you."

"OK, thank you." Bowie and Chief Logan had been conferring about the work that was being done in the Forward Torpedo Room. He made his way down the passage to his state room, which had a temporary phone line tied into the phone lines ashore.

"Dade, it's me."

"Oh, hi. Look, it's been a busy morning and I haven't yet had time to make those calls we talked about yesterday. I'll do that within the next couple of hours."

"That's what I'm calling about. It won't be necessary now. I've talked to Alice Detrick and she offered to go with me."

"You asked her?"

"No, no, I know that wouldn't be right. I was just talking to her, telling her that I'll be leaving as soon as possible and why. I told her that you were going to hire someone to accompany me, and she immediately volunteered."

"You didn't kind of hint around that you'd appreciate it if she—"

"No, nothing like that. It was entirely her own idea. As you know, we've become very close, and she just offered out of friendship."

"Well, I guess that's OK," Dade said hesitantly. "It's just that the skipper can't be in the position of asking or accepting personal favors from those in his command. It just doesn't look right."

"I understand. But we didn't ask, and it's Alice who's doing me the favor."

"Did she check it out with Tom?"

"No, but I suppose she will." She said he was coming home for lunch and she'd do it then."

"OK, I'm still uncomfortable about this, but it would sure help us out. Call me back when she calls you back."

24

August 22, 1942

Groton, Connecticut

After Dade and Tom Detrick dropped off their wives at the train station, they got into Dade's car. Before he started the engine, Dade turned and said, "I really owe you one for this, Tom. Hell, here you and Alice are, young newlyweds, and you offer to be apart for two months more than you really need to be. That's quite a sacrifice. So much so, that I almost told Rachael that we'd have to refuse your kind offer."

"Skipper, I'd like to take credit for it, but I can't. It was Alice's decision."

"Maybe the idea was hers, but you gave her your permission."

"No, sir, I didn't. Alice told me she was going to do it."

"Is this one of those modern marriages I keep hearing about?"

"Maybe you could call it that," Detrick laughed easily. "We normally talk over and reach agreement on everything, but we have kind of an exception clause. If one of us believes in doing something very, very strongly, then they go ahead even if the other disagrees."

"It's hard to understand that kind of arrangement working out. I always thought marriage was about compromise."

"Sure, so do we, in most things. It's just that sometimes you can't compromise except to allow the other person to do what they believe needs to be done. It doesn't happen often. In fact, I'll give you an example. The first time we couldn't agree on something important was my signing up for the last two years of NROTC in college. Alice was extremely, unalterably opposed. I couldn't be moved either. I felt that I wanted to do my part in defending my country and our way of life. We split up, but not for long. She decided us being together for the rest of our lives was more important than my doing a couple of years on active

96

duty in the Navy. There were a couple of other times, too. This was one of those times. Alice told me about Rachael's situation and told me she was going with her. They've become very close. I love Alice, and I'll miss her those extra two months, but if she feels she needs to do this, then so be it."

"You know I would never have asked this of you. And Rachael didn't ask Alice."

"I know, sir. She just took it upon herself to offer. Out of friendship."

"Anyway, this means a lot to me and to Rachel. Thank you."

"You're welcome, sir."

"I take it you don't plan to stay in the Navy once the war is over."

"My original plans were and are to become a civil engineer. To build roads, bridges, that kind of thing."

"That's a noble endeavor. You'd make a damned fine career naval officer though."

"Thank you, sir, but once this war is over, I want to build things, not destroy them. I don't ever want to have to kill people again either."

"But sometimes that's necessary."

"I know, and I try to be very good at destroying things and killing people. Frankly, I even take kind of a perverse pride in how well I do it. But, when the war is over, I'm gone to start a new life with Alice. Are you staying in? By the time the war ends, you'll have enough time in to retire, or at least be close to it."

"Oh, I'm not eligible until June of 1951, but as soon as the war in over, I'll be leaving too. I'll be resigning my commission and anxious to start a new life. I never wanted anything but a naval career since I was about 12 years old, but things happen in a man's life. Things he could never have anticipated. Things that make a man change his plans completely. Good things and bad." Dade was tempted to elaborate, to speak of all that had changed him since the Japanese attack on December 7th, sorely tempted. He had never told anyone but Rachael *everything*, not even Ray Petro or John Henry. He wanted, almost desperately, to be able to talk about some things to another man. Rachael knew him and loved him and she was wise and intelligent. But he longed to be able to talk to another man about some things. He respected and liked Tom Detrick, and wished he could talk about his experiences and thoughts, but was bound by his position as captain. It is and always has been, he knew, true that the commander of a unit was the loneliest man in it, and that was especially true of the captain of a naval vessel in wartime. It had to be thus. In the wardroom of a submarine, the lieutenants and lieutenants j.g. often used each other's first names, while the ensigns were normally addressed by the lieutenants as "Mister" or by their last names. At least until they proved themselves, which sometimes took months. The captain normally addressed the other officers by their first names, but no one addressed the captain by his first name, no matter how long he'd served under him. It was unthinkable. The captain was always addressed as "skipper" or "captain" or "sir." And, of course, the gulf between the enlisted men and the captain was even wider. The captain had the complete responsibility for the boat and the crew. He made all the major decisio ns. Whether or not the sub returned safely to port from a war patrol was, to a great extent, determined by how skilled and courageous the captain was. The lives of every man aboard were in his hands. He had to be set apart. Bowie could be friendly, but he could have no real friends except his peers, other submarine captains.

It was a hell of a thing, Dade thought, as he drove toward Detrick's quarters to drop him off. He could think of some good advice to give the young officer, not only about the Navy and submarines, but about life. He had learned a lot in the last eight months, a hell of a lot.

"Do you remember how you and John Henry clashed the first time you met?" Dade asked.

"I'll never forget it, skipper. He scared the hell out of me. In fact, he seemed so pissed off, I thought he was going to punch me out. And that wasn't the only time, either. He was very mercurial."

"He scared most people."

"Except you. Some people say that you were the only person who was never afraid of him. Why was that, sir? If you don't mind my asking," Tom quickly added.

"I guess it was because . . . . I don't know, I guess it was because I admired him so much and felt that I could learn a lot from him about submarines and commanding them. As long as you did an excellent job, John Henry didn't bother you. He might not be open and friendly or even like you, but he wouldn't bother you. Once I learned that, once everybody learned that, they were OK with him. Lots of submariners wanted to serve under him."

"I guess you know a lot of submariners want to serve under you."

"Yes. Ever since the second war patrol."

"And the third. You did an incredible amount of damage to the Japs and brought everyone home alive."

"Yes, I guess everyone wants to serve with a man who'll probably bring them home alive."

"Yes, but it's more than that, sir. It's the two carriers you sank as well as all the other ships. Men want to serve on a submarine they can be proud of."

"Yes, I suppose there's that." He stared ahead in silence fo r a long moment. "I still miss that old man. He was like a father to me." Damn it, he had said too much. Too much.

"I respected him too, sir. He was . . . . . . a good skipper."

"Yes."

"Alice tells me your wife may be able be help her get a job with O NI if she can't secure a teaching job."

"Yes, there's that possibility. ONI employs a lot of people with very specialized skills, and mathematics is one of them. The only downside is that they expect their people to work 60-hour weeks because they're always so shorthanded. But it's important work, and the ONI people are making a significant contribution to the war effort." For a long time there was silence. Dade yearned to talk to the young man about all the things he had so recently learned about courage, loyalty, love, friendship, and duty. There was so much to say, but he was the captain. Then he was pulling up in front of Detrick's quarters.

"Here we are, Tom. I'll see you on Monday, and thanks again."

"You're welcome, sir."

25

August 25, 1942

Laramie, Wyoming

When the train stopped to take on new passengers and baggage and let others off, Rachael and Alice stepped off it to walk on solid ground for a change and get some fresh air. It was about 11:15 am and sunny. The temperature was a pleasant 78 degrees and a light breeze blew.

"This is great," Alice said, "I just get sick and tired of all the constant vibration."

"I know. On a short train trip, you don't mind it. But days of it kind of wears you out."

"Was this morning the first time you had morning sickness?"

"No, it happened a couple of days before we left Connecticut. That was the first time. It's not so bad if I eat lightly and rest," Rachael replied, as they walked alongside the train. "Besides, I'm taking it in stride. God knows there are a lot more days of discomfort before the big event."

"You know, this is quite a big adventure for me. I've never been out of Connecticut in my entire life, well, except to go to New York City a few times to see plays or concerts. My home town is Danbury, and we're only about 50 miles northeast of New York City. I went to elementary and high school in Danbury, then it was on to New Britain to attend Central Connecticut State University. I've really done no traveling at all. I can't wait to see Hawaii. What's it really like?"

"Before the war, it was absolutely wonderful. Since Pearl Harbor, not as much. Its biggest industry was tourism, and it was very slow and relaxed. Now it's a bustling place, with more soldiers and sailors showing up from the States every day. The tourist trade is now nonexistent. It's still very prosperous, just in different ways now. Instead of entertaining tourists, the locals are entertaining all the thousands and thousands of military men and making money from them. In addition, there are more jobs than ever for civilians who are building military facilities or want to work as civilians for the War Department. There are still some wonderful beaches and picnic areas on Oahu though, and the climate is just about perfect. You'll like it."

"Do you think we're in any danger of the Japanese torpedoing our ship?"

"No, I don't think so. At least they haven't torpedoed any passenger liners yet, and, since their stunning defeat at Midway, they're probably concentrating their naval units in other areas. Besides, there'd be no gain in sinking a civilian passenger liner. Their priority is our naval ships and our supply and troop ships."

"You seem to know a lot about the war."

"It's a big part of my job at ONI to know."

"And you can't tell me anything about the job except that you're a Japanese translator."

"Right. In intelligence work, we have a little joke, 'I could tell you, but then I'd have to kill you.'"

Alice smiled. "It sounds terribly interesting, even exciting."

"It can be," Rachael nodded. "But there's a lot of tedium too. It's a lot of work, hard work."

An hour later, back on the train, Rachael continued to look through the window, bonding with her country just as she had on the way to Groton. During those terrible years in Japan, she wondered if she'd ever see America again, and, after about ten years, her memories from her girlhood in Minnesota had faded to the point that they began to seem, not memories of something real, but memories of a dream she'd had long ago. America had ceased to be real. And now, here it was, real, vibrant, an enormous land peopled by those who shared her native language, customs, history, values, and dreams. This was the land where anything could happen. It was not a half-remembered fable, but real. She could reach out and touch it. Alice had been reading, and now she had dozed off into a light sleep. Rachael smiled as she looked at the young woman she had become so very fond of in such a short time. Like most people born in America, she had taken it all for granted. Well, so had she, Rachael admitted to herself, until she had seen ugliness and brutality in a far-off land.

Americans thought that the rest of the people in the world were very much like themselves. That all people wanted the same things—peace, democracy, tolerance, justice, and mercy. But that wasn't true. People in some countries wanted war so they obtain victory over others they either despised, or wanted to exploit and enslave. Many people in the world thought that democracy was foolish; that a country needed strong and powerful leaders (*ein volk, ein reich, ein fuhrer*) who made all the decisions. Tolerance and mercy were considered weaknesses in many cultures, and justice, well that was a pretty elastic concept. It often translated as justice to certain classes or to those who supported whatever regime was in power at the time.

Maybe this war would disabuse Americans from their naiveté. In fact, it was sure to happen as they went and fought in distant lands. Rachael wished that she could spare Alice from some of the pain she herself had gone through in life. She especially hoped that Tom would live to see the end of the war. If Dade were killed, now she at least would have a part of him for the rest of her life. She would have his child. Perhaps it would have his eyes or his smile. It astounded her that, right now, a new human being was living and growing inside of her. It filled her with a sense of awe and strengthened her belief that God existed. Heaven knew, she had had many doubts about that over the years. Sometimes the world had shown itself to be an ugly place, peopled by cruel brutes. By the time she left Japan, her belief in a good and wise God who loved the people he had created, who listened to their prayers and often interceded in their lives to help and heal and bless them, that belief, had been so worn away that it was barely existent.

Then her whole life had been turned around. On her way back to Minnesota, friendless and nearly penniless, upon her arrival in Honolulu, she had been offered a high paying job at ONI, had been befriended by a young woman who was now her best friend, had met and fallen in love with Dade, lived comfortably in a tropical paradise, and remarried. All within the space of 13 months. She was happier than she'd ever been in her life. And now, she was to be a mother. There was only one cloud on her horizon—her worry that Dade might not survive the war. The thought of losing him, when it came, almost crippled her emotionally for hours. But, at least now there was her baby. Her baby would need her, especially if Dade were to be killed.

Alice's eyelids fluttered and she looked around to orient herself. "I guess I dozed off for a while."

"Yes. Don't worry though. You didn't miss anything. Mostly just open spaces. But I like the open spaces. You don't see that in Hawaii."

"You know, I'm embarrassed to admit this, but I'm a little afraid of the boat trip. Years ago, I read a detailed book about how the *Titanic* went down. Over 1,500 people were drowned." She shuddered. "It gave me nightmares for weeks."

Rachael smiled. "Don't worry, our journey doesn't take us near any icebergs."

"I know, but what if we're torpedoed? The *Lusitania* was a passenger liner and it was torpedoed."

"That was in 1915."

"Yes, but 1,200 people died when that ship went down."

"Again, the Japanese haven't attacked any passenger ships yet, and there's no reason why they would. Don't worry. If it makes you feel any better, I'm sure there'll be lifeboat drills, just in case. Also, if that happened, the ship would immediately send out a radio message giving our position and help would be there before you know it. This isn't 1912 or 1915."

"I suppose you're right. It just scares me a little. Drowning, I mean. The idea of desperately trying to take air into your lungs and all you get is water instead. The hopeless panic you must feel."

Alice's words made Rachael think of the men aboard a sinking submarine with water gushing in. She felt a chill go down her spine.

26

September 2, 1942

Groton, Connecticut

Armond Robhar was taking a turn through the boat, mostly nodding his head to himself in satisfaction at all he saw. The *Sea Otter* was shaping up nicely. She was a fine boat and would be finished on schedule. As Chief of the Boat, she was more his boat than the other members of the crew, except for the skipper, of course. Armond was, more than any other enlisted man, responsible for its overall operation and performance. He could see no serious problems with the boat, but the men were another matter. In peacetime, whenever a new sub was under construction, two-thirds of her first crew normally consisted of men who had already served on submarines before, and the remaining one-third consisted of men who had just graduated from Sub School. This time around, of 63 crew members, only 32 men had served aboard subs, and of that 32, only 8 had served on actual war patrols. Only half of the crew had served on subs and only an eighth had seen combat. All the men seemed willing enough and enthusiastic enough, but the lack of experience bothered Robhar. It wouldn't have mattered in peacetime. Fine. Inexperienced men would make mistakes and learn from them. But mistakes and inexperience in war often mean death for them and those around them. Possibly death for the whole crew.

He knew it couldn't be helped. America was cranking out thousands of planes and ships and tanks and now, with the war barely nine months old, there were not enough experienced men to man those instruments of destruction. A man could be taught the basics of how to be a soldier or sailor in a concentrated few months, but there wouldn't be enough experienced senior NCOs and senior officers for a

while. It also took a while for a man to become mentally tough enough for war.
No American man outside of prison had had a civilian job killing people. Well, he
would just have to make do, would have to work longer and harder in training the
inexperienced men. At least their morale and willingness to work seemed to be
OK.

Armond had begun his walkthrough in the After Torpedo Room and had been
working his way toward the bow. Now, as he entered the Forward Torpedo Room,
he saw about a dozen men clustered around Carl Logan, who was leaning casually
against the forward bulkhead, his right hand resting on one of the muzzle doors of
one of the torpedo tubes. He was "holding court." That's what the senior chiefs
in the Navy called it when a chief starts telling boots and new guys what it was
like back in the days of the Old Navy, when men were men. They'd spin sea
stories, tell of mighty legends, and recount tales of magnificent three-day drunks
and liberty ports filled with beautiful and willing women. "Holding court" was
considered to be beneath a real salt. The saltier a chief was, it was felt, the less
need he had to actively try to impress the younger sailors.

". . . one of the best liberty ports in the whole world," Logan was saying, when
Armond walked further into the room and remarked with a tolerant smile,
"'Holdin' court are we, Carl?"

Logan looked and saw that it was the Chief of the Boat. He looked
embarrassed, but gamely tried to hide it with a hearty, "Some of the lads were just
asking me about some of the places we been and so forth, Armond."

"Chief," a freckled young man barely old enough to shave, said, addressing
Armond, "Chief Logan said before that both of you served under John Henry
Hammerhand. We was just gettin' ready to ask about him."

"You asked the right man, son," Logan declared quickly. "The Chief of the
Boat served with John Henry for years, a lot longer than me. I only served under
him aboard the *Elver*."

Robhar looked at the eager kid's face and saw that the whole group had turned
to him. "Yeah, that's right. I served proudly with him for years, off and on, going
back to the S-boat days in the Asiatic fleet."

"Did he really have wolf's eyes?" another youngster asked, eyes wide.

"Yes, he did. His eyes were yellow with a bit of copper and rust tint. They
looked exactly like the eyes of a wolf. A wild and hungry wolf who was pissed
off mightily."

"See? I told you!" the kid said triumphantly to a buddy.

"Was he really the toughest captain in the whole Navy?" asked another, who
sounded doubtful.

"Yeah, there's no doubt of that. He also knew more about submarines than
any man alive, except, well, for Commander Bowie, who knows as much. I think
that's why the two of them got on so well. Hell, you could take any submarine and
all its gear aboard apart into as many pieces as you could, down to every individual

screw and bolt and rivet, and either one of them could reassemble the sub. Blindfolded. John Henry suffered no fools, but he was a fair man. If you knew your job and had your shit together, you didn't have anything to fear from the skipper. Sometimes he lost his temper, and there was hell to pay, but he was fair. Fair, but God help you if you fucked up. A man who fucked up once under John Henry never fucked up again. That is, *if* John Henry gave him a second chance after he disciplined the man. Some sailors that fucked up once—officer or enlisted, it didn't matter—never got a second chance. John Henry just threw their asses off the boat with a notation in their personnel jackets that 'the man is unfit for submarine duty.' A word to the wise: this skipper is the same way. He ain't as big or as loud or as scary as John Henry, but he don't tolerate fuckups."

"We heard John Henry killed a man in the boxing ring at the Naval Academy," said another, arms folded.

"That's not true. The man didn't die. For you new men, this is a good example of what scuttlebutt is like. There's usually some truth to scuttlebutt, but some of it is usually false too."

"Scuttlebutt says he killed his wife. Is that true?" came another question.

"We were stationed at San Diego years ago. Seems John Henry's wife disappeared one day and she was never found. The police questioned him, but there was never any evidence that he killed her. Odds are that she just ran off." Armond was getting a little uncomfortable. It was only natural that the men would want to know about the most famous captain who ever served in submarines. The man had been a true legend in his own time, and, like many legends, the stories were beginning to grow and become more colorful and dramatic after his death. While John Henry was dead and had left no family, he had been gone for less than six months, and Armond wondered if his old skipper wasn't still entitled to a little privacy about his personal life for a while longer, out of respect.

"Did he really blow his brains out?"

Armond almost ended the discussion at that moment, but didn't. Men, especially sailors, need their heroes, their legends, their superstitions. It was the glue that held them together. "Yes, that's true."

"Why?"

"That's no mystery. They finally forced him into taking a fourth stripe and gave him a desk job. He always said he couldn't take a job ashore, that he needed the feel of the deck plates of a submarine under his feet and the salt spray in his face as he stood on the bridge."

No one spoke for a moment, Robhar figured that was because they were unconsciously observing a moment of silence, showing respect for a great man. Finally, another man did speak. The boat's new yeoman, Grant.

"Was you with the skipper on the Truk mission?"

"Yes. So was Chief Logan here," Armond nodded toward the Forward Torpedo Room boss. So were six others on this boat, counting the skipper."

"From what I heard, the skipper must have a lot of balls."

"Fuckin' A!" Logan chimed in loudly. "Ain't nothin' scares this skipper. Hell, next war patrol, it wouldn't surprise me none if he sailed us into Tokyo Bay."

Robhar caught the sudden worried look on some of the faces of the group. "Well now, Carl," he smiled, "I don't see him doing that, unless he was ordered to do it for photographic reconnaissance, say, but even if that happened, I'll bet the skipper could get us in and out of there safely."

"True, Chief, true," Logan allowed.

"It seems to me we all should get back to work now. There's a war on." So saying, Robhar turned and left to go back aft.

Oliver Wirtz sat in the wardroom amid stacks of paperwork. He'd organized all the incoming into High Priority Items, Completed Reports, Requisitions, Personnel Actions, Leave and Liberty Requests, Documents Requiring the Skipper's Approval and Signature, Route to Appropriate Crew Member(s), and several other categories. While he had been XO of a school boat and was completely familiar with all the paperwork necessary to run a submarine, he had never been XO of a sub under construction. There was easily four times as much paperwork for this boat. He was beginning to get along with the skipper and the Chief of the Boat. Things were going according to schedule, and, with Madeline out of the picture now, and Timmy with his parents, there was no pressure in his off-duty hours. No more smart ass remarks or drunken binges, no concern that Timmy wasn't being properly cared for.

Nevertheless, he was lonely. Wirtz considered spending his free time at the Officers Club after work every day. Since he'd been permanent party for so long here, he knew a lot of guys. He could hoist a few with them, take part in some good-natured ribbing, maybe play a little poker for small stakes or play pool. He was an excellent 8-ball player. Or just have some conversations. Conversations about anything—sports, current events, movies, the latest scuttlebutt, war news— it didn't matter. He had few opportunities to talk to anyone at work except about work. And that's all the skipper and the other officers seemed to want to talk about.

Oliver decided to spend two or three nights a week at the Officers Club. Especially every Friday night, when there was always some live entertainment at the club, but he decided to just go back to the BOQ all the other nights and just read, sleep, and listen to the radio. Every Sunday, he'd call his folks in Indiana and say a few words to them and to Timmy.

Bowie was almost as much a legend as his mentor, John Henry Hammerhand. Oliver could never take his eyes off one particular ribbon in the fruit salad on his skipper's chest. The first one on the first row. The five white stars on a pale blue background that signified he'd been awarded the Medal of Honor. The Medal of Honor. Oliver would do anything to be able to wear that ribbon.

In all fairness, Oliver thought, Bowie never bragged about his being awarded the Medal at the White House by FDR himself. Neither did he ever brag about his famous war patrols. But one didn't need to brag, when he wore that rib bon. Bowie never bragged about his being a millionaire either, though scuttlebutt said he came from a famous Texas family that had had millions upon millions from their oil empire. But damn it, he wasn't friendly either. Except to the other seven men aboard who had served with him on the storied *Elver*. His "band of brothers." On one hand, Wirtz could understand being closer to the men who'd been tempered in the crucible of combat with you, but not to the point of the group becoming kind of a clique that made all others on the boat feel like outsiders. Well, at least there were three other officers aboard besides himself who were not *Elver* alumnae. Lt. David Greenbaum (who had not yet reported for duty) was slated to be the Torpedo and Gunnery Officer, Ensign Mike Day was the Assistant Engineering Officer, and Ensign Dan Remick was the Assistant Diving Officer. Of course, it wouldn't be appropriate for him, as the XO, to pal around with two ensigns, but he could still be friendly to them.

If only he hadn't gotten off on the wrong foot with Bowie when they met the first time. He realized now how idiotic he must have sounded saying that he couldn't wait to go into combat. Damn it, he *did* want to go into combat, like a lot of red-blooded men who wanted payback for Pearl Harbor. But he was also afraid of it, and that was normal too. He realized now that he should have just kept his mouth shut until he got to know the skipper a little better. If he had waited for even a few days, he would have discovered that the new skipper was not the kind of man you could impress with a stated eagerness to go into battle. Bowie's first impression of him—and you didn't get a second chance to make a good first impression—was that Wirtz was either stupid or had been lying to him. Damn.

Well, there was nothing for it but to work hard, say little, and prove himself. Prove not only his competence and maturity, but, when the time came, to prove himself in battle.

27

September 3, 1942

Groton, Connecticut

"I was expecting you to report a hell of a lot sooner than this," Dade said irritably to the officer who stood before him on the pier. "After all, we sail on October 14, and you should have been here to make sure the systems you're responsible for on this boat were being installed correctly, among other things."

Lt. David Greenbaum shrugged. "I agree with you, sir, but I didn't get my orders until last week, and I was supposed to report today."

Bowie sighed in frustration. "Yeah, I suppose it's not your fault. You bring your personnel jacket with you?"

"Yes sir," Greenbaum said, raising a thick brown manilla envelope.

"I'll go over it in detail tonight. What's your story? The short version."

"Naval ROTC at Ohio State. Class of '40, sir. I went on active duty right after graduation for what was supposed to be two years. Then came Pearl Harbor, and they told me I would not be going off active duty in June 1942, but was now in for the duration of the war."

"How do you feel about that?" Bowie demanded. "I had a Torpedo and Gunnery Officer on my first two war patrols who felt himself ill used because the Navy called him up for active duty after only one year of law school. That was before the war started, so it's not exactly the same situation as yours, but do you bear the Navy a grudge?"

"No sir, I don't. This war definitely threw a massive monkey wrench into all my carefully made plans, but then, it's done that for tens of millions of people all over the world." He shrugged again. "I don't waste valuable time being pissed off about things I have no control over."

109

"That's a sensible attitude. And exactly what were your carefully made plans?"

"I'm a musician, a composer, and a songwriter. And I'm great at all three callings. I plan to start my own big band and make millions in appearances, radio shows, and record sales. In the last two years I've written six songs that Glen Miller, Tommy Dorsey, and Harry James made famous, and that, incidentally made me a bundle of money too."

"That's very impressive. What do you play?"

"The trumpet. And, if it weren't for my going in the Navy, I'd already have my own band now."

"Are you that good on the trumpet?"

Greenbaum smiled. "I'm every bit as good as Harry James is and Bunny Berigan was."

"Was?"

"Berigan died three months ago. In fact, three months ago today."

"Damn! He wasn't that old."

"Thirty-three. I understand that it was primarily due to his alcoholism."

"Too Bad. You're really that good?"

"Yes."

"OSU, you said. What was your major?"

"Music."

"Ummm."

"Is that a problem, sir?"

"Frankly, I'd feel better if you had a background in engineering and math."

"Skipper, a man can have talent in several areas. And I've proven that on my last sub. I was Torpedo and Gunnery Officer there. Check out my fitness ratings when you look at my personnel jacket."

"I will. Have you seen any combat yet?"

"No sir."

"Well neither have most of the crew on the *Sea Otter*. Only an eighth of us. As you can imagine, that's not something I'm happy about."

"I understand, skipper."

"You didn't bring your horn with you, did you?"

"I did. It's in its case in the middle of my seabag. My previous skipper allowed me to play it for a while on the cigarette deck in the evenings. Some of the off-duty crew gathered around and listened. It was a good morale lifter."

Bowie thought for a long moment. "On combat patrols, I limit the number of men on the cigarette deck to four at a time when we're cruising on the surface at night. When we sight the enemy, we need to get below as fast as possible. But I like to give everyone a chance to get some fresh air at least once a day, even if it's only for 10 or 15 minutes. We'll give your horn a try. But under no circumstances are you allowed to play that thing below."

110

"Of course not, sir."

"Greenbaum, humility doesn't seem to be one of your virtues. I don't know or care how good you are with your trumpet or writing music. But, damn it, you'd better be as good or better as you think you are as a Torpedo and Gunnery Officer. And if you aren't, you'd better become that good quickly. Yours is one of the most important positions on the boat. All our lives depend on how well you do your job. If you fuck up, we can all die."

"I understand, sir."

"All right, go below and report to the XO. I'll talk to you again after I've read your jacket."

"Aye, aye, sir."

28

September 4, 1942

Pacific Ocean

"I wish you could calm down a little," Rachael said to Alice Detrick. "After all, the *Titanic* went down thirty years ago." The two women were sitting side by side on comfortable deck chairs and it was a beautiful day.

"I'm doing better," the younger woman replied. "I keep reminding myself the things that you told me. That, as a result of the *Titanic* tragedy, there now has to be enough life boats for all passengers, that the radio frequencies are monitored 24 hours a day, seven days a week, and that ships have improved their sea worthiness. I also remind myself that it took well over two hours for the ship to sink, and that we're not traveling in the North Atlantic and we won't be seeing any icebergs. I also feel better that we had that life boat drill a couple of days ago, and that we know which life boat we're assigned to. I'm feeling much better."

"Good. Enjoy the voyage. There'll be plenty of work for us to do once we get to Hawaii. I'll have to find a place to rent and get ready for Dade. If th ere are no junior officers' quarters available on base for you and Tom, you'll have to do the same. Then there's my job at ONI to go back to, and you'll be job hunting. We'll be very busy. Enjoy this rest."

"I'm doing my best. There's more than my fear of the ship going down that's bothering me, though. I'm thinking a lot about the war."

"That's only natural. Just don't let the fear of what might happen destroy the days you do have."

"I know," Alice nodded, "the Stoic philosophers you told me about. 'The past is unalterable and the future is unknowable. All we have is today.' Still, I worry. If I lost Tom, I don't know what I'd do."

"I feel the same way about Dade. How I wish we'd met twenty years ago. The only yesterdays we had together amount to a few days here and a few days there over an 8-month period, during which he was at sea most of the time. We spent the youth of our 20's and 30's apart, never knowing each other. All we have now, all that's left, may be a very short time, if Dade is killed in this war. I plan to live and enjoy each day with him as it comes, knowing that perhaps there is no future for us, no postwar years to enjoy our children and each other in a world at peace."

"That . . . . . . I don't know how you can maintain such equanimity. The only way I can cope is to believe, really believe, that Tom will live. To believe that his death just can't happen. To believe in—I don't know—a kind of magic."

"But you're too old to believe in magic, Alice."

"Yes, but if I try, I can make myself believe in it most of the time. It's all I have, you see. As you know, I have my doubts in the existence of a just and loving God who cares about us."

"It seems to me that it's easier to believe in God than in magic."

"But isn't it really the same thing? You can't prove or disprove magic just as you can't prove or disprove the existence of God. Logically, I mean. It all comes down to *choosing* to believe, rather than arriving at an irrefutable belief through a logical analysis of empirical evidence."

"I have my times of doubt in the existence of God, but I believe in him most of the time. And, yes, it all comes down to making a conscious choice to believe. Furthermore, sometimes it's very hard to believe. The scope of the war, the sheer barbarity, the incredible suffering and death and destruction make it very difficult. When we were in Groton, I began going to church every Sunday in an attempt to strengthen my belief in God. To eliminate the doubts I experience from time to time. It had little effect."

"The war. I don't know what to make of the war. I've said this only to you, because I think you'll understand: I don't hate anyone. I don't hate the Germans or the Italians or the Japanese. I respect you and your beliefs, but I think we're all just human beings who are very, very much alike. We all want the same things. Peace, a home, someone to love who loves us back. Friendship, security, enough to eat and to wear, a trade or job that gives meaning and worth to our lives, the respect of others. We want to be understood and cherished and valued. Wars happen because a few people who rule countries vie with each other for power and use their subjects as pawns. And all the pawns are persuaded or threatened into a belief that there is no solution but to begin killing each other until one side has been destroyed. They are told that it's their bounden duty to do this, and they believe it.

"So I don't hate the Germans. My mother's family came from Germany only thirty years ago, and they're good people. The Germans, as a whole, are decent people. It was Germany who gave the world Wagner, Beethoven, Schopenhauer, Brahms, Schumann, Hesse, Kant, Schiller, Goethe, and Luther. And the Germans are preeminent in science and industry. I can't believe that everyone or even most of the people in Germany are Nazis. Are evil people. And surely the Japanese can't all be evil either." Alice suddenly stopped herself, remembering the terrible experiences Rachael had had in Japan. "I mean," she began more evenly, "I'm angry about what the Japanese did at Pearl Harbor. I really am. But everyone says they hate the Japanese because of it. They say they hate the 'dirty Japs' and want to see them all dead. I'm sorry, but I don't hate the entire Japanese people," she finished defensively.

Rachael was silent for a very long moment. "Hatred and love are the two most powerful emotions we humans have. Some say that they are both sides of the same coin. I don't know about that; perhaps it's true. I do know that there are many different degrees of hatred and love. I also think that the degree to which you hate is determined by your own personal experience. For example, before the war, Dade was as indifferent to Japanese as he was to, oh, say Romanians. The only difference was that most professional American naval officers believed that one day war with Japan was almost inevitable. They planned for it and trained for it, but there was no hatred in their preparations. Indeed, they hoped that day would never come.

"Then on a quiet Sunday morning, that war did come, and the carnage at Pearl Harbor was almost indescribable. So suddenly, all those Americans who were there instantly hated, passionately hated, the whole Japanese people. They had lost friends, shipmates, and classmates. Many women lost fathers, husbands, brothers, and lovers. So they hated. They hated in direct proportion to the pain they experienced. I told you that Dade said that he hated the Japanese because it made his job easier. It's easier to kill people if you hate them. But he also said that, once the war had been over for several years and both Americans and Japanese put the war behind them, he'd probably revert to an emotional neutrality about them. He said that my hatred of them was nothing like his, that my hatred was more powerful, more visceral. And I think he was right. I will probably always hate the Japanese. I will always hate them for the way they treated me and my husband for twenty horrid years during which no one, no one, extended us the smallest kindness or civil word. I will always hate them for the time a Japanese man tried to rape me at knife point, for the brutal way in which Japanese naval cadets hacked my husband to pieces before my very eyes, spattering me and the walls and the floor and the ceiling with his blood and pieces of his brains and intestines and lungs and kidneys and stomach and bowels . . . . . . " Rachael stopped speaking and stared at the horrific vision in the past as vivid today as it had been on the night it happened. After a moment, she resumed. "I will hate the Japanese for their burning our home

114

to the ground along with all our possessions. Not that we had many, except for my books. The books that had kept me sane for all those years."

"It would be foolish and untrue to say I understand, because I realize I can't understand what you went through. Still, you're an intelligent, educated, and good woman. How can you possibly hate all the millions of people who live in Japan? How many of them are there?"

"Over 73 million."

"How can you hate 73 million people?"

"It's not difficult at all. Especially these days, when they're trying to kill Dade every time he goes out on patrol."

"But he's trying to kill them!"

"Yes, but they attacked us first, and without warning. They're fighting to enslave people and we're only defending ourselves."

"Yes, but—"

"I know," Rachael sighed heavily. "It's only the rulers of the country who are to blame for wars. All people want the same things. People are the same everywhere. But that's not really true, Alice. Countries differ in many ways and the most important difference is in their cultures. America shares many cultural attributes with European countries, because of course, the greatest majority of immigrants have come from Europe. Americans use a European language and most have the same religious beliefs as most Europeans, but the Japanese are very different from us. Look," Rachael sighed heavily, "it's easy to be tolerant and forgiving if you haven't been personally made to suffer. If Tom were killed out on patrol, would you still be so understanding of the Japanese and bear them no ill will?"

Alice frowned and thought hard, her face contorting at times. Finally she spoke, but without much conviction. "Well, of course I would be devastated by his death. Almost insane with grief for a long, long time. But I'd like to think that I would understand that the Japanese who sank his submarine were only doing their jobs, fighting for their country just as he was fighting for his."

Rachael shook her head slowly and sadly, then seemed to change the subject. "Do you know why my living as a missionary became almost impossible for me?"

"Yes, the way the Japanese treated you and your husband."

"No. It was because one day I realized that I had lost my capacity for Christian love. In *Corinthians*, Paul says, 'Though I speak with the tongues of men and angels, and have not love, I am become as sounding brass, or a tinkling cymbal. And though I have the gift of prophecy, and understand all mysteries, and all knowledge; and though I have all faith so I could remove mountains, and have not love, I am nothing. And though I bestow all my goods to feed the poor, and give my body to be burned, and have not love, I am nothing.' Paul wrote this epistle in Greek and the Greek word he used for love was *agape*. The Greeks had several words to express the different kinds of love there are, and by *agape* Paul is talking about the kind of love we should have for all of our fellow human beings. It means loving people even if they have done nothing to deserve it, and even if they don't return it.

"One day I realized that, while I had once had that kind of love for all people, I no longer had it. It was completely gone. So you see, my life as a missionary was not only fruitless and meaningless, it was hypocritical. Except for the love of my husband, I had no love for anyone, and there were days when I didn't even love him for forcing me to live in filth and squalor for the 'sake of God.' I had become an empty vessel, and there is nothing lonelier than being an empty vessel. Frankly, I don't think I ever will regain that kind of Christian love for all people. It was easy to have that love when I lived in Minnesota, and during the early times of my life in Japan. It's easy to love when no one has kicked you in the teeth and hated and reviled you and done evil things. Now I'm going to tell you the kind of thing that goes through my mind when I don't believe in God.

"Let me put it to you this way. Imagine you're a young Chinese mother in Nanking. Then the Japanese troops come and conquer your city. They lay waste to it, kill your husband and scores of thousands of other Chinese even though the city has surrendered. The Japanese troops see you on the street one day with your two children. They grab your 4-year old son, and grasping him by his ankles, swing him against a wall, bashing his skull and splattering his brains all over the wall. Then they rip your baby from your arms, throw it up in the air, and impale her with the bayonets on the ends of their rifles as she starts to fall back toward earth. They're laughing so hard they can hardly stand it. Then they proceed to brutally gang rape you. When they're all quite finished, they beat you unmercifully and leave you for dead. But somehow, you survive even though you wish you hadn't.

"That is exactly the kind of thing that happened all over the city for six weeks from the time the Japanese captured the city on December 13, 1937. They murdered about a quarter of a million Chinese men, women, and children. Such things were common. Tell me, would you hate the Japanese then?"

Alice Detrick's face had turned stark white in horror. "Yes," she replied slowly, "yes, I would."

"Of course you would, Alice. And you'd hate them if they killed Tom. And, do you know why?"

Alice shook her head slowly.

"Because you and I and all of us are animals. Smart animals to be sure. Animals who can write symphonies and discover penicillin and build machines that fly through the air, across a continent or across an ocean. But while we're much smarter than the other animals, that's the only difference. We select mates and have children and will kill, if necessary, to protect both. We're mostly loyal to the large groups into which we're born, just as wolves are to the other members of their packs. When another person or group of people seek to harm us or our pack, we will seek to harm or kill them. If the Japanese killed Tom or took him as a prisoner of war and tortured him, you would want blood. If you had undergone the kind of thing that I described, you would most assuredly hate them. You would want to kill them. It's only natural. Because you're an animal, Alice, just like me. Just like all of us. And, I think in my darkest hours, if a supernatural being ever created us, it was for the sole purpose of amusing himself for a while, and, when he got tired of us, he moved on. If he ever existed, he never really cared about us. Never."

29

October 12, 1942

Groton, Connecticut

Dade Bowie stood in front of the officers and men of the *Sea Otter*, assembled before him at a position of attention in four neat ranks. "At ease men. First, as you know, our farewell party is scheduled for tonight. Normally, the wife of the skipper traditionally plans this shindig with the help of several other wives, but, since neither my wife, nor the XO's, nor any of the other officers' wives are available, our Chief of the Boat's wife, Gladys, graciously stepped forward to volunteer, and has put together a great sendoff. The uniform of the day will be dress blues, and the dinner will begin at 1800 sharp. The cash bar will open an hour before, so there will be time for introductions and conversations before the meal. Many of you will want to introduce your guests, mostly family members, to your shipmates and officers. After dinner, the dance will commence and the band has been hired to play for two hours. At some point during the evening, I expect each and every one of you to personally thank Mrs. Robhar and the ladies who assisted her for all their hard work in making this event happen.

"While I also expect you all to be convivial, freely imbibe, and have a good time, I'd better not see anyone drunk on his ass. That would be extremely disrespectful to our guests. Tomorrow you will all be excused from duty to spend the day with your families, that is, those lucky enough to have family who either live in the area or who are visiting to see you off. The only requirement is that you report back to the *Sea Otter* no later than 2400 hours, since we sail at 0800 on Wednesday. I encourage you with all that's within me to treasure those moments with your loved ones. Savor every second, memorizing all the sights and sounds

118

and smells and feelings and words and embraces. We're bound for a long, hard war in the vastness of the Pacific Ocean and it may be a couple of years before we come back. In fact, we may not be back at all. We may find ourselves riding the boat down to crush depth. It's already happened to many American submariners in this war and it could happen to us.

"That's why it's so important for you to use this time to make good memories with your loved ones. When times get rough—and they will—you'll be able to draw strength from those times, from those bonds. You'll be able to draw purpose and hope from knowing that you're defending them and that they love you. Don't go to war with anything left unsaid, whether it's an apology for some wrong you've done or a simple declaration of love.

"Most of you haven't yet been in combat. Don't worry. We'll be drilling constantly on our way out to the Pacific and even when we're out on combat patrols. Eventually, you'll be able to do what you need to do automatically, no matter how tired you are. Those of us who have been in combat will help you learn. Most of you are young men. Some very young. In fact, last year, a few of you were in high school. Relax. That just means you might learn faster. Are you going to be afraid? Hell yes. Every one of us has been and will be. It's nothing to be ashamed of as long as you can conquer your fear. And you do that by — before you go into battle—thinking about how you'd feel if you let your country down, your family, your shipmates, and most of all, yourself."

Dade looked out over the faces of the men, studying each in turn. Most wore grim expressions. "Well, that's about all I wanted to say. Think on these things. Think about your loved ones and the great country you're defending, and think about your duty to not only them and your shipmates, but to yourselves." He stopped, knowing that there were other things to say, important things that would prepare them for what was in store, but not knowing exactly how to put them into words. The ideas were like smoke that swirled about him, tantalizingly near, but elusive.

"I'll see you all this evening, men. Dismissed."

30

October 16, 1942

Groton, Connecticut

While Wirtz conned the boat down the Thames River on her way out to the Atlantic, Dade stood on the cigarette deck looking back at Groton as it receded from view. It was a chilly fall morning and his hands were in his jacket pockets, his collar turned up. Would he ever see Groton again, or, for that matter, after they were in the Pacific, would he ever see the United States again? Before the war, his life was ordered and entirely predictable. Now it was complicated, not only by the uncertainties of the war, but by his falling in love with Rachael, his sudden wealth, and Rachael's pregnancy. It seemed that ever since the war began, one surprise followed another. The torpedo problem, John Henry's suicide, his close brush with a court martial that would not only have destroyed his career, but put him in a naval prison. The death of friends, Pearl Harbor, one Japanese victory after another for the first six months of the war. Finally, the decisive American victory at Midway. Helping Rachael fight and win her battle with alcoholism. Getting married. The Medal of Honor. No, things hadn't been dull or predictable since December 7th. It seemed like years ago now, but it had only been ten months. Ten scant months. God, he felt as if he had aged ten years. He lit a cigarette, took a deep drag, and expelled the smoke through his nostrils.

They'd have to watch for U-boats, of course, as they made their way down the Atlantic to go through the Panama Canal, but it wasn't nearly as dangerous as sailing through Japanese controlled water in the Pacific.

"Nice morning, ain't it, skipper?"

Dade turned to see the Chief of the Boat smiling at him. "That it is, Armond. It's good to be at sea again. I've missed it."

"Yes sir, I expect you've been missing Mrs. Bowie too."

120

"She's always on my mind. Night and day. I worry that the pregnancy goes well."

"It will, sir. Look, I hate to come to you with a problem at the very start of our voyage, but it can't be helped." Both men automatically looked around to see that no one was in earshot. The lookouts were fairly near up in the periscope shears, binoculars to their eyes, scanning their assigned sectors, but not close enough to hear voices in normal speaking tone.

"OK, shoot."

"It's Brooks—"

Bowie held up his right hand, and covered his eyes with his left. "Don't tell me. I've been studying the personnel jackets of the new men and let me see how much I can remember. Matthew Brooks. Home of Record, Wilkes Barre, Pennsylvania. Torpedoman's Mate. Graduated from high school last year. Worked as an auto mechanic for a few months before joining the Navy. That would make him about 19 now. Excellent fitness reports from boot camp up until the present day. No record of his being a disciplinary problem. He's assigned to the Forward Torpedo Room."

"On the nose, skipper," Robhar smiled. "The only thing I would add is that he seems to be a pretty smart kid and is hardworking. OK, here it is. Brooks went to Chief Logan. He said he needed to talk to you and only you about something very important. Logan reminded him we got a chain of command in the Navy, that if the kid has a request or a beef, he's to talk to Logan about it. If it can't be resolved at his level, then the kid goes to Mister Greenbaum. If it can't be resolved there, next stop is the XO. Last is you. But the kid insists he's gotta talk to you, and we have no idea what the hell this is all about."

"It is odd. But, given his good record, I'll see him. I'm going below to my stateroom now. Send him there right away."

"Aye got to, sir."

"OK, Brooks. I understand that you think you've got to talk to me and only me about something 'very important.' This is highly irregular, but I'm willing to listen." Dade was sitting on the only chair in the room, which was at his small desk. "Have a seat on my bunk and tell me what this is all about."

"Thank you, sir," the tall, blond, and muscular young man said. He was clearly uneasy. After sitting, he laced the fingers on his hands together and stared down at them, reluctant to meet Bowie's eyes. He was silent for a long moment. "Captain, I hope I'm not going to make a lot of trouble for myself over this, because I like the Navy."

"How would you be making trouble for yourself?"

"Well sir, this matter concerns an officer and I'm an enlisted man. I know officers have a lot more rights and privileges than enlisted men and a lot of things don't apply to them."

"Officers have more rights and privileges than enlisted men because they have more responsibilities, but everyone in the Navy has to adhere to its rules and regulations, Brooks."

"Yes sir. It's just that, while some things might be legal or allowed, that doesn't mean that it's always alright to do them. Some things are flat out wrong."

"I would agree with that, but let's get down to specifics. I assume that the officer you're referring to is either me or an officer under my command."

"An officer under your command, sir."

"And you believe that even though that officer did something he may have had the right to do, it was 'wrong'?"

"Yes sir. Flat out wrong," Brooks said fiercely.

"By wrong, do you mean unfair?"

"No sir, I mean immoral."

"Immoral? OK, son, tell me everything."

"Well, sir, my mother drove up from Wilkes Barre to be there for the party on Monday night and to spend all day Tuesday with me. It was a long way for her to drive alone, but we don't know when we'll be seeing each other again."

"Yes, I remember you introducing me to her at the party. A blonde woman in her mid to late thirties wearing a yellow dress. I remember thinking that there was a great deal of family resemblance between you two."

"Yes sir. Everything went fine at the party. Next morning, I went to her hotel to have breakfast with her. We planned to spend the whole day together. Well, I was so happy and so anxious to see her that, I don't know, I just didn't even knock. I just opened the door." The boy got an angry expression on his face and stopped talking.

"And?"

"And I saw Mister Wirtz sitting on the bed. He was in his shirt and pants, but he was putting on his shoes and socks. He was surprised to see me, but he didn't say nothing. Neither did my mother—she was getting dressed too—but her face got real red. I walked out and slammed the door behind me.

"I walked for a long time, maybe an hour. I was so damn . . . . mad and embarrassed and ashamed and disappointed, but mostly mad. Mad at Mister Wirtz. I wanted to punch his lights out, then stomp on his head, kick in his rib cage—"

Vast quantities of adrenalin had been dumped into Dade's bloodstream and he was experiencing precisely the same emotions Brooks was describing. "I want to make sure I understand this, Brooks. By Mister Wirtz, do you mean the XO of this boat?"

"Yes sir."

In a moment of rage, Bowie slammed the palm of his right hand on the small metal desk and it made a noise like a thunderclap. "Continue please."

"After about an hour, I went back to my mother's hotel room. She'd been crying. She told me in a small voice that she wished I hadn't seen what I did. She said she was so ashamed and asked me to forgive her. Said that she wasn't used to drinking alcohol and had a little too much to drink at the party and that Mr. Wirtz offered to drive her home. He bought her a couple more drinks in the hotel bar and the next thing she knew, she was in bed with him. He spent the night with her. Now, sir, maybe I'm just a small town boy, but don't you think it was wrong of him to take advantage of a grieving, lonely widow? She's very vulnerable in her condition."

"A widow?"

"Yes sir. My father got run over by a car about six months ago. She's been taking it pretty hard."

"By 'taking advantage' of her do you mean that he raped her?"

"No sir. No, I would have killed him if he had done that. No, she said it was her fault as much as his. That's why she was so ashamed. She said she had too much to drink and that he was 'a real smooth operator.' Still, don't you think it was wrong?"

"'A real smooth operator.' Of course, I have to hear both sides of the story before coming to a conclusion, but, if things happened as you say they did, yes, it was very wrong of Mr. Wirtz, and he should suffer the consequences. I will be talking to him about it this very day, and he'd better have some damn good answers for me. Have you spoken about this to anyone else?"

"No sir."

"I suggest you don't, for the sake of your mother's reputation and so you won't suffer because of it. A lot of sailors would think it's pretty funny and make jokes about it. Tasteless, vulgar jokes at your expense. I think you'd wind up getting in a lot of fistfights to protect your mother's honor and to get back at the men who would ride you unmercifully about it. There'd be no end to it."

"I understand, sir. I agree."

"Very well. I'll get back to you on this. It is, of course, a very serious charge, and I need time to think."

"Yes sir."

"You wanted to speak to me, skipper?"

"Yes, Mr. Wirtz. I do indeed. I'd like you to tell me about Mrs. Brooks." Dade was sitting at his desk, and had only become angrier since his talk with Torpedoman's Mate Matthew Brooks half an hour before.

The XO's face fell. "I was afraid that would get out. Her son was pretty angry."

"You're damned right he was pretty angry, Mr. Wirtz! But not nearly as angry as I am!"

"Sir, I had no idea the kid was going to just come barging into the room. My intent was to be gone before he got there to take his mother to breakfast! He was half an hour early!"

123

"You just don't get it, do you, Wirtz? It doesn't matter if he never found out about it. It was wrong. The charge 'Conduct Unbecoming an Officer' doesn't begin to address the seriousness of what you did. You're a disgrace to that uniform you wear."

"Sir, with all due respect, you haven't heard my side of the story."

"Which is?" Bowie snapped impatiently.

"She seduced me, sir. I don't know if you remember what she looked like at the party, but she is an extremely attractive woman. And, well, you know my domestic situation."

"Plenty of men in the Navy have marital problems, Wirtz. Hell, my first marriage ended in divorce. That didn't give me an excuse to fuck the mothers or wives of my crew. Besides, you're still married."

"Not for much longer, sir. My wife wrote a couple of weeks ago and asked for a divorce. Which wasn't much of a surprise. In fact, it was more of a relief. Anyway, I said I had only two conditions. First, that I have full custody of my son, and second, that I pay no alimony. Her family is rich as hell and give that spoiled bitch money as fast as she can spend it, and I'll be damned if I'm going to pay her for the rest of her life. She agreed and is having the papers drawn up. When they're ready, she'll send them to me, I'll sign them and send them back, and that'll be it."

"That's really neither here nor there. You've broken the bond of trust men and officers must have between them. How are the men supposed to trust us and respect us if you go around fucking their family members!? Are you really so stupid that you don't understand how serious this is?"

"Sir, as I said, the woman seduced me. She was extremely flirtatious and asked me to drive her back to her hotel because she'd had too much to drink. Once there—"

"Stop. Just stop. Unless she physically overpowered you and forced you to have sex with her, there are no excuses. None."

"Sir, both of us were consenting adults, and what happened between us is no one's business, including yours or, for that matter, her son's."

"Wrong. Even if you were not an officer and a gentleman in this young man's direct chain of command, even the fact that he is a fellow crew member puts what you did beyond the pale. Common decency toward a man with whom you go into battle precludes such despicable conduct. But you are a commissioned officer and in his direct chain of command. You've brought disgrace down on all commissioned naval officers and very probably incalculable harm to the morale of this crew on the eve of battle. You disgust me, Wirtz. You disgust me beyond all words. You don't deserve to wear that uniform, mister. Too many good and brave and honorable men have died wearing it."

"Sir—"

"Shut up. Just shut up and let me think. Just get out of my sight."

"Aye got to, sir."

Dade sat at his desk for a long time after Wirtz had left, trying to will his rapidly pounding heart to slow and to force himself to take slow, deep breaths. What the XO had done was inexcusable. On surface vessels, the men had to respect and have confidence and trust in the officers appointed over them, but, in the submarine service, that need was multiplied by a thousand times. Submariners were a different breed. For one thing, they were all volunteers for especially hazardous duty. Submariners were also smarter than the average sailor. Many sailors applied for sub duty and many were rejected. And a lot who were accepted didn't make it through Sub School. It was an elite service and all its members were proud to be a part of it.

Of course, with the massive buildup necessary for the war, Bowie was sure that it was now easier to get into subs, but he knew the standards would still remain high. Perhaps not as high as peacetime standards, but high. The incompetence or inattention of one crewmember at the wrong moment could send a whole boat down to crush depth. The peacetime Navy that Dade had spent most of his career in, had been small, and there had been no room for any officer who brought dishonor to it. An officer found guilty of this kind of Conduct Unbecoming an Officer would have, at the very least, been given a strong letter of reprimand and a subsequent fitness rating that would have effectively destroyed his career. While he would have been allowed to remain in the Navy, he would never receive another promotion. He would never serve at sea again. Instead, he'd spend the rest of his career at a desk doing administrative work at a Stateside naval base. He'd also be doing all of his drinking alone in the Officers Club, and not be invited to any social gatherings. He'd be shunned as completely as the Amish would shun a member of their sect who decided to join a cult that worshiped Satan.

But this was wartime, Dade thought, did the old standards still apply today? Certainly, Wirtz needed to be punished severely. Justice demanded it. The honor and sacred traditions of the Navy demanded it. Should he take it up with formal charges once the *Sea Otter* reached Hawaii or was it a different world because of the war? COMSUBPAC had wanted to send Dade, Harry Romano, and George Pulaski to a naval prison for disobedience of orders during time of war, but CINCPAC had kept the three of them on active duty because of the exigencies of war.

Bowie thought he'd probably not bring formal charges against the XO. Instead, he would write up the matter in Wirtz's next fitness report. That would be a blow to his career that he probably couldn't recover from. Still, he hesitated to do that to any man. His own career had almost ended ignominiously, and he remembered well how he had felt when it appeared all but certain that his beloved Navy would do that to him. Dade had loved submarines and he had loved the Navy. Did Oliver Wirtz feel the same way? He well might. After all, he was an Academy man, first in his class. He had, like all of the men who had spent four years there, been steeped in the history and traditions of the Navy. His career, the Navy, it all *had* to mean a great deal to him. What if, destroyed by his own broken marriage, and feeling the pressure of having to prove himself to a new skipper and other combat veterans, and the pressure of sailing off to what may turn out to be a couple of years at war, he *had* been seduced by a lonely, very attractive woman who knew exactly what she was doing?

No, it wouldn't wash. There was no excuse. Bowie wondered if, in trying to find at least some mitigating factors, he was really only trying to find some excuse for not taking any action. No, he had to act. But not now. He'd sleep on it. To clear his mind, he decided to write Rachael. To prepare, he took out her last letter and reread it.

September 24, 1942

Dearest Dade,

I finally found it! It took some doing, but I found a wonderful house to rent. It was the home of one of the top Makahiki executives who just retired and is moving back to the States. It's perfect, if a bit larger than we need now. I took your advice that we may as well start living like millionaires, so the rent is extremely high, but well within the price range we talked about. The front faces the ocean, which is about 300 feet down a rolling hill. The large lanai on the back faces pineapple fields almost as far as the eye can see. Between the pineapples and the many wonderful tropical flowers the owner planted on the estate, the aroma is heavenly. The owner took most of the furniture back to the States with him, so I've been doing some furniture shopping with an eye toward at least having the master bedroom, living room, dining room, and kitchen completely furnished by the time you get here. It's so quiet and peaceful here on the grounds. (Before I forget, our new address is: Seacliff Cottage, Makahiki Pineapple Plantation A-41, Oahu, Hawaii.) I've had lunch with Tracy a few times, and she filled me in on what's transpired since we left for the States. The biggest surprise is that she and Lance plan to be married in November. She still plans to work in L-2 for the foreseeable future, which surprised me only a little. As brash and cynical as Tracy makes herself out to be, she is, underneath it all, a true patriot. I see her working until the war is over. This is OK with Lance, except for the number of hours she puts in. He feels that 40 hours a week is enough, but she explained that the need for translators is beyond critical.

Alice was able to find a one-bedroom apartment in Honolulu, and is job hunting, but there are no openings in the area for high school math teachers. I have an idea that they may be interested in taking her on where I work though. I'll find out tomorrow, when I see Paul Duvall about my coming back and the conditions we decided on. I expect him to be disappointed that I'm pregnant and that my obstetrician wants me to only work half days, and then have several weeks off completely. He'll be more disappointed about the rest of it, but we do have our own lives to lead. I'm sure that, when I explain things to him, he'll understand though.

I just had a checkup with the obstetrician. (I did as you said and got the best one on Oahu.) Everything is fine. I've had so much fun and so many great conversations with Alice during the trip here and since we arrived. She's been such a comfort and joy to me, but I miss you terribly. I enjoyed seeing the States again and our time in Groton, but I've come to feel that Hawaii is my real home now. It was where a long nightmare ended for me and I began a new life. It was where I met Tracy, my best friend, and where I met you, my beloved husband. It's where I was hired to do very important work for my country at a place where I'm highly valued. It's where I married you. There are so many wonderful memories for me here and I love it so. I'm open to any other ideas you may have, but I think I'd like us to settle here permanently. Once the war is over, it will become less crowded again and the pace slower.

Of course, we can still take trips to the States for fun and sightseeing and shopping. Once Europe recovers from the war, we can go there too. Still, I feel that Hawaii is now my home. I hope you feel the same way. We wouldn't necessarily have to live on Oahu. Maui, Kauai, and the Big Island are possibilities too. Well, we have a lot of time to decide about those things.

Our first child is on his or her way, I have a job to return to, and you have a war to fight before then. I try to pray and sometimes succeed in believing that a Supreme Being listens and cares about us, about anyone. At other times, well, life does seem like "a tale told by an idiot, full of sound and fury, signifying nothing." Sometimes I think of John Henry's last letter to you. The one he wrote just before committing suicide. I know you remember what he said: "There is no meaning of life, no purpose or reason for our existence. We are born, live, and die with no more meaning to our lives than the lives of bacteria. The great secret of life is that there is no meaning."

I know I shouldn't say such things, but sometimes I believe them. Just as John Henry did. Just as you sometimes do. But we have to be able to be truthful with each other. Our love for each other has—from its first moments until now—always been predicated on that.

There is one thing I always believe, even on the blackest of days. I believe that you and I were meant for each other and that I will love you for the rest of my life. That has never changed and it never will. And, for me, that's enough to keep me going.

> *Love Always,*
> *Rachael*

Dade read the letter again, once again treasuring her last paragraph, drawing strength from it. He began to write:

October 16, 1942

Dear Rachael,

We're at sea now, headed south down the East Coast. We'll top off our fuel tanks in Florida (where I'll mail this letter), then it's south again and through the Panama Canal. The next stop after that is San Diego, then San Francisco, then home to you. We're still scheduled to arrive in Pearl Harbor on November 8th. We'll be running a lot of drills along the way because the crew needs it, especially the new men. We need to arrive in Pearl Harbor battle ready because I think they'll be sending us out on a war patrol as soon as we refuel and lay in food and other supplies. I think they'll give us a few days in port, but I wouldn't count on two weeks. It'll probably be five or six days.

The new boat is a good one. The biggest improvement over the *Elver* is that the *Sea Otter's* SJ radar is both far more reliable and has greater range. Unfortunately, the SD radar hasn't been improved. As always, it's nondirectional and has limited range. Of course, everything in the Sea Otter is brand new, and smells it. It's kind of like a "new car smell" except that this smell is a little different. It's composed mostly of fresh paint, freshly cut linoleum on the deck, and fresh new bedding. The Otter handles like a dream.

Unfortunately, a serious personnel problem has arisen today. It has to do with a "Conduct Unbecoming an Officer" incident that happened just before we left port. I know the charge doesn't sound serious, but sometimes these kinds of breaches have destroyed men's careers. Sometimes, men have deserved to have their careers destroyed, and this might be one of them. Since I know what it feels like to be told my career is over because of my conduct, I can't help but feel at least a little hypocritical in denouncing and punishing this man. While it's not the same thing (My offense involved willful disobedience of an order, while this man's offense has to do with his morals), in both cases, we both did what we should not have done. I wish this problem had not come up, especially now that we're on our way back into combat.

I miss you <u>all</u> the time and can't wait until we're together again. The house sounds wonderful! I worry that everything will be alright with the pregnancy and that our child will be fine. I pray from time to time too. Like you, I have my doubts. And, I don't know why, but my times of doubt have become less frequent. Maybe it's because I believe that it must have been God who brought us together, God who has seen me through the battles I've been in, God who gave us a child, and God who will see us through this terrible war. I can't prove any of that, of course, but, deep in my bones, I know it. Yes, I believe we were made for each other, and I believe that when the war ends, then we will smile and begin a life of peace and joy as we raise our children and have the time to see and appreciate all the beauty that exists in this world.

Love Always,
Dade

31

September 25, 1942

Pearl Harbor Naval Base

It was a beautiful, sunny day as Rachael drove up to the main gate of the base, and she smiled, remembering the first day she had come to the base. It had been April 15, 1941. Having no car, she had taken the bus. It had been peacetime then, of course, and the pass she'd been given by Captain Huxley had been sufficient to get her simply waved through the main gate, but the ONI building had a fence around it and Marines guards at its gate. She remembered the hard time the Marine guards had given her about having only a long-expired passport for identification.

She'd been so nervous, so overwhelmed by the people and what was to be her job. Now she felt as if she were coming home. At the fence surrounding the ONI building, two Marines studied her ONI credentials, smiled, and waved her through. She felt relaxed and happy. Paul Duvall would be glad to see her, but disappointed when he learned that her pregnancy would mean much shorter hours. Well, it couldn't be helped.

At the bottom of the stairwell, another Marine, this one a sergeant, sat at a desk with only two things on it, a log book and a loaded Thompson submachine gun. He was new. Rachael showed her credentials to him, and he pressed a button under the surface of the desk. There was a loud electric buzz, during which the door to L-2 could be opened. She opened it and stepped inside.

It was as busy as ever. Everyone was so engrossed in their work, no one looked up from their desks as she came in and passed by them on her way up to see Paul Duvall.

"Paul?" She said, and he glanced up, did a doubletake, then stood with a broad smile.

"Mrs. Bowie! Rachael! How good it is to see you again! Please," he motioned, "have a seat." They both sat, and Rachael was pleased to see Paul so enthusiastic. She smiled as broadly as he. "Are you ready to jump back in? God knows we've needed you badly."

"I'm ready to go back to work, but I won't be able to resume a 60-hour week, Paul. I'm sorry."

"Oh?"

"Yes, you see, I'm pregnant."

"What good news!" he exclaimed, failing to hide his disappointment, but trying valiantly.

"For me and my husband, it's quite wonderful news. However, I saw an obstetrician back in Groton, and one here in Honolulu, and they both urge some caution during my pregnancy. You see, I turned 40 back in May, and this is my first child. They told me that plenty of women in their 40's have children, but nearly all have had children before, when they were in their 20's and 30's. They say that there are some risks for a woman to have her first child in her 40's. When I told them that I'm accustomed to working a high pressure 60-hour week, they both said that was out of the question. That I could lose the baby."

"How many . . . . how many hours *will* you be able to work?"

"My plan is to work 20 hours a week—five four-hour days. Until halfway through my eighth month, then I'll be going home until the baby is born."

"Oh, my. Well, I suppose since it's what your doctors say you must do, I can't persuade you to do otherwise."

"No. I'm sorry, Paul, but that's the way it is."

"But you'll be coming back once the baby is born, of course," Duvall said anxiously.

"Not immediately. I intend to spend two months with the baby at home, then hire a dependable person to fill in four hours a day, while I resume a 20-hour work week here."

"Of course I'm happy to hear of your . . . . . blessed event, but, to be honest, I'm devastated that you want to work only a third of the time you've been working before and that you want to take so much time off just before and after having the baby. We need you very badly. Both translators and codebreakers are in high demand."

"I understand completely."

"Especially now. You see, while you were away, in fact just after you left, we intercepted the Japanese plans to take Midway Island and to lure what was left of the Pacific Fleet after Pearl Harbor out to a battle in the area to finish it off. This enabled us to send our carriers and other vessels to ambush the Japanese and deliver them a crushing blow. We sank four of their carriers, and turned back their invasion attempt. As I'm sure you've read in the newspapers, it has marked a turning point in the Pacific. As a result, our operation is looked upon with great favor by CINCPAC now. In fact, we've been told to double the size of the ULTRA project and been given the funds to do it. Captain Huxley was awarded a commendation for ULTRA's role in winning the Battle of Midway ."

"Captain Huxley was honored for it? Unless things changed markedly since I left, it was you and the people in L-2 who did all the work. You probably went to him with incontrovertible evidence of all the details of the Japanese plans and all he did was pass them on to CINCPAC. And you probably even had to plead with him to pass the information on."

"Yes," Paul Duvall blushed, "that's true. It took a lot of convincing to make him see that our information was correct and had to be acted on."

"Maybe what helped convince him somewhat was the fact that we were right that the Japanese were going to attack on December 7th, and that he told you we were wrong."

"Yes, that may have entered into it," Duvall agreed.

"So he's the hero here, and he did nothing except to pass on hard intelligence that you gave him. That hardly sounds fair to me."

"Well," Duvall shrugged, "I'm not here for any recognition. I'm here to do my part to defend my country in the best way I'm able. The point I was starting to make to you is that, now we need highly skilled people more than ever here. Now that CINCPAC and the CNO are finally listening to us and wanting us to expand the scope of our operations."

"I'm sorry, Paul, but now I may as well tell you there's one more consideration."

"Oh?"

"Yes, whenever my husband is in port between patrols, which is usually two weeks between two-month patrols, I want to have the entire two weeks off to spend with him."

Duvall sat back in his chair as if shocked by Rachael's words and needing support. "I, well, that's . . . . . . I mean, taken into consideration with all the other, uh, requested adjustments to your work schedule, I mean, that's . . . . . . asking quite a bit."

"I know, but you have to understand that as a submarine officer, my husband has one of the most dangerous assignments in the Pacific now and there is no end to the war in sight. Every time I see him might be the last. Up until now, I've continued to work whenever he was in port, and the only times we had together were nights and my one day off a week. We've decided that's not enough. It's not nearly enough. We're married now, we have a child on the way, and I want to spend as much time with him as I can."

Duvall was silent for a long moment. Next to Tracy Donahue, Mrs. Bowie was his best Japanese translator. She was also highly intelligent and he liked her. She was a valuable asset to L-2. He could also understand her wanting to be with her baby and with her husband. He supposed there was nothing he could do about

131

cutting her hours drastically for medical reasons until the baby was born. But *after* the baby was born? That was a different matter entirely. This was vital war work. The Battle of Midway proved that. Their work saved American lives and hastened the day when the war would end and all the killing would stop. She was smart enough to know that. "Mrs. Bowie," he said, with his tone sounding like he was issuing a reprimand, so he began again, more softly. "Rachael, during wartime, one can't always have what one wants." He pointed a finger at a wall. "People are dying out there. Every day."

"I know, Paul. Believe me, I know there's a war going on."

Duvall thought she now looked angry, and he frowned involuntarily. He never knew how to handle angry people, and considered it to be one of his flaws. Hardly ever angry himself, it was an emotion he didn't quite understand completely, and he was a little afraid of it, because there was no telling what a lot of people would do or say when they were angry. At the very least, it was difficult to reason with an angry person. "Yes, of course. I'm sorry. We all know there's a war on." He sighed heavily. "Well, of course you'll have to fill out the appropriate forms to request going from full time to part time. And for your maternity leave. And I will approve them, although I can't guarantee that Captain Huxley will approve your working part time after you return to work after the baby is born. And, as for your wanting two weeks off every two months when your husband is in port, I believe that he will not approve that. That's going a bit too far, Rachael. Our work is too important, and while I'm willing to let you have your way, Captain Huxley would never allow that. Surely you can continue to work four hours a day, even when your husband is in port? That still gives you plenty of time."

"I'll fill out the forms, Paul, but there's something you're overlooking. I'm not in the Navy. I'm a civilian employee of the Navy Department. If my requests aren't approved, I'll simply resign, and you'll get no hours from me. Dade and I feel strongly about this and my requests are nonnegotiable."

"You're saying that they are not requests, but demands. That it is your way or the highway."

"Essentially, yes. You see, with my husband's pay and some other money we came into, we don't need the money from my job at all. The only reason I want to continue to work in L-2 is patriotism. I want to do something meaningful to protect my country and Dade and all the other men out there fighting for their lives. I want very much to continue to do that, but not at the expense of ignoring my baby and not being with Dade day and night when he's in port. The days between patrols are precious to us, more precious than I can tell you. The war is hard on him, and he needs me very much during those days. And I need him."

"Fill out the forms, Rachael, and we'll work things out. I'm glad you're back."

32

October 17, 1942

Atlantic Ocean

Oliver Wirtz lay in his bunk staring at the gray overhead, frowning deeply. It had been a day now since the skipper had dressed him down about sleeping with Rosemary Brooks, and he hadn't been able to shake off a feeling of impending doom. Bowie was mad as hell. This could sink his career, or at the least, damage it for some time to come. But hell, he and Rosemary were both consenting adults. And it wasn't as if he had meant to take advantage of her. He liked her a lot. She was smart and funny and sexy. While she was 38, she looked ten years younger. She had a great figure, honey blonde hair, and violet eyes. Rosemary had made him laugh and relax and feel good about himself. This had been one of those very rare and very special times when you meet a person, and, with in a half an hour, you feel as if you've known them all your life. And you feel you can trust that person completely. She had spoken briefly of the loss of her husband months before and he had told her of his divorce being in the works. They spoke of so many things, easily, honestly. No one else seemed to exist for either of them at the party, and, he realized now, that both of them had recognized the same hunger in each other's eyes.

Sure, they both had quite a bit to drink, but he didn't think the alcohol had been a factor at all in why they had suddenly felt a fantastic bond between them. Some would call it love at first sight, and perhaps that's what it was. That kid Brooks and Dade Bowie probably assumed that Oliver had been nothing more than an asshole who got a woman drunk so he could fuck her and walk away with nothing more than a self-satisfied smirk. The truth was that he had walked away caring deeply about that wonderful woman.

133

The alcohol *hadn't*, he decided again, been a factor in their making love. They had been feeling the drinks, yes, but they weren't drunk. Perhaps the alcohol had acted as an accelerant, but the fire was going to erupt, to bust into a glorious bonfire, alcohol or not. They had sensed the need in each other and were drawn not by that alone, but by many things they had in common. Oliver couldn't even remember when he'd had a better time. Once in her hotel room, they began to kiss and to hold onto each other with a wild desperation, undressing as they made their way to the bed. They woke at dawn and made love again, slowly, savoring each touch, each sensation. Then they lay in each other's arms, talking about many things. Much as newlyweds might. He told her he'd write to her regularly. Unfortunately, her son walked in as he and she had been getting dressed, before he could write down her address. She was so shaken by Matt's unexpected barging in, that she began to cry and asked Oliver to leave as soon as possible so she could find her son and somehow try to patch things up with him. She was disconsolate, and there was nothing he could do but accede to her wishes.

Now Rosemary's son and Captain Bowie were trying to make it look like she and Oliver had done something dirty and disgusting. Or at least that *he* had. This was a bitch, because it had been a wonderful night for him. He'd had received sex without love from Madeline too many times. As she slowly began falling out of love with him (had she ever loved him?), her change in feelings for him manifested itself in bed. It was clear that it became just a mechanical act for her, devoid of all emotion. He began to hate himself for seeking sex from her. Sex without love became just a mechanical act for him too—something he did to obtain release. It made him feel ashamed and weak. It was really nothing more than masturbation.

But with Rosemary, it had been different. There had been no question that she was giving herself to him because she cared for him. This made all the difference in the world.

Things would have been fine if Matt Brooks hadn't shown up early and screwed up everything. Oliver wondered what she had told her son to smooth things over. Whatever she'd said, it evidently hadn't been enough.

He felt bad about saying that Rosemary had seduced him. The words had come reflexively out his mouth as a man might throw up an arm to block a guy's swinging fist coming toward him. Bowie had been very angry, and the defensive words had just come out. The truth was that either there had been no seduction or that they had seduced each other. What happened hadn't been Rosemary's fault. Nor his. Damn it. It was nobody's fault and nobody's business. Here he was, 26 years old, Rosemary 38, and he was being treated like a 16-year old caught screwing a girl in the back seat of his father's car.

The Officer Corps of the United States Navy had a puritanical streak. A midshipman quickly learned that at the Academy, so this state of affairs hardly came as a surprise to Oliver. Still, it was difficult to accept. No, it was impossible to accept. He'd fight it. He'd fight it and . . . . . . and he'd lose. Wirtz sighed, deeply, hopelessly, and continued to frown at the gray overhead. Only a few moments later, Bowie walked in.

"Oliver, I want to see you in my stateroom now."

"Yes, sir," Oliver replied, getting out of his bunk and following the skipper into the passageway. Once in Bowie's room, Dade took a seat at his desk and motioned for Wirtz to be seated on his bunk.

"I've given this matter some thought. Actually, a lot of thought. If this incident had happened in the peacetime Navy, I think you know you'd be dealt with severely. But we're at war now, and about to go into combat. We don't have the time that we did in peacetime to devote to matters like this. Our entire focus has to be on fighting the enemy. Furthermore, should word of this incident leak out to the crew, it would be prejudicial to morale. The men would lose respect for you and I can't have that. All in all, I've come to the conclusion that this is a matter better dealt with quietly. Here's what I've decided: You are to apologize to Torpedoman's Mate Brooks for your behavior toward his mother, here, in this room, in my presence. If he accepts your apology, I will order both of you to never speak of this again to anyone, and that will end the matter forever. No reprimand for 'conduct unbecoming' in your personnel jacket, no bad fitness report, nothing."

"Captain, I'm going to be perfectly honest with you here. It wasn't just sex. I really came to have strong feelings for Rosemary. We talked for hours before we . . . . . went to bed. I even believe I may be in love with her, and I believe she feels the same way about me."

"But just yesterday, you claimed that she seduced you. You laid the blame at her feet."

"I just blurted that out without thinking because I could see I was in big trouble and that was the first thing I could think of in self-defense. It was wrong of me to say that. The real story is that two lonely, hurting people met by chance and found they cared a lot about each other. If there was any seduction involved, we both seduced each other. My intentions toward her are honorable. We plan to write to each other and see each other again whenever possible. And that's the God's truth, sir. Rosemary and I are consenting adults and frankly, I don't see that this is any of her son's business."

"Well, that puts a somewhat different light on the story as I understood it yesterday. Nevertheless, you have to see it was wrong. At least the sex was wrong. Hitting the sack the first time you saw her. Especially with the mother of one of the men serving under you. That's about as 'conduct unbecoming' as you can get. You do understand that, don't you?"

"With all due respect, sir, was I supposed to get her son's approval?" Wirtz said in a burst of irritation.

"You were supposed to behave as an officer and a gentleman, damn it!"

"Captain, I'll obey your order to apologize to Brooks. I don't think it's appropriate or necessary, but I'll do it."

135

"Because you don't want a letter of reprimand? Is that your only reason?"

"Because it's an order, and I'm bound to obey all lawful orders."

"In a submarine, more than in any other type of naval vessel, we have to be able to trust and to respect each other. Especially in time of war. And anything prejudicial to that trust and respect can't be tolerated. Surely you can at least understand that."

"I do, sir. Yes, I do understand that. I will make a sincere apology to Brooks. When do you want me to do it?"

"Right now. Right this very minute, so we can put this behind us all. Step out into the passageway and tell someone to have Brooks report to me immediately."

"Aye aye, sir."

It was only about four minutes later that a nervous Torpedoman's Mate stood before Dade.

"Take a seat on my bunk next to Mister Wirtz, please, Brooks."

"Aye aye, sir."

"This is about your finding Mister Wirtz in your mother's hotel room." Brooks blushed and looked down at the deck, as Dade continued, "When I spoke to you before, I told you that, whatever happened, I thought it would be a bad idea if anyone outside this room ever learned of it. I do not want to see your mother's good name besmirched nor see you hounded and made the butt of vulgar jokes or see the *Sea Otter* and her crew made a laughing stock. We are all about to go into battle. I believe that Mr. Wirtz acted inappropriately and have strongly expressed that belief to him. He has indicated that he would like to apologize to you for his actions. Do you wish to hear that apology?"

Brooks looked up and made eye contact with Dade. "Yes, sir. Of course."

Oliver Wirtz cleared his throat and began to speak softly. "Brooks, when I met your mother at the party, I was taken with her. She is an attractive, intelligent, and very special woman. Both of us spent the whole time speaking to each other, oblivious to everyone else around us. We found we had much in common. For the first time in a long time, I had fun. My wife and I are in the final stages of a divorce that should have happened a long time ago, and she, of course, lost your father only months ago. She told me she loved him very much. At any rate, when I offered to drive her home, I had no nefarious intentions in mind. Anyway, one thing led to another, and you know what happened. I had and have every intention of writing her and seeing her the next time we're back in the States. I have strong feelings for her. Please don't judge me or her harshly. Both of us had been drinking, but what happened would have happened even without drinking. I haven't met a woman like her in a long, long time. If ever. I believe she has strong feelings for me. If we were back in the States, I would be dating her with an eye toward us having a future together.

"Nevertheless, making love with her that night was wrong. It was wrong for all the reasons the skipper mentioned. I would not do it again if I could live that night over. I meant no disrespect to her at all. It was just that I didn't know h ow long it would be before I got to see her again. How many months or even years? Or, perhaps, never, if the Japanese get the best of us in a battle. Perhaps none of us will ever be back. Again, I meant no disrespect. I only felt an urgent need to express how much I cared about her. And I know that she wanted to let me know how much she cared. But I was wrong. I apologize for the pain I've caused you."

Brooks had been listening attentively, making eye contact with the XO as Wirtz had spoken the heartfelt words in utter, clear sincerity."

"Do you accept the XO's apology, Brooks?" Dade asked.

"Sir, I . . . . well, I had no idea it was like Mr. Wirtz said. I mean, it was still wrong, and I wish I didn't know that they . . . . . spent the night to gether. It was a real shock, when I walked in and . . . . . I never planned to mention it to my mother ever again, but if she, well, if she knew what she was doing and had feelings for Mr. Wirtz, then I guess it's really none of my business." He turned t o Wirtz and said, "I'll write to her to tell her that you apologized to me and that you said you have feelings for her."

"'Honorable intentions' is the usual phrase," Dade said, with a trace of a smile. He believed Wirtz too.

"Yes sir."

"I think you'll find that she already knows that," Wirtz said, with a faint smile of his own.

"Alright," Bowie said to the two men, "that concludes this matter. None of the three of us will speak of it again."

33

October 23, 1942

Pearl Harbor Naval Base

The Chief of Naval Operations, Patrick Fogarty, had finished his remarks about the results of the inspection that he and his staff had been conducting during the previous two days, permitting himself a smile as he expressed how pleased h e was with what he'd seen and heard. He was effusive in his praise and equally complimentary about the detailed briefings he'd been given by CINCPAC and his staff. "Now," he said, "I need to have the room cleared so Admiral Van Husen and I can speak privately about a highly classified matter. Ethan," he said to his aide, "please leave the briefcase here."

As Van Husen's staff and Fogarty's staff filed out, Ethan Lombard unlocked the handcuff that bound the briefcase to his wrist and placed it next to the CNO's chair before leaving. In a moment, the room was empty and silent save for Fogarty and Van Husen.

"Let's move to the conference table, Cliff," the CNO smiled as he stood, reached down, and picked up the briefcase.

"Yes sir."

Once seated across from each other at the long, highly polished, rectangular wooden table, Fogarty set the briefcase on it, but made no move to open the combination locks at each latch. "First, have you ever heard of something called the 'Manhattan Project'?"

"No, sir."

"That's good, you're not supposed to have any knowledge of it. Not even its name. First, I'll tell you what little I know of it. It's a huge project involving tens of thousands of people, spearheaded by the best scientific minds in the country. Its budget is classified, but it runs into billions. That's billions with a 'b.' It's the most highly classified project going on right now and has absolute priority for any resources it says it needs. It's also run by a two-star general named Leslie Groves, who's in the Army Corps of Engineers. They're building what amounts to a medium sized city in Tennessee, surrounded by barbed wire fences and military police with guard dogs patrolling the perimeter. Everyone, and I mean everyone who lives and works there, is required to have a Top Secret clearance, and no one is permitted to speak of their work to anyone except their immediate bosses and co-workers. Any infractions, they're told, will result in prison. Just what they're building and why is unknown to all but a few who have the big picture. They also have locations in New Mexico and Washington State. Those of us senior officers in the Army and Navy who have been told of the existence of the project are told only that, whatever Leslie Groves says he wants or needs, we are to give it to him instantly and with no questions asked. And anything can be a request for some of our personnel, equipment, transportation of his people or gear, anything."

"A two-star Army engineer is calling the shots?" Van Husen asked incredulously.

"Yes," the CNO nodded, "and he reports to only the Secretary of War and to the President himself. He has absolute, godlike power."

"And no one outside the project has the faintest idea of what he's working on?"

"Well, I have an educated theory, but I'll get to that later. The answer is no. Not the Secretary of the Army, the Secretary of the Navy, not even the Vice President. In a closed, classified, Congressional committee hearing, when the members demanded to know just what the hell all this mountain of money was for, they were told that it was for the most important thing ever invented in all human history, one that would certainly end the war when completed. They swallowed hard and recommended approval of the funds."

"Damn. Do you think it really is that important, sir?"

"I do. Franklin Roosevelt is running this whole thing, and, although I don't especially like the man, he's as smart as they come. He knows something. Like all politicians, he's no stranger to hyperbole when it suits his purposes, but he had me and 'Wild Bill' Donovan over to the Oval Office to task us with a Top Secret operation directly related to the Manhattan Project, and, when he looked us in the eye and told us that both the Germans and the Japanese are working on the same thing, and that, whoever gets there first wins the war, we believed him. He was absolutely serious. Cliff, there's nothing bigger or more important than this mystery project. Of that, I'm certain.

"This is all we're cleared to know about the project. However, my chief of staff has a master's degree in physics, and we do know that, while there are many scientists involved, as well as engineers, most of the top people seem to be physicists. So he and I have been, quite naturally, speculating on wh at the hell it is they're working on. He's read some of the papers some of them published in the pre-war years in scientific journals and believes the project has to do with atomic physics—with the structure of the atom itself. We're assuming that they're working on a very powerful weapon and—I know it sounds crazy—but we think it's a kind of ray gun that disrupts the forces that keep the electrons orbiting around the nuclei of atoms, thus disintegrating the atoms and therefore the target. I have visions of making large ray guns—say about the size of searchlights—and mounting them on our ships and aircraft. Maybe all you'd have to do is run the beam over an enemy ship and have it instantly disintegrate into a pile of debris. Or mount them on bombers. As the bombers flew over enemy targets, they could completely disintegrate whole enemy bases or cities or troop concentrations. Whole buildings would just collapse completely, or anything touched by the disruptor ray."

"That sounds like something right out of Buck Rogers comics and movie serials."

"Yes, and that wouldn't be the first time science fiction accurately predicted actual scientific advances. Jules Verne gave us the *Nautilus*, the forerunner of the modern submarine. H.G. Wells wrote of modern aircraft when the only thing around was hot air balloons. Why not a Buck Rogers ray gun that could make things disintegrate? I admit George and I could be wrong, but, whatever this new thing is, it must be fantastic. FDR says it will change everything. I believe him."

"That's remarkable, sir."

"It is. But now it's time to get to where you come in on this. As I said before, we know that the Japanese and the Germans are working on the same thing. Unfortunately, we don't know how far along either of them a re. They could be ahead of us or behind. But we do know this: we must stop them from getting there first. We must stop them at all costs. There is a physicist in Japan named Dr. Hideki Nakamura. He's their best physicist and we know he's working on t his project. We only recently became aware of the fact that he has a son who is a grad student at MIT. The son has been there since his freshman year, but has spent every summer back in Japan until this past summer. Once the war started last December, he began to do a lot of thinking. He'd long been uncomfortable with the rise of militarism in Japan and the ruthless ways in which dissent was being put down anyway. Now, with a full-fledged war going on, he made his decision to stay on here in the States, and he has no intention of going back to Japan until the war is over, if then. Like his dad, Isokuru's field is physics, but he knows nothing of the details of his father's work because it's so highly classified.

"The people responsible for the security of the Manhattan Project have had several long discussions with the son. Not only is he pro-American, he says that his father leans in that direction too. His father was also an MIT man. True, that was many years ago, but he said his father often spoke fondly of his years in

140

America and his friends there. The two correspond regularly, but, since they know that all the letters are almost certainly being read by Japanese intelligence, they say nothing of politics or the war. Just a little chatter like polite questions about everybody's health, the weather, weddings, funerals, and so on. When asked if his father might be interested in defecting, Isokuru said he was about 80 percent certain he would if given the chance as long as he could take his wife with him.

"Getting the old man to our shores would, of course, deal a blow to the Japanese project. In addition, after debriefing him, the people in the Manhattan Project might decide he could contribute substantially to it. As I said, the Japanese might even be ahead of us on this effort. Now that's where you come in, Cliff. Isokuru says that every year, no matter what, his father and mother have a tradition of spending several days at her ancestral home on Kyushu, just south of Shikoku, to celebrate her birthday. That home is located on the north side of the island, overlooking the Japanese Inland Sea. It's also fairly secluded.

"The plan, called Operation Buntline, is to slip a submarine into a small inlet, and for a team of OSS commandos to snatch Nakamura and his wife. Hopefully, they'll come willingly. If not, they'll be brought back to the sub whether they want to come or not. If things go terribly wrong, and Nakamura cannot be taken back to the sub, the OSS has orders to kill him. We cannot leave such a key man in the Japanese project alive.

"Isokuru has provided us with a map of the family compound and a floor plan of the buildings. It's not going to be a walk in the park for the OSS people because another intelligence source tells us that, when the couple go to this house, it's guarded, not by regular Japanese army troops, but by the Kempeitai, or military police. The Kempeitai is not like our own military police. It has authority not only over all troops, but all civilians as well. Also, it has virtually unlimited powers, very much like the German Gestapo, and their ruthlessness surpasses that of the Gestapo's. The uniformed Kempeitai are elite troops, the plain clothes members act in a variety of counterintelligence roles, and both are formidable enemies. All we know for certain is that, when Nakamura and his wife are in residence there, two uniformed Kempeitai are stationed at the front gate to the compound, one at a smaller rear gate, and that a fourth patrols the perimeter with a German Shepherd. There may or may not be additional guards inside the compound or even inside the house."

"You say the OSS is to pull this off. Sir, we have our own, highly trained Marine Raiders. I don't see why the Army has to get involved in this."

"Frankly, I don't either, but Bill Donovan has Roosevelt's ear and the OSS is his baby. No, we're only to provide transportation for this mission, but that's going to be a tricky thing." The CNO worked the combination locks and opened the briefcase. "Let me show you on the map where this compound is. Look," he said, pointing with the tip of his index finger on a map of the island of Kyushu, "the sub will have to navigate up this narrow channel between Kyushu and Shikoku. While

141

the water in the middle of the channel is fairly deep, we can also be sure that the channel, as well as the coast of all the home islands, will be heavily patrolled by antisubmarine patrols. There is also apt to be heavy traffic in the channel. The skipper will have to know what he's doing, navigate precisely to where the compound is, get in as close as possible to the shore without running aground, and offload the commandos. Getting right in between two of the Japanese home islands where they are so close together and getting back out again is going to take a skilled man, and I want you to pick your very best. Give him strict orders to initiate no action against Japanese ships either on the way there or on the way back. He is to maintain strict radio silence throughout the mission with one exception. If, and this is very unlikely, we discover while the sub is enroute to Japan, that Dr. Nakamura will not be at the family compound, we will send a simple two-word message: Abort Mission. If the sub receives this message, it will simply reply: Acknowledged. This may well be the most important mission given any submarine in the whole war, so I want you to pick your very best skipper—not only a highly skilled submarine commander, but one who has demonstrated coolness under high pressure and shown courage. However, he is not to be fully briefed until the night before the sub leaves port. Until then, all he needs to be told is that eight OSS men and their equipment are to be loaded aboard his sub for transportation. Fortunately, we have the luxury of time for once. Dr. Nakamura's wife's birthday is not until December 14th.

"As we speak, the OSS commandos are practicing. In a secluded part of an air base in Florida, a full-scale mockup of the family compound has been built out of plywood and planks, including the main house. The son has given us the floor plan and we know which bedroom Nakamura and his wife will be sleeping in. They're getting to the point where they can complete the mission in absolute darkness without a single wasted motion. They're practicing scenarios where there are more Kempeitai guards inside the compound, some of the men are wounded or killed, the scientist and his wife physically resist being taken to the sub, and a number of other possibilities. They'll arrive here a few days before the sub's departure date.

"Now, I want to make this absolutely clear. During the travel to and from the objective, the sub skipper is in command. The OSS leader is in command of everything that happens once the team is ashore and until it returns to the sub. Period. Do you have any questions?"

Clifford Van Husen thought hard for a moment before answering, "No, sir."

"Very good. I'm leaving this material with you. It's for your use during the final briefing. I have here," he said, extracting one item after another as he spoke, "a map showing the location of the compound, floor plans of the buildings of the compound, a photograph of Dr. Nakamura, a list of the OSS team members and their backgrounds, what we know of antisubmarine efforts in the area, the location of Japanese military camps and bases on Kyushu, and associated materials. Keep all the materials in this folder, marked Operation Buntline, in your safe and share it with no one. No one. Even your chief of staff only needs to know that there is an Operation Buntline, and that you are handling it personally."

"Yes sir, and I infer that you don't wish me to mention the Manhattan Project by name."

"Correct. Nor, of course, any speculation about what the project is working on. Like the speculation I indulged in. The OSS men have been told only that the United States is working on a Top Secret project so important, so monumental, so advanced, that it will end the war. That there is literally no covert mission more important than this one, more essential. They have been told only that bringing this man and his wife back to the States, or, if that is impossible, killing him so that the Japanese will not benefit from his knowledge, is absolutely critical, and that nothing must stop them from successfully completing this mission. They were told that any and all collateral damage, if necessary to the success of the mission, is acceptable. That they must succeed at all costs. The night before the sub departs, you, the OSS team, and the skipper and XO of the submarine, will meet in this office, go over the whole mission in detail, and you'll then send the men on their way."

"Do you think it's literally true, sir? That the Manhattan Project will end the war?"

"FDR and top physicists advising him are certain of it, and, based on what little I know, I'm inclined to believe it too. But just when the project will be completed is something that isn't known at this time. It depends entirely upon the scientists and engineers solving a series of very complex problems. I don't know whether we're weeks away from success, or months. Hell, for all I know, it could be a couple of years. The people involved in this are working night and day. We could have a breakthrough anytime. Once they know *how* to do whatever it is they're trying to do, then there's the matter of manufacturing the thing. Say, for example, the Buck Rogers ray gun. Once they know how, the people in factories will have to set up assembly lines to produce thousands of them. And that takes time, even working 24/7 with massive funding and top priority over every other project.

"As I said, what makes this even more urgent is that we know the Germans and the Japanese are working on the very same thing. Whoever succeeds first, wins the war. The President was very clear on that. It could be that Dr. Nakamura can provide a piece or two of the puzzle and help us get there faster. Even if he can't, denying the Japanese such a key person will hamper their efforts."

"My curiosity about the Manhattan Project is certainly piqued. Now I'll be spending hours as I lay in bed at night wondering what the hell they're working on."

"I know. I haven't stopping wondering myself. The ray gun theory that George and I have is just speculation based on very little information. It could be something entirely different. There's a lot of classified research going on these days, some of it quite fantastic. The Office of Naval Research came to me a few months ago with a theory that we could actually make our ships invisible."

"That's even more incredible than ray guns!"

"Yes, but you can't really discount anything out of hand. What if it works?"

"Where does it stand, sir? That is, if you can tell me."

"Yes, I'll tell you with the understanding that you tell no one else. It's actually pretty interesting. I won't go into the physics of it, primarily because I didn't understand the explanations the scientists gave me. Neither did George, despite his Master's in physics and his keeping up to date on the latest developments. The concept is based on Einstein's Unified Field Theory. They designed sophisticated electronic gear to be installed on a Navy vessel which would envelop it in a huge electromagnetic field so powerful it would prevent light rays from reflecting off the ship, rendering it invisible."

"That's amazing."

"It is. Well, we had the equipment installed aboard a destroyer and tried it out at a remote area off the coast of Virginia."

"Did it work?"

"Perhaps, at least for a few seconds. Or it may have been simply my imagination and the imagination of the other witnesses to the experiment. Maybe we saw what we expected to see. At any rate, it was only for a few seconds."

"What happened?"

"I and the other observers were aboard a light cruiser about 250 yards away. When the switch was thrown aboard the destroyer, we heard a loud thrumming noise, which increased in volume until it was almost painful. Then the destroyer began to blur, then it . . . . . . well, it seemed to vanish. There appeared to be nothing there for about five seconds. Then the ship reappeared."

"So it worked!"

"For only about five seconds. The scientists said that this showed they were on the right track, that they only needed to do some more work. But you see, they couldn't explain at all why the effect lasted only five seconds, and we had already spent a great deal of money—a great deal—on this experiment. Furthermore, there were unanticipated problems. For one thing, when the ship reappeared, all the electrical circuits aboard the ship, from the bridge to the galley, were fried. All the vacuum tubes had exploded. The special gear that generated the effect was destroyed. But more importantly, there were problems with some of the crew members aboard the destroyer. Most had terrible, disabling migraine headaches. Many experienced convulsions that lasted for an hour or more. Their nervous systems were affected, some severely, and the scientists couldn't explain why."

"What happened next, sir?"

"I defunded their research. If they had had convincing answers, explanations that seemed reasonable, about what had caused the problems and how long it would take to fix things, it might have been different. But I had the sense that they were completely baffled."

"That's too bad. Invisible warships could really turn the tide dramatically."

"Yes. The only reason I brought this up is to illustrate the kind of just, well, remarkable things that are being researched today. And too, this project was not affiliated with the Manhattan Project at all. The latter has all the top scientists, is far better funded, and has absolute national priority, so what they're working on could well be even more revolutionary than invisible warships. Hell, this is the middle of the twentieth century; anything is possible. Intelligence tells us that the Germans have been making strides in missile technology and jet planes. Anything is possible.

"But there is no research project more important now than the Manhattan Project. The OSS team has already been briefed on just how important this mission is, without, of course, mentioning the Manhattan Project by name or being given any details about the project. Do the same with the skipper and XO of the sub you choose to use."

"I will, sir."

"Good. Good. A lot is riding on this, possibly more than we can imagine."

"I understand."

34

October 26, 1942

Pearl Harbor Naval Base

Clifford Van Husen sat on his highbacked leather chair facing 180 degrees away from his large mahogany desk, looking out the picture window at the harbor. It was good to be king. As CINCPAC, he was one of the most powerful men in the world and he enjoyed that power. He ruled all he saw through the window, the powerful warships, the planes taking off from the Naval Air Station on Ford Island, all of it and more. He had scores of thousands of men under his command, including divisions of Marines. Since martial law was still in effect in Hawaii, he was the de facto ruler of the Hawaiian Islands. The Territorial Governor still held office, but he was a mere figurehead. With the victory at Midway, the tide of the war in the Pacific had turned in favor of the Allies, and life was indeed good.

There was still a long, hard road ahead to the ultimate victory, as evidenced by the Guadalcanal campaign, but the Japanese would be defeated, and Clifford Van Husen would be the man who defeated them. Once the war was over, he would publish his memoirs, detailing how he had done it. He'd make himself available for radio, newspaper, and magazine interviews. He'd married into one of the most politically powerful families in the United States years before, and now he'd start to use that advantage to begin to float his availability for public office. He'd meet with the right people, make the right deals, and he'd be well on his way to becoming the most powerful man on earth. Before the war, he'd been planning on serving two terms as a U.S. senator before announcing his candidacy for the presidency. That had seemed unavoidable. But things were different now. Much different. As the man who had won the war in the Pacific, he could go straight for the Oval Office after he left the Navy. He smiled, opened up the humidor on his desk, and extracted a cigar. Yes, if he played things right, he could run for president in 1948. He clipped the cigar, lit it, and turned back to resume gazing out the window. He had about ten minutes before Rachael Bowie showed up. Tracy had told him that she was back in town and resuming work in L-2, translating the Japanese intercepts. Days after the attack on Pearl Harbor, he'd asked both his niece Tracy and her friend and coworker Rachael to act as his unofficial advisors on the Japanese. What prompted him to do that was one of Sun Tzu's precepts in the 6th Century B.C. classic "The Art of War." Sun Tzu had said, "If you know the enemy and know yourself, you need not fear the result of a hundred battles. If you know yourself but not the enemy, for every victory gained, you will also suffer a defeat. If you know neither the enemy nor yourself, you will succumb in every battle." Van Husen made up his mind to know the enemy, his world view, his values, his customs and his religious beliefs. To know what is sacred to him and what he holds in little esteem.

He had decided that Tracy and Rachael were the best consultants to learn about the Japanese. Both women spoke the language fluently. Tracy had gone to live with her father in Tokyo at age ten, had been educated in Japanese middle and high schools, and had graduated from Tokyo Imperial University with honors. Her father, Sean Donahue, had been an indispensable member of the embassy staff, and Tracy did a lot of work for the embassy. In the twenty years she'd spent in Japan, she'd met many of the most influential members of both the Japanese government and the top-ranking officers of the Japanese military. She got to know how they thought, and her advice was very useful to Van Husen.

Rachael had lived among the common people for twenty years, and had gotten to know the people who, in war, would be lower ranking soldiers and sailors. Both women had the highest security clearances and kept well abreast of what was going on. Through Sunday meetings for just an hour or so at his quarters each week, he'd learned a lot. At first, both women attended, but then they began taking turns as his education in Japanese religion, philosophy, history, and psychology had grown.

When Rachael had gotten married, then followed her husband back to new construction at Groton, Tracy came every Sunday. While Tracy was a university graduate and Rachael was only a high school graduate, Van Husen considered Rachael to be far more educated. During her twenty years in Japan, she had read voraciously—most of the greatest philosophers, essayists, economists, playwrights, novelists, theologians, poets, historians, and scientists, including Newton, John Locke, Charles Darwin, Albert Einstein, and Louis Pasteur. By her estimation, she had read over 5,000 books during that time, and she had an almost photographic memory. Furthermore, she not only read what amounted to all the important literature of the Western world, she understood it and thought about it. The woman's erudition had astounded Van Husen. She could quote effortlessly from sources as diverse as Homer to Adam Smith to make a point. Three hundred of the books she had read had been in Japanese and included diverse volumes on Japanese art, history, and religious beliefs.

While not a beautiful woman, Rachael was a desirable woman. Her raven black hair was shoulder length, she stood 5 feet 4 inches, and she had brown eyes. Though from the Midwest, her skin had a Mediterranean shade. She wore horn-rimmed glasses, and she would not turn heads on a public street, as would most of the women Van Husen had had affairs with. Still, there was something about her. About the way she carried herself. And something in her eyes. Something that spoke of wisdom and clarity and a secret knowledge. A secret knowledge of life itself that all the philosophers and novelists and poets had sought, but never quite achieved.

But she had achieved it. Damn it, she knew what life was about and why people did what they did, and she could see what was in people's hearts. Her smile was the smile of Mona Lisa. Clifford Van Husen had never met a woman like her and knew he never would again. He had to have her, to possess her. To enter her and be a part of all she was. All the wisdom and mystery and sanity and peace.

His heart began to pound as he thought about the time, before she married, when he could contain himself no longer, and he had let his feelings be known. It had been on February 8th at his residence. They were both having a drink on the lanai and she'd been wearing a dress that had been rather loose. Her thighs and the valley between them had been clearly outlined and, and, he had told her that he wanted a physical relationship with her. That he cared for her. He remembered his exact words. He'd said, "I don't think I've ever seen a woman with all your qualities: incredible erudition, intelligence, maturity, sense of humor, honesty, compassion, and a hundred other wonderful qualities, not to mention your powerful sexuality. Seriously, you're a virtual Helen of Troy. I've known many women who have a few of those qualities, but I've never seen them all wrapped up in one woman." What's more, he'd meant it. Damn it, he'd *meant* it! He'd gone on explain that the relationship would have to be kept secret, that while she couldn't actually move into his house, they could still sleep together a few nights a week as long as she left early in the morning.

And what had she done? She had *laughed*! She had laughed and said, "I had a better opinion of you until now. Fucking the hired help is so *déclassé*, Clifford." The casual vulgarity had shocked him. Furthermore, he hadn't struck out with a woman since, well, he couldn't even remember when or *if* he had ever struck out. Goddamn it, he was intelligent, handsome, witty, and the most powerful man in the Pacific! The women that he'd had had all realized how lucky they were to be bedded by CINCPAC.

And Rachael had called him *Clifford*. He hadn't been called *Clifford* since he had been a student at St. Stanislaus Parish School. The nuns had called him Clifford, and, when Rachael had called him that, he felt like a young boy being reprimanded by a black clad authority figure. He felt that Rachael had, like the nuns, put him in his place. In that moment, he hadn't felt like CINCPAC at all, but like a child being corrected by a woman.

148

No woman had ever treated him this way. His current paramour was a surgeon at the base hospital and looked like Rita Hayworth, and *she* was damned proud and honored that CINCPAC himself had picked her to share his intimate moments and thoughts with. Still he had begun to tire of her and it had only been three months. Plus, she was no Rachael Bowie. He had been humiliated when Rachael had rejected him, a feeling that had only improved slightly when she had told him that he was an attractive and intelligent man, but that she already had a lover.

Now she had married that lover. Dade Bowie. Could there ever be a worse match? While Bowie was clearly a gifted submarine commander, that was all he had going for him. That was all. He was a damned kid. He was what now? Thirty-two years old. Rachael was 40 and her mind was so superior to a fucking sub driver's that . . . . it was a gulf that just couldn't be bridged. What the hell could Dade Bowie talk about with her? Chaucer? Plato? Euripides? No, all the dumb bastard knows is submarines. But Van Husen could talk with Rachael about those very things as well as many others. OK, he wasn't as well read as she, but who was? The point is that he was pretty damned well read. And he was a hell of a lot more mature than a 32-year old sub driver. He was 58-years old and had seen and experienced more than Dade Bowie probably ever would.

And then there was the matter of sex. Clifford Van Husen was a skilled, accomplished lover. Hell, he had satisfied more women than he could count. Had driven them to heights of ecstasy. The thought of Dade Bowie and Rachael having sex flashed into his mind and repulsed him. That youngster couldn't give a woman like Rachael what she wanted. Probably all he knew was the missionary position. But *he*, Cliff Van Husen, would be able to drive her out of her mind with passion and desire and earthshaking orgasms. Now he pictured himself with Rachael, her beneath him, moaning in unspeakable pleasure, her full breasts heaving as she writhed with each of his thrusts—

His intercom buzzed and he jumped.

"Admiral, Mrs. Bowie is here to see you."

"Yes, well, send her in." As she came through the door, he noticed that she looked even better than he had remembered.

"Good morning, Admiral."

"Good morning, Rachael," he said as he rose. "You're looking well. That time off from L-2 certainly seems to have agreed with you." She seemed to have put on some weight. It looked as if . . . . . was she pregnant?

"It did," she smiled as they both sat. "Working sixty hours a week in a windowless basement takes a toll. The only time I ever got to see the sun here was on my one day a week off. Now I've seen the sun every day, caught up on my sleep, done some gardening, seen a bit of New England, and well, just had a wonderful time being with my husband every day."

Van Husen could have done without the reference to her husband, but he smiled broadly anyway. "Tracy told me you were back from the States and once again slaving away in L-2. I just wanted to welcome you back to the fold, and ask if you could continue—from time to time—to see me at my residence in your capacity as an unofficial advisor. I've learned quite a bit from both of you. A lot about the Japanese world view. You were quite right when you counseled me that the Japanese will fight to the bitter end. You told me that they wouldn't surrender, even in the face of certain defeat. Even in the face of certain death. Our experiences on Guadalcanal bear this out. As you undoubtedly know, we invaded Guadalcanal on August 7th, and we're still fighting for possession of the island. It's our first major land offensive in the war in the Pacific and the resistance we've been meeting is incredible—both on land and in the sea surrounding the area. I regret to say that the fight may go on for a couple more months before the island is fully secured." Was she pregnant? Her breasts seemed fuller and larger than he had remembered, and he had an excellent memory for such things.

"Thank you for personally taking the time to welcome me back. Although I'm not working full time right now. You see, I'm pregnant, and, for medical reasons, I'm only working twenty hours a week."

CINCPAC forced himself to smile even more broadly, "Pregnant? How wonderful! When is the baby due?"

"April 12th. As for continuing to consult with you from time to time on all things Japanese, I'd be happy to."

"You know, it was L-2 that provided us with the intelligence we needed to win the Battle of Midway. Thanks to L-2, we knew when and where they were coming, which ships were involved, and their complete strategy."

"Yes, I wasn't working then, but everyone filled me in when I got back to work the last week in September."

"And how is your husband?"

"Just fine. It was so good for both of us to have a normal life back in the States. He was home every night and we had all day together every Saturday and Sunday. Even though there's rationing in the States, you don't get the feeling that you do here—that the war is with you every minute of the day. You don't forget that there's a war going on, but it's far away in both senses. I feel better now, happier, well rested, and optimistic. Dade is very happy with his new submarine and its crew. It's the *U.S.S. Sea Otter*, and is due in port on November 8th. I can't wait to see him. I just wish the war were over. I worry about him so much when he's out on a war patrol."

"I wish the war were over too. I wish it every day."

"So do I and Dade. Every day."

"You must have had plenty of time to catch up on your reading."

"Oh, yes. Groton has a wonderful public library and then, of course, there are the book stores."

"I recall you and Tracy often quoted from Japanese writers and poets to illustrate different facets of the Japanese people. That never failed to impress me. As well as your frequent references to the best of Western minds. I sometimes wish there were time for you and me to discuss our favorite philosophers and poets."

Knowing damned well what Clifford Van Husen wished to do with her, Rachael only smiled pleasantly. His attempt to get her into his bed months before had offended her. What could have been a harmless pass that she could have taken as an unwanted compliment and shrugged off, had instead been insulting because of the way in which he'd gone about it. He had asked her—no, he had *offered*—it as some kind of golden opportunity he had expected her to jump at enthusiastically. His ego was enormous. Yes, he was a handsome man, an educated man with a sense of humor who had a number of talents. But he knew that. Knew it well. Besides, she had been in love with Dade.

"For example, I'd be very interested to know," Van Husen went on, "what your opinion of Emerson's essays are. They helped shape me as a young man. Particularly, his *Self-Reliance*."

"That's an excellent essay, but I liked his *The Over Soul* better. I believe he had a lot to say, and I think that he was clearly the most important leader of the transcendentalist movement. I also think his influence on John Dewey and Nietzsche was enormous."

"Yes, yes, exactly," CINCPAC replied uncomfortably. He hadn't understood very much of *The Over Soul* at all. He did remember that Emerson said when the Over Soul breathes through a man's intellect, "it is genius; when it breathes through his will, it is virtue; when it flows through his affection, it is love." He remembered that much, but he didn't really understand it. She was smiling that Mona Lisa smile. Was she mocking him? Had she decided he was merely a *poseur*? Or was it a friendly smile from one lover of philosophy to another? Did she know that he still wanted to lose himself in her body? Of course she knew, he decided. He could see the knowledge in her brown eyes. He broke eye contact and rose from his seat. "Once again, Rachael, welcome back. And if there's ever anything I can do, please don't hesitate to call me."

"Thank you, Admiral," she replied as she rose. "It's good to be back in Hawaii again."

Van Husen sat and noticed that his cigar, which he had set in his brown glass ashtray when Rachael had come in, had gone out. He picked it up, put it in his mouth and relit it, drawing the satisfying rich tobacco smoke into his lungs. He felt flustered, felt that he hadn't handled that encounter well. He began to replay it in his mind when his intercom buzzed.

"Yes?"

"Everyone's here for your staff meeting, sir. Shall I send them in?"

"No. No, I'm right in the middle of something important. I need another 10 or so minutes without any interruptions. I'll let you know when I'm ready."

"Yes, sir."

He stood and looked out at the ships in the harbor. *His* ships. And he thought of Christopher Marlowe's famous line about Helen of Troy in "Doctor Faustus":

Was this the face that launched a thousand ships
And burnt the topless towers of Ilium?

For over three millennia, men had been intoxicated with Helen of Troy. Aristophanes had written of her, as had Cicero, and Euripides, and Herodotus, and Sophocles, and Homer. And so many down through the ages. Yes, over a thousand ships had been launched and a 10-year war waged to restore Helen to Menelaus' side. Rachael was Helen of Troy. He was Menelaus, King of Sparta, and Dade Bowie was Paris, the young Prince of Troy, who had stolen Helen from him. If he were a king, would he launch a thousand ships and wage a 10-year war for Rachael? Hell, yes. But he didn't have to do that. All he had to do was wait.

Back in February, when she had said that she was already involved with a man and that that man was a naval officer, for a crazy moment, he had thought of David and Bathsheba in the Bible. David, the King, was taken with Bathsheba with just one look. Finding that her husband was a soldier under his command, David ordered her husband's superior officer to put the man at a place in the next battle where he was certain to be killed. Of course, Van Husen realized he probably couldn't get away with sending Rachael's lover on an especially dangerous mission that would all but guarantee his death. After a moment's thought, he realized even if he could, it would be wrong, because every other man on Dade's submarine would go down with him. Not only that, but he'd lose a valuable submarine. No, that was out of the question, he had decided.

But shortly after that, he learned that Rachael's lover was involved in the torpedo fiasco, along with two other sub skippers who had been modifying the torpedo exploders without authorization. COMSUBPAC had been bound and determined to see that all three were sent to a naval prison, only notifying Van Husen at the last moment. Van Husen had spent the better part of a night carefully analyzing each man's personnel jacket and patrol reports and had, the next morning, personally intervened in the Board of Inquiry to raise hell with the three men, and to impose a punishment that kept them going out on war patrols. The whole matter had exploded at the worst time—a time when the only weapons Van Husen had to use to take the war to the Japanese were his submarines, and those three—Dade Bowie, George Pulaski, and Harry Romano—were the best sub skippers in the Pacific Fleet. The submarines were all he had then, after most of the fleet had been destroyed on December 7th. All three had been highly decorated for bravery. From studying their records, he had arrived at a conclusion about all three. The reason they charged into harm's way and took such risks was actually due to fear. They feared fear itself. So much so that they feared that they might become immobilized by it in combat and shame themselves in battle. They feared fear more than they feared death. They kept on having to prove to themselves that they were brave men and the only way to do that was to do incredibly brave things.

Van Husen needed men like this. He could use men like this. The punishment he gave them was that they would continue to go out on war patrols until the very day that that Japan surrendered. During that period, regardless of what feats of heroism they might perform, there would be no more medals, no more commendations, and no more promotions. When the war was over, they would immediately be separated from the Navy. When Harry Reynolds, Van Husen's Director of ONI in the Pacific, suggested that this sentence was a bit too severe considering the mitigating circumstances, wondering aloud whether they would be sufficiently motivated to continue to excel, CINCPAC had smiled grimly and replied, "those men aren't going to live to see the end of the war. You know we're losing subs left and right. And the way that these three young men fight, their bravery, their tenacity, the risks they take, I'd be very surprised if all three are still alive a year from now, and there's *no* way any of them will be alive two years from now. You see, they'll continue to fight the way they do, despite the punishment I've meted out. Men like them don't fight as savagely as they do for promotions or medals or a retirement pension. They don't need to be supplied with that kind of motivation. Yes, they fight for their country and the Constitution of the United States, and they *like* to get medals and promotions and so forth. But they fight as well, as heroically as they do, because they're afraid." But Reynolds hadn't seemed to understand.

George Pulaski was dead now, killed in action. That left just Bowie and Romano, and they would surely follow. Bowie would be dead before the baby was even born. Van Husen would offer Rachael deepest condolences and, after a reasonable time for her grief to subside, he would make his move. By that time, she would, during their meetings, have come to the realization that Van Husen was a far better match for her. That he had more to offer her. There was his undeniable maturity. He was no callow youth like Bowie. There was his high intelligence, his sophistication, his wisdom, his dry sense of humor, his position, why the list was practically endless. He had already told her in February that he was married and that he intended to remain married, but that he and his wife had an understanding and that relations with other women, was, in her opinion, acceptable as long as he was discreet.

Of course, he hadn't told Rachael why he intended to remain married to his wife. She didn't need to know that he had married into his wife's family because they were wealthy and, more importantly, very well connected politically. Then he had a thought that made him smile. He could even continue the affair with Rachael in the White House. He could make her an Executive Private Secretary or something like that.

The important thing was to have Rachael. Once Bowie was dead, and once they had sex, Rachael would be his forever. If there was one thing Clifford Van Husen knew, it was how to satisfy a woman in bed. Once again, he pictured her moaning in unspeakable ecstasy beneath him, transported to heights of pleasure she had never known existed. Yes, all he had to do was wait, and, in the meantime, impress her with his erudition and charm. He went back to his desk and pushed the bar on the intercom.

"Alright, send everyone in."

35

November 8, 1942

Pearl Harbor Naval Base

"Welcome back, Slide," Admiral Onets said warmly to Dade, as he rose to shake the young man's hand. "Have a seat."

"Thank you, sir."

"I suppose you must be experiencing *déjà vu*."

"Sir?"

"Well, only last November you and John Henry came in here to report to me after sailing the *Elver* here from new construction in Groton. Now, here you are again, this time with another brand-new *Gato* class boat." He looked down at a log on his desk. "In fact, it was last November 26."

"Yes sir."

"The world has revolved on its axis 347 times since that day," COMSUBPAC said slowly, thoughtfully. "And so many things have happened. How could we have known that only 11 days after, the Japanese would attack Pearl Harbor and devastate the Pacific Fleet? And look at all the friends and classmates and shipmates who are gone. John Henry. He gave me plenty of headaches over the years, but I liked that man. Liked him a lot. CINCPAC won't admit it, but he had a grudging respect for that old sea dog too. And look at the subs and men we've lost, that are now, in that felicitous phrase, 'on eternal patrol,'" Onets mused.

Dade had never seen the man so mellow, and the warm greeting he'd been given surprised him. After all, Onets had tried to have him, George Pulaski, and Harry Romano court martialed and sent to prison only months before.

"I suppose you heard about George Pulaski's boat being lost."

"Yes sir, when I was back in Groton. We found out in August."

"I'm afraid I have some more bad news for you. Yesterday, we had to declare Harry Romano's boat, the *Dorab*, presumed lost at sea with all hands. They were two weeks overdue from patrol and we'd had no radio communications with them for three weeks. I'm sorry, I know the three of you were close."

Dade felt slightly ill, but controlled himself. "George had been set to retire two weeks before last Christmas."

"I myself had been scheduled to retire last December 31st. In fact, my wife and I had already planned my retirement party at the Officer's Club for December 30th," Onets said with a rueful smile. "At any rate, I wanted to speak to you about the Board of Inquiry."

"Sir, I believe CINCPAC was very clear that none of us who were there were ever to speak of it again."

"Yes, he was, but this is important. Look, what you did was wrong."

"I realize that, sir."

"Yes, but, in the weeks and months that have followed, I've come to the realization that the way in which I handled the incident was . . . . inappropriate. The choices I made in how to handle the problem were ill advised. Oh hell, I made a mistake too. If I had to do it all over again, I'd have made different choices. Better choices. I just wanted to let you know that there are no hard feelings on my part. As far as I'm concerned, we're starting with a clean slate. I know you to be a highly capable submarine commander and a brave man."

"Thank you, sir. I appreciate that."

"Well, that's the end of that then. It's all in the past. The dead past. How's the new boat?"

"Excellent, Admiral. She passed her sea trials and all tests with flying colors, including the radar. You know how temperamental the new SJ radar has been."

"Yes, a number of boats have reported problems with it."

"Well, the technicians seem to have discovered exactly what was wrong. The set in the *Sea Otter* has been working fine. Being able to rely on it is going to give us quite an edge."

"Good. How about your new crew? The quality of the crew of a boat is more important than the quality of the boat."

"As you may remember, sir, I was able to take seven crew members of the *Elver* with me. They're all solid men. None of the other men have been on war patrols. Some have, of course, served on subs before, even for years, but not in combat. Some have just graduated from Sub School. Two men have neither been in subs nor graduated from Sub School. I drilled them again and again at Groton and every day throughout the voyage here. They're coming along."

"Does 'coming along' mean they aren't ready?"

"I'd like some more training time for them, but I realize that's a luxury you probably can't grant."

"Ummmm. We'll get back to that, but first, how are you?"

"Me, sir?"

"Yes, when I relieved you of command of the *Elver*, it was entirely due to the results of your extremely complete physical. The physicians at the base hospital, you'll recall, painted a shocking picture."

"Yes, sir."

"Nevertheless, they assured me that a month of leave, a month in which you rested, ate three balanced meals a day, and underwent no stress whatsoever, would reverse most of the damage that your body and mind had sustained. Two to three months on the outside they told me, and you should be completely fit for duty again. Hence your leave, followed by your assignment to new construction. Now you *look* a hell of a lot better. Are you?"

"Absolutely, Admiral. I feel great. The doctors were right." Bowie raised his right hand and held it level, parallel to the floor. There wasn't the slightest tremor.

"Slide, you're *sure* about this? You're ready to sail your boat and your men back into combat? If you're not up to it, there's no disgrace whatever. I'd hate to lose you, but there are other assignments. Shore assignments."

Shore assignments. Bowie's heart quickened at the words. A desk job. He could be assured of living through the war! Then he remembered the Board of Inquiry and the punishment CINCPAC had meted out to him and his two friends. "But, sir, at the Board of Inquiry, Admiral Van Husen was clear that Pulaski and Romano and I were to serve one war patrol after another until the war ended."

"Yes, yes he did, but he couldn't have meant even if you became *unable* to go into battle."

Unable to go into battle. Wasn't that just another way of defining cowardice? Yes it was. Bowie involuntarily frowned. Furthermore, he knew that CINCPAC meant what he'd said; he was not a man who granted exceptions. Dade no longer had anything physically wrong with him. There was no doubt of that. But was he mentally incapable? What did that even mean? He felt fine. He was still afraid to go back into combat, but that was only normal.

It was odd. In his war patrols, he had always been apprehensive when conning his boat into an attack position, but not terrified. The terror only came after his torpedoes had been launched and there was nothing to do except try to evade the enemy. When the enemy sonar located him, when the depth charges began to shake his boat like a rat terrier shakes a rodent unlucky enough to be caught between its jaws, there was little he could do except make changes in his depth and course. It was *then* that he was always terrified. Perhaps because he always felt so helpless. He had, at least until now, always come through, however. He had yet to freeze with overpowering fear, to become incapacitated, to become unable to perform his duties. There was really no way out. He was both physically and mentally fit. He was just afraid, which was not a valid reason for being excused from combat. Besides, despite what Admiral Onets thought, he was sure that

157

CINCPAC would have him running war patrols until the end of the war no matter what the circumstances. CINCPAC had been quite clear on that. "I'm OK, sir," he said.

"You're quite sure?"

"Positive, sir. The doctors were right. All I needed was rest."

"Alright. Earlier, you said you'd like some more training for your new crew before going into the thick of things. As it turns out, I can accommodate you, in a manner of speaking."

"Oh?"

"Yes, you see, you and the *Sea Otter* are going to be going on a Top Secret mission codenamed Operation Buntline. You'll be departing 0600 on 25 November. Twenty-four hours before, the pier where your boat is tied up will be cordoned off and guarded by Marines. During the day, eight passengers and their gear will be taken aboard. None of your men is to ask these passengers any questions about anything and they sure as hell won't volunteer anything. Their leader will, however, introduce himself to you. No one except you and your XO can leave the pier for any reason. On that evening, you and your XO, along with the eight passengers, will meet with CINCPAC for a final briefing in his office at 1900. After the briefing, you, your XO, and the passengers will return directly to the sub. No one will be permitted to leave the pier or communicate with anyone not on the sub. Between now and 23 November, you're therefore free to schedule any training you wish in nearby waters. You'll have to be escorted by a destroyer to keep our own people from attacking you, but that's easily arranged."

"What else can you tell me about Operation Buntline, sir? For example, how long will we be gone?"

"I know nothing beyond what I already told you. I'm not cleared for it. Nobody is. You aren't cleared to know anything more until the night before you leave. I don't know where you're going or why or how long you'll be gone or anything. All I know is that CINCPAC got me on the horn late last month and said, 'Am I correct in assuming Slide Bowie is your best sub skipper?' I replied that you were and that you were bringing back a brand new *Gato* Class sub from new construction. He then proceeded to tell me what I just told you and that's all I know. By the way, how is your new XO? At least I understand that he's not a reservist."

"First, sir, I've found that some of these reservists are doing a great job. My diving officer, Tom Detrick being one such example."

"Yes, yes, I've heard the name."

"You may recall that it was he who figured out the torpedoes were running about ten feet deeper than set and why."

"He was that ensign? And a reservist too. Remarkable. I understand that you've taken him under your wing as it were, in much the same way John Henry became your mentor."

Dade smiled in surprise. "And you know this how, sir?"

"Oh, Slide, even with the war buildup, the submarine service is still small enough for word of everything to get around."

"Detrick is good, very, very good. He's a fine officer. As for my XO, I think he'll work out, but if it had been up to me, I would not have picked him."

"Yes, I know. Lack of experience. He's only served on Sub School boats. Down the Thames to the sea and back again. Captain Campbell has considerable pull and happens to be Lieutenant Wirtz's biggest promoter. I don't know why. Even if the man is good, without sea duty, he shouldn't have been foisted off on you. I regret to say there's nothing I can do about it except swap him out with an XO from another boat, but that would just mean that another skipper sailing into combat would have a man with no real experience as second in command. You deal with it."

"Aye aye, sir."

"How's the wife, by the way? I understand she's pregnant."

"Word does get around. She's fine. Back at ONI, but only working half days."

"Good. Good. Both you and I have been around long enough to know that, given these scant details, this mission is probably an exceptionally dangerous one. John Henry always spoke of your skill as a submarine officer and you've proven yourself in battle every time you've gone out. Good luck, Slide."

"Thank you, sir."

It was a little past 1400 as Dade followed the instructions to the house Rachael had rented. The pineapple plantation was vast, and, while the roads across it were unpaved, they were well graded and wide. Then, as he turned a curve, he saw it. Even though Rachael had described it well, the sight still took him aback. It was beautiful, with well-tended tropical flowers, trees and bushes that bespoke a gardener who was a true artist. The house was larger than he had expected, and its architectural style befitted the tropics, with a huge lanai and plenty of windows. It reminded Dade of Lance's estate near Diamond Head, only not nearly the size of that sprawling complex. While Lance's house was on the beach, this house sat perched 300 feet back from it, at the top of a hill. He parked the jeep in the circular driveway, then opened the front door. There was little furniture in the large living room, just a brown leather couch, a matching easy chair, a coffee table, and a couple of floor lamps and end tables.

"Rachael?" he called tentatively, but heard no response. He continued through the dining room, and the kitchen. Then he saw her, emerging from a hallway. They quickly moved toward each other and embraced, holding each other tightly for a long moment before either spoke.

"I was just taking a nap."

"How are you? And the baby?"

"We're fine. It's been so long. I've missed you so. This two and a half months have seemed like years."

"To me too." Then they kissed. It was a long kiss, with all the wonder and promise as their first kiss.

"Have you eaten?"

"Not since breakfast aboard the boat."

"Come on then. Let's go into the kitchen and I'll fix you something."

He followed her, smiling, now that they were together again.

"What do you feel like? The refrigerator and pantry are fully stocked, ready for your arrival."

"Just a sandwich is good. Anything."

"OK, grilled ham and cheese coming up along with a bottle of ice-cold beer."

"Perfect."

He sat at the breakfast nook, she opened up a bottle of beer, gave it to him, and went about preparing the sandwich.

"How long do you have before going out again?"

He told her of his meeting with COMSUBPAC, concluding with, "So you see, I'll be around for a while until we go into quarantine on 24 November, the day before we leave on the mission. I'll be running the men through some more training in local waters, but I'll be home most nights. I'll have the men out on night exercises a couple of nights, but just a couple."

"That's good news—the part about us beginning together until then, but I don't like the sound of Operation Buntline. It sounds dangerous."

"Oh, it's probably just transporting coast watchers to a few Japanese-held islands. That and maybe picking up a few. My role is probably just that of a glorified nautical bus driver."

"You don't believe that," she said matter-of-factly.

"No."

"And for the same reasons I don't. If it were just routine transportation for coast watchers, it wouldn't be so highly classified that not even Admiral Onets wouldn't be cleared for it."

"I know."

"Then the quarantine on the pier for a day before you sail, taken in conjunction with CINCPAC himself giving you the briefing the night before you sail, and the cloak and dagger aspect of your mysterious passengers. Finally, them assigning it an operation title. This is something big."

"I know." She was bent slightly over the stove, spatula in one hand, her back to him. He stood and walked over to her and turned her around. Her eyes were beginning to tear up. Dade kissed her. "I'll be alright. Remember, I'm Slide Bowie, a naval legend. I'm invincible. I'm immortal."

"Yes" she said, tears suddenly streaming from her eyes, "I keep forgetting that you're immortal. It's silly of me, I know." They held each other for a long

160

moment. "Go back and sit down. I'll have your sandwich ready in a couple of minutes."

He sat and took a long pull from the beer bottle. "I'll be alright," he said again softly.

"I know."

"So what's going on?"

"A lot of things, actually. I was able to get Alice a job at ONI as a cryptographer. Paul Duvall was very taken with her grasp of higher mathematics. He said her talent would be wasted in teaching high school math. She loves the job too, except for the 10-hour days. Still, she's very happy. She says it's a real challenge."

"That's great."

"And I'm glad you're sitting down for this news—Tracy and Lance are getting married."

"How the hell did that come about? I thought Tracy was the quintessential party girl."

"Not any more. Remember she moved in with Lance right before we left. Well, they've been getting closer and closer and she's really fallen hard for him."

"It doesn't have anything to do with him being incredibly wealthy?"

"No. She's had affairs with wealthy men before. Not men as wealthy as Lance, of course, but no, Tracy's never been a gold digger. I don't think it matters a whole lot that he looks like Errol Flynn, either. She just loves being with him. He's smart and witty and, what's more, he really loves her back. I think it's wonderful. One of the reasons they're getting married is that they've decided they want to have children."

"Tracy a mother? That's awfully had to envision."

"Oh, I think she'll make a great mother. She's changed a lot."

"She must have."

"We had a long talk last week about having children. She was kind of getting cold feet about it. Not about the pain of childbirth, but about the possibility that the child could be born mentally or physically disabled or deformed. Or that, she and Lance could be the perfect parents—do everything right—and still one or more of their children could turn out to be murderers or rapists or prostitutes or drug addicts."

Dade felt a small shiver of fear travel down his spine as he realized for the first time that that could happen to him and to Rachael too. He hadn't really considered that. "That's true, isn't it? Having children is like shooting dice."

"No, Dade. Only in that there is risk involved in both. But there's a big, big difference. When you're in a crap game, the only thing you stand to lose is money and the only thing you stand to gain is money. If you win, the risk you take with children (and the odds are much more in your favor), then you win love. You have people you love who will love you back all your life."

"But if you lose, your loss is a broken heart."

"Yes, it's the same risk you take when you make a commitment to a lover or a spouse. If you win, you're rewarded with love; if you lose you have a broken heart."

"It's a far more serious thing than betting money."

"Yes, there are no guarantees. But there are no guarantees at all in this life. Not really. And you take the greatest risks for the greatest prize of all, love. Something that no amount of money can buy. And what's the alternative? Not to take that risk of falling in love or having children? Some people decide to do just that. You see them every now and then. Afraid to take a risk, they spend their time and energy on their careers or on travel or hobbies. Something safe. They're afraid of a broken heart and dreams that might turn to dust."

"And they die alone," Dade nodded.

"That's not the tragedy, Dade. The real tragedy is that they *live* alone. They go through this life never having experienced the greatest gift a human being can receive. Having never even tried. Having been afraid to take that risk. It reminds me of something that Helen Keller said. "Avoiding danger is no safer in the long run than outright exposure. Life is either a daring adventure or nothing.""

"So Tracy's afraid?"

"Not any more. She never had a second thought about marrying Lance. They're very much in love. It was having children she was afraid of for a little while. She's fine with it now. She wants to begin having some children as soon as possible before she gets as old as I am," Rachael laughed good naturedly.

"How old is she now?"

"She just turned 34."

Dade shook his head, "That old," he smiled.

Rachael came over and handed Bowie a plate with the sandwich and sat down across the padded booth from him. "Yeah, right."

"Have they set a date yet?"

"A week from today on base. By the way, we're invited over to dinner at their house. Tracy said to let us know when would be good for you."

"OK. You know, I'll never forget the night we met at his house. I remember everything about it. Everything."

"So do I. I'm so glad we found each other. You were so nervous that night. Just back from that Wake Island mission when you almost lost your life. You drank a lot that night but it didn't seem to help."

"No, not much. What helped more was talking with you back in your apartment. It's funny. That was only about eleven months ago. So much has happened in such a short time. When I was talking to Admiral Onets earlier, he reminded me that it was only a year ago that John Henry and I brought the *Elver* back from new construction." They both sat in silence for a while as Dade began to eat. After swallowing the first mouthful and washing it down with beer, he tried to strike a more upbeat tone. "So, with a place like this, I imagine we have some hired help?"

"We have a married couple who worked for the owner before he moved. They were both born in Mexico, but are now American citizens, and have been living in the islands for ten years. Maria is our housekeeper and cook, and Juan is our gardener and general handyman. They live only a mile away, and have been wonderful to me. I gave them the day off, since I just wanted us to have the house to ourselves your first day here."

"That's too good to be true! A woman who can cook Mexican!"

"I knew you'd be pleased," Rachael beamed.

"That means enchiladas, burritos, tamales, chimichangas, migas and chorizo—"

"Whoa, pardner, not for every meal though! That has to be understood."

"I'm sure there's room for compromise."

They sat in silence for a while until Dade finished his sandwich. "That was good. Thanks."

"Can I get you anything else?"

"Another beer would be good."

"Coming up," Rachael said as she rose and moved toward the refrigerator. After she opened the bottle and set it in front of Dade, she sat down. She hesitated before she spoke, but this had to be done. "Dade, when the President offered you shore duty for the rest of the war, and you turned him down, you said it was a matter of the duty you felt you owed. Of course, that was true as far as it went, but it wasn't the real reason—the major reason—was it?"

Dade paused thoughtfully before speaking. "No. I was very tempted, very tempted to take him up on it. But if I had, I could have never been sure for the rest of my life if I had accepted his offer out of cowardice."

Rachael knew that, but she had to get him to see it, to face it. Dade averted his eyes from her gaze and picked up the cold, condensation covered beer bottle. Using his thumbnail, he concentrated on peeling the label down the middle. He thought he knew what she was probably thinking. She probably wanted to say, *But what about me, Dade? How could you go back to a succession of one combat patrol after another until your luck runs out? A lot of your friends have already gone to crush depth. How could you do that to me?* He believed those thoughts were running through her mind now, and that they had in days past and would in days to come. And she had every right to feel that way. He also knew she'd never give voice to those thoughts. The decision, rightly or wrongly, had already been made and nothing could change it now. He had been tempted, but told her it was a matter of duty. Duty and honor. And it had, but it had been about more. It had been about proving that Hardy Fish was wrong, that Dade was no coward.

November 21, 1923. He would never forget that night. After Dade's father had died, his mother had married Hardy Fish, a blacksmith by trade, and the strongest man in Mariposa County. She saw it as a desperate measure, but could think of no other way to save the family farm. Farm work was tough, and Dade was only 12 and his younger brother 10. The latter was mentally retarded, and was not expected to ever have his mind develop beyond that of a 5-year old. Dade's mother, Francine, later told Dade that she had made herself see some good qualities in Hardy before marrying him. Qualities that weren't there, she later tearfully admitted.

Fish was a drunk and a cruel man, and began a reign of terror that ended only with his death years later when Dade was finishing his third year at the Academy. When he was a child, Dade had suspected Fish of beating his mother, but had never seen him do it until one night he heard the unmistakable sounds of blows and her cries coming from the parlor. He rushed out of his bedroom to find that Fish had Francine up against a wall. Her nose, bleeding profusely, was evidently broken, and she was also bleeding a lot from a big cut above her left eye. When she saw Dade come into the room, she screamed "Dade! Get out of here! Go back and stay with Roy!" But Bowie just stood there. Then Hardy Fish told him to get back to his room, but Dade stood his ground. He was terrified, but determined to save his mother. Fish told him a second time to leave, but, instead, Dade yelled, "Stop hitting my mama! You stop hitting my mama!" He advanced toward Fish, who advanced right back.

"You figure you got enough sand to make me, you little piss ant?" Fish had thrust his face into Dade's so only six inches separated them. "Go ahead, hero. Save your mama. Go ahead, and I'll smash your face in and break both your fuckin' arms."

Dade had just turned 13 years old, and while he was, at 5 foot 10 inches, two inches taller than Fish, he was a skinny, gangling boy weighing 135 pounds to Fish's 240 pounds, which consisted almost entirely of bone and muscle. Fish had been in countless fights with many men in the county and had beaten all of them, often breaking various of their bones. He usually never stopped beating on a man, even after his victim lost consciousness. Fish would continue, kicking the man, stomping on him, until he had decided the man had received enough punishment. "Now I ain't gonna to tell you again, boy," said Fish, pointing a finger right back at Dade. "Git back in your room with your idiot brother."

Dade knew Fish could and would follow through on the threat and enjoy doing it. Paralyzed with fear like a damned rabbit, Dade couldn't move a muscle. He wanted to. He had wanted to, but he was scared. Hardy Fish could kill him. A long moment went by. Then Hardy Fish pushed Dade so hard, he fell over.

"Haw! Haw! Haw! I didn't think so. You cowardly little piss ant! Now get back in that room before I squash you like a bug!"

"Go Dade," said Francine. "Go back to your room. It's all right, son." Her left eye had started to puff up. Hating himself even more than Hardy Fish, Dade did as she said.

Forever after that, until he left home, hardly a day went by without Hardy Fish reminding him of that night, reminding him that he was a coward. Fish sadistically delighted in it.

Dade had told Rachael of that night long ago, and she had tried to make him see that he had not been a coward. That he had been a justifiably frightened boy, that what he had done was understandable, was what his mother had told him to do. That it had been an ugly, ugly incident, and that it was the shock that haunted him, not evidence that he was a coward. Dade tried to convince himself that Rachael was right; he wanted to believe her. But he had never quite convinced himself. He hadn't ever brought up the incident again to her. What would have been the point? Instead, when he spoke of his fear and his propensity to take great risks in combat, he spoke in terms of duty and loyalty to a higher cause than himself. But he knew that Rachael probably knew it had more to do with that horrible night than anything else. That Hardy Fish's pronouncement that he had proven himself a coward that night exerted a greater influence upon him than almost anything else in his life. Almost certainly, Rachael knew that. She could read him. But she had agreed to support him in his decision to go on war patrols until the war was over anyway. "I'm sorry," he said finally.

"I know. It's alright."

36

November 14, 1942

Oahu

"Thank you for coming, Rachael," Clifford Van Husen said warmly, as he met Rachael at the door of his residence. "Please come in. It's a beautiful day for being on the lanai. Let's relax there."

"That sounds good." She followed him and they sat on two chairs in the shade of a large tree. The crashing of the ocean waves could be heard below them, and a steward came in.

"I believe I'll have an iced tea," he said. "Rachael?"

"I'll have the same, thank you."

"Again, I want to thank you and Tracy for all the time you've devoted to schooling me on Japanese history, culture, religious beliefs, and how they view the world. Your efforts have been extremely useful. No, more than that. Very valuable. Today I have one very important question for you. Just recently, I found out that, when the Doolittle raiders bombed Tokyo, they were given strict orders not to bomb the Imperial Palace, for fear of killing the Emperor. Now, frankly, that strikes me as unconscionable. Why in the hell *not* kill the leader of the country with which you are at war? After all, there is the old adage that, if you cut off the head of the snake, that ends the matter. I mean, we don't keep from bombing the Reich Chancellery for fear of killing Hitler. Indeed, we're *hoping* to kill him with our bombs.

"You and Tracy have explained to me that the Japanese people revere the emperor as a god. Surely, if we killed him, that would take some of the wind out of their sails. You see, the officer who told me about the Doolittle prohibition against bombing the Imperial Palace said, although he can't be sure of the reason behind the order, his understanding is that killing the Emperor would only stiffen the resolve of the Japanese to go on fighting. But I think that's absolute poppycock. Those bastards couldn't stiffen their resolve any more than it is already. Look at how hard they fight! Look at what's happening on Guadalcanal! They're outnumbered and they die rather than surrender. How the hell could their resolve be even more stiffened? No, I think that, if we kill the Emperor, they'll lose some of that resolve.

"What I'm thinking about is parachuting in a crack commando team consisting of Japanese American soldiers or getting them in by submarine and rubber boats. To have them get to the Imperial Palace and assassinate the Emperor. Alternatively, we could have a bombing raid on the Palace. What are your thoughts?"

It was a lot to take in and Rachael thought for a while before she spoke. "There are a number of factors here, many of which are unknowable. First, the Imperial Palace and the Reich Chancellery are not alike because Hitler and Hirohito have different roles in their countries. Hitler is a political figure who is head of state and commander-in-chief of all German armed forces. Hirohito is primarily a religious figure, the head of the state religion, Shinto. While he is technically a head of state, the power of the military has been growing steadily for over ten years. In 1932, Prime Minister Inukai Tsuyoski was assassinated, pretty much ending civilian control of the military. In 1936, there was a military coup attempting to take over complete control of the country, but that failed because other parts of the military were loyal to the Emperor and the status quo. It will interest you to know that Tojo fought against the coup. The Emperor is a quiet man and, for most of his life, been known to be a pacifist. However, as the military became more and more powerful, even having a veto over the approval of cabinet ministers, his actual power has, in turn diminished. Yes, he is the titular head of state, but the cabinet ministers formulate policy and plans and submit only the most important to the Emperor for 'approval.' It is entirely possible that he has become a rubber stamp. Tracy knows much more about this than I do, because of all the work she did at the American Embassy and the fact that she has actually met and spoken to a number of cabinet ministers. Still, she left Japan in early 1940, and so much has happened since then. As far as we know, or believe we know, Hirohito was initially against war with the United States, but was persuaded by Tojo, who became Prime Minister in October 1941, that it was the only realistic course of action to ensure a bright future for Japan. There are six people in Hirohito's wartime cabinet and, after discussion, they vote on what actions will be taken. Our understanding is that the only time Hirohito votes is when there is a tie. We also understand, that, while the cabinet meetings take place in the presence of the Emperor, he normally remains silent. While it is technically true that the Emperor commands the armed forces of Japan, in reality, Tojo is actually the one who gives all the orders. Since we can't speak with the Emperor or attend cabinet meetings, it's impossible to know whether the Emperor has become a figurehead with little

167

or no power, whether he does exert considerable influence on occasion, or well, anything. We do know that, at this stage, the Emperor fully supports the war and has great faith and confidence in Prime Minister Tojo.

"Now let me digress just a bit, because this is very important. The Japanese people do view the Emperor as divine, but, as we told you before, this is not divinity in the Western sense. They know he will die and they know he has no supernatural powers. He is divine because he is the direct descendent of the sun goddess, who created Japan and her people. The first emperor was Jimmu Tenno, who ascended the throne in 660 B.C. Hirohito is the 124th emperor. If he were to be killed, it is entirely likely that the Crown Prince Akhito, would simply take his place. That could make things worse, because Akhito is only about nine or ten years old. Almost certainly a child that age would become easily influenced by Tojo. For all we know, maybe there's a little of the pacifist left in Hirohito and perhaps he even serves as a moderating influence. Perhaps, as the war goes on, Hirohito may be more prone to sue for peace. Would the Japanese people be angry if the Emperor were killed? Absolutely. Also extremely saddened.

"I have no way of knowing what the reason was for the order to make sure the Imperial Palace wasn't bombed. If it was to avoid 'stiffening the resolve' of the Japanese to go on fighting, I agree that doesn't make much sense. For what it's worth, I think it was more a matter of respecting the devout religious beliefs of the Japanese people.

"Neither Tracy not I are seers. All we can offer are our opinions. This is what I think. If Americans were to kill the Emperor, it would probably have no effect on how hard the Japanese fight. They're already committed all the way and will fight to the death. No matter how badly we're beating them in the rest of the Pacific, we will eventually have to invade the home islands and, when we do, there will be no surrender. If they have nothing else left, they'll be fighting us with bamboo spears and rocks and clubs. Including the women and children."

"That's a chilling prospect, but I believe you're right. OK. This was important to me and I want to thank you again for stopping by. Now let's talk about something much more pleasant. I'll be seeing you at the wedding tomorrow."

"You're going?" said Rachael with surprise.

"I wouldn't miss it for the world. I'll be giving the bride away. After all, I'm the only family Tracy has left. Well, technically I'm not family. I guess she's told you that. I'm 'Uncle Cliff' because I was her father's best friend."

"Yes, she did tell me. I do know that she loves you just as much as a real uncle."

"I know," he nodded smiling, "but sometimes Tracy is hard to handle. Still, I love her as if she were my own. I thoroughly approve of her young man, I must say, though. There's no disappointment there. I like him a lot. Your husband and he were roommates at Annapolis, I understand."

"Yes. And they both went into submarines."

"You've only been married a short time yourself."

"Just this past May 3rd," Rachael said.

"And married life agrees with you?"

"I'm very happy. The only cloud on the horizon is the war. I worry about Dade when he's on patrol."

"Understandably. As you probably know, we've lost 20 percent of our submarines since the attack on Pearl Harbor. Even so, the odds are that he'll survive." A little lie, Van Husen thought, a little phony sympathy, would help him in the long run.

"But, as you yourself said, this war is going to last for years, perhaps into 1947. Even if a man is very lucky, he can only throw the dice for so long before he loses. If we lose 20 percent of our submarines every year, the odds of Dade's survival diminish every year. It's simple probability theory."

"Yes, well, I don't believe we'll take losses that high every year. Our crews become more experienced with the passage of time, and we'll keep making improvements in our submarines. Your husband is perhaps our best submarine skipper. He's gotten himself out of some serious scrapes when the odds were against him before. I think he'll do all right, and I'm a very good judge of men. In my job, I have to be."

"Have you ever met my husband?"

"Actually, I have. I personally gave him and Captain Hanrahan their pre-mission briefing before their first war patrol. Then too, I read the patrol report carefully when they returned. When Admiral Onets recommended that your husband be awarded the Medal of Honor for his actions on his second war patrol, I studied that paperwork carefully, along with the second patrol report. I've followed your husband's war exploits with great interest since then. I feel I know him.

"You see, like every man who aspires to the highest ranks in the military, I've been a lifelong student of military history—everything from the Peloponnesian War to the battles that are currently raging in this war. I study not just strategy and tactics and logistics, but I try to understand why men do certain things in war. And one of the things that men like me study is heroism. What makes a man a hero? You see, if you can understand that, then perhaps you can then know how to go about making your men heroes. Or, at least, perhaps you can recognize men who—when thrust into battle—will become heroes. Actually, it's not as simple as it may seem. Sometimes a man will suddenly perform a heroic act simply because he has just seen a good friend on his right killed and a good man on his left killed, and he suddenly becomes enraged—enraged to the point that, at least for perhaps five or ten minutes, he's filled with revenge. He becomes bloodthirsty and all fear leaves him. There is no more desire for self-preservation, only the overpowering urge to kill the enemy. So he charges a machinegun nest or pillbox and he becomes a hero.

Will he ever become a hero again in other battles? Perhaps, and perhaps not. Some men in the infantry win medals for an act they performed while drunk. Not often, but it happens sometimes. What is hard to find is a man who will act heroically time after time, in every battle. Those men are like gold."

"And my husband is such a man."

"Yes. Yes, he is. I've examined the background of men like him, to see if there are any commonalities that he and the few other men like him I've found share. I've looked at interests, education, family, values, beliefs, anything I can think of."

"And?"

"And I haven't found any pattern at all. I have a theory that there is a commonality, and that it is their childhood. But there's no way to know, of course. Military records have no information on the childhood and early adolescence of our men. Part of it could be genetic, but again, no military records have that kind of data. The only good thing is that I have learned how to identify these men when I see them. Not instantly, of course. But after their first time in combat, when I see exactly how they responded, when I look at all the details, then I know. I only wish I had a hundred sub skippers like your husband in the newest fleet boats. Damn, that would be something," Van Husen said, his eyes glistening. "I could shorten the war by two years. As it is, I have to count myself fortunate to have four or five such men."

"I knew Dade was a very brave and very special man the first night I met him."

"Love at first sight?"

"The beginning of love at first sight," she smiled.

This was taking a chance, but Van Husen couldn't help himself. "Since we're friends, I hope you won't take offense at an observation of mine."

"Oh?"

"Yes. You and Slide seem to be an odd match. I mean, your backgrounds couldn't be more different. In addition, you're older, more mature, incredibly well read, and possess an extremely high intelligence. Your husband, is, well, a highly skilled submarine commander, but I'm unaware of any other attributes he has." *Damn it! He had gone too far. All he had to do was wait until Bowie died like Pulaski and Romano and so many others, and the way would be clear. As he'd spoken, he could see her lips press together in a tight horizontal line and the beginnings of a thunderstorm appear in her brown eyes.*

"You don't know my husband at all. All you want to do is use him up, as if he were a store of torpedoes or ammunition, or some inanimate object. If I may make an observation myself, you don't see many of his attributes because you don't have them yourself. Maybe you don't even know that they exist. You see people as objects you can use to win campaigns and a war with, so his bravery is something that catches your eye. But you have no idea how much it takes out of him to go above and beyond his duty every time he goes out there. You don't know about his honesty, his sensitivity, his honor and decency."

Van Husen hadn't seen this coming at all. Damn it. He had to convince this woman that he cared whether her husband lived or died. More than that, he had to convince her that he wanted Bowie to live. If he couldn't do that, he had no chance of having an affair with her after Bowie died.

"Please forgive me, Rachael. I meant no disrespect to your husband or you or your marriage at all. It was a very poor choice of words. You're right. I don't really know your husband as anything other than a very courageous man. I've never had the chance to do so. Scores of thousands of men are under my command. I can't know them all, and, frankly, it's probably best that I don't. If I knew them all, knew them as unique and special individuals, I wouldn't be able to bear their deaths. I have to send thousands of fine young men out to die. Someone has to, and that's me. It's difficult enough as it is.

"In addition, I put my foot squarely in my mouth when I made what in hindsight was a foolish observation. If a woman of your quality is in love with Slide Bowie, then it's very obvious that he must have some wonderful attributes. Please accept my apology."

Rachael looked deeply into Van Husen's eyes. She couldn't be positive, but believed he was insincere. All his facial expressions, his choice of words, and his mannerisms seemed to her to be too practiced. Like many powerful men, he was an actor. It was also probable that he still wanted to bed her. When he had propositioned her months ago, she had been single, available. Now she was not only married, but pregnant. No. There were too many younger, more attractive women on Oahu. Available women, who would be thrilled to be CINCPAC's mistress. No, he couldn't still want her. He had too many other, more alluring, more pliable choices.

"Your apology is accepted. I have to be leaving now. I'll see you tomorrow," she said as she rose and smiled.

"I'll look forward to it. The weather is supposed to be perfect for the occasion."

37

November 15, 1942

Pearl Harbor Naval Base

Oliver Wirtz sat at the bar, nursing a scotch and water. It was 1425 on a Sunday afternoon and he had some time to kill. The past week had been spent in training in nearby waters with a destroyer. They had practi ced countless torpedo attacks on the destroyer as it zigzagged both at the speed of merchant ships and at destroyer speeds. They had practiced gun action, and crash diving. Now they could go from the surface to periscope depth in 40 seconds, which Oliver thought was respectable, but the skipper had insisted that they could shave five seconds off that. The *Elver* could do it in 35 seconds. Wirtz was tired of hearing about the *Elver* from the skipper and the other men who had been on her. It was the *Elver* this and the *Elver* that. Under Slide Bowie, the *Elver* had, in fact, achieved some remarkable victories, but damn it, the *Elver* men were no longer aboard her. It was the *Sea Otter* they should be focusing on.

But, all in all, things were coming along well. After the blowup over Rosemary Brooks, things had settled down. As the days at sea went by en route to Pearl Harbor, Oliver was able to prove over and over again to the other men in the wardroom, to the Chief of the Boat, and to other members of the cr ew that he was a competent XO. *Elver* alumnus Ed Milmer, the Engineering Officer, had been clearly surprised and delighted to learn that Oliver knew so much about the engines and other key mechanical and technical aspects of the boat. Slide Bowie had been impressed with Oliver's navigational skills and how well he functioned as assistant approach officer in the torpedo attack training. He also got along well with Detrick and Greenbaum. By the time they reached Pearl, in fact, he felt he had bonded well with the crew. Even with the skipper. In fact, Slide was back to calling him 'Ollie,' and they'd had discussions about many things. Of course, he still had to prove himself in combat, but he was positive he would. Toward that end, Oliver had set up a number of hypothetical combat situations in his mind and ran through them often in detail, practicing exactly what he would say and do. He felt ready. All he needed was the opportunity to prove himself. It was a fact of military life — the new guy constantly having to prove himself. It had started with his first summer at the Academy before school had started at the hands of the upperclassmen. But it never stopped. Every time a soldier or sailor went to a new duty station, he had to prove himself. As the lowest ranking men on the commissioned officer totem pole, newly minted naval ensigns and Marine second lieutenants were under special, constant scrutiny. Even as you rose through the ranks, you had to keep proving yourself to the new people you were assigned to. Even when a man arrived to become skipper of a submarine, he had to prove himself to the crew. There were two exceptions. The first one was if you had an excellent reputation that preceded you because you had already proven yourself in previous action. Like Bowie. The second was if you were promoted to skipper of the same boat you'd been serving on. And a man who had won the Congressional Medal of Honor didn't have to prove himself to anybody.

No, Bowie didn't have to prove himself, Oliver thought, as he finished his drink and ordered another. But he did and he would. Bowie had spent a lot of time explaining the lessons he had learned in combat in the wardroom. He was actually a good instructor, and Oliver had learned a lot already, like the methods Bowie had used to make Japanese destroyers think they'd sunk the *Elver*.

First, Bowie had explained, he had some fake debris prepared that they could send out via a torpedo tube that would float to the surface. Things like life jackets, the wooden wedges used to temporarily plug leaks, pieces of cork insulation, and so on. This stuff was kept ready to go in the forward torpedo room. Another trick was blowing a lot of diesel fuel from one of the fuel ballast tanks. The *Elver* had launched the debris and blown the fuel simultaneously during depth charge attacks so the Japanese wouldn't be able to hear the sub blowing the fuel or using the torpedo tube.

There were six fuel ballast tanks, identified as 3A and 3B, 4A and 4B, and 5A and 5B. They were open bottomed tanks used to carry either seawater or reserve fuel oil, and, if and when the fuel was used, seawater was admitted to take the place of the oil used. Because oil is lighter than water, when mixed, the oil floats at the top of the tanks so it could be drawn off and used after going through filters to remove any seawater that might remain. When the fuel ballast tanks are used as reserve fuel tanks, the flood valves are locked shut, the vents disconnected, and a special plate bolted across the vent opening in the superstructure. On his previous war patrols, Dade had had all six fuel ballast tanks filled with reserve fuel oil, but for 5A and 5B, the flood valves would not be locked shut and the vents would not be disconnected, which would allow him to blow the oil from those tanks. On two occasions, when the *Elver* had found itself in a desperate, life-or-death situation, he had simultaneously blown fake debris through a torpedo tube and released a large amount of fuel from tanks 5A and 5B. The tactic had worked twice when everything else had failed.

Things were going so well with Dade that Oliver thought it might even be time to start addressing him as 'Slide,' at least in private. While no one in any submarine wardroom would dare call the skipper by his first name or nickname, no matter how friendly and outgoing he was, there was a single exception. The XO could do that, at least in private, if the skipper allowed it. There were no specific conditions by which the XO could know it was OK; it was entirely a judgement call. If he did it, and the skipper told him not to do it, it would be awkward for a moment, but that was all. Yes, Oliver thought, the next time he and the skipper were having a conversation and there was no one else around, he would call the skipper by his nickname.

It had been clear from the beginning that Bowie viewed Detrick as the fair-haired boy of the wardroom, and, Oliver had to admit, the young man was smart as hell and easy to get along with. Greenbaum was an odd duck, a reservist who was just finishing up his mandatory two years of active duty following commission when war broke out. The man saw himself as a songwriter, musician, and band leader rather than a naval officer. He was understandably frustrated by the fact that the war was keeping him from his chosen profession, but at least he wasn't bitter about it or a shirker. He was a fine Torpedo and Gunnery Officer. He was also a fine trumpet player, for many were the nights when he practiced on the cigarette deck when the boat was riding on the surface at night. He was one of the best trumpet players Oliver had ever heard, bar none. Greenbaum had a sardonic wit, but was not much for casual conversation. Oliver got along fine with Milmer, and, for that matter, with the two young ensigns attached to the boat. Mike Day was the Assistant Engineering Officer, and Dan Remick was the Assistant Diving Officer.

The skipper hadn't told Oliver any of the details about their upcoming Top Secret mission, saying only that he himself didn't know much yet. Wirtz had done a lot of speculation before giving up. He'd just have to wait to find out. It seemed logical that the mission was probably both very dangerous and very important, which, of course, worried him a little. Worried him, but also excited him and made him look forward to it. The more important and the more dangerous it was, the better the opportunity to prove himself to his skipper and his shipmates. Then he would be part of that special fraternity—the men who had served with valor in deadly combat. He would fit in with the *Elver* alumnae. He would be part of that "band of brothers." He would be the envy of those who hadn't proven themselves in combat. He would walk a little taller and straighter and brim with a new self-confidence. Rosemary would be proud of him.

Rosemary. He took her last letter out of the left inside pocket of his jacket and read it for the tenth time:

Dear Ollie,

It seems truly incredible that I'd fall in love with a man I met only once. Of course, that was quite a night. As we talked at the party, I quickly felt that I had known you all my life. I surprised myself by going to bed with you that night. Shocked myself, actually. I had only been to bed with one other man in my life. My husband. And that wasn't until our wedding night. But that night with you was a wonderful night, an enchanted night. I was humiliated and ashamed when Matt walked into the room the next morning, and I'm afraid I just fell to pieces. The look on his face, the hurt, was too much for me to bear, and I began to make excuses. I said we'd had too much to drink, I said a lot of things. I was so happy to hear that you and he had talked and things are now OK between the two of you.

Matt is a good boy, smart and brave and strong, and I'm sure he must be a fine sailor. I fear for both of you and pray everyday that you both will survive this war and come back to me. I miss both of you very much, and every time they publish casualty lists in the paper, I'm a nervous wreck as I check for both your names. I know the way it's supposed to work is that, if something happened to Matt, I'd get a telegram from the War Department before they released his name to the newspapers, but sometimes it doesn't happen that way, and the first notice a family gets is through the papers. What a terrible way to find out!

Life goes on here as it always has in a coal mining town. Wilkes Barre is prosperous, with full employment, and I've always enjoyed living here. I was born and grew up here and have always assumed I'd die here. I live in the East End, and everyone knows everyone. When the weather is good, I spend most evenings sitting on the porch swing, nodding and saying hello to the neighbors as they walk by. Sometimes people will come up on the porch and visit for a while. I also like to take walks down to the town square, where we have two movie theaters. I get a lot of enjoyment listening to the radio and reading. The weather here is very cold now, with freezing rain, so I don't get out much except to the neighborhood grocery and to church.

As you can see, I'm not very good at writing interesting letters. I'm sure you and Matt have much more exciting things going on in your lives. Hawaii must be wonderful. Please tell me about it, about what you're thinking, and what you plan to do once the war is over.

Love,

Rosemary

Oliver smiled, refolded the letter, and put in back in his pocket. What he planned to do after the war? That was simple. He'd always planned to make the Navy his life's work. What would Rosemary think of that? He couldn't imagine doing anything else, had never thought of doing anything else. He knew it was too soon to even think of marriage, yet he was. That night *had* been enchanting. He had felt too as if he had known her all his life. Of course, he had been vulnerable because of his impending divorce and she because of the death of her husband. He was sailing off into war and so was her son. Still, there had been something about her. Something real, real in a way that Madeline had never been.

Marriage. How would Rosemary feel about taking on raising Timmy? After all, she had already raised one son to be a man. And Matt was *her* son. She had given birth to him, not some other woman. She was 38 years old. She had probably never thought she'd be raising any kids again. That was another thing—the age difference. Oliver was 26. Rosemary looked like she was 28, but she wasn't. How does she feel about the age difference? Everything had gone so well in the time they'd had together that there had seemed to be no possible impediments to their love. How would she feel about being a Navy wife? Even when the war was over, he'd still have to spend long periods at sea. Would she be willing to sign on for that? To leave the town she had been born in, grown up in, and spent her whole adult life in? Surely, she was asking herself the same questions. Wirtz shook his head vigorously, as if to clear it. He was getting ahead of himself. This was crazy. Time would tell, and he had plenty of time. They'd be writing to each other for months to come, and get to know each other much better. Maybe they were right for each other and had been brought together by some kind of miracle. Maybe they'd get married and their love would only grow deeper and deeper. Or maybe they would conclude that they had only been two lost and lonely, vulnerable people who had embraced each other out of desperation one night, and there was nothing more to it than that. Time would tell.

But, damn it, he was in love with Rosemary Brooks.

38

November 22, 1942

Seacliff Cottage, Oahu

Dade and Rachael had finished dinner and were sitting in the living room listening to the Glenn Miller Orchestra on the radio. The band had begun the program with its signature, *Moonlight Serenade*, and had transitioned into the lively *Chattanooga Choo Choo*, when Rachael spoke. "So Wednesday morning at 0600 is when the *Sea Otter's* crew is being placed under quarantine until after you return from the mission?"

"Yes. By 0600, armed Marines will seal off the pier where she's docked. No one will be allowed on or off the pier until after we sail with two exceptions. First, the eight mysterious passengers and their equally mysterious gear will be admitted to the pier and their leader will make himself known to me. They'll be taken aboard, assigned living spaces, and their gear stowed. Then, that night, they and Oliver Wirtz and I will report to CINCPAC himself for a final briefing. All of us return to the sub and no one can leave it or communicate with anyone not aboard until we set sail the following morning at 0600."

"And you have no idea where you're going or why or how long you'll be gone?"

"Right."

"I don't like it."

Dade shrugged, "Neither do I. To me, the big red flag is that even COMSUBPAC isn't cleared for it. The extremely high classification says extreme danger to me, but then again, that high danger may be something the passengers are in for, not the crew of the sub. It could be that all we have to do is drop them off someplace. Maybe a remote area. American subs have been sneaking in and out of the Philippines successfully for months to supply the guerillas, and the

177

Philippines have over 22,000 miles of coastline. It could be a milk run for us, with the passengers being the ones who should be worried."

"I hope that's true. Didn't you tell me that it was CINCPAC who said he wanted you for this mission?"

"Basically. Admiral Onets said he asked if I was the best sub captain available for a very important job and Onets told him that I was."

"But Admiral Onets is the one who normally decides what sub captains go on which mission, surely."

"Yes. The Pacific is divided up into various different submarine patrol areas, each of them numbered. And, of course, some patrol areas, like the ones off the coasts of the Japanese home islands, are much more dangerous than others, like the Gilbert Islands. Now submarines are constantly coming and going from their assigned patrol areas, some need extensive repairs before going out again, and we're always getting subs coming in from new construction. COMSUBPAC's staff officers, including Lance, draw up suggested postings on which subs will go to which areas, and their dates of patrol. Then they submit the recommended postings to Admiral Onets for final approval."

"I assume that one of the factors they take into account is the skill of the skippers and how much experience the crews have."

"Oh, yes. Those are the biggest factors, especially the skill of the skippers. Actually, another factor is the aggressiveness of the skippers. This year, they've relieved some skippers of command because they 'lacked aggressiveness.'"

"What does that mean?"

"That they tried to play it too safe. Some didn't even launch their torpedoes using the periscope. Instead, they kept the scope down and launched on sound bearings. They didn't want to take chances. They were considered good skippers before the war started. They did great in the peacetime exercises, but were a disappointment when it came to the real thing. Only a few were relieved though. A lot of others are OK skippers, but still have an aversion to taking real risks."

"And, you, of course, take risks. A lot of risks. They must be thrilled with your level of aggressiveness."

Dade only nodded.

"So they take the most skilled and aggressive sub commanders and assign them to the most dangerous patrol areas, then?"

"Yes, that's generally how it goes."

Rachael sat in silence for a while. Finally, Dade continued. "Look, I know exactly what you're thinking. Why don't I become less aggressive? Not so much so that they relieve me of command of a boat, but enough so that they'll assign me to the safer patrol areas. Of course, that thought has crossed my mind. I think of you and our baby and . . . . . . well, I've thought of it, but I can't see my way to doing it. A lot of things enter into it. I don't think that anyone makes a major decision in his life for only one reason. Human beings are complex, so complex that we don't even understand ourselves and why we do things. For example, there wasn't only one reason why I joined the Navy. When I made up my mind that I wanted to be a naval officer, there were a number of reasons—patriotism, adventure, a free first-class college education, an interesting job, travel to the far corners of the globe, prestige, good pay and benefits, job security, to protect and defend the Constitution of the United States, a good pension, free medical and dental care for life, a desperate desire to get out of Mariposa County and all the bad memories there, and, I don't know, maybe a dozen other things I wasn't even consciously aware of."

"Yes, just as a woman doesn't marry a man just because she loves him. She has to be sexually attracted to him. She takes into account whether he'll be a good provider, a good father, and strong enough to protect her from danger. She also wants him to be free from addictions like alcohol and gambling. She wants to be sure that he's not the type to run around with other women after they're married. She wants him to be honest and open and feel that she can talk to him about anything. She wants to be sure that he loves her."

"Yes, exactly. People never do important things for one reason. And often we aren't sure what our main reason, the critical reason is, even in retrospect. I've thought long and hard about becoming less aggressive in my upcoming war patrols. But it wouldn't be right. The Navy took me in, gave me a college education, and spent years training me to be a leader and how to command a submarine, the most complex weapons system in the world. Year after year, it fed me, clothed me, gave me medical and dental care, world travel, still more advanced training, and all of the perks that officers get. My end of the deal was that, if war ever broke out, I would lead submariners into combat and do my very best to destroy the enemy. To go out as many times as it took, knowing that each patrol might be my last. Knowing that I might be killed in battle. That was the unspoken contract, and I entered into it knowingly and willingly and now that the war is here, I have to fulfill my part of the contract. It's like, well, it's like a major league baseball team took me on, and spent a lot of time and effort in developing me. They started me out in the minor leagues, spending a couple of years developing me. Then they put me in the starting lineup in their major league, paying me a lot of money for doing something I really love. And I do my job well. I mean really well. I mean I'm another Babe Ruth, sending that ball right over the fence out of the ballpark almost every time I come up to bat. They know what to expect when I step up to the plate.

"How can I then, for personal reasons, slack off? Figure that all I owe them are some singles and doubles instead of home runs? They're counting on me. My bosses, my coaches, my teammates, the fans. No. I owe it to them to do my very best. To try to blast that ball right out of the park whenever I swing that bat."

"That's an interesting analogy, Dade, but it's not an accurate one. No one in major league baseball dies when he steps up to the plate."

"Look, if you want me to tone down my patrols, not take many risks, just tell me. I'll do it for you and the baby."

"No, I'm not going to ask you to go against what you think is right, what you see as your duty. I won't do that. If I did, and you agreed to do it, you'd be no good to me as a husband and you wouldn't be a good father to our children. You have to do what you think is right. If you slacked off and your only reason was to please me, you wouldn't be able to look at yourself in the mirror for the rest of your life and that would be like a daily dose of poison in our relationship. Do it only if you think it's right."

Dade looked at the fire dancing in the fireplace as if seeking an answer in its flames. "You're right. If I did it, I could never be sure for the rest of my life if it was something I did for you or for myself because I lacked the courage to give it everything I had. I know I'd also feel that I was letting the team down. If I stopped doing my best, then I'd be replaced by men who might die out there in the most dangerous patrol areas and I'd feel like their blood was on my hands. If I die, I die, but it would be wrong to have other men die in my place."

"Well, then it's settled once and for all. I promise I won't bring it up again."

"I love you, you know."

"I know."

"I'd do almost anything for you, but I can't do this. Like you said, I'd be no good as a husband or a father if I didn't do my duty. It's a matter of honor."

"It's settled, Dade. It's alright. When I spoke to Admiral Van Husen back on the 14th, he mentioned briefing you and John Henry before your first mission. Then, of course, he took over the Board of Inquiry proceedings. I'm curious. What's your opinion of him?"

"He's a very intelligent man, very capable. In the briefing for the Wake Island mission, sparks flew between him and John Henry because, since we all knew we could, at best, only delay the Japanese from taking the island, not prevent it, John Henry questioned the whole mission. Then, I don't know, the briefing degenerated into CINCPAC angrily saying that the scope of his job was so immense that he didn't have the luxury of bleeding for all the dead, for caring about them. Only commanders at much, much lower levels could take the time to care about their men and to grieve for their loss. That kind of made sense, but, I don't know. I think it's as simple as this: he doesn't care because he doesn't care. He's a very ambitious man. You have to be to get to be CINCPAC. I think the only person he really cares about is himself, but then, I could be wrong. Why?"

"Just wondering. I've formed my own opinion from my interactions with him. I agree that he's a very intelligent man and ambitious. I also think he's a narcissist. But there's a complexity there that I haven't been able to figure out. He's direct, which creates the appearance of honesty, but I'm not sure that real honesty is part of his makeup." She considered, then decided not to tell Dade about Van Husen's proposing that he and Rachael have an affair. When it happened in

February, Dade had been at sea on his second war patrol and when he returned, he'd had enough on his mind. Besides, she had been single at the time and enough of a modern woman to have solved the problem herself with a simple refusal. There had been no need for Dade to have one more thing to disturb him. And there was certainly no need to tell him about it now. It was nothing. She went on, "As far as not caring about the men under his command because there are so many of them, that does make a kind of sense, I suppose. A defense mechanism. Or, it could be that he's merely a high functioning psychopath (many great leaders are) and has no genuine feelings for any human being other than himself. Psychopaths understand normal human emotions and are even able to imitate them in order to manipulate people. There's no way we have of knowing. Anyway, some psychopaths are actually geniuses. He could be one of them, and, if that's the case, he may still be the best man available for his job." She shook her head. "I just wish I knew when to expect you back from this mission."

"We only have so much fuel and so much room for food, so we know that the latest would be about the first of February. Are you feeling OK? Everything with the baby going OK?"

"Yes, I haven't had morning sickness now in a long time, and aside from being more tired than usual, I'm fine. But it's a good thing I'm only working half days now. Anymore, I need a nap in the afternoon."

"Just don't hesitate to call the doctor if anything doesn't seem right."

"I will. Don't worry. You need to keep focused on your mission and come back to me."

"I will. Remember, 'Slide' Bowie is a naval legend. He's invincible in battle."

"That's right. How silly of me. I keep forgetting that."

39

November 24, 1942

Pearl Harbor Naval Base

"That must be them," Dade said to Oliver as they stood on the bridge of the *Sea Otter*. Both men watched as the Marine guards let an Army deuce and a half rumble onto the pier. "Let's go greet them." Both men descended to the deck and crossed the brow onto the pier as the truck came to a stop parallel to the submarine. It was 0800. A man got out of the cab and walked up to the two naval officers. Checking their insignia of rank, he saluted Dade.

"You must be Commander Bowie, sir."

"Yes," said Bowie, returning the salute as he studied the man, who wore Army fatigues with captain's insignia. "Are you the team leader?"

"Yes sir. My name is Captain Jones."

"Since you guys are Top Secret, cloak and dagger types, that's probably not your real name is it?"

"No sir, it's not," the man replied with a trace of a smile. "Jones" was about 6 feet 2 inches and looked like he weighed about 210 pounds, mostly muscle. He had a deep scar on his right cheek, gray eyes, and was heavily tanned. He walked and held himself with absolute confidence. "The biggest reason for the phony names in this particular type of OSS team is that most of us have relatives living in Germany or occupied France. If we were captured—"

"I understand. This is Lieutenant Oliver Wirtz, my XO. He'll assist you and your men in getting your gear on board and stowing it, as well as finding places for your men to sleep. I understand there are eight of you in all?"

"Yes, sir. There's me, my second-in-command, Lieutenant Smith, and six others. Have your men been told that they're not to be asking us any questions about who we are, what unit we're from, where we're going, and why?"

"Yes. That's understood. You and Lieutenant Jones are welcome to take your meals with my officers in the wardroom. The rest of your men will eat in the crew's mess aft."

"OK, sir."

"My understanding is that you, your men, my XO, and I will meet with CINCPAC in his office at 1900 tonight and that we set sail at 0600 tomorrow morning."

"That too is my understanding, sir."

"Do you have any questions?"

"No sir."

"Very well, Lieutenant Wirtz will see about getting you and your gear aboard. I'll see you later."

Bowie looked at his watch as he and the other nine men filed silently into CINCPAC's office. It was exactly 1900. No one had said anything on the walk over. The Army personnel hadn't even spoken among themselves. They were obviously a well-disciplined unit, intelligent, and tough. They seemed to be cut from the same cloth as Captain "Jones." They were all in excellent physical condition and moved with an air of competence and confidence. They were older than the average soldier by a few years and there was a deadly seriousness about them.

"We'll take seats around my conference table, gentlemen," CINCPAC said as the men entered. A Marine guard had been stationed outside the door and Admiral Van Husen addressed him. "We are not to be disturbed for any reason. No one is to enter." The Marine nodded in reply, and Van Husen closed the door. Once everyone had been seated, Van Husen took his place at the head of the table.

"We're here to discuss Operation Buntline in detail. Anyone may interrupt at any time if there are questions. The purpose of the operation is to evacuate a Japanese scientist, Dr. Hideki Nakamura, and his wife, from his wife's ancestral family compound on the Japanese home island of Kyushu. Dr. Nakamura's son, Isokuru, who is a grad student at MIT, tells us that his father, who also went to MIT, lived in the States for several years, and is favorably disposed to our country and democracy, will almost certainly come willingly if given the opportunity, as long as his wife can accompany him. While Dr. Nakamura is engaged in a highly classified project in a secret laboratory complex with impenetrable security on the outskirts of Tokyo most of the year, he and his wife have always—since the early days of their marriage, had a tradition of spending several days at her family's compound to celebrate her birthday. This operation is scheduled to take place on 14 December, her birthday.

"Their son has provided us with a detailed map of the compound and the buildings in it, as well as floorplans of the buildings." CINCPAC turned to look directly at Bowie and Wirtz. "The OSS team has, for a long time, been practicing assaults on a full-scale model of the compound constructed of plywood and planks in a secluded part of an air base in Florida. They've run through different scenarios in both day and night. Over and over again. I have here a diagram of the compound. Captain Jones, I'd like you to go through your plans so I can evaluate them." CINCPAC rose and used thumb tacks to affix the large diagram to the bulletin board on the wall. When he was finished, he sat.

Captain Jones rose and walked over to the diagram. "Thank you, Admiral. By way of introduction, this is the first operation the Office of Strategic Services has mounted in the Pacific Theatre. Up until now, we've operated only in Europe, so no one in the Pacific knows our work firsthand. For that reason, General Donovan has authorized me to tell you about the kind of work we've been doing. We want you to feel confident that we're a good fit for this operation. We're members of the Army, but our training and organization has been modeled on t hat of the British Special Operations Executive. Since our team was one of the first, we received our advanced training from British instructors in England and Scotland before the United States even entered the war. We wore Canadian uniforms and had Canadian papers. We participated in a number of operations in occupied Europe last year before America entered the war. This year our team has successfully performed three high risk missions—all in occupied France. Each time, we parachuted in, and after completion of our missions, we made it to the coast, where we were picked up by submarine. On the first mission, we attacked Gestapo Headquarters in Rouen one night, where we freed all the Resistance fighters from the lockup and killed all German personnel. Before we set fire to the building, we took with us a number of Gestapo files listing the names of the double agents who were working for the Germans. On the second mission, we ambushed a convoy carrying the commanding general of the First SS Panzer Corp s outside Reims. We killed the general, a number of his staff, and came away with detailed maps and other classified documents giving the complete order of battle of the corps. During that operation, we wore German uniforms and so achieved complete surprise. Nevertheless, getting away was pretty dicey, since we were outnumbered ten to one by elite troops. On our last mission, we made our way into Paris and kidnapped a German scientist on vacation. He was a key figure in their rocket program, and we brought him safely back to England.

"These are the kinds of missions we do, that we were trained for. We always operate deep inside enemy territory and we're always on our own. We can't call in artillery or mortar fire. We can't call in air support. If we 're wounded, we can't yell 'Medic' and have someone run to our side to patch us up. We can't call for reinforcements or help of any kind. We all speak both German and French. Half of us speak German like natives because it was spoken in our homes, the o ther half French, for the same reason. The second language we speak fluently, but with an accent. We are all highly motivated volunteers, and, frankly we know you can't go up against the odds that we do for long before your luck finally runs out, no matter how skilled you are. It's simple mathematics, and we're OK with that. We're committed. Three of us are Jews, who have made it out of Germany only one step ahead of those who were rounding up Jews. The rest were born in the United States, but consider this war to be the most important one in the history of the world. If the fascists win this one, it's all over for freedom and self-government. We're *totally* committed.

"Unfortunately, none of us are fluent in Japanese, however Dr. Nakamura speaks English fluently. He did, after all, attend MIT. Although that was well over three decades ago, we can be reasonably sure he maintains his proficiency in the language in order to keep up with all the scientific papers that are regularly published in the field in English. Many top flight scientists also read German for the same reason. While there shouldn't be any problem in communicating with Dr. Nakamura in English, anything can happen, and we may find it essential to communicate with others in the compound. For that reason, three of us have undergone an intense eight-week course at Army Language School and are able to ask and answer basic questions in Japanese as well as to give instructions. I'm afraid that will have to do. There wasn't enough time to learn anything more than the bare basics. Another unfortunate thing is that, unlike when we're operating in Europe, we can't pass ourselves off as locals or as members of the occupying enemy army. To continue on for a moment with some more bad news, our intelligence of the target is not nearly as complete as we would like it to be. Finally, the guards are not regular army troops, but members of the Kempeitai, the Japanese version of the Gestapo, only more ruthless and brutal. Well, the lads and I like a challenge. Now to the plan.

"We'll leave the submarine in two inflatable rafts and hit a small beach area directly behind the compound, which sits on a plateau overlooking the beach. It will be a moderate climb up to the plateau. While the slope is steep, we won't require any ropes or other climbing gear. The distance from the beach to the compound is approximately 250 yards.

"The compound is surrounded by a two hundred-year old stout eight-foot high wall, made of rammed earthen walls, constructed by making a mixture of selected aggregates, including sand, gravel, silt, and a small amount of clay, and ramming this mixture with wooden poles into place between flat panels, or framework. The ramming compresses the mixture, and when it dries, it's extremely solid. In fact, its hardness is comparable to our modern concrete. Some walls made using this method have stood for a couple thousand years. The wall is about two and a half feet thick. There are two gates. First, the main gate, has two wide doors, big enough to admit horse drawn wagons and carriages. These days, of course, the horse drawn vehicles have been supplanted by motor vehicles, which can also fit through the main gate. When Dr. Nakamura and his wife are visiting, there are at all times two Kempeitai guards manning the front gate, one on either side. Both men are armed with Type 99 7.7 mm Arisaka rifles. As you can see, the main gate faces due west. There is a smaller gate on the eastern wall large enough for use by people only. It is guarded by a single guard armed with a rifle, and the gate is secured from within the compound, barred and locked with a padlock. The purpose of this gate is to provide the residents of the compound easy access to a tea house about 70 yards away, down the long slope that the compound sits atop. The tea house (in the West, we'd call the small structure a gazebo) offers a beautiful view of the sea below and, for generations, the family has spent many hours there, reading, meditating, and so forth.

"There is a fourth guard, who patrols the outer perimeter with a German Shepherd. He too is armed with a rifle. The guards are changed every four hours. We will be assaulting the compound at 0200, halfway through one of their shifts. Now let's look inside the compound. This long rectangular building you see to the right as you enter the main gate used to be the stable, but, since the family no longer keeps horses or horse drawn vehicles, it's now used as a two-car garage as well as for storage.

"The long building to your left is used for servants' quarters as well as a kitchen where all meals are prepared, including the ones which are served to the family in the main house. The main house consists of two large bedrooms, two smaller bedrooms, a dining area, a living room, and a library. Mrs. Nakamura's parents sleep in this bedroom here, and the Nakamuras in this one here," Jones said, pointing.

"We don't know how many guards will be within the walls. It's reasonable to expect, however, that there will be an additional four guards as well as a sergeant of the guard. It's also reasonable to expect that most of them will be asleep when we strike. They probably won't begin to bestir themselves until it's time for them to relieve the guards on duty. We can't count on that, however. They could even have an interior guard patrolling the courtyard.

"The first order of business is to kill the four exterior guards, quickly and silently, as well as the dog. The lack of cover immediately around the compound walls precludes us from getting close enough to do that by knife, so we'll use crossbows."

"Why not silenced weapons?" CINCPAC, who was listening intently, asked.

"What people refer to as 'silencers' is a misnomer, sir. They are actually 'suppressors,' which muffle the sound, but, on the still night air, anybody within 70 yards would hear the sounds and immediately identify them as gunshots. It's only in the movies that suppressors make a barely audible *pfffit*. Everyone will be in position and the crossbows will all let fly at the same time. Everything will be timed down to the second.

So four men (Team A)—two armed with crossbows—will take out the guards at the main gate, then fan out, two men to the left building and two men to the right. At exactly the same time as the bolts are flying from the crossbows of the team at the main gate, two men from Team B will use crossbows to take out the roaming guard and his dog. The remaining two men from Team B will take out the guard at the small gate on the eastern wall and run around to enter the compound by the main gate. At this point, all team members will transition to suppressed submachineguns. When we trained with the British and went out on missions with them, we used Sten Mark 2(S) 9-mm submachine guns. That model has the suppressor integrated into the barrel. They use 30-round stick magazines.

"Once we have cleared the two buildings to the right and left and the courtyard, Team A will enter the main building, clear that in case there are any guards inside, then go to the bedroom Dr. Nakamura and his wife are staying in, explain the situation to them, and get them moving. Meanwhile, three members from Team B will be in front of the residence in case any unanticipated Kempeitai put in an appearance, while the remaining team member will pick the padlock securing the gate in the eastern wall and remove the horizontal plank reinforcing it. We'll be leaving with Dr. Nakamura through this gate."

"One of your guys can pick locks?" Dade asked.

"We all can pick locks; it was part of our training."

"In the dark?"

"In the dark," Jones nodded with a smile, "and very quickly."

"What if, for whatever reason, Dr. Nakamura refuses to leave?" CINCPAC asked, although he knew what the answer was supposed to be.

"Sir, Dr. Nakamura is going with us whether he wants to or not. His son says he spent seven years at MIT, and enjoyed his time there. That he has fond memories of America and its people. I will tell him that, if he and his wife come with us, they will be immediately reunited with their son back in the States. I will explain that our scientists would like to ask him some questions about the project he has been working on for Japan, and that he may well be invited to participate in our special project, but I will explain that another option open to him would be teaching at one of our many universities and colleges. I will say that we do not consider him to be a prisoner and we will not treat him as such. When we take him back to the States, he may do anything he wishes, except that he cannot leave the country until after the war is over. We have every reason to believe that he'll willingly come with us, but, if he doesn't, we're fully prepared to handcuff him and his wife, throw them over our shoulders, and carry them back to the sub. Now, in an operation like this, any number of things can go wrong. No one knows this better than we do. As we're getting into position for the attack, we could be spotted by one of the guards, who could alert everyone both inside and outside the compound. There could be more Kempeitai than we estimate inside. As we try to take down the exterior guards silently with crossbows, one of us could be a little off and one of them could live long enough to fire a warning shot that would alert the men inside the compound. As we're killing the Kempeitai inside the compound, one of them might manage to stay alive long enough to get off a radio or telephone message for help, and the nearest Japanese army base is only three miles away. And those are just a few things that could go wrong. I can think of about twenty more.

"But that's always the case with high risk missions like this. The OSS sent us, not only because we have performed missions like this successfully behind enemy lines, but because they believe we're the best team. General Donovan was told—told by the President of the United States—that the accomplishment of this mission could shorten the war by a couple of years, and a lot of American soldiers, sailors, Marines, and airmen can die in two years of war. We were told we *had* to succeed, whatever the cost."

"If things do go wrong, terribly wrong, and it is not possible to get Dr. Nakamura out?" CINCPAC said, again, knowing what the answer should be, but wanting Jones to say it.

"In that case, our orders are to kill Dr. Nakamura in order to deny his expertise to the Japanese."

CINCPAC nodded with satisfaction.

"If things go wrong," Dade said, "and it's not possible to evacuate all your wounded, I assume you going to leave them behind."

"None of us will be captured alive. If capture is inevitable, we'll use our L capsules."

"L capsules?"

"The 'L' is for lethal. They're cyanide, causing death within 15 seconds. We wear them taped to our necks. We've worn them before on high risk missions when there was a danger we'd be captured by the Gestapo. We had no desire to be captured by the Gestapo and we have much less desire to be captured by the Kempeitai."

"How long from the time you set out from the submarine to the time you return?" asked CINCPAC.

"If the sub can get us to within 100 yards of the place we need to land, we'll leave the sub at 0200 and expect to return no later than 0345."

"That's if everything goes well," Dade said.

"Yes, it could be longer if it doesn't. But if we're not back by 0415, you can assume the mission has failed and put to sea without us. It means the enemy has been alerted and has either killed us or we've taken our L capsules because we're wounded too badly to get back to the sub. I believe that, under those circumstances, you'll want to exit the area before dawn and get to some deep water fast because Japanese patrol craft will have gotten the word and be looking for you with a vengeance."

"Let's look at the nautical charts," CINCPAC said, advancing to pin a large one over the diagram of the compound. He turned around and pointed at the island of Kyushu. "Come up here, Bowie. This is where you're going."

"And this is where I need you to drop me and my men off," Jones said, "This small peninsula that juts out of the north end of the island and points northwest to

188

Shikoku, one of the other major home islands. At the tip of the peninsula is the city of Saganoseki. At this very spot." The tip of his right forefinger rested at a spot midway down the southwestern side of the peninsula. "Can you do it?"

Dade studied the chart closely. Fortunately, the maps the U.S. Navy had of the Japanese home islands—unlike some of the other places where it had to fight in the Pacific—were accurate. The soundings off the coast where the drop off and pick up point was, indicated that the water there was deep enough to get to within a hundred yards of the place Jones had pointed to, but, at 70 feet, just barely enough to submerge. They could launch the two boats, then flood down to sit on the bottom for an hour, then resurface, but this was going to be a tough job. "First, this is in Submarine Patrol Area 2, the toughest patrol area in the Pacific. To date, we've lost five subs in this area. Those subs and their crews are now, as we say in the Silent Service, 'on eternal patrol.' They never returned and are presumed lost. We're talking here about going through the Bungo Strait into the Japanese Inland Sea. The Japanese patrol it heavily because there are constant convoys and naval task forces running up and down this side of the home islands. In the area we're talking about here, there's only about 21 nautical miles between Kyushu and Shikoku. Then, on top of that, we're going to take the sub up to where it's only 100 yards away from Kyushu in just barely enough water to submerge if we sit on the bottom. If a patrol boat or tin can spots us here, we're totally vulnerable. And, within minutes, we'd have more Japanese ships than you could shake a stick at boxing us in, keeping us from getting back to deep water."

"Of course, you're correct," said CINCPAC. "This is a dangerous area, particularly for this kind of mission. Tin cans are aggressively patrolling up and down the coasts and in the channel between Kyushu and Shikoku. That's a fact and there's nothing we can do about it. We do have some intelligence regarding the patrol boat activity in the specific area where the drop off is. There is a Type 31 patrol boat that shows up every four hours, noses around in the bay for about 25 minutes, then goes on its way. The Type 31 is armed with two 120-mm guns and one 25-mm antiaircraft gun. Its top speed is 18 knots."

"Do we know its schedule?"

"Yes. It should be leaving the bay around 0125."

"So we'll have until say 0500 until it enters the bay again?"

"Yes, barring any unforeseen change in its schedule."

"How reliable is this intelligence?"

"Absolutely reliable," Van Husen said with perfect confidence.

Dade guessed that CINCPAC had had another submarine up that way with orders to watch the bay for a week or so. The sub's crew would have been sworn to secrecy and told under no circumstances were they to enter the bay, only observe from outside. That would explain Van Husen's confidence.

"I'd hate to be bottled up in that bay. If it arrives early, we'll have to fight our way out on the surface. If we surprise them, we'll have a decent chance of taking them, but if they have enough time to get a radio message off, the tin cans patrolling the channel would be arriving pretty fast."

"True," nodded Van Husen, "but at least you don't have to worry about being spotted by any aircraft."

"Until dawn."

"Yes, but by then you'll be out to deep water."

"I'd like a dark night for this operation. A very dark night."

"Me too," echoed Jones fervently.

"What phase will the moon be in?" Bowie asked.

"Waxing crescent," CINCPAC replied.

"Well, at least that's something. How about sunrise?"

"0642."

"I just hope we have plenty of clouds, lots of dark clouds."

"That'd be nice," said Jones. "As long as we're wishing for things, rain would be good. The sound of rain pouring down will muffle the sounds of our movements on land."

"To get back to your original question, sir," Dade said, addressing Van Husen, "can we pull this off? Of course I can't speak for the ground mission, only for the sea end of it. The answer is yes, yes, in the sense that there's a school of philosophy that says that all things are possible. It can be done, but the odds are against us."

"What would you say the odds are—not for the ground mission, of course, but the sea portion of the mission," Admiral Van Husen asked, as he took his seat at the head of the table.

Dade thought hard. He wanted to be as accurate as possible. "About 35 percent."

Van Husen nodded. "Considering the importance of the mission, those are acceptable odds." He turned to Jones. "What are the odds of success of the ground portion of the mission?"

"Actually, roughly the same, sir," answered Jones immediately. He had calculated the odds weeks before.

"Very well. The mission is a go. Slide, you are to maintain complete radio silence until you're within a day's journey from Pearl Harbor on your way back, at which time, you'll give your ETA. You will, however, be monitoring the radio in the unlikely event that we send an abort mission message. Understood?"

"Yes sir."

"Furthermore, you are on this mission and this mission only. No matter how favorable the circumstances, you will not engage any enemy ships on the way out or on the way back. Clear?"

"Yes sir."

"Furthermore, you are not to discuss any of the details of this mission with the other officers and men in the crew. Nothing beyond the fact that you are taking

Captain Jones and his men to a place where they are to perform a highly cl assified mission and pick them up when they're finished. Clear?"

"Yes sir."

"Another thing. If it looks like you're either going to be captured by Japanese vessels or sunk in relatively shallow water, the first thing you must do is to burn the ULTRA codebook. That *must* be done."

"I understand, sir," Dade replied.

"Very well," CINCPAC said, hands folded on the table. "You men and the crew of the *Sea Otter* are to be confined to the boat and the pier where it's tied up until you set sail at 0600. A tin can will escort you out to the open sea. There will be no communication from this point on with anyone not involved with the mission. Last chance. Does anyone here have any questions? Any questions at all?" He searched each face. "That's it then. One last thing, and you've heard this before, but I must stress it. This is one of the most important missions of its kind ever mounted so far in this war. If it is successful, it could shorten the war by two or more years. Think of that. Bear that in mind constantly. Whatever risks you have to take, whatever sacrifices you must make to accomplish the mission, take them, make them. Don't hesitate for a second to do what needs to be done, even if it means your life or the lives of some of your men. That's all, gentlemen."

Dade and Wirtz walked alone on the way back to the pier, a little behind the group of OSS men. For a while, they walked in silence. Finally, Wirtz half whispered to Dade, although there was no one in earshot. "That was some briefing."

Dade simply nodded in response. "I mean," Wirtz said, "I never imagined I'd be involved in anything like this when I volunteered for combat duty in the Pacific. Have you ever been on a mission like this, skipper?"

Dade shrugged. "Like this one? No, but John Henry and I were sent on a Top Secret mission with the *Elver* the day after the attack on Pearl Harbor. We had the same rah rah speech from CINCPAC about how important the mission was and how we had to accomplish it even if it meant the loss of the b oat and everyone on her. We didn't accomplish the mission, but found out later that it made no difference, no difference at all." Bowie sighed wearily in the chilly night. "To be fair, that was a mission conceived entirely by CINCPAC himself, while this one comes from a hell of a lot higher up. And having the OSS involved—supposedly the best team of this sort they have—well, it's obviously a joint Army-Navy operation at the highest level. The Secretary of War himself may even be involved. It does seem to be very important, but then, again, it could just be a half-baked notion dreamed up by some staffer back in Washington based on inaccurate intelligence. At our level, we have no way of knowing. But one thing I do know is that it's all too easy for our superiors to say that a mission must be accomplished 'at all costs' and that the mission is vastly more important than all of our lives.

I've been told that before and it wasn't true. Nevertheless, I'll give them the benefit of the doubt and act as if it is true. It could even *be* true."

"Those OSS guys are pretty intense."

"Yes, the L capsules and so forth. They seem to be true believers."

"They have to be. To parachute into occupied France and do what they do. You've gotta be a true believer to risk death or worse—capture by the Gestapo. I'd want an L capsule too. They're a quiet bunch. Even among themselves."

"I know. They're a different breed. I have to admit that I'm impressed with them. If anyone can get the job done, it's them."

40

November 25, 1942

Pearl Harbor Naval Base

Paul Duvall sat at his desk nervously, trying to summon up the courage to confront Rachael and to go over carefully in his mind the words he would use. He had laboriously written out the speech and practiced it in the few hours a day he had to himself. He'd been trying it out in front of the mirror to get down the right facial expressions and just the right earnestness in his eyes, the right gestures with his hands. He hated personnel administration, hated it with a passion. He was one of the best theoretical mathematicians in the United States and had been happy teaching advanced graduate courses at the University of Oklahoma and doing research. But the military had taken note of the papers he had published on cryptography, and, before he'd quite known what had happened, he found himself a naval officer in charge of breaking Japanese military and diplomatic codes at ONI in Hawaii. It was all very exciting, especially when he found out that that was what they had recruited him to do. The Japanese codes were challenging. Quite elegant, actually.

But he was not, and had never been a people person. Fortunately, nearly all the people who worked for him were as introverted as he, so that wasn't much of a problem. But now, now he had to dragoon Rachael Bowie into working a lot more hours. The translators were falling behind, and a new threat had just been identified. A very big threat. While he could understand and appreciate Rachael's medical condition, his boss, Captain Huxley, had told him in no uncertain terms that he had to wring more hours out of the translators. That there could be no excuses. Most already worked 60 hours a week, but untranslated Japanese intercepts had been piling up, and the most important were about something the Japanese had named, "Operation Blue Samurai." To make matters worse,

193

Rachael's best friend Tracy had recently married into an enormous amount of money, and he had overheard Tracy tell Rachael that now, she too, was going to think about working shorter hours. He couldn't have that. He'd just have to be tough.

"Paul, you wanted to see me?"

"Yes, Rachael, please have a seat."

"Thank you."

"I . . . . well, the only way to do this," he stammered, his prepared and memorized speech forgotten, as he looked at her swollen abdomen. "That is, I know that we agreed you could work shorter hours because of your . . . . condition, but, as you know, we're falling behind."

"Yes, I know."

"It's Blue Samurai that has me nervous. Captain Huxley too. As you also know, Miss Donahue, I mean Mrs. Fillmore, is of the strong belief that 'Blue Samurai' might be the Japanese code for the invasion of Australia. And, of course, since it was our unit that provided CINCPAC with detailed information on the Japanese plan to take Midway, leading directly to the first real success we had in the war in the Pacific, the higher ups are listening to us. We've gained enormous credibility and value in their eyes. I mentioned that to you when you came back, but I just want to emphasize how much they value us now. And both you and she do so much more than simply translate. You go the extra mile and do first rate intelligence analysis."

"Thank you, Paul. We do what we can."

"Do you agree with Mrs. Fillmore about Blue Samurai?"

"Yes, I think there's a strong probability that it's to be an invasion of Australia."

"I don't need to tell you how serious the situation would be if the Japanese took Australia."

"It would be catastrophic, of course. It would set back our war effort for possibly up to a year, not to mention the pain and suffering of the Australian people."

"Exactly!" Paul said, thumping the palm of his right hand on his desk. "Exactly," he repeated more softly. She was making his case for him. "This is the biggest thing going on now in the Pacific. It presents the greatest threat. In its own way, it's as serious as the attack on Pearl Harbor. Why, we would have to change our strategy completely and move quickly."

"Yes."

"Do you or she have any idea of what the timetable is on Blue Samurai?"

"Soon. Ships are being directed to rendezvous at Truk. But they intend to do it piecemeal, so that a huge fleet won't be spotted moving together. The last ships they send will be the troop ships. I think, but emphasize that we can't be sure yet that the objective is Australia, that the attack will take place sometime between one and two months from now."

"We probably need to alert CINCPAC now."

"I think it's premature, Paul. We need much more information to be sure."

"For all we know, we already have that information, because we've fallen behind in translating. In fact, that's the very thing I wanted to talk to you about. Would it be possible to increase the number of hours you work every week? At least, at the very least, until we solve the riddle of Blue Samurai?"

"I'd like to help, but my obstetrician is the one who suggested I work only 20 hours a week. When women after 40 become pregnant for the first time—"

"I understand, but surely, since this is an emergency—"

"But don't you think there'll be many more emergencies in this war, Paul? We've already had a number of them, just since I began working here."

"True, true enough."

"And it's going to be a long war. All the strategists say so."

"Yes. But the frequency of emergencies doesn't mean that each of them is nonetheless real, posing grave threats to our men out there fighting on land, sea, and in the air."

Rachael sighed heavily. "I know when I'm beaten, Paul. I'll begin working 40 hours a week tomorrow. However, I have an appointment with my obstetrician in two weeks, and if he says I should work fewer hours, it's him I'm going to listen to. I want nothing to go wrong with this pregnancy. I'm sure you can understand that."

"I do, and thank you Rachael."

Rachael related her conversation with Paul to Tracy, and asked, "Do you really think Blue Samurai is an invasion of Australia? From what little I've seen, it looks like it, but what do you think?"

"It's funny, a week ago, I would have said it was 98 percent certain, but the more I look at the intercepts, the more I feel that there's something strange about the traffic."

"How so?"

"It's hard to explain. This is going to sound crazy, but it's almost as if it's too easy to figure out. You were away when we were working with the intercepts that allowed us to put together the whole Japanese plan to take Midway, but it was a really big job, one that, when the pieces finally fell into place, there was just barely enough time to disseminate it to CINCPAC. We went through thousands of messages to get the Japanese order of battle and the exact timetable. It took us a lot of analytical time to tease out the names of the Japanese commanders and the names and types of each of the ships involved, the details of the amphibious attack against the island, the objectives on the ground, air attack plans and targets, and army unit designations. I mean, it was tough. Blue Samurai, on the other hand, lays everything out in detail in some unusually long messages, and there's an abundance of other corroborating messages confirming the details. I just have the feeling that . . . . that maybe they're playing us. Us being ready for them when and where they were closing in on Midway when we still didn't have much of a fleet left to send, well, they had to at least suspect that was more than a coincidence. I think that made them suspect we're reading their encrypted radio traffic and that Blue Samurai is possibly a red herring. I think that maybe there is no plan to invade Australia. That they want to see if we suddenly rush to reinforce Australia, and, if we do, it will prove we're reading their most secret traffic.

"The problem is that it's just a hunch, nothing more than a feeling, and, obviously, with something this important, I need more than a feeling. I need proof."

"Of course, I'll do anything I can to help. Where should I start?"

"Right now, I'm rereading all the traffic about the operation that's been translated so far. What you can do is to translate all the decrypted traffic that we haven't gotten to yet and that might have a bearing on it. There's an awful lot of messages, so don't waste any time. If you're going through a message that appears to have nothing to do with Blue Samurai, just forget it and go on to another."

"Right."

On the following afternoon, after Rachael had finished eight hours of translation, she felt tired. A lot more tired than when she'd been working ten-hour days months before. She walked out to the parking lot and got in her 1942 Lincoln Zephyr Continental. It had a V12 engine and rich interior appointments. Made in the early part of the year, it was one of the last American cars to be built in 1942. The year wasn't even half over before it was announced that there would be no more cars made for the civilian market until the war was over. The car was one of the first things she'd bought when she returned to Hawaii in September. Dade had been insistent that, along with a house that befitted their new lives as millionaires, she should buy a car just as luxurious. She loved the car, and, when he got back to Hawaii in November, so did Dade. The upholstery was leather and the paint a royal blue that sparkled as if it were made of spun glass. The transmission was as smooth as butter and the ride as soft as a cloud. The Lincoln still had that "new car smell," and, as she drove home in the setting sun, she smiled. Her weariness was made easier to bear by the knowledge that the work she was doing was important, that it could save the lives of many American soldiers and sailors. That was actually the best part of the job. The pregnancy was probably another reason she was tired lately, but that had its good side too. The result would be another human being, a combination of Dade and of her. A unique human being they could love and share things with. She wondered how many children they would have. They hadn't talked about that. Since they could well afford it now, she wanted to have five. Yes, five, she thought. A good number. That meant a pretty busy decade ahead for her, but it'd be worth it.

As she drove home, she thought of all the things that had happened to her in the past two years. Things that she could have never foreseen. And so many of them good things. The only problem was the war. The damned war. Something neither she nor the scores of millions of people in the world who were directly affected by it had any control over. It was like being at sea in a small boat when you suddenly found yourself in the middle of a deadly typhoon. You would either live or die and you had no way of affecting the outcome. You were helpless before it. No, it was worse than being caught in a typhoon. A storm was a force of nature, not a sentient being. It did not intend to kill human beings; it just did. In war, both sides fully intend to kill human beings, many human beings. A war was far worse. People, *other human beings*, were out there *trying* to kill Dade.

She wondered if her children would ever have to fight in a war and frowned. World history suggested that they would. To get her mind off that unpleasant thought, she began thinking of Blue Samurai. She thought that Tracy was right; there was something suspicious about the Blue Samurai intercepts.

41

December 2, 1942

Pacific Ocean

Bowie went up to the cigarette deck to have a smoke. The night was chilly and he turned up the collar on his jacket. He saw Captain Jones there, facing aft, looking up at the stars. "Enjoying the night sky?" Dade asked with a smile.

Jones turned and said with an air of wonderment, "I've never seen this many stars in my life, and I've looked at the sky often. It helps to calm me."

"Me too," he replied, joining Jones at the railing.

"How many stars can you see with the naked eye?"

"Under perfect conditions, which we have tonight, with no clouds and little light from the moon, and, being in the middle of the Pacific Ocean with no manmade light around us for many hundreds of miles, about 5,000. You always see about twice as many stars at sea than you do on land. It's one of the benefits of being a sailor."

"Five thousand," Jones repeated in awe. "It makes a man feel small and insignificant."

"Being in the middle of the Pacific Ocean has the same effect. Combined, they sometimes make me feel like nothing more than a speck of dust in the cosmos."

"Do they ever make you feel fey?"

"Fey?"

"It's a Scottish word I picked up there when the team and I were in commando training. It has two meanings. One is the feeling that your death is fast approaching. The other applies generally to having extrasensory perception, having visions or clairvoyant powers—that kind of thing."

"No."

"I have. About twenty minutes ago, I became certain—*certain*—that I will die on this mission. It wasn't simple fear. I've been very afraid before. This was a certainty. I felt as if some, some supernatural being, was speaking to me inside my mind. He told me I would die on this mission. I've never had an experience like it, and, somehow I know that it's true. I know it's true."

"I'm sorry."

"I wasn't expecting that reaction. I thought you'd try to tell me it was my imagination, just a manifestation of my very natural fear."

"No, I believe you. I've also experienced things beyond what we think this life to be. You're speaking to a man who has been visited by and conversed with ghosts. I believe, like Hamlet, that, 'There are more things in heaven and earth, Horatio, than are dreamt of in your philosophy.' I can't prove it, of course. My wife thinks it was bad dreams or hallucinations, and I let her think that. In fact, I let her think she's convinced me of it. But I know, just as you know. When something truly supernatural touches you, you know it."

"Yes. I'm saddened by this, of course. I had hoped and expected to lead a much longer life. To see the war end, to fall in love, get married, have children . . . . to see and do so much more." Jones put his hands on the railing and looked up at the sky in silence for a few moments. Dade lit a cigarette and said nothing.

"Do you think there's a heaven?" Jones suddenly asked.

"Yes," Dade replied simply. "A ghost I knew well when he was alive, told me there was. He said he didn't achieve admittance right away though. He said he found that he first had to purge himself of all hatred."

"I suppose that was what some call purgatory."

"Yes, I suppose so."

"Hatred helps me to do my job."

"Me too."

"I've overheard a lot. Your crew talks up a storm."

"There's not much else to do in a submarine."

"I understand you were awarded the Congressional Medal of Honor."

Dade nodded in reply.

"I'd be interested in the story."

"It's not very interesting. I took a lot of risks, some say more than I should have. I could easily have lost the boat and the entire crew. But things turned out OK, so they gave me the medal."

Jones grinned. "I'll bet that isn't the way the citation reads. You know, Captain, I think I like you."

"I think I like you too. I'm sorry about your impending death though. I wish there was something I could do about it."

"So do I. Well, at least I'm not leaving a wife and kids behind. Just my parents, and they know that I'm in the OSS and they know the kinds of things th e OSS does. It will hurt them, but it won't come as a complete surprise. I'll write them a long letter before we get to Japan and give it to you to mail when you get back to Pearl Harbor. Life is funny. We thought we were leaving all the craziness behind when we left Germany."

"How old were you when you left?"

"Sixteen. Originally, we lived in Munich, where my father was an architect. Even so, the 1920's were hard on nearly everyone. Economically, I mean. But, by 1930, we were living very comfortably. My father's work became well known and he was offered a position with a famous international architectural firm, so we moved to Berlin. I was fourteen at the time I joined the Hitler Youth."

"The Hitler Youth."

Jones laughed. "Yes, all the boys were in it. In the early days, its focus was on athletics, camping, hiking, and so on. Both my parents were apolitical, but neither liked the Nazis, primarily because of the *Sturmabteilung*, the Storm Troopers. Hitler recruited them in the 1920's from the dre gs of German society. Most were thugs, uneducated, and what Americans call losers. Hitler took them out of the gutter, gave them fancy uniforms to wear and convinced them that they were valued patriots who would bring Germany into a thousand-year era of greatness and abundance. They gloried in their status and Hitler used them for security, for crowd control, and so on, but mostly he used them to crack skulls with clubs. To beat senseless anyone who dared criticize Hitler or the Party in public. They vandalized the offices of newspapers that found fault with Hitler, beat up shopkeepers, beat up union officials, and terrorized people. They'd walk down the sidewalk like they owned it and greet everybody with a 'Heil Hitler' and the arm salute. Those who didn't respond in the same way were often stopped and told to explain why and that their explanation had better be pretty good or else. After a while, most people just felt it best to flip an arm up and mumble a 'Heil Hitler' back. Most Germans weren't in the party and hated or feared the Storm Troopers, but they figured if they just did that little ritual and kept their heads down, they could go about their business in peace. By the time they realized that, if you give in to animals (no matter how small the compromise), it leads to another compromise and another, until the animals rule you, it was too late. By the late 1920's, Hitler was constantly on the move, going up and down the length and breadth of Germany, giving speeches. He'd show up at fairs, graduation ceremonies, weddings, athletic events, building dedications, and so on. He was everywhere, giving speeches to dozens or to thousands. Many radio stations broadcast his speeches and they were very, very effective. I went to several of the speeches he gave, in Munich and in Berlin. My God, he could whip up a crowd! He spoke with passion and urgency and, I don't know, there was some kind of raw power in his speeches. I was pretty much immune from them, primarily because my family listened to some of them on the radio and my father would dissect his speeches for me, pointing out inconsistencies and absurdities.

"At any rate, when I was 14 and we moved to Berlin, I wanted to join the Hitler Youth. It wasn't because I was a big fan of Hitler; it was for the sports and outdoor activities and because my schoolmates were in it. My father was initially against it; he said they'd make a Nazi of me. My mother sided with me, saying it would do no harm because they had taught me good moral values and I was too smart to be reined into Nazism. 'But the Hitler Youth wear uniforms!' he objected. 'So do the British and American Boy Scouts,' she said reasonably. 'Perhaps,' he replied, 'but not with a red armband with a swastika in a white circle just like the *Sturmabteilung.*' The upshot was that he let me join as long as I promised to quit if there started to be political activities or hooliganism like the Storm Troopers.

"I joined in the summer, and had a lot of fun. There were some bullshit pep talks about the New Order that was coming, which I shrugged off. I loved the hiking, the camping, soccer, track events, archery, and swimming. I excelled at swimming. In fact, at the end of the summer, they gave out awards to the boys who did the best at each sport. The medals were sterling silver and I won the one for swimming, and who should show up for the awards? Yes, Hitler himself. He leaned over and pinned the medal to my uniform and shook my hand, and that's when I saw them."

"What?"

"The eyes of a madman. An evil madman. That was in 1930, three years before he came to power. And, now that summer was over and we were back in school, most of the Hitler Youth meetings were held indoors after school, and the lectures began. The need to keep the purity of the Aryan race, the duplicity of the Jews, the visions of the Fuhrer to expand the frontiers of Germany. You know, that stuff. And the brown shirts on the streets became more and more aggressive. Sometimes they'd literally beat a person to death. They set fire to buildings. I quit the Hitler Youth then, and, as I expected, there were repercussions. Why? Why, they demanded. Had I no patriotism? Did I lack faith in the Fuhrer? I had a pretty good excuse prepared. I told them that I would no longer have time for the Hitler Youth, since I had to obtain a job so I could work after school and on weekends to save up enough money for college. Most of them bought it, but harbored suspicions that that wasn't the real reason. I became an outsider and lost a number of friends.

"I got a job in the neighborhood grocery store and did a number of things there—unloading trucks of produce, stocking shelves, keeping inventory, working behind the counter, and so on. The store was owned and run by a Jewish family, and it had been in the family for three generations. The Rosen family had two kids who also worked there. One, Hans, was my age and we became very good friends. His sister was Greta and she was a year older. She was also beautiful and smart and had a wonderful smile. Her brown eyes would light up when she smiled, and, for just a few moments, when she smiled, you felt that the whole world was a better place. I quickly developed a crush on her, but kept it well hidden, or so I thought.

"But, after I turned 15, I couldn't keep it bottled up anymore. Somehow, I summoned up the courage to ask her to go to the cinema with me. She told me she'd like to, but that her parents would not be happy with her dating a Gentile, because they were very old fashioned. Anyway, we worked out a deal with Hans. It was always the three of us who went out together to the cinema, for a picnic, to the zoo, to a concert, and so on. We represented it to her parents as just three friends and coworkers having some fun together. But, once we got to where we were going, Hans left the two of us to ourselves. By the time I was 16, Greta and I had fallen in love. We spoke of marriage. Not then, of course, we planned it for three years or four in the future. My plan was to become an architect like my father. We made a lot of plans for the future, discussing things like how many children we would have, where we would live, and so on. It was a wonderful time. But the atmosphere in Germany was becoming more and more oppressive, and every time I saw brown shirts patrolling the streets, I became more worried, not only for my country, but for Greta. Jews were being beaten up just for being Jews. Their businesses were being vandalized, and Greta and I began to feel that we might have to leave Germany to have any kind of life together. We were thinking, in fact, of moving to America." Jones paused for a long time before continuing to speak.

"Then, one day, two leaders of the local *Sturmabteilung* were seen dragging her into an alley, where they raped and savagely beat her. She regained consciousness in the hospital and named the two men before dying. In addition, three witnesses came forward and identified the men. The two men were arrested. Now, from the Middle Ages up until 1924, there were trials by jury in Germany, but not afterward. After hearing evidence, judges decide whether the accused is innocent or guilty. In this case, there were three judges. The courtroom was filled with uniformed *Sturmabteilung* each day of the trial, an intimidating presence to both judges and witnesses. One witness took the stand to say that, on second thought, he really couldn't be sure that what he told the police was accurate. When asked why both of his eyes were blackened, his nose broken, there were deep cuts and scrapes on his face, and why one of his arms was in a sling, he stated that he had tripped and fallen down the stairs in his house the night before. Another witness exhibited similar uncertainty. Later it was found that someone had placed a bomb in the driver's seat of his car. The bomb was not rigged to go off; it was clearly just a friendly warning of things that *could* happen to him. The final witness was in the hospital in a coma. The defense attorney made much of the fact that the alleged victim was, after all, a Jew, and that it was well known that the Jews hated the New Order and often told lies about it and its followers. Finally, one of the judges was a member of the Nazi Party. I'm sure the other two judges took into consideration what had happened to the witnesses and what might well befall them if they came up with a vote to convict. The brown shirts were found not guilty.

"Well, needless to say, I was devastated. I wanted to kill the two brown shirts. More than anything, I wanted to kill those two pigs, who had smirked as they left the courtroom in triumph. I even began to plan how and when and where I would do it. In the meantime, I wasn't the only one who was devastated. My father saw this as the final straw. We must leave Germany. He actually wept. His family had lived in Germany for generations. He had volunteered to fight in the German Army in the Great War. Had even won an Iron Cross for valor in action. But now, now it was clear that nothing would get better in Germany, only worse. Worse for everyone.

"Fortunately, the international architectural firm he worked for had an office in New York City. He had even been there on a business trip, and knew that America was prosperous and free and that many Germans had gone to America over the previous decades and were welcomed. It turned out to be blessedly simple."

"You don't speak with a German accent. Anybody would take you for American born."

"Oh, my accent was gone completely by the time I finished high school in the United States. I kind of have a gift for languages. It was one of the reasons my enlistment papers were flagged for OSS review when I joined the Army. That was a plus, as well as, of course, as my being born and raised in Germany and some other talents I have."

"I would have thought that they'd never give a security clearance to anyone who was in the Hitler Youth. I would have thought that they'd think you had probably been completely indoctrinated and made into a true believer in the Thousand Year Reich."

"The Hitler Youth did come up in my interviews, but I had only been in it for six months and had quit when they started the heavy indoctrination. The OSS people also spoke to my parents and quickly learned that their abhorrence of the Nazis is what caused us to come to the United States and become citizens. And, when I told them about Greta, that too showed them I was no Nazi sympathizer. That, even after years, I wanted payback for Greta. I wanted very much to kill Nazis. Then too, there was my high school and college records. I was very active in sports and got excellent grades. I got my commission through the ROTC program."

"I was just thinking. It's probably safe to say that you're the only man in the United States Army who has had a medal pinned to his uniform by Adolph Hitler himself."

Jones laughed easily. "That thought had never occurred to me, but I'm sure you're right."

"By the way, what's your real first name?"

"Will, short for Wilhelm."

"Mine is Dade, but only use it when no one else is around. I don't even let my XO call me by my first name.

"Thanks."

"I think we're very much alike."

Both men stood for a while in companionable silence, both looking at the stars, each with his own thoughts. Dade lit another cigarette. "My wife works for ONI and is kind of an expert on the Japanese. She speaks, reads, and writes the language fluently and lived there for more than twenty years. She says that the Japanese will never surrender. Never. She says the only way we can end the war is to eventually invade all the home islands and fight street to street, house to house, hill to hill."

"That's a pretty grim assessment."

"Yes, but she's explained why to me, and I think she's right. Do you think Hitler will ever surrender once it's clear that he can't win?"

"Hitler surrender? No. As I said, he's a madman. He's an evil psychopath who will die before he'll surrender. For that matter, he'll see all of Germany destroyed before surrendering. You see, he doesn't care about the German people or the nation. He never did. After all, he wasn't even born there. He was born in Austria. No, he'll never surrender. We'll have to kill him; there's no other way. I've proposed to General Donovan that I take a small team into Germany for the express purpose of killing him. It could be done, you know. I could take half of this team in and do it. Of course, it would be a suicide mission. While I know we could succeed in killing him, we'd never get out alive."

"You'd do that? Go on a suicide mission?"

"To kill Hitler? As we say in America, 'in a New York minute.' It could save hundreds of thousands, perhaps even millions of lives on both sides, from American and British and other Allied soldiers, to all the European civilians who are having their homes and businesses blown up, to the countless Jews the Germans are still rounding up to . . . . hell, yes. Yes, that would be worth my life."

"You're a brave and good man. More than that, you're a noble man. I think that you're probably a better man than I am. You're a believer. I used to be, but the war has made a cynic of me. I'd figure that killing Hitler might not accomplish what you think it will. That he'd just be replaced by another psychopath. He surrounds himself with that kind of person, doesn't he?"

Jones appeared to seriously consider Dade's remark. "Yes, he's appointed Himmler, Heydrich, Goebbels, Bormann, Goering, and some other psychopaths, but of them, the only one who had the presence, the power, the ambition, the intelligence, and the ability to capitalize on the assassination of Hitler and seize the power for himself and continue down the same road was Reinhard Heydrich, the *Reichssicherheitshauptamt*, that is, the head all German security forces. But

Heydrich was assassinated in Prague by a team of Czech patriots who had been trained in England by the Special Operations Executive. The operation, called Operation Anthropoid, was kind of botched by a jammed Sten gun, but they also used a grenade. The wounds from the shrapnel became infected and Heydrich died a few days later. That was just this past June.

"At any rate, General Donovan believes any assassination of Hitler now would be premature. So far, the German Army has been victorious in the war. It was pushed back from Moscow, and things don't look too good for its troops surrounded in Stalingrad right now, but it has yet to have a significant defeat. Donovan believes that the time to assassinate Hitler is when the tide of war has turned against Germany, with the Russians closing in from the east and the other Allies from the west, and it is clear to any reasonable man that Germany must surrender before invading troops enter the Fatherland itself. That would be the right timing, he says, and I suppose he's right. I don't know. I just believe that the sooner that man is dead, the better for the world."

"A suicide mission. I don't see myself ever volunteering for one. Every time I take this boat out, there's always the *possibility* that I'll die. I've been in situations where the *probability* was that I'd die. But going out with the *certainty* that I'd die, now that's just something else again."

"But our situations are probably dissimilar. For example, I'm single. You probably have a wife and kids."

"A wife whom I love more than I can say and a kid on the way."

"And, as you said, I'm a believer. Winning the war is all I live for. It's the most important war in all of human history with the biggest stakes."

"My job is a lot simpler than yours. It's just to sink as many Japanese ships as I can. There's nothing complicated about it and there are a lot of other sub skippers doing the same thing. I doubt that any of us think about the big picture, the impact of our missions on world history."

"I can understand that. And I can understand your aversion to suicide missions."

"But surely you can't be thinking of the big picture and world history when you pull out your knife or pistol and it's time to kill."

"No, when that time comes, I always think of Greta."

42

December 6, 1942

Seacliff Cottage, Oahu

The three women sat on the lanai sipping iced tea. It was a lazy Sunday afternoon and there was a comfortable lull in the conversation as Rachael, Tracy, and Alice looked out across the sea. Alice felt completely at ease and content with her life now. She couldn't believe how quickly she had, well, become a different person in just the past six months. She had become a grownup. Born and raised in Danbury, Connecticut, she had led a happy and comfortable life in a middle-class home where she was loved and cared for. Then, she was off to New Britain to attend Central Connecticut State University. After receiving a B.S. in Mathematics in June 1941, she stayed on to work twice as hard, managing to fulfill the requirements for her M.S. in the same subject in just a year. It was while she was an undergrad that she'd met Tom Detrick. He was a Yale student and one year ahead of her, graduating with a degree in civil engineering in June 1940.

For a number of reasons, they decided to wait until she graduated to get married. However, by the time that happened, Tom had been commissioned an ensign through ROTC and begun his mandatory two years of active duty. It was at this point that Alice had decided that this was the perfect time to pursue her master's degree. While it wasn't as if nothing had been going on in her life, she still felt somewhat less than a full adult. In all this time, the only times she had ever left Connecticut were a few occasions when she and her mother or she and her friends had taken forays into New York City to see shows or go shopping. That was it. She had fallen in love, of course, which was a major life event, and she and Tom had made plans to get married when she got her master's, but she couldn't shake the fact that she had never been anywhere or done anything. At 22, she had still felt like a teenager. After all, she was still listed as a dependent on her parents'

206

joint income tax return. And she *was* a dependent. Even in grad school, they paid for her room and board and her tuition and books. They even gave her an allowance.

Then, suddenly, this year, she had had so many experiences and adventures. The month after she got her Master's, she married Tom, and became not only a wife, but a Navy wife. Yes, now she was not only a Navy wife, but her husband was a submarine officer, a brave man who had been in combat and was at sea again, even now, fighting in the biggest war in human history. *And* she was fighting it herself in the Office of Naval Intelligence, as a codebreaker. She was using her considerable skills in mathematics to break Top Secret Japanese military communications, working side-by-side with one of the most respected mathematicians in the United States, a man whose papers she had read avidly in college. She was making *much* more money than she would have teaching high school, and teaching would not have challenged her as this job did. She actually looked forward to going to work most days. With Tom at sea, she didn't even mind the number of hours she was expected to put in.

And Hawaii was so different from Connecticut in every way. Sometimes, in the early days, she'd felt that the only similarities were that English was the major language, and that the American flag flew from poles in both places. She loved the tropical climate, the wonderfully aromatic and beautiful flowers, the palm trees, the cooling trade winds, and the smell of the sea. She loved the beaches and browsing the wares in the International Market.

Here, her two best friends were not college kids her own age, but two women who were much older and experienced than she. They were also different from each other in many ways. Just as Alice had never met anyone like Rachael, she had never met anyone like Tracy. While Rachael was 40 and very settled, Tracy was 33 and a very free spirit. She was outgoing, vivacious, and fun loving. When Tracy had mentioned offhandedly once that she'd had sex with dozens of men, Alice had smiled, thinking she was joking, or at least exaggerating. When it turned out that it was literally true, Alice had been shocked. This had been old news to Rachael, however, who, noticing Alice's discomfiture, smiled and said, "You never mentioned how many dozens, Tracy." Tracy had thought for a moment, and, before she could answer, Rachael had said, "Alice, I think, is somewhat stunned, as was I when I first learned how active you were. Before meeting Lance, that is."

"Well, it's something that I'm neither proud of nor ashamed of. I don't mean to sound immodest, but from my mid-teens on, I always had boys and men trying to get into my pants. I mean, it happens when you're beautiful. And I've always loved the attention and the sex itself. Some people think of their bodies as temples, but I always looked upon mine as an amusement park. I had a lot of fun and I'm not sorry about that. Part of it, I think, is due to the fact that I never thought I'd find a man I wanted to spend the rest of my life with. I think that's why I was so . . . . . flighty."

"And then you met Lance."

"Yes, he certainly was an earthquake. I think the Richter scale goes up to 10, and it's a logarithmic progression, so that an earthquake measuring 2 is 10 times more powerful than one measuring 1, and a 3 is 100 times more powerful than a 1 and so on. Well, Lance is a 38 on the scale. My God! He rocked my world. I haven't seriously looked at another man since."

"Tracy and I both met our future husbands on the same day," Rachael said to Alice. "We had dinner at Lance's beach house."

"I was just thinking," Tracy said, "all three of us were married this year. Rachael, you and Slide were married on May 3, I married Lance three weeks ago, and, Alice, you and Tom got married, when?"

"On the Fourth of July."

"And you're how old now?"

"I'm 23." Alice was happy and proud that, despite her age and lack of experience in life, Tracy and Rachael treated her as an equal.

"And all of us becoming Navy wives the same year."

"And all our husbands submarine officers."

"At least," Tracy said, "I'm glad that Lance has a desk job." She turned to Rachael. "How do you do it? How do you handle Slide being at sea for two months at a time, never sure that he'll return at all?"

"I don't. That is, I don't handle it well. When I was working 60 hours a week, that helped a little in that it took up so much of my time and concentration, but it was still hard. I still worried a lot. Now that I'm working 40 hours a week, there's more time available for worry. I have my reading, of course, and my getting ready for the baby, and I pray. I pray like crazy, even though sometimes I wonder if that does any good. Given all that happened in Japan to me and my first husband, given this brutal war with all its attendant suffering for millions and the deaths of millions, and, given just living for forty years, it's hard sometimes to believe in God. I want to. I want desperately to, but sometimes I just can't. But we've talked about that before."

"How do you cope, Alice?" Tracy asked.

"Well, of course I'm working 60 hours, and, like Rachael said, that helps a lot. And I pray too. I began to doubt the existence of God in college and still have my doubts. I mentioned that to Rachael the first time I met her. So I guess I don't handle it well either. I know how many submarines we're losing and it scares me. Sometimes I have nightmares, when I see Tom drowning in his submarine. In other nightmares, I see a Western Union boy bicycling up to me. I'm standing on the street watching him and we're making eye contact, but he's pedaling in slow motion. I want him to hurry up, to get it over with because I know what's in the telegram. He knows too, and that's why he's giving me this evil smile. And I know he's purposely pedaling in slow motion because he wants to prolong my horror."

"That's dreadful," Tracy said.

"At least we can all do our part at ONI," Rachael said to change the subject.

"I just wanted both of you to know," Alice began, a little nervously, "that it means so much to me that you've both taken me in, so to speak. I mean, I was basically a school girl who had never been out of the small state she was born in, with no real experience in life, and you've given me your support and friendship. You've both lived a lot longer than I have and lived in different countries, you speak, read, and write an Asian language fluently, and—"

"Please, Alice," Tracy said, clearly pretending to be offended, "I haven't lived a 'lot longer' than you. Why, at only 10 years older than you, I could be your sister—your slightly older sister."

"That's true," Alice smiled warmly.

"Furthermore," Rachael added, "neither of us can understand the higher mathematics you work with, and Paul Duvall says you border on genius."

"Well, thank you. I'd hate to be in this alone, with Tom at sea and in danger all the time. My job and living here in Hawaii could be a heady experience if it weren't for the war. Both of you . . . . . . your friendship and acceptance mean more to me than I can say."

"You're an unusual and very bright young woman," Rachael replied after a while. "I knew that in the first 10 minutes after I met you. Your friendship means a lot to us too."

43

December 7, 1942

Pacific Ocean

Dade was taking a turn through the boat, something he did three or four times a day. One of the first things he'd learned from John Henry was that a sub skipper had to know every member of the crew. Since the crew of a sub was so small, this was an easy thing. There were five officers besides himself, two CPOs, and 54 other crew members. John Henry had impressed upon him the need to know every crew member's strengths and weaknesses as well as his biography, to include his home town, a little about his family, what he'd done in civilian life, his schooling, and his plans for the future. Dade accomplished this the same way that John Henry had, by stopping and talking to men for a few moments on his turns through the boat. Dade had been doing this now ever since the boat was under construction in Groton last summer and now had a complete idea of each man's personality and background. He'd also studied their personnel jackets thoroughly and was well satisfied that he had a good crew. He didn't even mind the fact that Oliver Wirtz had been foisted off on him as XO. Not anymore. After a couple of false starts back in Groton and that crazy incident involving Brooks' mother, things had settled down and Wirtz was proving himself to be a capable and competent XO. Dade was even beginning to like him a little.

Bowie stopped in the tiny and cramped radio room to chat for a few minutes with Tony Grove, a man he hadn't talked to for several days. Grove was, Bowie knew, a native of Pittsburgh, had worked in the steel mills for two years before deciding that the Navy had to be a better way to make a living, an enthusiastic Pittsburgh Pirates fan, and had been a Ham radio operator in civilian life. "How goes it, Grove?"

"Pretty damned quiet, sir. I mean, I'm always listening for that abort message that you told me would probably not be sent, but, with us operating under absolute radio silence, there ain't a lot to do. Just to keep my hand in, so I don't forget Morse Code completely, I copy down messages sent to and from other subs, but I don't decode them. I figure, what's the point?"

"Right. Good idea to practice, though."

"Yeah, even copied a couple of messages with the ULTRA prefix. I know what a big deal those are, but they weren't addressed to us."

"ULTRA messages," Dade repeated thoughtfully, remembering how, on previous patrols, ULTRA messages had sent the *Elver* flying through the night to intercept Japanese ships, including the naval task force that had resulted in his sinking two aircraft carriers. "Yes, they're a big deal all right. Do you still have the ULTRA messages you copied?"

"Yes sir, right here. The first one was sent to the *Oarfish* by COMSUBPAC, the second was the *Oarfish's* response."

"OK, give them to me."

Back in his stateroom, Dade took the ULTRA codebook out of the small safe above his foldout desk, mounted to the bulkhead, a code that only skippers and XO's had access to, and began decoding. When he'd completed decoding the second message, he sat back in his chair, his thoughts in turmoil. The ULTRA had notified the *Oarfish* that the *Susaki Maru*, a 7,200-ton Japanese troop transport was en route to Guadalcanal with the Japanese 21st Infantry Regiment, seasoned troops who had been fighting in China. The regiment consisted of 2,985 men and the transport was being escorted by two Fubuki Class destroyers. The message gave the ships' port of departure, the time and date of the departure, and their base course and speed. The message said it was imperative that the *Susaki Maru* be sunk.

Oarfish's response was disheartening. It said that, due to heavy battle damage sustained, two of its engines were off line and it would be impossible to intercept the troop transport. This was serious. Dade thought of how many American lives had been lost on Guadalcanal and how the issue was still in doubt. Americans had invaded Guadalcanal on August 7th and the fighting still raged on, on both land and sea and in the air. The fighting was ruthless and brutal and sometimes it seemed that the Japanese might even succeed. They were winning most of the naval engagements around the island, making it extremely difficult for the Navy to supply the men ashore. The Japanese had also been able to send reinforcements in to bolster their troops. If they were able to land the 3,000 seasoned troops aboard the *Susaki Maru*, Dade thought, that would not only mean many more dead and wounded American Marines and soldiers, it could even tip the balance, driving the United States out of the Solomons. The *Susaki Maru* had to be sunk. He put the codebook and messages in the safe and went to the radio room.

"Hey Grove, were there any other ULTRA messages sent after those two you gave me?"

"No sir."

"You're sure?"

"Positive, sir."

"OK, thanks." That meant, Dade knew, that there were no other subs close enough to intercept the *Susaki Maru*.

Back in his stateroom, he showed both messages to Ollie, who instantly grasped the urgency of the situation. "I need you to get out the charts and find out if we have enough time to intercept that ship and still get to our objective on time. I think we might."

"But remember what CINCPAC said, skipper. We're not to engage any enemy ships on this trip. Period. Even if we could intercept this ship, we're under orders to not undertake any actions other than our assigned mission."

"But surely, Ollie, you see the importance of preventing 3,000 crack enemy troops from getting to Guadalcanal. The situation there is desperate."

"Yes sir, but—"

"Just do it, Ollie. One step at a time. Maybe it's not possible anyway."

"Aye aye, sir," Wirtz said stiffly, stood, and left.

"OK, skipper. It's just barely possible. But only if we change course immediately and travel at all ahead full on the surface. Even so, we'll only have two hours at the point of interception. If the tin cans can acquire us fast, maintain contact, and keep us from attacking for a long time, we could still be late according to the schedule we have to keep to give us enough hours of darkness to carry out the mission. And that's if they don't even damage us. Or they could sink us, meaning we will have failed to accomplish the mission."

"Alright, lay in the course and increase speed to all ahead full."

"Sir, once again, CINCPAC—"

"I know, Ollie," Dade said, holding up his right hand. "but this is war, and a naval captain has a certain latitude in his orders if there are exigent circumstances. And these, my friend, are exigent circumstances. If 3,000 fresh and well-trained Japanese troops are thrown into the battle for Guadalcanal, it means we could lose the island. The island we've been desperately fighting for for four months. And we need that island, Ollie. We need it. Now go ahead and follow my orders."

"Aye aye, sir"

Captain Jones liked just walking around and studying the submarine, asking countless questions of her crew. It was the most complicated, fascinating machine he had ever seen, from its diesel engines to its electric motors to its $10,000 apiece steam torpedoes to its electronic gear. He was especially enthralled by the Torpedo Data Computer. He was in the control room when Oliver ordered the change in course and speed, and, since one of his skills in the work he did was reading people, he saw something in Wirtz's eyes, something in his expression. Something that told him something was wrong and that the XO was trying to hide it. "What's up, Ollie?" he asked with a friendly smile.

"Nothing much," Wirtz replied, avoiding eye contact.

"Are we on schedule? Everything proceeding according to plan?"

"We'll get there in time all right," Wirtz said, but he had hesitated for just a second before speaking, and that was long enough to confirm Jones' suspicion that something was wrong.

"Where's Captain Bowie?"

"In his stateroom."

Jones made a gap in the heavy curtain that covered the hatch to Dade's stateroom. "Do you have a minute for me, skipper?"

"Sure, come on in."

"Thanks. Say, is everything OK?"

"You mean in general?"

"I mean with the mission. Ollie just ordered a change in course and speed after feverishly consulting some calculations. In my line of work, you get to notice signs that something is wrong."

"Have a seat," Dade said, waving a hand in the general direction of his bunk.

"Thanks."

"I ordered the change. It wasn't according to plan, so you're right in that regard and Ollie is a little, ah, uncomfortable with it, but it's no big deal. I know you're cleared for Top Secret material, but the information I received not long ago, the information that is the reason I made the course change, is classified above Top Secret."

"I thought we were on strict radio silence and the only message that we would ever get would be an abort message, which we were told was extremely unlikely."

"The message wasn't addressed to us; it was addressed to another submarine."

"Then I'm confused."

Dade sighed deeply and wondered how much, if anything, to tell Jones. Jones would, of course, find out what Dade was up to when they began their attack on the *Susaki Maru*. He'd need to be able to concentrate then, and not have Jones questioning his actions as he made his approach. Better to get it all settled now. "OK. May I have your word that you won't reveal to anyone—and I mean anyone for any reason—that we have an intelligence source that is so amazing that we can sometimes get detailed information on Japanese ship departures and destinations and cargoes?"

"Of course, I give you my word. And, I don't want to rain on your parade, but that's not such an 'amazing' piece of information. I'd be surprised if you weren't getting some intelligence reports like that from time to time."

"Believe me, it's a very big deal."

"OK. Go on."

"You've been following the fight for Guadalcanal?"

"Yes."

"I received information that a Japanese troop ship carrying 3,000 crack Japanese troops who are veterans of the fighting in China is en route to Guadalcanal. I also have enough information, I believe, to intercept it and sink it. Furthermore," he went on, raising his voice to drown out an anticipated objection, "we'll still have enough time to get to our objective in Japan on schedule."

"But CINCPAC gave you explicit orders not to engage any Japanese ships. Period." Jones' face darkened. "Please ask your XO to join us."

Dade immediately picked up the handset and asked that the XO report to his stateroom immediately. Both men said nothing until Wirtz entered. "Have a seat next to Captain Jones, Ollie. It seems he wants to talk to both of us about the slight detour we're going to take to intercept the *Susaki Maru*." Wirtz sat and nervously looked at Dade and then at Jones.

"Lieutenant Wirtz, if I understand this correctly, we have just made a change in course for the express purpose of attacking a Japanese ship. Is that correct?"

Wirtz looked at Dade, who nodded. "Yes, that's right."

"Do you recall CINCPAC specifically ordering Captain Bowie not to engage any Japanese ships on this mission?"

"Yes."

"Look," Dade interrupted, "as I said, there are 3,000 seasoned Japanese troops on that ship, veterans of the fighting in China. If they get to Guadalcanal, we might wind up losing the whole campaign in the Solomons. This is important."

"So is the mission we were sent to do. In fact, a lot more important. You heard CINCPAC explain how this mission is one of the most important missions ever mounted so far in this war. You remember he said that if it's successful, it could shorten the war by two or more years. When we were training for the mission back in the States, the director of the OSS himself told me that there is no mission that has higher priority and that we have to accomplish it at all costs."

"'At all costs,'" Dade erupted. "I was told the same thing about a highly classified mission last December. My skipper and I were, like on this mission, briefed by CINCPAC himself, and told that it was *imperative* that we accomplish the mission, even if it meant the loss of the boat and all our lives. Well, we went out and came within a hair of losing the boat and all our lives, but, despite our best efforts, failed to accomplish the mission. Guess what? It made no difference at all because the Japanese invasion ships we were to stop were stopped by Marine coastal artillery batteries on Wake Island and turned back. Our failure to accomplish this Top Secret do-or-die *imperative* mission made no difference at all. We almost died trying to do it, but, in the end, the joke was on us. This mission may turn out to be for nothing too. It could be that intelligence is wrong and that

Dr. Nakamura won't be there. It could be that his people are behind our scientists and that he'll have nothing of value to contribute, or that he isn't pro-Western anymore and will refuse to cooperate—or worse, feed our people false information. It could be that we'll be detected by Japanese patrol ships and sunk before we can even land you guys. It could be that, God forbid, you and your men are killed trying to get him out. And OK, I understand that anything can always go wrong, and I'm prepared to try my best. I'll do my damnedest to accomplish this mission. As I said, after I sink that troop transport, we'll be off to Kyushu, we'll arrive on time, and you guys can go ashore as planned and grab Nakamura. And the successful accomplishment of the mission may help end the war sooner. I'm not counting on that, because after a year of war, I don't trust our bosses anymore. We submariners had to operate with torpedoes they insisted worked but didn't, we had to . . . . . look, one of the things I've come to understand is that it's the easiest thing in the world for a man who wears stars on his shoulders, to tell a group of men he doesn't give a damn about, that the mission he's sending them on is the most important mission of the war and that they must be fully prepared to lose their lives and the lives of their men, that they must accomplish the mission at all costs. I don't *know* that Operation Buntline will amount to anything. But I know, that if I keep 3,000 veteran Japanese troops from reaching Guadalcanal, there's no doubt I've done something important."

"Maybe your intelligence is wrong and that troop transport isn't where you think it'll be. Maybe it's not even at sea."

"No. Our intelligence from this particular source is never wrong. That's why it's Top Secret. I know where that ship will be and I know it has 3,000 Japanese troops aboard."

"Even so, you can't guarantee that you'll sink it."

"Yes I can. I can guarantee that I can sink it."

"To be fair," Oliver spoke, "what the skipper can't guarantee is that we can elude the two destroyers that are escorting it. If the destroyer captains are good— and to escort a ship containing such a valuable cargo they have to be—once they see the tracks of our torpedoes and know where we fired from, they'll be on us fast. The difficult part will be eluding them. We'll crash dive after firing, going deep very fast, but if they're able to acquire us on their sonar, we could be in for a rough time. It could be hours before we're able to slip away."

"Or isn't it possible that you won't be able to elude them? That they'll sink us?"

"That's always that possibility in submarine warfare," Dade said. "But, even if they sank us, we will have killed 3,000 Japanese soldiers bound for Guadalcanal. Counting the loss of your men, we would have traded 70 American lives for 3,000 Japanese lives and possibly ensured victory in the Solomons."

"But that would mean we would not have accomplished our mission of delivering Dr. Nakamura to Pearl Harbor."

215

"True. We would not have traded a bird in the hand for a possible two in the bush. But you're being unduly pessimistic. My goal is to wind up with all three birds."

Jones studied Dade's face for a long moment before shaking his head forcefully. "I can't condone this. You're talking about a willful disobedience of orders. One which seriously jeopardizes the success of this mission."

"I'm sorry you feel that way, but, if you'll recall, I'm in charge of the sea portion of this mission and you're responsible for the land portion. I'll get you to the objective on time."

"Not if two Japanese escorts sink us or damage us badly enough that we can't make it to the objective in time."

"It's a risk I'm prepared to take."

"Well, I'm not." Jones sat fuming, then turned to Oliver. "You were there in CINCPAC's office. You heard the orders he gave. As XO it's your duty to relieve Captain Bowie of command and take his place. Now."

Oliver's eyes grew large and his heart began to hammer in his chest. "On what grounds?" he asked.

"Dereliction of duty. Willful disobedience of orders. I can think of a number of possible charges. You need to place him under arrest and change course for Kyushu."

"You don't understand, Captain, that's mutiny. And there's no more serious charge in the Navy than mutiny aboard a warship in time of war. It doesn't get any more serious than that."

"Do you mean to sit here and tell me that you're perfectly OK with your skipper disobeying strict orders given him by CINCPAC?"

"Frankly, I am . . . . . . uncomfortable with his decision, and I would not have made the same decision myself. However, Captain Bowie is in command. He is the captain of this boat, and the oath we all took requires us to obey the orders of the officers appointed over us."

"Unbelievable. Simply unbelievable. So I take it you're willing to face a general court martial too?"

"I . . . . . . " Oliver suddenly wished he were back in one of the Sub School boats. They thought a lot of him there, and there was no doubt he could have spent the entire war there. What the hell had he been thinking of? Now he was on his way to fucking mainland Japan itself under a hard to know Medal of Honor winner who wanted to make a detour to attack a troop transport. It was scary, but it kind of made sense. Meanwhile, an OSS captain was threatening to see him court martialed if he didn't arrest the skipper and relieve him of command. Son of a bitch. He was wrong no matter what he did. He'd give anything to be back at Groton now. Anything.

"Well, Mister Wirtz?"

"Look, give me some time to think about this. You don't know what you're asking. There's an old saying that the closest thing to God on this earth is the captain of a Navy warship at sea in time of war. He has the power to do almost anything."

"Including disobeying orders?"

"Yes, that is my understanding. When at sea, if exigent circumstances present themselves, he may decide to modify his orders. Of course, he is responsible for his decisions and may, at some later date, be called upon by higher authority to justify them."

"This is clearly not a decision he could justify, either now or later. Damn it, what the hell is the matter with you, man? The biggest part of going to war is having the stones to do your duty when the time comes. And, Mister Wirtz, for you, that time has come. If you can't find the courage to do your duty, then I will. I have seven well-armed and trained men aboard, and I'll arrest both your asses and take command of the boat myself."

Oliver folded his hands and looked down at them intently, as if expecting to find an answer there. Dade spoke. "Let's all take it easy and not do anything in haste. This is an important moment for all three of us. Ollie, how long until we intercept the *Susaki Maru* and her escorts?"

Wirtz looked at his watch. "About fifteen hours."

"OK, Captain Jones, let's all take an hour to think about things. But as you think about your options, there's something you should know. If Mister Wirtz here decides not to throw in with you, your plan to take command of the boat yourself isn't very realistic. You wouldn't know what commands to give and the crew wouldn't follow you anyway. My Chief of the Boat will definitely not go along with you either. To put it into an analogy you might be more familiar with, my position is very much like an Army company commander's, except that my rank is equivalent to an Army lieutenant colonel instead of a captain, the usual rank of a company commander. The Chief of the Boat is equivalent to a company's first sergeant. Now imagine the infantry company in the field, about to go into combat. For some reason that hasn't been explained to the men in the company, there is a handful of Navy men attached to them. Suddenly, the man in charge of the Navy group 'arrests' me, my XO, and my first sergeant, declaring that he's now in charge of the company. What do you think would happen? That's something to consider carefully. If Mr. Wirtz decided to arrest me and relieve me of command, and to cooperate with you completely, you might have a chance to get what you want, but I wouldn't count on it. As I said, the Chief of the Boat won't go along with it, and it's to him that most of the crew would turn to for advice about what to do. Oliver, what you have to think about is our men on Guadalcanal and how you would go about defending yourself on mutiny charges. Let's meet back here in an hour."

Oliver stood on the cigarette deck, wishing he were a smoker. He'd noticed that smoking seemed to calm a lot of men and it also seemed to help them to think.

217

He grabbed hold of the thumb of his left hand. Number one: The skipper was the skipper. Number two, he thought, grabbing his index finger: He was sworn to obey the orders of the . . . . . . wait a minute. Didn't the oath specify *lawful* orders? He tried hard to remember. It had been so long. Slowly it came to him, *will obey the orders of the President of the United States and the officers appointed over me* . Yes, that was it. Simple words. Clear and forthright words. Three, he was now on the middle finger, CINCPAC had issued clear and unequivocal orders that they were not to engage any ship either on the way out or on the way back from the mission. Those were clear orders. Four, CINCPAC had also ordered complete radio silence, so they could not radio Hawaii, explain the situation, and get CINCPAC's permission to go after the *Susaki Maru*. That was definitely not an option. Five, touching his little finger, Captain Bowie could sink the Japanese ship, of that he had no doubt, and there was no question that that would greatly aid the men who had been locked in a desperate and costly struggle with the Japanese for months. Thousands of Army, Navy, and Marine personnel had been killed and wounded fighting for that strategically important island. Three thousand veteran Japanese troops suddenly introduced into the fight could even turn it into a Japanese victory, setting the Americans back for months.

Six, now he was on his right thumb, this constituted exigent circumstances, or, it could constitute exigent circumstances. The meaning of "exigent" was certainly a subjective judgment. Dade Bowie could have one understanding of it, Captain Jones another, and the officers in Oliver's general court martial board another. Seven, the definition of mutiny was clear. It was the seizure or the attempt to seize control of a vessel from her commanding officer. Eight, scuttlebutt had it that Bowie had almost been court martialed before for disobedience of orders, but then again, that was only scuttlebutt. Nine, Dade Bowie was an odd man, a man who was kind of a mystery in ways, and, except around a few men like Chief Robhar or Lieutenant Detrick, introverted. But he was a decent man, a fair man, and a legend in the Silent Service. He was also a Medal of Honor winner, and, although he often said he was afraid of combat, Oliver was pretty sure he said that only to give the men courage. The truth was that he wasn't afraid. That brought Wirtz to number ten: Clearly Bowie believed he was doing the right thing. So much that he not only risked a general court martial, but spoke of the very real possibility of the *Susaki Maru's* escorts sinking the *Sea Otter* in a calm manner, saying that, even if that happened, it would be worth it to kill 3,000 Japanese soldiers who would otherwise have gone on to join the fight in Guadalcanal and perhaps even win the battle for Japan. If he was that sure, that determined, Oliver mused, he must be right. Well, no, that didn't logically follow. What it meant was he *believed* he was right.

It was odd. Oliver had always thought that the first time he had to summon up a hell of a lot of courage fast was when the *Sea Otter* went into actual combat. But they weren't in combat yet and here it was. His first real test. Back the skipper or back Captain Jones, and both men made convincing arguments. His first real test of courage and he was all alone. It was probably much easier to be brave when you were surrounded by men who were facing death with you. Being brave alone was another matter entirely. He looked at his watch. Still half an hour before he had to make his irrevocable decision. He considered praying for guidance, but quickly dismissed the idea. He had prayed for guidance before and had never been rewarded with anything that he could possibly construe as a divinely inspired reply. When it came right down to it, he thought, a man is always alone. He looked out across the sea, then the sky, seeing no answers there. For an insane moment, he even thought of flipping a coin. Heads and he would relieve Bowie of command, tails and he would stand by the skipper. But that was crazy. What had Jones said? *The biggest part of going to war is having the stones to do your duty when the time comes.* A real man, a man with courage, wouldn't decide the matter with a coin toss. A coward, a dithering, scared coward would do something like that. A man made his decision based on his honest judgment of what the right, the honorable thing was, then summon up the courage to do it, regardless of the consequences. It was then that Oliver finally knew what to do, and he felt a peace about it.

Wirtz and Jones got to Bowie's stateroom at the same time, and he motioned for them to have a seat. "I'm going to go first," Dade said, "because both your decisions are predicated on mine. I've thought things through carefully, and my orders to intercept the Japanese troop transport stand. Captain Jones, when the war started a year ago, I was a true believer. I never questioned the orders I was given or the competency of my superior officers. Especially flag officers. Then I found myself and other sub skippers using defective weapons and receiving orders that made no sense. I saw a lot of good men die for nothing. For nothing. Now, I don't know about Operation Buntline. Maybe it'll make a difference and maybe it won't. But I *know* sinking the troop transport will make a difference, a big difference. Maybe even a decisive difference. And, if we die in sinking that ship, we won't have died for nothing. We're going to sink the *Susaki Maru*. Oliver, what have you decided?"

Oliver cleared his throat, which had become dry on his way to the captain's stateroom, and spoke clearly. "You have my complete support, skipper. It is my belief that you are operating within the limits of your power in this circumstance. Unfortunately, our orders for strict radio silence precludes us from getting permission from CINCPAC to attack the *Susaki Maru*, so we have to go with your judgment alone. I will follow all the orders you give and do my level best to see that we succeed."

"Thank you, Oliver. Captain Jones?"

Jones frowned deeply. "I believe you are wrong, sir. Our orders from CINCPAC were explicit. We are not to engage any Japanese ships. We were given one mission only, and, in my opinion, any other action that jeopardizes our completing that mission cannot be condoned. However, if I were to relieve you and your XO on the high seas and countermand your orders, I believe that there would be a very real possibility for confusion and chaos among the crew. The analogy you gave an hour ago was, I must admit, probably spot on. Therefore, I'm in. I do not approve of what you want to do, but I will take no action to stop you. I will only hope and pray that you can still get us to Japan according to schedule. And finally, Captain, you're not the only one to see good men die for nothing in this war. I've seen it too. It happens in every war."

"Yes, I suppose it does, but I don't have to like it or go along with it. If I and my men die in this war, I plan to make damned sure it's not for nothing." Dade sat in silence for a moment before speaking again. "Well, that's settled. Good. Thank you, gentlemen."

When the two men left, Dade stared straight ahead at the small safe on the bulkhead. Now that he had Rachael and now that they had a baby on the way, he wanted more than ever to live. Hell, now he was even a millionaire, and he and Rachael could have a wonderful life, living wherever they wanted, traveling, never worrying about money again. They had spent long hours making plans for their life after the war. He probably wanted to live more than any man aboard the *Sea Otter*. It would have been easy to disregard the *Susaki Maru* and the 3,000 Japanese soldiers she carried. It was only by a fluke that he'd found out about it. He could have followed his orders to the letter and neither CINCPAC nor anyone else could have blamed him for that. But could he have lived with himself? Probably not, especially if the Japanese were victorious at Guadalcanal. A lot of the Americans on Guadalcanal had wives and kids too. What made Dade Bowie's life more important than theirs?

And what if Operation Buntline really was all that CINCPAC said it was? What if it could shorten the war by two years? That made it a hell of a lot more important than a major setback on Guadalcanal. If that were true, then he couldn't risk not accomplishing that mission. The brass had been wrong about so many things though, beginning with its refusal to heed the warnings about the attack on Pearl Harbor. It boiled down to whom you could trust and there was no way on earth to know.

44

December 8, 1942

Oahu

Clifford Van Husen lay in his bed in his private quarters, hands interlaced behind his head, staring at the ceiling, wearing only undershorts. His lover, a surgeon at the Pearl Harbor Naval Base hospital, sat in a nearby easy chair. She was dressed in a thick, Turkish bathrobe, and reading a novel.

"You're unusually quiet, Cliff. Penny for your thoughts."

He spoke without turning to look at her. "Just thinking about a mission, Marion. It's highly classified and I can't tell you anything about it. It's very high risk, but there's the possibility it may turn out to be one of the most important missions of the war. I'm told it could conceivably even shorten the war by two years. On the other hand, the prize we seek may be useless. There's no way at all to tell until it's been completed."

"It sounds intriguing. Are you in one of your 'the loneliness of command' moods?"

"Yes, I suppose so. I'm wondering if I picked the right man to lead the sea portion of the mission. He's technically competent and he's a very brave man."

"However?"

"However, he has in the past disobeyed orders and taken extreme risks. A while back, I had occasion to spend several hours reading everything in his personnel jacket, including all his fitness reports. I also read all the patrol reports he had filed. I tried to understand what makes him tick."

"Why?"

"For another reason that I can't talk about. The thing is, it's hard to be objective about him. I mean, I don't like him. Anyway, I think that perhaps I should have sent someone more . . . . . ."

"Reliable?"

"Predictable."

"Why don't you like him?"

Mostly because I want his wife, CINCPAC thought, but that isn't what he said. "I think he's an extremely two-dimensional person. He's not well rounded, not well educated. Driving a sub and attacking enemy ships is all he knows. And he's young, very young. What's odd is that his wife is an extremely well educated, very mature person. She's older than he too. It's an odd match."

"It takes all kinds," Marion, said in vague dismissal and returned to her reading.

Van Husen felt a flash of irritation. Yes, he was going to have to break it off with this one too. Sooner rather than later. Yes, Marion looked like Rita Hayworth, and yes, she was good in bed. Terrific, in fact. And she was discrete about their relationship and she was smart. But he had become bored with her just as he had become bored with all the others before her. He couldn't *talk* to her. Just as he couldn't talk to the others. Not about anything that mattered. She was a well respected surgeon and had even published groundbreaking articles in the most important medical journals. But, for all that, she was a superficial person. She could speak intelligently of current events, popular books and movies, and of her travels. But damn it, so could almost everyone else in the world. Well, hundreds of millions of them anyway.

Van Husen loved his work and he loved exercising his power as CINCPAC. He was one of the most important men in the entire Pacific. No, he was *the* most important and powerful man in the Pacific, and he gloried in it. And power was the ultimate aphrodisiac. There was no woman he couldn't have. Even if he had been an ugly man with no charm, just being CINCPAC was enough to score with women. And he wasn't ugly. He was an uncommonly handsome man, 6 feet tall, ramrod straight, with blue eyes and a mane of thick white hair. He was central casting's idea of a four-star Navy admiral.

The problem was that there was a woman he had tried to get and couldn't. Rachael. He had turned on the charm and propositioned her and she had turned him down flat. He had been shocked. A woman had rejected *him*? And now she was married and pregnant. That would end it for most men, but Van Husen was not like most men. Cliff Van Husen never conceded defeat.

Besides, there was something about her. Marion was younger and far more physically attractive. Her blonde hair, her incredibly fair skin, her statuesque legs that turned heads wherever she went, her violet eyes, her mouthwatering breasts, everything about her served to make her a powerful magnet for every man with blood in his veins. But those were all visual things. Van Husen needed more. He needed a woman who was his intellectual equal.

Rachael Bowie was not a beautiful woman. Neither was she unattractive. She had a good figure and a wonderful smile when she did smile with happiness. But so did a lot of women. Millions of them. It was her other smile that fascinated him. That Mona Lisa smile that she wore most of the time. That mysterious smile coupled with that strange look in her brown eyes. It could mean almost anything, but Van Husen's theory was that it was a smile of sad amusement at the human comedy. He thought it was because she understood it all, that she knew the past, present, and future of the human race, that she could read people with unerring accuracy, that she was the wisest person he had ever known.

He had never wanted to possess a woman as much as he wanted to possess Rachael Bowie. Why? Why was he obsessed with her? Maybe because her knowledge and wisdom constituted power—a different kind of power than he had, but an enormous power. She knew things, many things that he did not. Things he needed to know, to understand. She was like the Pythia, the high priestess of the Oracle at Delphi, who was consulted on matters of state, military operations, the law, and family and personal matters. On everything. The Pythia knew all—past, present, and future. Rachael was like that. He was sure of it. If he could connect with her, really connect, and she were convinced of his complete sincerity, he would be able to ask her any question and receive the answer. He could see it in her eyes. He could even ask her what the meaning of life was, and she would be able to tell him in terms that he could understand. It sounded crazy, but he knew it was true.

And this power of hers made her so sexually desirable that he could hardly bear it. To enter her body, to possess her. To fuse, to merge with her, might even give him some of her power. Even if it didn't, the very act itself would be a transcendental experience. His orgasm would undoubtedly be the most soul jarring, profound, and fantastic one he had ever experienced. He noticed he was breathing hard and that he had an erection like granite.

"I see you're not thinking of the mission anymore, Cliff," Marion said seductively, as she set her book on an end table.

No, but I sure as hell wasn't thinking of you. He made a smile that he hoped didn't look as phony as it was. "How observant of you, my dear. Why don't you join me?" He could at least pretend she was Rachael. No, not for any more than a few seconds.

Dade went up to the bridge, passed a few words with Lieutenant Greenbaum, who was the Officer of the Deck, and made his way to the cigarette deck, then down the ladder on the starboard side to the main deck below. It was 1910 hours and cloudy. There was a damp chill to the air, and he zipped his jacket up tight and pulled the collar up around his ears. Then he began to slowly walk toward the stern. He stopped in front of the access hatch that led to the after engine room, and stood staring at the *Sea Otter's* wake. His hands were in his pockets, and he thought of having a cigarette, but decided against it. Operation Buntline was a crap shoot. That's all it was. There was no way anyone involved in the planning or execution of it could know if it would achieve the results that they hoped for. But war was full of crap shoots. War itself was nothing more than a giant crap shoot with the stakes being lives. In this war, millions of lives.

At least the fresh sea air felt good against his face and he drew it deeply into his lungs. The privacy was good too. The closest men to him were the lookouts in the periscope shears, and only one of the four was assigned to look aft. And his binoculars scanned the sky and the sea, not the deck of the boat itself. They now had three hours until they intercepted the *Susaki Maru*. Then, one way or another, it would be over.

"Don't do it, Dade."

It couldn't be. Dade turned around to find himself looking directly into the yellow eyes of John Henry Hammerhand. The hair on the back of his neck stood up and he felt a chill go down his spine. He struggled to speak, then finally got the word out. "Skipper."

"Don't do it, Dade. Don't go after the *Susaki Maru*."

"Why, sir?"

"Because you'll lose the boat. All of you will die."

Dade could think of nothing to say, marveling that John Henry looked exactly as he did when he'd been alive. He appeared to be solid and substantial, not translucent like the ghosts in movies. Bowie knew that, if he reached out a hand to touch Hanrahan, his hand would not go through him, and that scared him even more than if he'd been translucent.

"If you go after her," Hanrahan said expressionlessly, "the two escorts will be on top of you almost instantly. You'll begin your approach at 2231, and a sharp-eyed lookout on the newer escort will see the wake of the very first torpedo you fire, and, by the time you fire your forward tubes and crash dive, they'll be almost on top of you. The first pattern they drop will shake the *Sea Otter* so hard you'll be sure she's coming apart, and, before you know it, before you can catch your breath, the second pattern will hit.

"Your lighting will go out, and you'll switch to emergency lighting. Lots of light bulbs and gauges will be shattered, and there'll be plenty of cork particles in the air. Cable stuffing glands in the conning tower and the starboard shaft stern tube will be leaking heavily. This is going to rapidly fill the motor room bilges and then flood the starboard circulating water pump and standby lube oil pump motors. The top and sides of Main Ballast Tank 1 is going to buckle in the forward torpedo room. The bulkhead between the forward torpedo room and the forward battery compartment will buckle. The pressure hull is going to be dished inward between the forward escape trunk and the torpedo loading hatch. There'll be pressure hull plating and framing distortion in local areas as far aft as the forward engine room, including the conning tower, the safety and auxiliary tanks, and the after lube oil tanks.

"You'll be fighting for control of the boat as you desperately try to stay on your feet. The skippers of the two Japanese tin cans are top ASW guys, which is why they were assigned the job of getting 3,000 troops to Guadalcanal. As you manage to level off at 300 feet, the damage reports you get won't be good. You'll find that gaskets have been blown out of the safety tank and the Main Ballast Tank 2A master vent valves. The engine air induction system is flooded and considerable water was taken into the engine room bilges through inboard drains and inboard hull valves. All four main engines are flooded through leaking inboard and outboard exhaust valves, and the boat is becoming heavier and heavier.

"And here they come again. Roaring in, one after another, the tin cans lay down two patterns that are right on the money. Now the cable stuffing glands in the port shaft stern tube will be leaking heavily as well. Water will be pouring in. Both reduction gears will have developed a pounding noise and the starboard shaft will be groaning loudly, due to strut bearing damage. But the Japs don't need that to keep nailing you. They've got a solid return on you from their sonar, you're leaking oil, and you have an external high pressure air leak from bank No. 2. Furthermore, your rudder post packing has jammed, causing the rudder to groan and seize. Torpedo tubes 7 through 10 are flooding through muzzle door gaskets. You won't know it at this point, but both of your periscopes are no longer operable.

"You're taking on more and more water. The pumps that are working can't keep up with it. You have to run at all ahead full and a hard rise on both bow and stern planes just to keep her level. Now the forward and after fuel oil filling line hull valves are jarred partially open and plugs on topside standpipes backed off, allowing still more oil to leak to the sea and rise to mark your location. Oil is now also leaking from normal oil fuel tank 6 and from fuel ballast tank 5. The radio antenna trunk is flooded. There are numerous electrical grounds in many systems. Despite your best efforts, you're now at 420 feet and still slowly sinking.

"Two more patterns. Now there's serious leakage in the conning tower around the binnacle tube flange and more water coming through the after bulkhead door. You evacuate the conning tower and seal the hatch to continue the fight from the control room. The pressure hull plating is dished inward between frames 119 to 130, both port and starboard. The emergency lighting in the aft half of the boat goes out. The inboard vents on normal oil tank No. 1 and Fuel Ballast Tank No. 3 jar open under the shock of the depth charges and shower the forward torpedo room and the crew's mess with oil. The whole boat is groaning in agony like a dying prehistoric monster, unable to lash out at her tormenters. More frames begin to buckle. The speed of your descent is rapidly increasing. You don't have a prayer and you know it. You've known it for at least 15 minutes now and so has the rest of the crew. Your depth is now 496 feet and your down angle is 30 degrees when the last pattern hits. All the lights go out, the boat rolls sickeningly 45 degrees to starboard, and you lose your footing. Somehow, somehow, you're still alive, something which amazes you, until the boat reaches crush depth three minutes later. And that's it, Dade. That's the end."

Dade was stunned with the finality of John Henry's last three words. "Are you sure, sir?"

There was a flash of impatience in Hanrahan's eyes and an exasperated frown. "Of course I'm sure, Dade. How obtuse can you be? I come back from the dead to save your life, and you think I might not have my facts right?"

"Sorry, skipper. I didn't mean to—"

"That's alright," the ghost of the big man said, the frown disappearing in less than a second. "The answer is yes, I'm positive. I've seen it happen several times, from a number of places inside the sub and from outside as well. If you go after the *Susaki Maru*, that's exactly what will happen. I could give you even more details if you like. You'll die at 0008 hours, about five hours from now. I've seen it happen. But you can avoid it by not intercepting and attacking that ship. You have the power to do that."

"If I attack, do I sink the *Susaki Maru?*"

"Oh yes, she goes down like a rock, her bow completely blown off with one torpedo, and another torpedo hits the hold where they're storing all the ammunition. Yes."

"So I keep those 3,000 Japanese veteran troops from getting to Guadalcanal."

"Yes, but you and the crew and the boat are all lost."

"That means I'd fail to carry out my mission. I wouldn't get to Japan to get that scientist."

"That's correct."

"Is that mission really that important? If we go there, will we be successful?"

"I don't know the answer to either of those questions. The only thing I've been permitted to see is what happens if you attack the troop transport. And, by the way, me getting to see that and getting permission to come here and warn you is a very big deal. Things like this don't happen very often."

"What do you think I should do, skipper?"

"Dade, I can't presume to tell you what to do. It's your decision. I can only tell you you'll die if you attack. I have a fondness for you and would like to see you live and go back to Rachael and your baby, but it's your decision."

"Of course the prospect—the certainty—of death if I attack the transport makes me want to rule that out entirely, but then I think of our boys on Guadalcanal and in the waters around it. About all the men who have been killed and maimed to get and keep that rock, and I think of trading 70 American lives for 3,000 Japanese lives and maybe, by doing that, help win the campaign in the Solomons. On the other hand, what if the mission to Japan really is as important as CINCPAC says?"

"I just wanted to let you know that one of those choices definitely means your death."

"So might the other one."

"That's true," Hanrahan conceded. "I don't know what happens if you sail to Japan instead. You could wind up losing the boat there too. Well, I've done all I can and it's time for me to go back. It was good seeing you again."

"It was good seeing you again, sir. I miss you. I miss you more than I can say."

"And I you, son."

"What's it like on the other side?"

"Oh, Dade," the older man said with a smile, "there are no words to describe it. It's also something that no human being can really understand."

"I take it that there's a God."

"Of course there's a God. I didn't realize it when I lived on this earth, unfortunately. My life would have been very different if I had."

"Oftentimes Rachael and I have our doubts."

"Everybody who's ever lived has had doubts. It's normal. I have to go now, son," John Henry said, putting a large right hand on Bowie's shoulder and squeezing it hard. "Take care." And he was suddenly gone. Dade was surprised at how substantial Hanrahan's hand had felt. Dade stayed on the deck for a few moments more before he went below in search of Oliver. He found him and Jones sitting in the wardroom having coffee. "Ollie, please calculate a direct course to Kyushu immediately and give the appropriate orders to put us on it."

"Aye aye, sir," Wirtz said, and immediately got up and left.

Jones eyed him speculatively. "What made you change your mind?"

"You're not the only one who can receive messages from supernatural realms."

"Oh?"

They were the only two men in the wardroom now as Dade sat down. He looked over at the entrance to ensure that no one was coming in. "'There are more things in heaven and earth, Horatio, than are dreamt of in your philosophy.'"

"A ghost then?"

"Yes, that of my old skipper."

"Was it good news?"

"It was just some information that I took into consideration in my planning. I'm going with the idea that this mission is as important as CINCPAC and you say it is."

"Great. Welcome to the club, Dade."

45

December 9, 1942

Pearl Harbor Naval Base

Early that morning, Tracy flashed Rachael a tired but triumphant grin. "I found what I was looking for in the traffic. There's no time to tell you about it now. Paul and I have to brief Huxley and Admiral Reynolds before a big conference with all the top brass after lunch. I'll let you know after that what I found and what they decide. Wish me luck." With that, she was off and Rachael began her day.

That afternoon, Tracy was more than a little nervous as she and Paul Duvall walked into CINCPAC's office and headed to the long, highly polished mahogany conference table. They were five minutes early, but most of the attendees were already there and seated. Tracy hadn't seen so many stars since her embassy days and seldom even then. Uncle Cliff sat at the head of the table with his four stars. Then there was Army General Russell Moyers wearing his three stars. Seated to his left was Admiral Robert Neuman, another three stars, and to his left sat Admiral Bradford Pelmano, with his two stars. There was a Marine two-star general she didn't know, and two-star Admiral Reynolds, the Director of ONI in the Pacific Theatre. She and Paul took two seats toward the foot of the table, and then Captain Huxley and Captain Elmer Caine, CINCPAC's chief of staff, both rushed in and took seats

Tracy felt out of place for a number of reasons besides all the star power. She was also the only civilian present, the only woman, and the youngest by far. Several of the men glowered at her, then at Admiral Van Husen, as if to ask, "What the hell is *she* doing here?"

"Gentlemen, thank you all for coming. I must make an important decision today, a decision made extremely difficult because its outcome will have an immediate and major influence on the next steps we take in the entire Pacific. It is not too much to say that it may be one of the most important decisions I've made in the war to date. The decision is mine alone to make, and I will take on my shoulders full responsibility if I should make the wrong choice. However, before making that choice, I wanted to lay out the facts to you and to seek your opinions and advice.

"First, all of you here are cleared for receiving intelligence gathered from our Top Secret ULTRA program. As you know, because ULTRA is our most reliable and accurate source of information, not to mention that the intelligence comes from the very highest level of the Japanese High Command itself, we have always taken great pains not to reveal to anyone, even to most of you, exactly what that source is. We 'sanitize' our intelligence reports derived from our source to try to conceal what that source is. Now I'm sure that you have all made educated guesses on what the source is, and some of you have probably guessed correctly that the source is radio intercepts of the most secret and highly classified messages sent out by the Japanese Navy as well as the traffic between Tokyo and its embassies throughout the world. I ask, of course, that you not share the knowledge of this source with anyone in your command."

The generals and admirals nodded quick affirmation, and Van Husen went on. You will see presently why I've revealed that to you just now. The source has everything to do with the problem at hand. At this table, we have Admiral Reynolds, the Director of all ONI activities in the Pacific, who runs the ULTRA program here, his deputy, Captain Huxley, Commander Duvall, and one of our senior translators, Mrs. Fillmore. As most of you know, it was ULTRA intelligence that, not only informed us that the Japanese were going to try to take Midway Island and lay a trap for our fleet when it sailed out to respond to the threat. It was the interception, decryption, translation, and analysis of Top Secret Japanese Navy radio messages that enabled us to know their plans, including their timetable, order of battle, and, well, everything. In a very real sense, it was the ULTRA people who made our decisive victory at the Battle of Midway possible. Going into a bit more detail, Commander Duvall tells me that this coup was mostly due to Mrs. Fillmore's keen insight and analysis of the messages during the 60 hours a week that she routinely puts in. We owe a great deal to Mrs. Fillmore, and—you will presently see why—I'm going to give you additional information about her background. When her mother died at age 10, she went to live with her father at the U.S. Embassy in Tokyo. She attended Japanese public schools and is a graduate of Tokyo Imperial University. She spent years working with her father at the embassy, and met and spoke with many influential Japanese, including Hideki Tojo and Admiral Isoroku Yamamoto. In fact, she has personally conversed with both men a number of times at embassy functions, as well as with other important figures in Japan. She speaks, reads, and writes Japanese with an educated, perfect fluency, and, when her father died, we were able to hire her on here in 1940. I have prevailed upon her and our other senior translator, Mrs. Bowie, to advise me on Japanese culture, history, customs, and psychology, and this has proven invaluable. I've always been mindful of Sun Tzu's admonition to know one's enemy.

"Now, with that background out of the way, I'll proceed. Quite simply, our ULTRA people have intercepted high level Japanese messages concerning a planned invasion of Australia."

The effect on the military men was electric. Van Husen may have just as well have announced that the building was on fire and the exits were blocked. "My God!" exclaimed Marine General Moore, "Are you sure of this?"

"When?!" demanded General Moyers.

CINCPAC held up a hand. "One step at a time, gentlemen. Admiral Reynolds, will you provide us with the details of the intercepts?"

"Yes sir." Reynolds picked up a page from a folder he had just opened and began to read. "The Japanese have codenamed the invasion of Australia, 'Operation Blue Samurai.' According to the intercepts, the invasion fleet will consist of 6 battleships, 4 aircraft carriers, 10 heavy cruisers, 12 light cruisers, 42 destroyers, and six submarines. There will also be a number of tankers, but we don't yet have the exact number of those. The flagship of the invasion fleet will be the Yamato, and the Admiral in charge of the operation will be Yamamoto himself. In addition, there will also be enough troop transports and cargo ships to transport 110,000 troops, their supplies, and amphibious landing craft. The Japanese will get the troops for the invasion by taking two of their divisions from China, one from Korea, one from the Philippines, one from French Indo China, and the remainder from strategic reserves based on the home islands. It goes without saying that, except for the men in the strategic reserves, all of these troops are veteran combat troops who have seen a lot of action. I have here the names of the ships involved and the identifications of the Imperial Japanese Army units that will be used."

"That's not necessary right now," CINCPAC quickly interjected. "Give us a quick look at what assets we have in Australia to oppose an invasion."

"Yes sir. Before the war in the Pacific started, the Australian Army raised four infantry divisions to come to the assistance of the British in the fighting in the Middle East and the Mediterranean. The 6th Infantry Division fought in the North African Campaign, but was pulled back to Australia this year, as was their 7th Infantry Division. Their 9th Infantry Division is still fighting in North Africa. Their 8th Infantry Division wasn't sent. By the time they were ready to go, it was clear that they were needed here in the Pacific. They fought at Singapore, Rabaul, Ambon, and Timor, and the division has essentially ceased to exist. The men of the 8th who weren't killed in action became Japanese prisoners of war. Now the Aussies have raised six other infantry divisions and three armored divisions, all of which are in Australia at the present time. The 6th and 7th Infantry Divisions took heavy losses on the other side of the world, so many of the troops are replacements, but the original men in them are highly skilled combat veterans who did a lot of heroic fighting over there. As for American troops, MacArthur has the 41st Infantry Division and the 32nd Infantry Division. Both were formed from National Guard units and, except for elements of them now fighting in New Guinea, they are unblooded. Elements of the Australian 7th Infantry Division are also fighting there. Australia also has about 80,000 people in its Volunteer Defence Corps, which is modelled on the British Home Guard. Except for about 1,000 people who serve full time, the rest of the volunteers serve only part time, but are well motivated. In addition, we have the Fifth Air Force to help defend the country. It consists of three fighter groups equipped with P-39's and P-40's, and four bomber groups, equipped with B-25's, A-20's, A-24's, B-26's, and B-17's. Of course, they'd be going up against Japanese Zeros from the four aircraft carriers, and, at this stage of the game, the Japanese pilots have far more combat experience than most of our pilots. And, of course, there is the Royal Australian Air Force, which is not very large yet, and has a shortage of aircraft, but most of their pilots have combat experience.

"However, there are problems. Australia's coast is long and virtually no fortifications have been built along it. There's nothing resembling the Fortress Europe beach obstacles, like pillboxes with interlocking fields of fire, artillery pieces registered on the beaches, minefields, and so on. Shifting troops rapidly from one place to another is almost impossible. Even before the war began, there was no extensive rail network and there weren't a great deal of locomotives and railroad cars. Most of the transportation of goods from one city to another was and still is done by ship. The network of roads is likewise inadequate for the rapid movement of large amounts of troops and supplies from one place to another to meet the need of repelling an invasion. And if it's one thing we've all learned in modern warfare, mobility is everything. The Germans taught the world that when it kicked off this war. The population of Australia is 7.2 million, virtually all of whom live in a coastal city or in towns and villages not all that far away from the coast. The Japanese don't have to take a lot of territory to conquer the country. If they move very fast, blitzkrieg fashion, and if we aren't able to anticipate where the landings will take place, well, we could have a major problem on our hands."

"You don't know where they'll land?" asked General Moore.

"Not yet. We hope and believe we will be able to ascertain that as we continue to intercept, decode, and translate further Japanese messages. We do however, have a date. It's January 3rd, a Sunday."

"Good God, man!" exclaimed General Moyers. "That's only 25 days away! Hardly enough time to do anything. Yes, we can send some additional aircraft and pilots, but not many. In addition, with one exception, all of our available infantry divisions are either engaged in combat or en route to other places where they're going to be committed to operations already planned or underway. All of us at this table," he looked around, then corrected himself after casting a disparaging look at Tracy and Paul Duvall, "*most* of us understand what kind of logistical nightmare this presents. It's not a simple thing to assemble and equip and train an infantry division, secure enough ships to transport them when and where you need them, to load those ships, brief the men, solve strategic and tactical problems on how and where the elements of the division will be used, offload them and their supplies and get them overland to where they're needed."

CINCPAC seemed unperturbed. "Let's take one thing at a time, gentlemen. Admiral Reynolds has given us a quick look at what we have on the ground in Australia. Now I'd like the considered opinions of the Army and Marine representatives at this table. *If* the information we have is accurate, and, *if* we are unable to stop the invasion fleet from getting to Australia, do you think that the invasion could be thrown back into the sea with what MacArthur has on hand? That is, assume for the purpose of this exercise that we would be unable to send them any material assistance."

The men looked around at each other in confusion. It was a hell of a problem; one they didn't want to think about at all. After a few moments, Army General Russel Moyers spoke. "First, losing Australia is unacceptable for a number of reasons, all of them quite obvious. Are we all agreed on that, gentlemen?" Moyers looked around the table at the face of each flag officer in turn, including CINCPAC's, and received solemn nods in reply. "Next, in answer to Admiral Van Husen's specific question, I am doubtful the forces there could hold on. That is, once a beachhead or beachheads are established, and that seems likely. The amount of air power those four carriers have, coupled with the heavy guns of the battleships and cruisers taking care of shore bombardment, their prospects look grim indeed. In addition, I must point out that, to date, the Japanese Army has suffered no major defeats. In the Philippines, it handed us the worst defeat in the history of American arms. Nevertheless, anything is possible in a war, and the Aussies will be fighting on their home ground. They're splendid fighting men. They proved that in the Great War and they proved it in this war in the Mediterranean, especially fighting against the elite Afrika Korps. They, along with the two American divisions, just might be able to pull it off, but, if they do, it'll be a very, very close thing. It pains me to say this, but no, I don't think they can hold on without help. At least not for very long. Not in a protracted campaign."

Marine General Moore nodded agreement. "It is *possible* that they could hold on, but as, as General Moyers said, not for a long time without help."

"The next question I have is for Admirals Pelmano and Neuman. "*If* the information on the composition of the invasion fleet is correct, do we have the capability of stopping it?"

Pelmano and Neuman looked at each other, then off into the distance as they carefully considered the problem individually. Neuman spoke first. "Sir, as I'm sure you know, in order to even have a chance, we'd need to practically use every damned ship in the fleet. This fleet is even larger than the one we encountered in the Battle of Midway. A whole hell of a lot larger. It would be almost a desperation move on our part. We'd have to put virtually all our naval eggs in one basket."

"We *won* at Midway," Van Husen said.

"Yes sir, but there was a certain amount of luck that we had too. It could have gone either way there for a while."

Admiral Pelmano agreed. "We were lucky. The enemy made two big mistakes, and we had a couple of breaks."

"Sending practically every available vessel we have racing to intercept the invasion fleet," said CINCPAC. "Is that something you'd recommend?" he asked Neuman.

"I . . . . well, we'd have to take a lot of ships out of the Solomons. Ships that are critically needed there. We'd also have to reassign ships from a number of other operations. I would only recommend this *if* the intelligence is accurate and *if* we'd be prepared to possibly lose the naval war raging in the Solomons and *if* it is a given that we must save Australia at all costs."

"If we lose the naval war in the Solomons, we lose the land war," interjected a morose General Moyers. "It's tough enough now getting supplies through to our troops on the ground, and trying to protect them from Japanese naval bombardment. But the worst problem is that the Japanese keep on being able to supply their men and also bring in reinforcements. They have naval superiority in the area and we've lost a number of ships trying to stop the constant successful resupply of the Japanese troops on Guadalcanal. If you pull American naval units from the Solomons, it could be disastrous for our men on Guadalcanal. That fucking island is drenched with American blood. We've lost thousands of fine young men in hanging on. I sure as hell would hate to lose it at this point. We've been fighting there since the first week of August."

"If we decided to reinforce Australia, which infantry divisions are available to send them?"

"Now that's a real problem, sir. We have both the 1st and the 2nd Marine divisions on Guadalcanal. They're fully engaged and committed, as is the Army's Americal Division. Evacuating them is unthinkable. For one thing, it would mean all the fighting and dying that's been done since August would have been for nothing. All that blood and treasure, all those lives, all that heroism for nothing. We'd lose the Solomons. Second, evacuating men who are engaged with the enemy results in a great loss of life itself. The enemy tears into your rear when you retreat. That's why retreat in combat is a movement made only in desperation. Now we *do* have the Army's 25th Infantry Division here on Oahu. They're preparing to ship out for Guadalcanal the day after tomorrow. We could send them to Australia instead. Back in the States, there's the 7th Infantry Division, which was formed in 1940. A few months ago, someone got the idea to give them a lot of vehicles and some armor, name them the 7th Motorized Division, and send them to fight in North Africa. That didn't pan out for one reason or another so they're going to rename the unit the 7th Infantry Division and send them to fight in the Pacific. They're in California right now and should be ready to ship out soon. I'll check on their status as soon as we finish this meeting. But there's no way we could get them to Australia before the invasion."

"Sir," said Admiral Neuman addressing CINCPAC, "one thing confuses me. In this meeting, you've said '*if* the information is accurate.' I believe you used that phrase twice. It has always been my understanding that the ULTRA reports are always 100 percent accurate. Have I been mistaken?"

"No. The ULTRA information has always been 100 percent accurate. After all, they are taken from the most secret transmissions that the Japanese Imperial Navy uses for communications between its own bases and ships. ULTRA intelligence has always been 100 percent accurate so far."

"I infer that you have a reason to believe that this particular piece of intelligence may not be accurate though, sir?"

"Yes. This is where it becomes incredibly difficult. I mentioned Mrs. Fillmore," he nodded toward Tracy, "before. I spoke of her living in Japan beginning at age 10 and attending all Japanese schools. I don't think that I mentioned she did postgraduate work at the Tokyo Imperial University in Japanese classical literature. She spent 21 years in Japan and has a larger Japanese vocabulary then most Japanese. It was largely due to her insights that we were able to find out exactly what the Japanese planned at Midway and in such detail. She believes that this Operation Blue Samurai is a ruse. Mrs. Fillmore, explain why."

Tracy was never one to be awed by military rank, but the number of stars on the collars and shoulder boards of the men sitting around the table did make her a little nervous. Nevertheless, the nervousness began dissipating when she began speaking. By her fourth sentence, she was completely at ease. "Thank you, Admiral Van Husen. First, the Japanese Imperial Navy sends literally thousands of messages every day. We don't have the resources to decrypt, translate, and analyze all of them. So that's the first problem. Which ones do we ignore? For example, we read everything that comes from Imperial Navy Headquarters, messages to and from high ranking naval officers, to and from capital ships, and so on, but generally don't pay much attention to weather reports, cargo ships' manifests, and routine position reports of minor vessels. Determining when and how the Japanese planned to attack Midway was quite a task. We had to sift through several thousand messages to fit all the pieces in place. You see, after we intercept, decrypt, and translate the messages, we have to find a coherent pattern. We liken it to putting together a very large jigsaw puzzle. Picture, if you will, a jigsaw puzzle approximately twice the size of this very spacious room and fifty people trying desperately to solve it while a clock is ticking and time is running out. Somehow, we did it nevertheless. And we continue to generate significant intelligence successes. But it's not easy. What first made me begin to suspect that Blue Samurai was a ruse was that it was too easy to solve. Everything was laid out, clearly, and succinctly. And, just in case we missed a few messages, there were a number of others. Operational details were all conveniently laid out in a way we haven't seen before. It just seemed to be too easy."

"That isn't a logical argument, Mrs. Fillmore," Admiral Pelmano said with a frown. "Please tell me we're going to be guided by more than just women's intuition in this matter."

"Bear with me, gentlemen," she replied with a smile she had to force. "Things were odd enough that I read the translated messages over and over, but found nothing. Then I went back and read all the messages in the original Japanese. It was only then that I found this simple one-sentence message from Tojo to Yamamoto. It reads, 'Blue Samurai will be the definitive test.'" The men all stared at her, unblinking and silent.

"Languages reflect the culture of the people who speak them," she went on patiently. "For example, the Eskimos have more than thirty different words for blubber, while we have only one in English. All thirty of those words have distinctly separate meanings, each meaning a different type of blubber, a different tasting blubber, and so forth. But all of those words would normally be translated into our one English word. And the translation would be adequate as far as it went. Adequate for the purposes of most native English-speaking people. In English, we don't have many words for test. We have the word itself, as well as exam, examination, trial, quiz, and a few others. But the Japanese have many more words for different types of tests. When I first read the message in English, I thought the sentence could mean things like the operation being 'a test of our strength,' or 'a test of our resolve,' or 'a test of our strategic planning.' Something like that. It was only when I went back and was reading the messages in the original Japanese that I found that the word one of our people had translated as 'test' was a Japanese word that, yes, means test, but the connotation is that it's a test which involves deception. One of the subjects I studied at Tokyo Imperial University was etymology, and—"

"Etymology?" asked Marine General Moore.

"Yes, that's the study of the source of words, exactly how they're used, and how their meanings often change over time. You see, in this message, this Japanese word for test has, since the Tokugawa Shogunate, meant a test in which there was deception. That was back in the Edo Period, from 1600 to 1868. And its meaning has remained unchanged." Tracy stopped speaking and sat back in her chair.

"It's unclear to me what kind of a ruse you're saying this is," Admiral Neuman said evenly.

"I'm saying that they're testing us. I'm saying that, ever since the Battle of Midway, they've suspected that we've cracked their code and that they want to find out by sending a message so important that we'd have to take certain actions. They don't plan to invade Australia. At least not now. Blue Samurai is bait. If we go rushing troops and ships to Australia, then they'll know for certain that we're reading their messages. They'll change codes and we'll be completely in the dark about what they're up to for quite possibly a long time.

"Look. They plan an elaborate attack on Midway in the utmost secrecy. Then, as they approach, suddenly there's most of our available Pacific Fleet to block them. They'd be crazy to write that off as coincidence, and they're not crazy. This is a red herring. It may even be serving two purposes. One, to find out if we're reading their messages, and two, to use it as a diversion while they strike somewhere else."

"That's it?" General Moyers said incredulously. "You're asking us to believe this is a ruse because of the translation of a single Japanese word?"

Tracy nodded emphatically.

"Commander Duvall," asked CINCPAC, "if the Japanese Navy were to change codes, how long would it take us to crack a new one?"

"It's impossible to say with certainty, but, if we're lucky, I'd say somewhere between two and three months. If we're unlucky, and they decide to use an entirely new kind of encryption machine, it could take us up to six months."

CINCPAC shook his head. "I can't imagine trying to fight this war for months without the ULTRA information that that we've come to rely on. If it hadn't been for ULTRA, the Japanese would now have Midway, and the men we have fightin g in the Solomons now would be here, bracing for a Japanese attack on the Hawaiian Islands. They'd be digging trenches, stringing barbed wire, setting up pillboxes, and so forth. Midway would have been a major defeat for us, and we'd all be hunkered down here, with the Japanese still undefeated."

"With all due respect, sir, I can't imagine losing Australia," said General Moyers. "We have to do something. How about if we took the middle ground, keep all our forces in the Solomons, but send Australia all the air assets we can spare immediately, along with the 25th Division? They'd get there before the invasion. We could also see about getting the 7th Infantry Division sent from California to Australia. We probably couldn't get them there before the inva sion, but it's the best we can do. We also have to warn General MacArthur immediately so he can begin to make plans."

"Sir," said Captain Huxley, "it's common knowledge in Hawaii that the 25th is slated for the Solomons, and that its departure date is the day after tomorrow. There are also Japanese spies in Hawaii who we can be certain know this. If we suddenly change the destination to Australia, the Japanese are going to know that we're reading their messages."

"I disagree that the 25[th Division's] destination is 'common knowledge,' Captain. The destination is classified."

"I understand, sir, but, when you move 12,000 men, word inevitably gets out. In this case, I can assure you that it has gotten out."

"I'll take your word for that, Captain," Moyers glowered, "but that's easily fixed. Once the convoy is at sea, we'll simply send a coded radio message changing their destination."

"Yes sir, but there's still the matter of their arrival in Australia. The arrival of a division doesn't go unnoticed. Believe me, the enemy will notice. That, in addition, to our, at the same time, suddenly sending a large amount of aircraft to Australia and making arrangements to obtain the 7th Infantry Division for immediate deployment to Australia, would clearly show the Japanese that we read the encoded messages regarding Blue Samurai."

"So, Captain, I take it that your recommendation is that we do nothing? That we just take a chance that this young woman is right?"

Tracy didn't like the tone the general had used when he'd said, 'this young woman.' Neither, she noticed, had Admiral Reynolds, who answered the question posed to Huxley. "It is ONI's recommendation that we send no additional material assistance to Australia at this time, because we believe Blue Samurai to be a deception intended to determine whether we're successfully reading their messages."

"I take it then, that you are also against advising General MacArthur of a possible invasion?"

"That is correct, sir."

"I know Douglas well," interjected CINCPAC, "and he wouldn't be able to keep himself from taking some precautionary actions, such as putting his troops on alert or shifting them about, and I'm certain that the Japanese have spies in Australia who would be looking for exactly this kind of reaction."

Moyers looked around the table at the other flag officers. "Gentlemen, did we not agree a few moments ago that we must not lose Australia?"

"I believe we also agreed, along with you, sir, that the Aussies are excellent soldiers," said Marine General Moore. "You yourself said that they 'proved that in the Great War and they proved it in this war in the Mediterranean, especially fighting against the elite Afrika Korps.' Remember, you also made note of the fact that they'd be fighting on their own home ground. I think that's an important factor. Those men fought like lions for Britain in North Africa. Can you imagine how hard they'll fight to protect their homes and families? The Aussies are tough customers. Half of the Australian *civilians* will probably become guerilla fighters and saboteurs if the Japanese invade. Those people, along with the two American infantry divisions that are there will give a good account of themselves. The more I think about it, I don't think it will be a close thing. At least, I'm confident that they can hold on for from four to six months, and that's certainly more than enough time for us to send help. There's a very good chance that, by that time, we'll have wrapped up our campaign in the Solomons, and we can send them a couple divisions from there. I'm thinking of the 1ˢᵗ and 2ⁿᵈ Marine Divisions. In short, I'm betting that, even if we don't send help now, we're not going to lose Australia."

"Any way you look at this," said Admiral Neuman, "it's a gamble. There's no way we can be sure. But we're forced to gamble, and I agree with General Moore. The most we could send in terms of fighting ships right now is a task force with no more than two carriers, and that's not much of a match for the fleet the Japanese are talking about sending. And the idea of losing our ability to read their most secret messages for from two to six months is unthinkable. We rely on ULTRA intelligence heavily."

"I agree, sir," said Admiral Pelmano, "plus the fact we do have two American infantry divisions already in Australia to help out. I realize that some elements of both are fighting in New Guinea, but still . . . ."

Moyers spoke. "I can't believe that we're making what may well turn out to be one of the most important decisions of the war based on a young female civilian's *feelings* about a single Japanese word."

CINCPAC's face was expressionless. "Does anyone have anything else to say? Now is the time, gentlemen." No one spoke. "Very well then, please remain silent for a few moments while I think this over and make my decision." He got up and walked to the large picture window behind his desk. Even though it was now a year and two days since the attack, the harbor and base still bore many scars. Van Husen thought of that day as he had so many times during the last year. It was all as vivid in his mind as if it had happened yesterday. He could remember every moment with crystal clarity—all the sights, sounds, and smells—everything everyone had said and that he had said—everything. He was the man who had presided over the destruction of the fleet he was responsible for.

The victory at Midway had served to rehabilitate his reputation and restore the confidence the CNO, the Secretary of the Navy, the media, and Congressionals had in his abilities, but the campaign in the Solomons was taking much longer than he had forecast, and the losses had been heavy. He could not afford to make a mistake on something this important.

Tracy was brilliant and had been right on the Pearl Harbor attack. She'd been right about Midway too, but the evidence on Midway had been solid and there had been no business about the connotation of a single word. That was all she had. It did make sense that the Japanese had to wonder how and why their secret operation to take Midway with overwhelming force and the element of complete surprise had been met with pretty much almost all that was left of the Pacific Fleet. *And we can't lose the edge we have with ULTRA. But we can't lose Australia either*. The precise connotation of one word. That was pretty thin gruel.

If Blue Samurai was the invasion of Australia, Australia could probably hold out for months. Even without the 25ᵗʰ Infantry Division or additional air assets.

Given a few months, he'd be able to send substantial help to Australia. Guadalcanal would certainly be in his hands then, and he could send the 1st and 2nd Marine Divisions, leaving the Americal Division and the 25th Infantry to hold the crucial island. Australia could hold on for a few months even if he didn't give MacArthur warning of the invasion. If the invasion happened though, and anyone outside of this room let the fact be known that Van Husen had foreknowledge and hadn't warned MacArthur, there'd be hell to pay. Even if he explained he had reason to believe it was a ruse. They'd tell him that he should have notified MacArthur anyway. As a precaution, if nothing else. The thing was that MacArthur wouldn't be able to help himself. He'd take concrete actions based on the warning. Van Husen would, if he were in MacArthur's place. Anyone would; it was only natural. Then ULTRA would be blown. Perhaps for as long as half a year, which was an eternity in a war.

It would be hell, if the invasion happened and he hadn't notified MacArthur of the possibility. Douglas MacArthur would blame Van Husen for the early Japanese victories as they poured onto the continent. Son of a bitch. If he made the wrong decision, he was fucked. Really fucked. He watched a fighter plane take off from Ford Island and wished he could change places with the young man in that cockpit. No worries on his mind, just doing a routine patrol. Then he'd have a couple of beers and be off to see his girlfriend. Not a worry in his young head. No momentous decisions to make. CINCPAC tried to imagine the girlfriend. She'd be a nurse, he thought. Yes, at the base hospital. She'd be 21, with hair the color of straw, and she'd be from Indiana. The young pilot would be an ensign, just a few months out of flight training in Pensacola. She'd have chosen nursing out of a sincere, youthful desire to help people. They both would have joined the Navy for travel and adventure. They had gotten both and were now on what would prove to be the biggest adventure of their lives. He smiled sadly, wishing even more that he could magically change places with that young man in the fighter who had no idea how good he had it.

He turned away from the window, walked back to the table, and sat down. "I believe that Blue Samurai is a ruse. We will take no action whatsoever. It is absolutely imperative that no one at this table recount any of the things we discussed here this afternoon. You must mention it to no one. Not to your chiefs of staff, your intelligence officers, no one. Are there any questions? Very well. We stand adjourned."

46

December 11, 1942

Pacific Ocean

One thing Dade was especially happy about was the improved SJ radar that had been installed on the *Sea Otter* during construction. The set that had been installed on the *Elver* had been completely unreliable, working only about 40 percent of the time. But the scientists and the technicians back in the States had worked all the bugs out by the time the *Sea Otter* had hers installed at Groton, and it had worked like a charm every day since they'd left to head to the Pacific and the war. The SJ was a surface search radar which could spot ships and give their bearing and distance. It was limited to line of sight, that is, from the antenna to the horizon, which, in the case of where the antenna was mounted on the *Sea Otter*, meant it could cover a radius of 20 miles from the sub. It could also pick up low flying aircraft.

They were close enough to Japan that they spent the days travelling submerged and ran on the surface only at night. Dade liked to give the crew a chance to get up on deck at night for some fresh air and a breeze. With the SJ working as it should, Bowie felt comfortable with letting as many as eight men up on the cigarette deck at a time. If they suddenly had to dive, there had to be time for the four lookouts, the Officer of the Deck, the Junior Officer of the Deck, and eight men to get below in time, and he felt that any more men topside might be pushing it.

Every night, Lieutenant David Greenbaum played his trumpet for an hour on the cigarette deck, and men took turns on who got to be topside when he was playing. Without a doubt, he was a true professional, and knew all the men's favorite songs that Glenn Miller, Tommy and Jimmy Dorsey, Harry James, and the other popular swing bands were playing. Greenbaum had explained to Dade that he needed to play a minimum of an hour a day to keep in practice for when the war ended. Bowie saw no harm in it, and it proved to be a huge morale booster. The only other entertainment on the boat was reading, cards, listening to records played over the 1MC, and movies. The movies were shown in the largest room in the boat—the forward torpedo room—about three times a week. Each sub only got about 15 movies to last for a two-month patrol, so most men saw each movie two or three times. But the movies were good ones, many of them just released and with Hollywood's most famous stars. Occasionally, they'd show a British movie too, like the popular "Thirty-Nine Steps."

It was almost 0100 hours when Dade went topside to find only Will on the cigarette deck, looking up at the stars and smoking. Bowie lit a cigarette himself. "Hi Will."

"Hi Dade. I just can't get enough of this night sky at sea, not since that first night I was up here."

"Me neither." They stood in easy, companionable silence for a while, then Will reached into his jacket and pulled out an envelope.

"Dade, this is a letter to my parents. Would you mail this to them when you get back to port?"

"I'm tempted to tell you to mail it yourself because you're probably going to live. I'm tempted to say that millions of men throughout history have believed they were going to die in an upcoming battle, but that many, many of them lived. But I won't. To try to talk you out of your premonition would be to disrespect your certainty. It would be to disrespect you. I know enough about life to know that there's a whole other world that we can see only seldomly in glimpses, as if a curtain is parted by a faint breeze and—just for a moment—we can see the future. Sometimes we can see the past. I don't understand any of it, but I know it happens. It's happened to me. So, yes," Bowie said, taking the envelope, "of course I'll mail it when we get back. Is there anything else I can do for you?"

"No, not a thing."

"No girl left behind?"

"Oh," Jones said, smiling gently, "there was a girl in London. I was more in love with her than I could possibly express. And she loved me too. She was a young physician doing her internship in Charing Cross Hospital. She worked in the ER, desperately trying to save victims of the German bombing of the city. Some nights, when there'd been big raids, and she finally got a break after 18 or 20 hours, exhausted, her gown covered with blood and gore, she just sat and cried, and I held her in my arms. It was the children, she told me, the children most of all, that got to her. Seven-year old girls who had lost their legs, or little boys who would never grow up. Or a million other things like that.

"We clung to each other and we made love with an intensity I never knew was possible. I think we were trying to shut out death. At the time, I was making commando raids into occupied Europe too, and I'd seen more than I really wanted to. We were good for each other. So good I asked her to marry me. It was then that she told me she was already married and that her husband had gone missing in North Africa in December 1940. She hadn't had any word from or about him for a year and a half. It was possible that he was a POW, but his name hadn't been on the lists of POWs. It was more likely that his body is covered by several feet of sand and may never be found. She was willing to bet that it was the latter and start a new life with me, but I kept picturing this poor son of a bitch coming home after the war had ended to find the women he loved with another man—a foreigner—and possibly with one or two children by this new man. I knew how I'd feel if I were the poor bastard. I think I knew how she'd feel, and I definitely knew how I'd feel if I had to give her up then. Three lives would have been ruined forever."

"Damn!" Dade said softly. "And I thought I had problems."

"So I broke it off, of course. That was the only honorable thing to do. She cried, I cried. I still do from time to time. I can still hear her voice, see her smile, taste her kisses, and remember how, whenever we were together, even if there was an air raid going on, everything was all right. She used a shampoo that made her hair smell of strawberries. Her name was Laura."

"That's probably the noblest act I ever heard of. You're a better man than I. After I fell in love with my wife, I don't think any power on earth could have made me give her up. Especially because of another man who may not even be alive."

"It was the hardest thing I've ever had to do. Well, it all turned out alright anyway. If we had stayed together, had gotten married, she'd be a widow in a few days anyway. I have, as Alan Seeger said, 'a rendezvous with death.' Are you familiar with the poetry of Alan Seeger?"

"No."

"He predicted his death in a poem. He was a soldier in the Great War, and died in battle in 1916. In the last lines of the poem, *I Have a Rendezvous with Death*, he says:

> *But I've a rendezvous with Death*
> *At midnight in some flaming town,*
> *When Spring trips north again this year,*
> *And I to my pledged word am true,*
> *I shall not fail that rendezvous.*

Dade nodded. "I've never been sure I was going to die before going into battle. On my first war patrol, there came a time during the battle that I was certain I was going to die, but not before. And, when I got that feeling, I was too busy trying to keep me and the crew alive that I had no time to think about my death. I can't imagine what it must be like to know before the battle that you're going to die."

"It's not so bad," Will shrugged. "You feel a little sorry for yourself, but the overall feeling you have is one of peace."

"No anger? No feeling that it just isn't fair?"

"No. What helps is that I believe that there's a life after this one."

"I believe that too. In fact, I can guarantee you that there is."

"The ghost you spoke to?"

"Yes. And months ago, I was getting regular visitations from another ghost. But I made my peace with him and he won't be back. No, there's an afterlife alright, but I don't know what it's like. I mean, I don't think it's anything like people wearing white robes and having wings and halos and playing harps."

Will laughed. "I don't think that either. I think it's probably nothing like we imagine. In fact, I think it's probably nothing like we're *able* to imagine."

They stood in easy silence for a while longer. "I guess your men will also have letters they'll want sent if they don't come back?"

"No, we're a superstitious lot, those of us on these teams. We believe it's bad luck to leave a letter behind like that. There've been more than a few cases of people dying who do that. Of course, people die who don't leave those letters too, but the superstition persists."

"But, in your case, it's OK, because you know you're going to die."

"Right."

"I hate this fucking war."

"Me too."

47

December 14, 1942

Off the Coast of Kyushu, Japan

Oliver Wirtz looked away from the periscope for a moment and blinked his stinging eyes several times. They hurt badly. He looked at his watch and saw that it was 0126 before turning back to look in the periscope. The *Sea Otter* held its position at the northern end of the mouth of the small bay, waiting for the patrol boat to leave. It had entered the bay at 0106. The weather was not completely what both Dade and Jones had hoped for, but it was nothing to complain about. It was a cloudy night, and it was only occasionally that the crescent moon shone through. Oliver was afraid, very afraid. That dark land mass out there was Japan itself. It was close enough to swim to, for God's sake! The boat was rigged for red, every light glowing a dim red, so they'd already have night vision when the hatch was cracked.

Oliver consoled himself with the fact that everyone was probably scared. When speech was necessary, everyone spoke in a near whisper, as if the Japanese were close enough to hear them. Even the skipper spoke softly.

"It won't be long now," Dade said to Captain Jones, who stood beside him, gear strapped to his uniform, face blackened, and wearing a wool knit watch cap. Jones nodded in reply.

"Here, Ollie," Dade said. "I'll take over for a while."

Wirtz gratefully relinquished his post at the periscope and stood next to Jones. He wanted to say something to the man, but couldn't think of a thing. It must be something, he thought, to be so brave. To actually go ashore onto the soil of Japan itself with only seven other men and only small arms, knowing you were going

244

into a fight. Knowing you couldn't call anyone for help. Knowing so many damned things could go wrong you couldn't even count them. He admired this man greatly and wanted to tell him so, but the only words he could think of would make him sound stupid. Everyone's face was lit by the light from red bulbs, making Oliver think that they looked like they were at the entrance to hell. An involuntary shiver went down his spine.

"There she goes," said Dade. "The patrol boat is leaving now. We'll give it a couple of minutes and then we'll move in. Things are on schedule so far." He continued to watch as the patrol boat exited the bay and turned southeast. After that, he took one last, long, slow 360-degree look and ordered, "All ahead one-third. Prepare to surface."

"All ahead one-third. Prepare to surface."

After two minutes, Dade spoke again. "Surface."

"Surface. Surface." The klaxon sounded three times. *Ahoooooouga! Ahooooooga! Ahooooooga!*

"All hands detailed to assist the Army personnel with their equipment and boats on deck. All Army personnel on deck."

"All hands detailed to assist the Army personnel with their equipment and boats on deck. All Army personnel on deck."

Everyone moved very quickly and silently. In a matter of minutes, the OSS men were clambering into their inflatable boats. "OK, we're going to sit on the bottom for exactly 60 minutes. If you guys get the job done early, get on the shore and keep flashing the letter 'V' over and over. We'll constantly be scanning through the search scope on high magnification, looking for your signal."

"Dot dot dot dash, got it," replied Jones. "Remember some of us may be coming back wounded, maybe seriously."

"I'll have our pharmacist's mate standing by."

"We may also have Japanese soldiers chasing us. If you could give us covering fire in that eventuality—"

"I'll take care of it."

"Remember, if we're not back by 0415, that means we're dead. Leave without us. OK, that's it then," Jones said, extending his hand. "It was nice meeting you, Dade. Good luck to you, your wife, and baby."

"Thanks, Will," Dade replied, shaking his hand. "It was a privilege knowing you." Both men knew they wouldn't be seeing each other again. "I'll miss our talks."

Then Will was in one of the two boats and the men began to paddle rapidly toward the enemy shore. "All hands below! Clear the bridge! Prepare to dive!"

In only minutes, everyone was below. Dade stood in the conning tower over the hatch and shouted below to Detrick in the control room. "Flood her down gently and set her on the bottom, Tom."

Detrick repeated the command and, as water flowed into the ballast tanks, the boat slowly began a descent. It was like riding in a very slow elevator, but the trip was short, ending in a slight bump, then all was still and silent, bathed in the glow of the red lights located throughout the *Sea Otter*. Dade looked at his watch, and saw that it was 0204. He thought for a few moments and then picked up the handset and spoke to the entire crew on the 1MC.

"Men, this is the captain speaking. The Army team that just went ashore is due back here at 0345. It's possible that they'll be early, and, in that event, they'll signal us from the shore with one of their flashlights. The recognition symbol will be the letter 'V' in Morse code. We'll be watching through the search scope for that signal. Either at 0345 or earlier, if they're running early, we'll surface and prepare to take them back aboard. They'll be bringing two elderly Japanese civilians with them. It is possible that some of the team will be wounded, so Frost, prepare for that eventuality. When we surface, all gun crews will man their assigned guns for two reasons. First, the Army team may be pursued by Japanese soldiers, in which case we will give them covering fire. Second, in the event a Japanese patrol boat appears, we'll have no choice but to fight it out on the surface. We won't see water deep enough to maneuver in until we're back in the channel. In the meantime, all we can do is wait." He put the handset back in its clip and ordered, "We'll be using the search scope. Up periscope."

"Search scope. Up periscope."

"Oliver, watch for that signal."

"Aye aye, sir."

"Chief Robhar to the Captain's stateroom."

"Chief Robhar to the Captain's stateroom."

In the control room on his way to his stateroom, he asked Tom Detrick to follow him. Once both men were in his room, he asked them to have a seat on his bunk and he sat in his chair. "You two are very smart guys, and have no doubt figured out by now that this mission is something above and beyond any other mission you've been on, heard about, or even imagined. It's been represented to me by . . . . . . well, a very credible authority that it has the possibility of even shortening the war by as much as two years. The war has made me kind of cynical, but I believe this may be true. A lot of things can go wrong ashore, and I believe it's necessary to have an emergency backup plan. Of all the members of this crew, you are, I think the best. If things reach a point when I deem it necessary, I intend to go ashore to support the Army team in their mission. We won't go unless I have good reason to believe that something has gone wrong. If that happens, you and I will take one of our small inflatables and go ashore. I know exactly where we're going and the floorplans of the buildings in the compound. The mission is to bring those two Japanese civilians back to the sub. Chief, I'd like you to get the arms we'll need. Detrick, are you checked out on the tommy gun?"

"No, sir, but I qualified as an expert on the M1 and the .45."

"Very well, Chief get tommy guns for you and me and an M1 for Mister Detrick. Oh, and .45's for all three of us. Get us a lot of extra ammo too."

The Chief of the Boat nodded grimly. Detrick's face betrayed no expression.

"Now this may not even be necessary. I hope it's not. I hope that everything goes according to plan. But we need a backup plan in case it doesn't. Any questions?"

Both men shook their heads. "OK, that's it then. Thank you." After they'd left, Dade sat in his chair and thought. He knew that things weren't going to go according to plan. The OSS team would lose at least one man. And if Will was going to die, it seemed probable that others would too. If this were happening in a book or movie, the commander in his place would have asked for volunteers. That's the way it was usually done in fiction. But this was real life, and Dade needed his two best men. Volunteers were overrated. All too often a man who volunteered for a supremely dangerous mission was simply a fool who lacked the imagination to envision his own death or maiming, or someone who was brave and strong and skilled only in his own mind, but not in reality. Bowie sighed deeply. There was no time to write a last letter to Rachael. At least not enough time to write all that was in his heart. That would take more time than he had. A lot more time. He supposed he was doing the right thing, but couldn't be sure. That was the thing about nearly all the major decisions he'd had to make during this past year of war. At the time, he could never be sure he was doing the right thing. In the peacetime Navy, a man could make a mistake and the worst thing that could happen was that he'd get a bad fitness report. That affected his chances for promotion, of course, but considerations like that seemed so trivial now. Now, when mistakes could mean the deaths of many men, including one's own. Peacetime was as far away now as childhood, and wartime stretched out for unknown years ahead. There was a chance that no one on the *Sea Otter* would ever see peacetime again. Who was it who said, "Only the dead have seen the end of war"? He remembered now; it was George Santayana. That was a grim thought, but undoubtedly true.

Dade felt as if he were moving toward something that was predetermined, fated. That there was a destiny assigned to every man and that his idea that he had any control over it was an illusion. Whatever was happening and would happen in the next couple of hours had already been written. Yes, Rachael had told him that Islam was deterministic, that the Arabic word *Maktub* literally meant, "It is written," to signify something that must happen. That God wills it to happen, so no man can keep it from happening. Perhaps his death in an hour or two was written. John Henry had told him what would happen if he attacked the Japanese troop transport, so, obviously that had not been written. Bowie had had a clear choice. But perhaps the reason John Henry could not tell him what would happen on this mission was that the outcome *was* written and could not be changed. It was not that Bowie had a premonition of his death, like Will had. No, it wasn't a certainty. But it was a very, very real possibility, even a probability. He and Tom and the Chief weren't trained commandos like the OSS men. But he knew he should go, that he should *try* to see that this mission was accomplished.

He looked at his watch and stood, then looked down on his tiny desk at the framed three-by-five photograph of Rachael. More than anything else in the world at this moment, he longed to hold her in his arms. He picked up the picture frame and held it against his heart for a moment, then set it down and left to go to the conning tower.

It was 0305. Dade picked up the 1MC handset. "This is the captain speaking. We're about to surface, men. Everyone get ready to move smartly. Gun crews are to get to their stations fast and prepare for action. In addition to having the deck gun and the two 40-mm guns manned, I want you to break out the two .50-cal. machine guns and set them up, one forward and one aft. If that patrol boat comes back early, or another comes by, we'll need to fight on the surface, so be ready. Lookouts, be especially sharp. It's also possible we may have to give covering fire if the OSS team is being chased by Japanese soldiers. Frost, stand by for casualties. OK, men. Surface the boat."

"Surface the boat."

As the water cascaded from the decks and the hatches popped open, men rushed to their assigned stations. They did it quickly and silently, and Bowie was proud of them. Japan itself lay to the starboard and port, as well as aft. Japan, with its teeming millions and their complete devotion to their Emperor and to their nation. Once everyone was in place, Dade consulted his watch. It was 0315, and his eyes strained for the sight of the OSS team along the shoreline, but he saw nothing. Wirtz had not seen the "V" sign in Morse while they had been submerged. Uneasy, he walked over to Robhar, and quietly said, "Get the boat ready and you and Detrick get the weapons. We launch from the same place we launched the OSS team. The Chief nodded and walked off quickly. Dade walked along the deck toward the stern, hands in his pockets. It was cold. He turned and walked over to Oliver, who stood near the cigarette deck, scanning for a sign of the OSS team.

"Oliver, I think something may have gone wrong. If we need to, Chief Robhar, Tom Detrick, and I are going ashore to see if we can't help out."

"But sir, they're not due back until 0345. And, in the briefing with CINCPAC and when we saw Captain Jones off, the understanding was that we were to wait for them until 0415, and, if they weren't back by then, to leave without them. There was nothing in the plan about us sending a shore party. Nothing at all." Then they all heard the shots. They were somewhat muffled. Some of the sounds sounded like cracks, and others like pops, but it was clear they were all coming from firearms up the slope at the top of the hill.

"There it is now. I had a feeling about this. Operating on my own initiative, I'm leaving now. There's no further need for silence now that there's a serious firefight going on. Get the diesels running. I want to top off the battery charge as fast as possible. We may need every bit of juice we have in order to evade."

"Aye aye, sir."

Both men watched Detrick and Robhar carefully set the small boat in the water. Tom and Armond wore .45 automatics on their pistol belts, and Detrick had an M1 slung over his shoulder. Robhar approached Dade and handed him a Thompson submachine gun, then, one by one, four spare magazines. Dade put two in his front pockets and two in his rear pockets. One had already been inserted into the gun.

"Thanks Chief, you and Mister Detrick stand by. Oliver, if that patrol boat or another one appears, you should keep your bow toward him to present as narrow a silhouette as possible. It's a dark night and the dark mass of the land behind the boat will help hide you. Tell the deck gun crew to concentrate on his forward 120-mm gun as he comes toward you. Tell our forward 40-mm crew to concentrate on his forward 25-mm antiaircraft gun. Tell the forward .50-cal. crew to keep on raking his bridge. Don't open fire until he's 300 yards away unless he spots you before that. Have all four engines ready to answer bells. You'll have to maneuver fast. He may try to ram you. Blow the hell out of him, and get out of this bay at flank speed. You've got to get to water deep enough to dive and maneuver in. Then you've got to get out of the channel back into the open sea. They'll be tin cans coming from all over. They'll expect you to take the shortest route to the open sea, by hugging the coast of Kyushu. Fool them by heading straight east and hugging the coast of Shikoku on the way out."

"And leave you and the others behind, skipper?"

"Yes, if we're not back aboard by then, leave us. You'll have only one chance to get out of this alive and get the crew back safely, and you'll have to act fast and decisively."

"I understand, sir." Oliver swallowed hard and blinked his eyes a few times. This was nothing like being XO of a Sub School training boat. It was nothing like his day-to-day duties had been thus far as XO of the *Sea Otter* either. Whenever he had pictured the combat he'd see in the Pacific in a submarine, he'd pictured tracking a target through periscope observations, and firing torpedoes when the TDC solution light lit. Not gun action in a Japanese bay in the early morning hours.

"OK, this is it then," Dade said. "Chief, let's go. Ollie, the boat's all yours. I know I can count on you. Just remember these people aren't supermen. If you see that patrol boat or any other coming into the bay, remember that they're just as afraid of you as you are of them." He clasped Wirtz's left shoulder with his right hand and squeezed hard."

Oliver nodded. "Just make it back here, skipper."

"We'll do our best." Then, it seemed like only a moment before he was in the boat with Tom and the Chief, both of them paddling furiously to shore. Things were going so quickly he hadn't even any memory of climbing in. They hit the shore.

"OK, guys, follow me. We're going to be going into the back gate of a walled compound. It's supposed to have been opened by one of the OSS team from the inside. If it's not open, we'll have to go around to the main gate. Be careful, be ready to fire at any moment, but only at uniformed Japanese soldiers." Then Dade took off at a run. He no longer felt cold. Instead, he was invigorated by the run up the pathway that led up the slope. It was an easy run because of all the adrenalin that had been dumped into his bloodstream. Then he suddenly stopped by the teahouse. When he had accepted the Thompson from the Chief, he had forgotten to pull the bolt back. The submachine gun fired from an open bolt. Pulling the trigger would slam the bolt forward and fire the first round at the same time. After pulling the bolt back, he said with a little embarrassment, "I forgot."

"We're OK, sir," the Chief smiled. "I only thought of it when we stepped out on the shore, and Mr. Detrick's got his M1 locked and loaded, safety off. We're ready for anything."

At that point, Dade realized he'd hadn't thought about another thing. Unlike the OSS team, he and his men had no L capsules. If they were captured alive by the Kempeitai, they would die long, agonizing deaths by torture. "Right. OK, let's go."

They were at the top of the hill before Bowie had expected to be, and the gate was open. It was dark, but the main house was lit. Then there was a bright flash and an explosion. The back door of the main house, which was a sliding door, had been blown open, perhaps by a hand grenade, and Dade saw four figures in Kempeitai uniform, armed with rifles, about to go in. Their backs were to Dade and his men. Instantly, Dade stopped and sprayed a long burst of fire at them. As he did, Tom and the Chief came alongside him and added their own firepower. The Japanese never had a chance. The first of them fell into the large hole blown in the door earlier.

In order to avoid being downed by friendly fire, Bowie shouted, "U.S. Navy coming in the back door! Don't shoot!"

"Who's Superman's girlfriend?"

"Lois Lane."

"Come on in, Navy!" shouted an American voice.

Dade was unprepared for what he saw. The bullet-riddled front door, off to his right, had been blown off its hinges, and there was the body of an American soldier beside it. The large windows on the front of the house had been shot away and there were bullet holes everywhere. Bits of broken glass covered the floor of the living room, as well as broken furniture. There were more bodies too, some Japanese Kempeitai, some American. There were pools of blood, large pools, in many places, as well as spent cartridges, empty magazines, and other military items strewn, seemingly haphazardly about. Dade noticed an arm clad in an olive drab sleeve. It lay at his feet, and had come from an American body seven feet away. On the arm was a wrist watch, and he saw that the sweep hand of the watch still made its way around the dial, as if everything was normal. Off in one corner, huddled and trembling, were an old Japanese man and woman in kimonos. Other than them, only two other bodies showed signs of life. One was Will Jones, obviously wounded badly. He was in a sitting position, with his back up against a long, low table on the floor scarred by shrapnel. He held his submachine gun at the ready, his attention toward the front of the house. The other, one of Will's men, was crouched, facing the back door. Dade ran over to Will, whose first words were, "What in the hell are you guys doing here?"

Dade knelt beside him. "Things got kind of dull back at the boat, so we decided to take a walk."

"You came at exactly the right time. Maybe you guys can yet save the day. Stan and I were just about to," he glanced over at Dr. Nakamura, "exercise our last option. There's no way the two of us can get him out of here. I've been hit with three rounds and shrapnel from the grenades they threw through the windows. I'm bleeding out internally. If I'm lucky, I've got maybe 15 or 20 minutes left. Stan's been hit in the shoulder and abdomen. A rifle bullet broke his right leg. He's not going anywhere either. Listen. We don't have much time," he said. Dade saw how pale his face was and how he had to strain to both breathe and talk.

"There were a lot more Kempeitai billeted here than we thought. I make it out to be about 25. We took out all the exterior guards as planned, but when we hit the courtyard, all hell broke loose. We had surprise on our side, but these were good troops. Stan and I are the only ones left alive. There's about five or six Kempeitai left alive, I think, and they're all out of grenades. At least no more have been sailing through the front windows. I killed their officer and at least two of their senior NCO's, so they're kind of unsure about what to do next. Trouble is, when I killed one of the NCO's, he was on the phone, and we have to assume he was calling for help. I don't know how long it will be before that gets here, but I think it'll be soon.

"All Stan and I can do is offer our services as a rear guard. I explained everything to Dr. Nakamura and he and his wife are coming along willingly. You and your guys get them to the sub fast. Drag me out to the rain barrel to the right of the rear gate and Stan to the shed to the left of it. Do it now and do it fast. We might have only minutes. We'll cover your withdrawal."

"OK, do you need anything else?"

"Yes, we're almost out of ammo."

"We'll give each of you our tommy guns with four loaded stick magazines for each. That still leaves us our M1 and our pistols."

"Good. Thanks. Let's do it now!"

"Chief! Tom! Get over here!" Dade explained what they were doing. He told Tom to take the Nakamuras in tow, while he dragged Will out to the rain barrel and Robhar dragged Stan behind the small shed. As he gave Will his submachine gun and magazines, he asked, "Anything else?"

"No, we'll be OK. If we stay alive long enough to use all this ammo, we have our L capsules. Take off fast! Run!"

The five people began to run, but it quickly became obvious that Mrs. Nakamura couldn't keep up. Dade simply scooped her up in his arms and took off running again. He was surprised how little she weighed. Both she and her husband were small people, even by Japanese standards. Dr. Nakamura began lagging too, so Chief Robhar picked him up as well. The three men ran, with Detrick and his M1 bringing up the rear. As they got to the place where the boats were beached, they heard heavy gunfire erupt above and behind them.

"We'll take one of the Army boats; they're a little bigger," Dade said, as he helped a terrified Mrs. Nakamura into one. In a moment, all five were loaded and the three Navy men paddled furiously toward the submarine, spurred on by the continual gunfire. Once there, they were met by Oliver Wirtz and the men who had been manning the aft .50-caliber machine gun. As they were helped out, Dade said, "Forget the boat! Just get the Nakamuras down the after torpedo room hatch!" To Wirtz, he said, "All ahead flank! Course Zero Nine Zero! Get us out of the bay as fast as possible so we have deep enough water to dive! All lookouts and gun crews below! Clear the bridge! Prepare to dive! I'll be on the bridge to give the order when we're ready. Everyone else below now!"

Oliver raced to relay the orders, while Dade stood for a moment to listen to the gunfire. Bowie thought it was slackening off. Then he ran to the bridge. As he ran, he felt the deck beneath him begin to vibrate as the four powerful diesels began to push the *Sea Otter* to its maximum speed. Sure, he thought, the patrol boat wasn't due back for another 30 minutes, but if Kempeitai reinforcements had been called, the man receiving the call could very well have alerted the Japanese Navy, since the Americans could only have been put ashore by submarine. If the Navy had been alerted, the patrol boat would be pounding its way back here at maximum speed and its battle stations manned and ready for trouble. Other boats could be on the way too.

Now the *Sea Otter* was surging ahead toward the mouth of the bay, the deep water in the channel tantalizingly close. Dade peered forward, then walked around and glanced aft. Everyone was below and all hatches were closed except the one to the conning tower. As the sub burst into the channel, he hit the klaxon twice and ordered, "Dive! Dive!", then jumped into the hatch, sliding down the ladder by holding its sides until his shoes thumped on the deck. The quartermaster closed the hatch behind him. "Periscope depth," Dade ordered.

"Periscope depth." In preparation for this mission, Dade had carefully memorized the chart of the area. For seven nights on the way here, he had studied hard to commit it to memory, including the soundings in the channel. To test himself, he had finally drawn the chart from memory, then compared it to the real thing. The two charts were completely identical. Therefore, Dade knew that the depth of the water where they were now was 300 feet, and as they continued further into it, the depth increased to 500 feet. "Up scope."

"Up scope." It was still dark. Dade didn't expect to see another ship, and he didn't, although he slowly covered 360 degrees twice. "Down scope."

"Down scope."

"Sonar contact bearing zero nine zero," Quigley said, his voice tense. "Sounds like a patrol boat. From the rpms on his screws, I'd say he's doing about 18 knots."

"Very well. That's the Type 31's top speed. He's early."

"Should we rig for silent running, sir?" Oliver asked.

"No, right now he has only one thought in mind—to charge into that bay and find out what the hell is going on. He's hoping to find a sub in there. He'll be at battle stations and have his searchlights fore and aft lighting things up. He won't be paying attention to his sonar now. Plus the only chance we have is to put as much distance between us and that bay as fast as possible. When they figure out what happened, there'll be more and more and more tin cans showing up to search for us. In another hour or two, we won't have a chance." A few moments went by as Dade consulted his watch. A moment before, he had automatically put the lanyard hooked to a stopwatch around his neck, and checked his watch again. His watch was more than a watch. It was a precise Swiss chronometer Hank Turner had given him upon his graduation from Annapolis. Dade used both in dead reckoning navigation. His *idiot savant* skill of being able to perform many mathematical calculations in his head at once and his taking into account his knowledge of the rate at which a submarine slowed or sped up when changing speeds enabled him to navigate with precision underwater. In fact, he was known throughout the Silent Service for his uncanny accuracy.

"Contact now bearing one seven four. Speed unchanged."

"Very well. Come right to course one six five."

"Come right to course one six five." Now they were running parallel to the coast of Shikoku, headed southeast. The patrol boat would be in the bay now, nosing around. Dade wondered briefly if finding the inflatable boats would slow them down while they investigated that, or, whether not immediately seeing the sub would send it out racing into the channel to find it. As he'd told Oliver, he believed that the Japanese would be betting that the sub would take the most direct route out to the sea, hugging the coast of Kyushu. As long as there were no sonar contacts except the patrol boat, they would not rig for silent running yet, but he decided to reduce the speed to save energy on the batteries.

"All ahead two-thirds."

"All ahead two-thirds."

Dade looked at his watch again, picturing where they were now on the charts. He had a brief thought of Will. He'd be dead by now, along with the rest of his men. Eight good men gone. Eight heroic men. He hoped that what they had died for would turn out to be worth it. But then, so many people were dying needlessly in this war. How many submariners had died in the early months of the war because the damned torpedo exploders wouldn't work right? How many Marines and airmen died because of inaccurate intelligence reports? Hell, you could go crazy just think—

"Sonar contact bearing one three zero."

"Very well. He's out of the bay now and he'll be after us. I'm betting he's going to be looking along the southwestern part of the channel." Dade thought it would be nice to get a fathometer reading, but he was concerned that an alert man on the patrol boat's sonar would hear the single ping, although it was unlikely at this range. "Up scope."

"Up scope"

Dade scanned 360 degrees before trying to estimate how far the *Sea Otter* was from the coastline of Shikoku. He wanted to stay as close as possible as long as they could count on at least 300 feet of water beneath the keel. He looked at his watch. "Down scope."

"Down scope." So far, so good, but the first tin cans would be showing up any time now. Dade decided to remain at all ahead two-thirds for the time being.

"Another contact, bearing zero one nine. High speed screws."

"Very well." There was the first destroyer. This was going to be tough. Dade thought of the Japanese scientist aboard and wondered again if the man was worth it. He'd better be. Goddamn it, he'd better be. "Up scope."

"Up scope."

Because it was dark, he expected to see neither of the ships they were tracking by sonar; they were too far away, but he did a quick 360-degree search to see if there were any others that may be nearby and not moving. Then he looked hard at the dark coastline to the east. "Down scope."

"Down scope."

"A third sonar contact. High speed screws. Bearing three four zero."

"Very well. All ahead one-third. Rig for silent running. Make your depth 200 feet."

"All ahead one-third. Rig for silent running. Make your depth 200 feet." If he was right according to his dead reckoning and memory of the chart, the depth below the keel was now at least 300 feet. Someone on one of those three Japanese ships, almost certainly one of the tin can captains, had taken control and was directing the search operations over the radio now. And there'd be more tin cans on the way. If, Dade thought, he were that man, he'd have the patrol boat continue to search along the southwest part of the channel, he'd take the middle, and he'd have the remaining tin can search along the northeast part of the channel. But that was a problem. The sonar in use by the Japanese had an effective maximum range of 3,000 yards at optimum conditions. This meant that, if the ships were positioned perfectly, the two end ships 3,000 yards from the shore, and 6,000 yards between those two ships and the middle ship, they could cover 18,000 yards, or 8.89 nautical miles. But that wouldn't be nearly enough to cover the channel's width, which was about 21 nautical miles wide at this point, and for miles yet to come before it got even wider. If the hunter banked on the sub hugging either the southeast or northwest coast, and kept two ships within 3,000 yards of the two coasts, that accounted for two 6,000-yard swaths, leaving only one tin can to search the 30,000-yard swath in the middle. One tin can to search a 14.81-mi. swath. A really, really, good ASW skipper and crew could do this and maybe even succeed with a little bit of luck by using the sprint and listen technique. The faster a tin can was going, the less effective its active sonar. This is why trying to find a sub often meant sprinting to where you thought he might be, slow down or even stop, listen, then, if you didn't find him, sprint to another place and do the same thing.

But the Japanese skipper had another option. He could space out the three ships equally, with about 10,000 yards between each of them and 10,000 yards between the two end ships and the coasts, and have them search up and down the channel. This would amount to 19.75 nautical miles, effectively covering most of the channel. Except that there would be 7,000 yards between the coasts and the end ships that would not be covered by sonar at all. It would also mean that there would be 4,000 yards between the first ship and the middle ship and between the third ship and the middle ship that would have no sonar coverage.

A third option was to place all three ships equidistant from each other at the mouth of the channel, and have them conduct sweeps in single file in one continuous tight oval, from one end of the mouth to the other end of the mouth.

Which of the three strategies would the Japanese skipper use? Dade decided he'd take the first one, and he bet the Japanese skipper had that in mind too. This meant he had to navigate down the middle of the channel, down that 14.81-mi. swath now being searched by one tin can. He also had to bet that the Japanese skipper would be zig zagging as he sprinted and listened in order to cover more ground and to be more unpredictable. Also, Dade had to act fast before more t in cans showed up. He'd have to roll the dice. "All ahead two-thirds."

"All ahead two-thirds."

"Bearings and approximate speeds on the sonar contacts," Bowie ordered.

"Contact One bears zero seven six, and he's slowed down. Sounds like about 10 knots. Contact Two bears zero one four and is slowing to about 10 knots also. Contact Three bears three three five and is doing about thirty knots."

"Very well," Dade acknowledged, picturing all the ships superimposed on a chart of the channel. They could do this. Just, please God, no more tin cans. Contact Three hadn't slowed much yet because that was evidently the ship that was going to search along the northeast part of the channel. He was right. The Japanese skipper had decided to go with the first option. It would be nice to have a range on Contact Two, but if Dade used his active sonar, it would give them away instantly.

"New sonar contact! Bearing one eight zero! Faint sound of high-speed screws coming fast! Sounds like a tin can at max speed. He's a long ways behind us."

"Very well." OK, Bowie thought, OK. He consulted his watch again and scanned the chart in his mind, estimating where each of the four ships hunting the *Sea Otter* were now and where they'd be going. If Contact Three had slowed to get better results from his sonar, it meant he was in position and was about 3,000 yards off the coast of Shikoku.

He had to get through the cordon before Contact Four joined up with the other three ships. Two destroyers searching that 14.81-mi. swath would make it nearly impossible to get through. The best they could hope for in that eventuality was a temperature gradient, a layer of water that's at a different temperature than the water directly above it. A gradient shields the sub from sonar because the abrupt change in temperature bends the sonar waves around it. It was a great way to elude tin cans, but almost never around when you needed one. He walked over and glanced at the bathythermograph without much hope. Nope.

The *Sea Otter* would be tougher to find if he slowed his speed to one-third, but, with more tin cans on the way, there was no time. Dade consulted his watch. Time for a course change. "Come left to course one four seven."

"Come left to course one four seven." He was going to take a straight line course out of the channel. There was no time for anything else. He would stay 10,000 yards off the northeastern coast. They'd listen carefully and be prepared to take immediate evasive action, but there was no real time to spare. "Quigley, I'm most interested in Contact Two. What's his bearing and speed now?"

There was a long pause before the sonarman replied, "I don't hear him at all now, skipper! He must have stopped dead in the water!"

"Keep me informed on him." Dade frowned deeply. Standard protocol would be for the *Sea Otter* to come to a complete stop now too, and wait until that tin can started moving again. But there was no time. No time. He had to take chances to get out of this. "How about Contact Four?"

"Contact four bears one nine zero degrees. He's getting closer, but still a little ways off."

"Very well."

Dade couldn't slow down, and he didn't want to make any more noise by running at full speed either. He looked at his stopwatch. They were in deep enough water now. The sounding here was 650 feet. There was only one other defensive measure he could take. "Make your depth 420 feet."

"Make your depth 420 feet."

It was already uncomfortably hot and humid. With the air conditioning and fans off, it didn't take long for the heat generated by the machinery and the bodies of the crew themselves to make things bad. The oxygen level was now slowly decreasing and the carbon dioxide level increasing, although it would be a while before that became a concern. Dade remembered how, on his first war patrol on the *Elver*, that had become almost a matter of life and death. Dade guessed the temperature was in the high 80's now and rising fast. The humidity was about the same. Men in every compartment were sweating and uncomfortable, but the only concern on their minds at this moment was the Japanese hunters above and near them. He looked at Quigley. While he was a Petty Officer 2nd Class, he was only 20 years old and looked younger. He was a skinny, freckle-faced kid only two years out of high school and, to a large extent, the lives of the entire crew rested on his skill and judgement. When Dade had been told he could bring (with COMSUBPAC's approval) seven men from the *Elver* with him to the *Sea Otter*, Quigley was his third pick. The first two had been Chief Robhar and Tom Detrick. Quigley was good, damned good. In fact, at Sonar School, they had been so impressed with him that they tried to make him an instructor, but Quigley had wanted sea duty. Yes, he had proved himself time and again aboard the *Elver*. Still, there was something odd about one of the most important men on the boat looking like a high school sophomore.

"Contact Two bears one four six degrees! He's picking up speed!"

So he was astern of the *Sea Otter* now. Dade's first reaction was one of relief. He had passed them by. But he could just as easily turn around and overtake the sub instantly. Destroyers could do better than 30 knots without breaking a sweat. He could be ahead of them in minutes and be listening for them up there. "Quigley! Is Contact Two getting louder or growing fainter?"

"Louder, skipper."

"Very well. How about Contact Four?"

"Coming on. His bearing is one seven zero."

Damn. There was no time left. Soon he'd be in the immediate area. Right now, he was probably being given instructions on where to search once he got here. There was no time. Dade would stay on this course at this speed and trust to luck and prayer. Right. Prayer. *Look, God, I know it's been a while. But get me through this one too. It's not just me on board this boat. There are 61 other men aboard too, and they all have families. Oh, and the Nakamuras. Maybe Dr. Nakamura can shorten this war. That would save hundreds of thousands of people. Maybe even a million or more. But, yes, to be honest, mostly I'm thinking of me. I need to see Rachael again. I don't want everything to end just as my life is beginning to have joy and meaning. I want those children. I want grandchildren. I want to live in a new world where wars aren't fought anymore. Please, get me and my men through this. Amen.* "What's the bearing and approximate speed of Contact Two?"

"He bears zero nine zero now, passing by us at about 15 knots."

"Very well." Dade looked around the conning tower at the tense group of men. Greenbaum sat at the TDC, carefully regarding his folded hands. There was nothing for him to do, nor was there much for anyone to do except for Quigley. The few other crewmen actually doing something right now, like the steersman and the planesmen, only maintained the *Sea Otter* at the same course, speed, and depth until ordered otherwise by Bowie. And Bowie saw changing none of those things in the immediate future. Acting calm was tough on men when their lives were in immediate danger and they knew it. And, at times like this, seconds seemed like minutes and minutes like hours. Men looked casually at their watches, at the switches and dials and buttons and levers in front of them, stole furtive glances at each other, then began the cycle all over again by looking at their watches. They were all praying, Bowie thought. They were all praying, just as he had. They all wanted to live just as much as he did and for all the same reasons. You had people you cared about back there and who cared about you. Even if it was just one person—a wife or girlfriend or mother. Even if it was just one person. Dade thought of Oliver, who was standing next to him. Oliver had four people. His parents and his son and Rosemary. Dade just had Rachael for now, but she was more than enough.

"Contact Two bears zero zero five and is slowing. Now he's stopped."

"Very well." *Great. So he's stopped directly in front of us and is straining to pick up the slightest indication, from a solid sonar return to the sound of the Sea Otter's screws to someone dropping a wrench on the deck.* "How far ahead do you think he is, from the intensity of his pinging?"

"Hard to say, skipper, but probably between 4,000 and 5,000 yards." So spoke a skinny 20-year old kid who held the lives of 62 American sailors and two Japanese nationals in his hands. Not to mention a $6 million submarine.

"Very well." Dade fought an intense internal battle. "Make turns for 2 knots. Steady as you go."

"Make turns for 2 knots. Steady as you go."

If the Japanese destroyer was now 4,000 yards ahead, 2 knots would bring the sub within his sonar range in 15 minutes. His optimum range. Would he lie dead in the water that long, listening before moving on and sniffing at another place? Then again, Quigley said he could be 5,000 yards ahead, which gave them about 30 minutes before coming into his sonar range. Certainly, he wouldn't wait 30 minutes before moving on. Or, he could be less than 4,000 yards ahead or more than 5,000. And if the *Sea Otter* sent a single ping toward the destroyer to get his exact range, he'd nail them for sure. "Where does Contact Four bear?"

"Contact Four bears one six zero."

"Very well." Dade wiped away the sweat from his forehead with the handkerchief he kept in his back right pocket and looked around again. Everyone was sweating profusely. If Contact Four hadn't appeared, he'd have more time, but there was no time to screw around. The *Sea Otter* had to get out of the channel as fast as possible. It was all a crap shoot. "All ahead two-thirds."

"All ahead two-thirds."

The temperature had risen to about 100 degrees and the humidity was about 100 percent. Breathing was difficult. If he could just slip past Contact Two, they stood a good chance. "Let me know when Contact Two starts moving again."

"Let you know when Contact Two starts moving again."

Dade looked at his watch again and tried to think of something inspirational to say to the tense men gathered around him in the cramped confines of the conning tower, but couldn't. They would live or die based on a combination of their skills, the skills of the Japanese who hunted them, and pure blind luck. If the past year of war had taught him nothing else, it had taught him that luck played a very large role in whether a man lived or died in battle. Maybe it was mostly luck, which wasn't a very comforting thought at all. Unless you were of the unshakable opinion that you were a lucky man. The thing about luck though, was that it always ran out. Given enough time, a gambler would always lose. A man could win in the short run, but never in the long run. That's why a city in the desert named Las Vegas flourished. In the long run, the house always won. And a war which was expected to last until well into 1947 was definitely the long run.

Contact Two began to move 19 minutes after it stopped, and the *Sea Otter* continued on her way, along course one four seven until she was in the open sea. Soon all the contacts were astern and the sounds of their screws fading. The Japanese skipper in charge obviously believed that she was still somewhere in the channel, possibly hiding. Dade knew that once the Imperial Navy learned that Dr. Nakamura was missing and apparently aboard an American submarine, it would launch one of the most intense searches ever made. A search that would make the British search for the *Bismarck* look like a small affair. The Japanese would know that the sub could only be bound for either Hawaii, Midway, or Australia, and would search along the most direct routes from the mouth of the Inland Sea to those places. For that reason, Bowie chose an indirect course, which would extend the travel time by a week, but would give the sub a much better chance of getting home.

48

December 16, 1942

Pacific Ocean

They were running on the surface now at night. Enough time had gone by that the ship was on a more or less normal routine now. Things had been so hectic that Dade hadn't had a spare peaceful moment since before they'd entered the Inland Sea on the way to the peninsula where the Nakamura compound had been. He hadn't even known that Detrick had been wounded back at the compound until he saw him wearing a sling hours after the sub had made its way into the open sea.

"It's nothing, skipper," he'd said. "Just a slight graze. I don't think I even really need this sling. Frost cleaned out the wound and put some sulfa powder in it. Then he stitched it up and put a bandage on it. It's actually not a very big wound at all. He said I should use the sling to try to keep me from moving the arm too much so it wouldn't put strain on the stitches. At least for a week or so."

"Well, do it then. That was a damned fine job you did with me and the Chief. You're a good man."

"Thank you, sir."

After they'd been at sea for twenty hours, Dade had spoken to the men about the Nakamuras over the 1MC:

"This is the Captain speaking. As you all know, we have two Japanese nationals aboard. They'll be coming to Pearl Harbor with us. Doctor and Mrs. Nakamura are our guests, they are not prisoners, but people who have voluntarily decided to go to the United States. They are to be treated with the greatest respect and with genuine friendliness. Dr. Nakamura speaks English, but his wife does not. Please show them every courtesy. I need every lookout and every radar and sonar operator to be on his toes every second he's on duty. The same goes for the Officer of the Deck and the Junior Officer of the Deck. Dr. Nakamura is a VIP and they won't be happy with his leaving. Expect half the Imperial Navy to be trying to hunt us down now."

The night was chilly as Dade stood at the rail of the cigarette deck, looking back at their wake and enjoying a cigarette. Suddenly, Dr. Nakamura was beside him. "It is permitted to smoke now?"

"Yes," Dade replied.

Nakamura lit up and exhaled a long plume with satisfaction. "I smoke too much," he admitted, "but it helps me to think."

"Yes, it helps me sometimes too."

"I just wanted to thank you and your men for your . . . . . . well, for all you have done for us."

"You're welcome, sir, but the greatest thanks should go to the eight Army men who went ashore to pick you up."

"Yes, and, unfortunately it is not possible to thank them. All of them are dead?"

"Yes. And they were all fine men; they were all heroes. On the voyage to Japan, I got to know their leader very well. If there had been more time, he and I might have become best friends. I had great respect and admiration for him. I liked him a lot."

"I am sorry. I am sorry for the war. It is not something that most Japanese wanted. For a short while, it looked like we might even be successful in setting up a democracy. But then, in November 1930, the militarists assassinated our prime minister, Mr. Hamaguchi, and they took over completely. The following year, we invaded Manchuria, and we were off on a road that would only lead to total war. I think that, in every nation's life, there is a point of no return, and that was ours. But opposing the militarists meant death."

Dade simply nodded and both men continued to smoke in silence for a few moments before Nakamura spoke again. "Do you know why the United States wants me?"

"I only know that you're the top scientist in a project very much like one my own country is working on. I think they believe that you may be able to help them."

"Is that all?"

"Pretty much. I know nothing of the project itself. It's very highly classified."

"Yes. Well, you see this puts me in an awkward position. The Americans almost certainly want me to work on perfecting a weapon, just as the militarists in my own country did."

"I believe that's a fair assumption."

"Yes, but, you see, I am a pacifist."

"Are you a Buddhist?"

"Yes, how did you know?"

"My wife told me that about 60 percent of Japanese are Buddhists. Since you said you're a pacifist, I presume you are guided by the Five Precepts of Buddhism, one of which is to refrain from killing any living beings."

"Yes, that's correct. It interests me that a Westerner knows of the Five Precepts."

"My wife is a very learned person, and she's taught me much about theology, philosophy, and history, among other things."

"A learned woman is a rare thing in Japan. In my 52 years, I have met only a handful. We have always been a traditional society and the role of women has always been to become wives and bear and raise children. Things are changing a little now, but not much. Are things so different now in America? I went to MIT in 1908, earned my PhD in physics, and taught for a year there before returning to Japan in 1916. Since then, I've read many scientific papers written in English, but haven't had any real contact with Americans since 1916. And now, of course, listening to radio broadcasts in English is punishable by death. I haven't read an American newspaper or magazine in years. My son has written us about what Boston is like now, but my knowledge of present-day America is scant."

"It's very different than it must have been in 1916, but I wouldn't know. In 1916, I was only six years old and living in rural Texas."

"Your wife sounds like a remarkable woman."

"Yes, she is. She's the most intelligent and best educated person I ever met. I was very lucky to find her. I've learned so many things from her. She lived in Japan for more than twenty years, and is fluent in the language, as well as knowing a lot about Japanese history, culture, and traditions."

Nakamura's face lit up. "Then she is a friend of the Japanese people?"

"No. No, she's not.

"I am sorry. When this war is over, we will need both Japanese and Americans to help us come together as friends. Someone like your wife could be one of those people."

"I don't believe that's in the cards. At least as far as my wife is concerned. To get back to Buddhism for a moment, perhaps you can help me understand why, if 60 percent of Japanese are Buddhists, they support the war."

"There are two reasons. First, there are different offshoots, different sects of Buddhism, and not all embrace the five precepts. At least, not in their actions. I think it's somewhat like your Christianity in the West. Many people say they are Christians, but not all really scrupulously follow all the teachings of Christ. Second, when the Japanese government *requires* everyone to participate in the war under penalty of prison or death, one can lose his religious fervor rapidly. The point is that I do follow Buddhism, including the Five Precepts."

"But you worked on this project for your own government, and you say that they wanted you to produce a weapon."

Nakamura sighed heavily. "It is not a simple thing. I and other scientists around the world have been researching atomic physics for years. This project will, I and many others believe, produce a source of unimaginable power. The world is close to a breakthrough, and that breakthrough will be the most significant event in human history since man discovered how to control fire. Picture a power source that could light all the cities of the world with cheap and safe electricity. A power that could be used to propel great ships on the ocean that would only need to be refueled every 30 years, a power that could irrigate vast deserts to grow food for millions, a power that could be used in medicine to save countless lives, to provide salt water desalination, and to enable us to explore space!

"Yes, this power can also be harnessed to provide a weapon of incredible devastation. But I think I can safely say that none of the atomic physicists who have been working on these theories for a decade had in mind a weapon until the war started and governments became aware of the destructive potential of the atom. At least, neither I nor any of my colleagues did. But, you see, I could not—as a scientist—simply walk away from working on what, as I said, will turn out to be the greatest advancement in human history. So, yes, perhaps I have compromised my religious beliefs to a degree. In part, I have used as a justification the fact that the enemies of Japan were undoubtedly working on the same thing, and, that if they were the first to make the breakthrough, that weapon would be used against my homeland and its people. The fact that I am now on a submarine bound for America only serves to prove I was right.

"I love my country as, I'm sure, you love yours. Under the militarists, Japan has become an aggressor nation. In starting this war, and invading other countries that have done us no harm, we were wrong. Unfortunately, we may well 'reap the whirlwind.' Even though that's a phrase from the Western Bible, that is also a Buddhist concept—that one must suffer the consequences of wrongs he does. But I love my country. Men come and go, but Japan is forever. One day the militarists will be gone, gone either because the Americans will win the war and eliminate them, or because the Japanese people will rise up and depose them. Either way, one day they will be gone. One must think of the long game.

"Captain Jones told me that, while the Americans would appreciate my telling them how far along our Japanese project is, they would not require me to actively participate in their program. That they may offer me a job, but that I could refuse it if I wished. If that happened, he said I would be free to seek a job of my own, perhaps in teaching at an American university, even my alma mater, MIT. Do you think that's true?"

"Yes, I do. It would be foolish to expect you could force a scientist to make groundbreaking discoveries if his heart isn't in it. In addition, if they decide your assistance isn't needed, my understanding is that the only restriction on your movements is that you will not be allowed to return to Japan until after the war is over. At least that way, the Japanese government would be denied your intellect in its project."

"Yes, well, that sounds entirely reasonable." Both men remained silent for a few moments, both watching the phosphorescent wake of the *Sea Otter*. It was strangely relaxing. Dade lit another cigarette.

Nakamura cleared his throat and spoke. "I do appreciate your coming for me and my wife. And I'm sorry about the eight young men who died. I hate this war. I hate all violence. As a theoretical physicist, I never thought I'd find myself in the center of a world war. I thought I'd spend my life in the world of the mind, of ideas, unlocking the secrets of the universe. Everything quite safe, serene, and removed from unpleasantness. And here I stand on the deck of an enemy submarine, leaving my home. Perhaps for years, perhaps forever. No one can see the future. Well, at least I'll see my son soon. That will be a joyous occasion. Do you have children, Captain?"

"One on the way."

"Ah, then he won't have to fight in this war. Hopefully, he will live his entire life without having to fight in a war."

"That's the kind of world my wife and I hope for."

"Your wife sounds most interesting."

"She's more than interesting. She's very wise. She's a few years older than I, and has had many experiences, most of them bad. They've acted as a crucible. She's also read thousands of the greatest books ever written and learned from them. I never realized how little I knew about life and human nature until I met her. I never realized how shallow and ignorant I was. Oh, I'm an expert on submarines and submarine warfare. But that was all I knew. Now I know so much more and, if I can just get through this war alive, I'll be leaving the Navy and beginning a whole new life."

The slight, frail Japanese scientist lit another cigarette too. "'A whole new life.' That is not a small thing. Many people around the world would give anything for that. Even die for it."

"Yes, I'm a lucky man."

49

December 17, 1942

Oahu

Rachel struggled to consciousness from an unusually deep sleep. At first, she was unaware of what sound she was responding to. She was only aware that it was insistent. She rolled over a few times and tried to ignore whatever it was, but finally realized it was the doorbell. Confused, she looked at the clock on the nightstand and saw that it was 0210. Her first reaction was an icy fear. Something had happened to Dade. Suddenly wide awake, she lay there and thought for a moment. No, that wasn't the way they handled death notifications here, at least for submariners. When a sub was lost or presumed lost, the men who had families here on Oahu were visited by a chaplain and another officer, who notified the wife in person, and it was always during the day. The men whose families were back in the States were notified by telegram. No, Dade was alright. He had to be. The bell continued to ring, over and over again. Rachael got to her feet, put on a robe and slippers, and walked to the front door.

When she opened it, she saw an almost hysterical Alice Detrick. It was raining hard, and the lightning and thunder only served to make her appearance more dramatic. Her hair was thoroughly wet and plastered to her frantic, panicked face.

"Alice! What's wrong?"

"Rachael! May I come in please? I need to talk to you!"

"Of course, please. Can I get you some coffee or tea?"

"No, no thank you."

"Well, let's go into the kitchen to talk. I'll put on some coffee—oh, I also have some cocoa. I could make us some hot chocolate. That's a much more soothing drink when things aren't right. How does that sound?"

"Yes, yes, that would be nice. But can we sit down for a moment first? I need to talk to you."

"Of course, let's sit at the table." Once seated, Rachael waited for Alice to settle down and find the words she needed.

"Tom is in terrible danger!"

Rachael's first reaction was to say, *Join the club, young lady! So is my husband and every submariner on patrol. It's something you learn to live with, like any other grownup.* She wanted to say this, almost said it, not only because it was true, but because she was a little irritated that Alice came to her house at two in the morning to make this pronouncement. That was one of the things about her pregnancy, she'd noted. The fact that she seemed to feel emotions more intensely. Good things made her much happier than normal, and things that would normally make her slightly irritable made her angry. Allowing for this, she waited for a moment before speaking. Finally, she said, "What prompted you to suddenly feel so overwrought? The men are always in danger. On every patrol. You know how many submarines we've been losing since the war began."

"I had a dream two nights ago. I saw a man in a Navy uniform standing in dim moonlight. He was staring off, looking at something I couldn't see. I felt this terrible sense of dread. Then, slowly, he turned to the left, and I could see it was Tom. I could also," she sobbed, "see blood streaming down his left arm."

"What else?"

"Then I woke up. But I had the same dream the next night, and again tonight!"

"I see. Both I and Dade have had some experience with nightmares, Alice," Rachael said soothingly. Dade had a reoccurring nightmare that he was being visited by one of his best friends, Ray, who had been roommates with Dade and Lance at the Academy. Ray's sub never came back from its last patrol. It was a very realistic dream and it terrified Dade. It came again and again. I had, for a long time, a nightmare in which I relived the murder of my first husband, when those Japanese naval cadets chopped him up with samurai swords before my very eyes, blood and gore spattering the walls and the cadets and me. Every now and then I still have it. Do you believe that the dream is some kind of premonition or message that Tom was or will be wounded?"

"Well, yes, I suppose I do. I guess if I thought it was just a dream, I wouldn't be so upset. I mean, I've had nightmares before, but this was different. Very different. Don't you think it could be more than just a dream?"

"Dade would probably say yes. He believes that supernatural things happen. As for myself, I don't completely discount that, but I don't know of any convincing evidence that a dream can be anything more than a dream. I don't think anyone really understands the human mind. Maybe no one ever will. We don't even know what goes on in our own subconsciousness, even though that's something that never stops functioning, even when we sleep. Sometimes people have nightmares because they're afraid of what may happen, or they feel guilt over something they've done or left undone. Sometimes because it takes time to fully face something horrific that we've seen. We don't want to face it in our waking moments, so we're forced to face it in nightmares until it no longer has any power over us. Sometimes we dream of things we miss, loved ones who have died, good friends. Sometimes we dream crazy impossible, bizarre dreams which seem to have no meaning at all.

"I think it's probably as simple as this: you're worried about Tom, and with good reason. All of our men at sea are in danger. And it's worse for those of us who are married to submariners. They're gone for two months at a time and we can't even write to them. The men on surface vessels send and receive mail on a regular basis. When our men go to sea, it's as if they've sailed off the edge of the earth. It's tough, for us and for them. Tom has been on three combat patrols and has come back each time. Picture him always coming back. I know that's not always possible. We all have our dark days. But there are only two things you can do for Tom. They're the same two things I can do for Dade. First, when you're with him, always make him know that everything is OK here, that you're alright and that you love him. If he goes to sea knowing that there's nothing for him to worry about back here, he'll be more effective on his job and more likely to survive. The second is pray. That's all we can do. Everything else is completely out of our control."

"Everything?"

"Yes. I'll make that hot chocolate now." Rachael got up and began to get a saucepan.

"Does it ever get any easier?"

"A little easier, but it's never easy."

"Why would I have that dream? Three nights in a row?"

"Because you're afraid."

"I guess I'm lucky to be working 60 hours a week. There's not much time to worry."

"Except at nights, including when you're asleep."

"Yes. I get so engrossed in my work that the time just seems to fly by. And Paul Duvall is a mathematical genius."

"So you've said, several times," Rachael smiled. "Look, a day off would still be good for you. I wasn't due to be going into work tomorrow anyway, because I have a complete physical scheduled for tomorrow morning. I hit my fifth month of pregnancy a few days ago, and my obstetrician wants to check a few things. Why don't you call in sick tomorrow? We can have lunch together downtown, take in the afternoon double feature at the Rialto, then you can join me for dinner back here. I can ask Maria to make a great Mexican meal. The two movies are *Citizen Kane* and *Buck Privates*."

"Call in sick? But what would I say?"

"Say that you were too tired to cook last night, so you ate at a small restaurant and you got food poisoning. That's good for a day. How long has it been since you had an unscheduled day off?"

"Never. Well, there's nothing that's absolutely critical on my desk right now."

"There you go!" Rachael said positively, "Maybe this recurring dream is your mind telling you that you need a little break. There's no sense in driving back to your place in this storm tonight. Stay in the guest room and call in from here in the morning."

"Thank you, Rachael. I don't know what I'd do without you."

"Let's have that hot chocolate now and speak of happier days to come. It won't be long before the *Sea Otter* is back in port."

50

December 20, 1942

Pacific Ocean

"Skipper," Oliver said, when he saw Bowie in the passageway, "do you have a few minutes?"

"Sure," Bowie replied, "come into my stateroom." A moment later, after both men were seated, Dade at his desk and Wirtz on his bunk, Oliver said, "I've been meaning to talk to you about this for some time now. I've been trying to find the right words, unsuccessfully actually, so I figured I may as well go ahead anyway."

"It sounds serious."

"First, I want to thank you for the way you've treated me. I know you didn't want me for your XO, and, of course we got off on the wrong foot with the Rosemary Brooks affair. But since then, you've taught me a lot and overlooked some rookie mistakes I made, and well, I feel good about being the XO of this boat. In fact, I feel proud to be the XO of this particular boat. I wasn't completely ready for combat. I mean, not for sailing into the Japanese Inland Sea and putting people ashore on Japan itself. Then, when you and Chief Robhar and Tom Detrick went ashore when the shit hit the fan, leaving me in command, I have to admit I was pretty scared and wondered if I could do what had to be done if that Japanese patrol boat had turned up before you and the others got back or if I could have successfully gotten the boat through the Japanese ships hunting us and back to the open sea by myself. I was so damned relieved when you came back aboard, hell, you can't even imagine it."

"Nobody's ever really prepared for combat, Ollie. I know I wasn't. I trained for years for it, but when it happened, it scared the hell out of me. It's never the way you think it's going to be."

"Does it get easier?"

"A little. When you've lived through a battle, you've proven to yourself that, no matter how bad it looks and no matter how scared you are, you *can* live through a battle, and that's a comfort. But you'll always be scared."

"I was hoping that wasn't the case."

"It would be a lot easier if, after a certain amount of combat, something clicked and you no longer had any fear, but it's enough to know that fear is something you've conquered before, so you can conquer it again. Besides, fear can make you fight pretty damned hard. The will to live is a powerful thing. A man who won't give up is a mighty adversary."

"Thanks, sir. That helps. I guess what I'm trying to say is that I want to thank you for giving me the opportunity and for helping me to become a better naval officer than I was before coming aboard the *Sea Otter*. I mean that."

"Experience is one of the best teachers. *I'm* a better naval officer than I was before coming aboard the *Sea Otter*. And I want you to know that, if you'd had to fight that patrol boat and make it back to the open sea on your own, I'm pretty damned sure you could have done it. You were ready for it. Otherwise I never would have left you in command. The way this war is going, it won't be all that long before you have your own boat. And when that happens, you'll do OK."

"Thank you, skipper. That means a lot to me."

"By the way, if it's not getting too personal, how have things been going with Rosemary Brooks?"

"Fine, sir. We made a pact to each write a letter a day, and we've been holding to it. Our letters are long ones and we've talked about everything in them. Our childhoods, our political and religious beliefs, our hopes for the future, everything. I really think we're right for each other. When we get back to port, I'll have about 45 letters from her waiting, and I'll be able to mail all the ones I've been writing every day during this patrol."

"That's great. She seemed like a very special person to me back at that party. I'm happy to hear that things are going so well. That son of yours and your parents—all in good health, I hope?"

"Yes, sir. As of the last letter I got from them. We just all miss each other."

"One day, all this will end. We can all hold onto that."

51

January 9, 1942

Pearl Harbor Naval Base

Everything was finally done. The crew had been warned in no uncertain terms that they were not free to discuss anything about this mission with anyone. That it was classified Top Secret. Bowie's patrol report had been typed up by his yeoman and given to a Marine armed courier who was to take it immediately to CINCPAC. The Nakamuras were the first people to leave the boat. They had been escorted by ONI personnel to a Navy staff car waiting at the pier and taken to a secret location. The men had received the mail that had been accumulating for them back at Pearl, and the traditional welcome feast of fresh fruit and ice cream was being enjoyed while they waited for the buses that would take most of them to the *Royal Hawaiian*. CINCPAC's chief of staff, Captain Elmer Cain, had come aboard briefly to congratulate Dade on a job well done and to tell him that he was to see Admiral Van Husen in his office at 0800 the following morning. Then the relief skipper and his XO had come aboard to go over the list of things that needed to be done while the boat was in port. Since she had sustained no battle damage, it was mostly a matter of fixing minor glitches and routine maintenance. Then finally, at long last, everything had been done and he was free until 0800 the next day. Normally CINCPAC didn't hold office hours on Sunday, but he had made an exception in this case.

With the crew gone, the Nakamuras gone, and Captain Cain gone, there was only the relief skipper and his XO aboard, going over the boat in detail with a clipboard and checklists. Dade felt an emptiness. He hefted the small bag containing the clothes he had worn while on the mission and his shaving gear, slung it over his shoulder, and went ashore. In the parking lot at the end of the pier, Dade took the scrap of paper with the bumper number of the jeep that had been assigned him during his time in port, found the vehicle, and sat down heavily behind the wheel. Suddenly, he was overcome with exhaustion. He sat there for a moment, trying to summon up enough energy to start the engine, but a whirling kaleidoscope of visions filled his mind. His talks with Will Jones, his seeing John Henry on deck delivering that chilling message, the firefight in the Nakamura compound, the narrow escape through the Inland Sea back to the open sea. He saw that arm again. The arm lying on the floor with the watch on it still ticking. He sighed deeply. He had almost bought the farm again. How much longer could his luck hold out? He gripped the steering wheel and squeezed it as hard as he could. Not long, he answered himself. Not as long as he was doomed to one combat patrol after another until the war was over. Both Harry and George were now dead and the war stretched out for years ahead. It didn't take a mathematical genius to compute Dade's odds.

But there was nothing he could do about it. Nothing. He could only do his best, but a lot of good men had done their best and were now on "Eternal Patrol." He had to live. He had to live for Rachael and the baby. And, admittedly, for himself. There were so many things he wanted to do. He was tired, so tired. He looked at his watch. It was 1604. He'd be home in time for supper. That would be good. A good meal, holding Rachael, a good night's sleep. Yes, he'd be OK. And he had nothing to worry about when it came to his meeting with CINCPAC tomorrow. He had accomplished the mission. No, everything was right with the world now. It was pointless, more than pointless, it was destructive to worry about the vague, unknowable future, about what would happen in the years to come. Rachael and her Stoic philosophers had taught him that. He smiled, started the engine, and put the jeep into gear.

Dade came through the front door, lay down his bag, and headed for the kitchen, where, his nose told him, there were both hot tamales and enchiladas. Maria was at the stove, and Rachael sat at the table. When she saw him, joy followed surprised disbelief. She rose and walked over rapidly. They embraced without a word. It was a long, tight embrace that seemed to last forever, but still not long enough. Finally, they parted, smiling at each other.

"You look familiar. Don't I know you from some place?" Dade asked.

"Could be. I've been around."

"Seems to me that you were thinner then."

"I was, but some sailor knocked me up. I don't know which one though. There've been so many. I suppose it could even have been you, but I don't recognize your face."

"That's OK, I'll grow on you." Dade glanced off to see Maria chuckling and shaking her head. Then Rachael beamed.

"I didn't expect you back so soon. Are you alright?"

"I'm alright. How about you? How about the baby? Is everything OK?"

"Oh, yes. Yes. When did you get in?"

"A few hours ago, but it took some time to get away."

"You must be hungry."

"And tired."

"Your timing is perfect. Maria was just about to put the food on the table."

"I smelled it. How about a cold beer to go with it?"

"I'll get you one."

Later, as they lay at last in bed, Rachael said, "Tell me all about it, from beginning to end."

He did, leaving nothing out, and she listened intensely. When he'd finished, she said nothing for a while before speaking. "Once again, I could easily have lost you forever. I hate this war. On one hand, I'm a little angry that you went ashore. No one would have blamed you for leaving when the OSS team failed to return. On the other hand, I'm proud of you for doing it."

"That's pretty much how I thought you'd feel about it. It just seemed that there was so much at stake that I felt I had to. Then again, maybe this man won't be of any assistance to our scientists and engineers at all and maybe his loss to the Japanese program won't be that big a deal. We have no way of knowing these things. The only thing we have to go on is what we're told by those who give us orders, and we know two things. Sometimes those people are wrong and sometimes they lie to us."

"Yes. It must have been terribly tempting to go after the *Susaki Maru*. That way, you know you would have accomplished something. Something very important. What made you change your mind when you were on the way to intercept her?"

Dade decided not to tell her about the appearance of John Henry. He knew that she didn't believe in ghosts. They had been all through that when he had kept seeing Ray Petro. Rachael believed that ghosts were the products of a person's mind. That they were dreams or hallucinations. Besides, even when John Henry had given him the warning, he still considered going ahead anyway. He wouldn't tell her that. That he had been ready to accept certain death to kill 3,000 Japanese troops en route to Guadalcanal. He was almost certain she'd understand. Most women would not. Most women in her position would have probably considered that a kind of desertion. Desertion of them and their unborn babies. If it hadn't been for his knowing that Rachael and the baby were financially set for life, he might not have considered a suicide run on the Japanese transport. But they *were* set. Bowie hadn't had to worry about that, so he felt free to do it. Rachael would have understood it if he explained it to her. He could tell her he thought of doing it even if it meant certain death because he would have been sacrificing his life so that they might live in a better world. He was almost certain she would understand. But he *wasn't* certain, so he said nothing for a while. "I just kept weighing the options, and I decided that the Nakamura mission was probably of greater importance," he finally said.

"Let's hope it was. Was any crew member injured?"

"Tom Detrick was. When we were ashore, he was wounded. A Japanese bullet grazed his arm. It wasn't serious though. I didn't even realize it happened until long after we got back to the *Sea Otter*."

"Which arm was it?"

"The left arm, why?"

"Just curious. He's OK?"

"Sure. We're all OK, except for those brave OSS guys. They were real heroes. In just the short time I knew him, I really got to like their leader, Will. I feel that I lost a good friend. You know how John Donne said, 'Any man's death diminishes me?'"

"Yes, 'because I am involved in Mankind; And therefore never send to know for whom the bell tolls; it tolls for thee.'"

"Well, I'm not at the stage where I feel that way about the death of every man. Maybe I never will feel that way, but I certainly feel that way about the deaths of those eight men. I sure hope that they didn't die in vain."

"So many people die in vain in every war, Dade. Throughout history. It's part of the nature of war. Futility. Meaningless suffering. Sheer stupidity. War is mostly insanity. Criminal insanity."

52

January 10, 1942

Pearl Harbor Naval Base

Clifford Van Husen looked across his large, highly polished desk at Dade Bowie with mixed emotions. This was the man that stood between him and the woman he wanted to possess more than any woman he had ever met. There was some undefinable thing about her that obsessed him. This was also the best submarine commander in the Pacific, a brave man, a Medal of Honor winner. Bowie probably didn't fully appreciate that, if Van Husen hadn't stopped that ridiculous Board of Inquiry in its tracks, Bowie's career, possibly his entire life, would have been ruined. There was little doubt Bowie and the other two sub skippers involved thought themselves ill used at the punishment he had handed out to them. Well, the other two men were dead already and Bowie would probably not last much longer. And Bowie himself knew that well. Perhaps, by this time, he had even become a fatalist. It would only be natural. Finally, CINCPAC spoke.

"I've read your report carefully, Bowie. You did an excellent job. Copies of your report were sent yesterday to the CNO, the OSS, the Army general heading up the project, and the White House. Half an hour ago, I received a phone call from the President's Naval Attaché. It's early afternoon their time. He said that the President told him to call me and say that the President was *extremely* happy with the success of Operation Buntline. *Extremely* happy and that I was to be commended for it. Therefore, I'm in a pretty expansive mood now, and more than willing to share some of the glory. I'm putting Robhar and Detrick in for the Silver Star, and, of course, Lieutenant Detrick will automatically get the Purple He art. I'm also going to make an exception to my diktat of several months ago when I said you would no longer receive any recognition for any valorous acts you might perform in the future. Using your initiative and displaying great courage, you snatched victory from the jaws of defeat by going ashore and rescuing the Nakamuras. Besides, if I decorated your men but not you, it would raise questions, and I don't want any questions. The mission was an unqualified success, so let's leave it at that. I'm putting you in for the Navy Cross."

"Thank you, sir."

"Of course, the citations will be somewhat vague, simply stating that you and your men displayed great valor in fierce combat with the Japanese during an operation classified Top Secret."

"I understand."

"You know, since I entered the Academy more years ago than I care to think about, I've made it my business to study successful military leaders. Not only the legendary ones, like John Paul Jones and David Farragut, but lower ranking officers, men no one has ever heard of, but who inspire their men in combat. I'm curious. Just what words of inspiration did you say to get those two men to volunteer to go ashore into Japan itself to join a firefight which our side appeared to be losing?"

"They didn't exactly volunteer, sir. I just picked my two best men and told them we were going."

"And they immediately and unhesitatingly replied, "Aye aye, sir," and followed you?"

"Yes sir."

"Why two men? Why not more?"

"There are two reasons, sir. First, although I had memorized the layout of the compound and the floorplan of the main house, and although I knew the OSS plan, there was no time to go over that with the men I took with me. About all I could do was tell them to follow me. That worked well with two men, but, with a group of men, in the dark, it would have been impractical. Second, there was a very good chance we wouldn't be coming back, and I wanted to limit the number of casualties."

"Those two men must have a hell of a lot of confidence in you."

"I guess so, sir."

"Well, I've never thought you were a bad leader, Bowie. You have your flaws, but being a bad leader is not one of them. Your men appear to respect you, and that's one of the most important things a leader must have. The respect of his men."

"Yes sir."

"You'll be interested to know that the Nakamuras are on a plane bound for the United States right now," CINCPAC said, as he looked at his watch. "In fact, they'll be landing at San Francisco in an hour."

"I just hope that man was worth it, sir. Worth the deaths of eight good men."

"So do I, although that's something we may never know."

"I do have a question for you, sir. Did the *Susaki Maru* make it to Guadalcanal?"

Van Husen's eyes narrowed. "What do you know about the *Susaki Maru*?"

"That it was bound for Guadalcanal with 3,000 seasoned Japanese troops who'd fought in China."

"And you know this how?"

"On the way to Japan, I had our radio operators give me the ULTRA messages sent to other subs, and I decoded them. That's how I also found out that the sub assigned the job of intercepting and sinking the troop transport wasn't able to do it due to damage it had taken. I was concerned, knowing how fierce the battle for Guadalcanal is, how hotly contested it is. I was afraid that 3,000 fresh experienced Japanese troops might give them a victory."

CINCPAC didn't answer immediately. Instead, he extracted a cigar from the humidor on his desk, clipped the end, and lit it. He settled back in his chair, and exhaled a plume of smoke. "The *Susaki Maru* made it to Guadalcanal. We tried to get some planes to intercept and destroy it, but they failed. They couldn't find it due to poor visibility. A storm was raging throughout the area. Two nights after the arrival of the fresh troops, the Japanese staged an all-out banzai attack on Henderson Field. They took enormous losses, and so did we. It was a very close thing. If the Japanese had succeeded, if we had lost Henderson Field, we might have lost the battle for the island, and it would have been a major setback in the larger battle for the Solomons. And a setback in the war, for that matter. Why do you ask?"

"Because I was sorely tempted to intercept it myself. We were close enough that we could have engaged it and its escorts and still made it to Japan in time for extracting the Nakamuras."

"First, you were given explicit instructions not to engage any enemy ships. Second, you could have been sunk by the escorts and therefore never made it to Japan."

"My thought was that a naval captain has a certain latitude in his orders if there are exigent circumstances. I know I could have sunk that troop transport. And, to be frank, sir, I couldn't be sure I could escape after doing that. To escort such an important cargo, I think that those tin can skippers and crews were probably tops at antisubmarine warfare, but I thought that, even if they nailed us, trading a sub for 3,000 crack Japanese soldiers was a pretty good trade. I figured it would save at least hundreds of Marines and soldiers, and, as I said, maybe even make the difference in the battle for the Solomons."

"But if you had been sunk you would not have accomplished your mission."

"I know, sir. But the chances were that I'd have accomplished an even more important mission. I wanted to contact you by radio to get your permission to do it, but, of course, we were under strict radio silence. I felt very strongly about this,

Admiral, so much so that I ordered a change in course to intercept the *Susaki Maru*."

"So you disobeyed my orders."

"No sir, if I had attacked the transport, I would have disobeyed orders. But, as we headed toward the intercept point, I realized that the mission we were given should take priority. It was a difficult decision, sir. I knew that, if that ship got through to Guadalcanal, many Americans would die, possibly needlessly if the Nakamura mission turned out to be a bust. Hell, our intelligence could have been wrong and maybe he wouldn't be there I thought. Or maybe we wouldn't be able to get him out. That almost happened. Or maybe he's so far behind our people, he can't contribute anything of value. That's very possible. Or he might refuse to cooperate. That's possible. Or maybe his loss won't slow the Japanese down because they have another guy who's just as smart. That's possible. It's the old bird in hand being worth two in the bush. But I decided to stay with the orders we'd been given. To tell the truth, I'm still not sure I did the right thing."

"Young man, you've got a hell of a lot of nerve telling me that. I guess you feel that your saving the mission singlehandedly by going ashore on Japan itself with only two other men to get Nakamura out confers upon you some kind of immunity from almost blowing the whole thing based on your own uninformed evaluation of the worth of the mission you were assigned. I guess you think that, since the mission was a success—due to your own initiative and valor—you're untouchable?"

"Sir, I'm just being absolutely honest with you. I *thought* about intercepting the troop transport, but I didn't. In the end, I followed orders and accomplished the mission. I just hope that it was worth it. Worth the 3,000 Japanese troops that got to Guadalcanal and worth the lives of that entire brave OSS team."

"As I said, we may never know if it was worth it," CINCPAC said softly. As Bowie had been speaking, Van Husen had appeared ready to erupt like a huge, angry volcano. But the moment had passed. He sat back in his chair, took a very deep drag from his cigar, and watched the smoke plume as he slowly exhaled. "We may never know. We lost men, many men, because that ship got through. We could have lost the island. It was a close thing.

"I don't have any real knowledge of what this big secret project is about. Few people do. In the end, it may come to nothing. In the end, it may have made more of a difference to the war effort to sink that transport. I can only follow orders, and, damn it, I wish you'd just follow orders without thinking about them. Last year, you nearly destroyed your career by disobeying orders. You and your two friends came damned close to a general court and a naval prison. I found out about that Board of Inquiry at the last minute and I stepped in and saved your sorry asses. You probably don't realize that. You probably think that I told you that you'd receive no more promotions, no more commendations, and that you'd be going on combat patrols for the rest of the war because I'm a mean, cruel, heartless

278

motherfucker. And I let you all think that because I really don't give a shit what men under my command think of me, especially the ones who have done something to piss me off. But, just because I'm in a good mood right now, I'm going to give you the benefit of my thoughts.

"First, the no more medals or commendations. Hell, you'd already been approved for the Medal of Honor, and your partners in crime already had Navy Crosses. Once a man has achieved that kind of recognition for valor, he doesn't really need anything else, does he? One of your pals was even having a Hollywood movie made about his exploits, with John Wayne playing him. So that was no loss. The only reason I'm putting you in for the Navy Cross now is because anyone reading that report knows you clearly deserve it and I don't want to have to explain why I didn't write you up for one. But you have all the glory you need already. So did your friends Romano and Pulaski. Besides, men like you don't fight for glory.

Second, the no promotions. You're already a commander. The only way you could get four stripes is to take a desk job, and a desk job is out for the next reason.

Third, the prospect of nothing but war patrols for the rest of the war. Let me put it this way. The two men you selected to go ashore with you in Japan. How did you select them? What were the criteria?"

"As I said, sir, I picked them because they're the best men in the crew. When the chips are down, you have to choose the best men."

"But they could easily have been killed or worse. Perhaps captured and tortured to death. Don't you have any feelings for these men?"

"As it happens, I do. I consider both of them to be friends."

"But you put them in grave danger without a second thought."

"Yes, but only because it was necessary. There was no choice."

"Exactly! Don't you see? That's exactly the reason why I kept sending you three out for the most dangerous missions in the most dangerous patrol areas! Because you always have to send your best men on the most important missions. That was no punishment I gave you three! I would have sent you out on patrol after patrol until you were either killed or the war ended even if there had been no Board of Inquiry! Don't you see it's the same thing as your selecting Robhar and Detrick to go ashore with you? Well, the comparison isn't exact, because you cared about those men, while I don't give a damn about you or the rest of my sub commanders. That didn't sound quite right. What I meant was that I have no emotional attachment."

"But sir, men, all men have limits. There's only so much stress that a man can take before he becomes less alert, less capable of sound judgment in life or death situations. It happens with combat troops in the Army and the Marines, and it happens with naval personnel too. It happened to me. That's why Admiral Onets relieved me of command of the *Elver*."

"Yes, yes, I'm aware of that. But the doctors at the base hospital said that, given a month or two out of combat, three meals a day, and plenty of rest and exercise, you'd be right as rain again. And, quite obviously, they were correct! You come back from new construction, and, on your very first mission, prove that you still have what it takes!"

"So it's your intention, as a policy for the duration of the war, to just take your best submariners and keep using them in the most dangerous missions, patrol after patrol, until you've, in effect, used them up? That doesn't sound fair to me, Admiral."

"What's the alternative? To use less competent, less courageous men, to perform the most important missions? That's ridiculous! By your own admission, you have to use your best men in the most dangerous situations."

"Is this your policy for the skippers on surface vessels? For the Marines?"

"No. For the most part, this only applies to submarines. Submarines are different, Bowie. For the first six months of the war, the submarines were the only tool I had with which I could take the battle to the Japanese. Rebuilding the Pacific Fleet made our victory at Midway possible, and now we have more tools in our tool box, but submarines remain our most potent weapon. I can't afford to fuck around with our submarines. Without them, at least for the foreseeable future, we're screwed. I need as many subs as I can get, and I need to have them commanded by my best skippers. What's the alternative?"

"Sir, it's not as if your pool of men never changes. It's increasing all the time. The Sub School is graduating qualified men at a faster pace than ever."

"Yes, but they're all unproven."

"Give them a chance to prove themselves."

CINCPAC sighed deeply in frustration, and took another long, thoughtful drag on his cigar before answering. "How many years have you spent in submarines, Commander Bowie?"

"I graduated from Sub School in December 1934, so it's been over eight years now."

"And before that?"

"I spent two years on the *U.S.S. Arizona*."

"And you've been at war since December 7th. In fact, as I recall from your personnel jacket, you were wounded that day, right here in the harbor, trying to shoot down Japanese aircraft. You've sunk a large number of enemy ships, including two aircraft carriers, and have proven yourself time after time in combat. So just where do I go to find a man with your experience for patrolling in the most dangerous areas or for the most important special missions?"

"Most of those men are now dead, sir. Killed in combat. Soon you won't have anyone except unexperienced and unproven men. You see, when a sub goes down to crush depth, it takes with it, not only its skipper, but the other officers whom the skipper has been grooming for their own commands. His XO, and the rest of the wardroom. They're all gone. If the *Sea Otter* goes down, along with me go two of the officers who were with me on the *Elver*, along with five other very valuable enlisted men who were also on the *Elver*. Sir, you can't keep playing only your first string, especially when they're being killed off, one by one."

"'First string.' That's an entirely invalid comparison. This is war, not a fucking football game. Men die in war. A lot of them. And my job is to send men off, knowing that many of them will never return. It's also my job to win this war, and, by damn, I will. I'll do whatever it takes to win this war in the Pacific. That may mean 200,000 dead American soldiers, sailors, and Marines, or maybe even more before this is finished, but I will do whatever I have to. That doesn't mean I'm some kind of monster, son. I don't like seeing my fellow countrymen die, and I'm not unsympathetic to the families they leave behind. After all, I *am* human. But I *will* do my job."

"Sir, with all due respect, don't you find it somewhat ironic that the sub skippers who lack the aggressiveness or skill or willingness to take risks are, in effect, *rewarded* by being given the safer patrol areas, while the best skippers are penalized by being given the most dangerous?"

"We've just been through this. I have my reasons, logical, pragmatic reasons. Look, I think I know what goes through your mind and the minds of the other best skippers from time to time. Why not become less aggressive, less inclined to take risks, and have poor or mediocre patrol results? From time to time, I'm sure that idea has occurred to you and some of the others. It's only natural."

Dade said nothing.

"But that doesn't bother me at all. I didn't get to wear four stars on my collars by being a bad judge of men. In fact, I'm an excellent judge of men. I know your type, Commander Bowie. You and men like you may have fleeting thoughts like that, but they come and go in seconds. You won't do anything less than your best. You not only do your duty, but you go above and beyond it. You always have and you always will. Would you like to know why?"

Bowie could only give a slight nod.

"It's because, at some point very early in your life, you looked at yourself and didn't much like what you saw. So, you set a goal, found a purpose, a noble cause to which you could devote your life. Most men seek meaning to life. You decided to protect and defend the Constitution of the United States. You set for yourself the goal of being not just a good naval officer, but a perfect one. An expert in his field, a great leader, a man of indomitable courage and honor. And, when you got to Annapolis, those goals were nurtured and encouraged. You were immersed in U.S. naval history and its heroes. You became a true believer. You believe that your honor is more important than your life. You have to continually prove to yourself that you are what you've always hoped to be. Romano and Pulaski were the same way. I don't have to worry about men like you slacking off. You'd hate yourselves if you did and you know it. Though men like you may dislike or even detest me, even though you may be angry at what you perceive to be unfairness — you said you were *penalized* for your successes—I know that I can always count on you," Van Husen said with a smug smile.

"You chose a naval career too, sir. Aren't you a true believer?"

"I am a true believer in the Constitution of the United States, and I believe our cause to be noble. I always wanted to be an excellent naval officer. I served my share of sea duty, but I have never been in combat. If I'd had to serve in combat, I would have, of course, and I would have done my best. But it never happened, and I am not disappointed about that. You see, I never had set being a hero as one of my life's goals. A true believer, as I use the term, wants war so he can have the opportunity to become a hero. Me, I've just been content to be an administrator. Now that war has come, my role has become remarkably more complex and challenging, and I do my very best. I take pride in doing my very best. I put in as many as 12 hours a day, every day, and sometimes more."

"I appreciate your sharing your thoughts with me, sir. I know you're a busy man. What you said about me, about 'true believers.' I don't know. Perhaps you're right. After preparing to fight a war since age 18, I must admit that sometimes I wanted it to come. And yes, like many other men, I've entertained fantasies about becoming a hero."

"And you've done it."

"Right now, all I want is for the war to end. When war is a fantasy, it does no harm, but when it becomes a reality, you see how gruesome, how horrible, what an unspeakable evil it is. I've hated the war for months now, and even when I was out of it for a few months in new construction, I read about all the civilian suffering in Europe. The death and dismemberment of innocent people is one thing, but when you can lose both your home and workplace in a single bombing attack, that's terrible too. Yes, you can count on me. I could never do less than my best on patrol. I owe it to my country, my family, and my crew."

"I'm glad we had this little talk, Commander Bowie. Perhaps we both learned a little."

"Yes, sir. Thank you." Dade rose to leave. Before he reached the door, Van Husen spoke again, and Dade turned to face him. "As you know, your wife has been an informal advisor to me on Japanese customs, beliefs, history, and psychology. I have developed a great respect for her opinion on various matters. It would be most regrettable if she were to become a widow."

"My feelings exactly, sir," Dade said, then turned and left.

Rachael was waiting for Dade on the lanai. She smiled as he approached. "How did it go?"

"Alright, I suppose. I'm getting a Navy Cross and Armond and Tom are getting Silver Stars. And, of course, Tom is getting a Purple Heart. Van Husen was in a great mood over a call from the White House expressing FDR's 'extreme' happiness over the successful completion of the mission. He felt so good he even had an actual conversation with me."

"A friendly conversation?"

"No, not especially friendly, just him expressing his opinions. It's difficult to like him, but I guess he's good at his job."

"I'm in no position to evaluate how good he is at his job. At military strategy, I mean. As a man, well, at first, I thought he was a very well educated, highly intelligent man who was also very complex. Now, after advising him on and off for a year, except for the time we were back in the States, I've realized that, after you peel away the various surface layers, he's not complex at all. After you peel back the layers, you find only one thing—appetite. A raging, monumental appetite."

"An appetite for what?"

"For power, status, women, money—the usual things a narcissistic man wants. The things that he thinks will give him pleasure." Rachael knew that if she told Dade about Van Husen's propositioning her early last year, he'd be disturbed. That was when Van Husen told her of his ambition to become President of the United States a couple of years after the war. "What do you think of him?"

"I think he's amoral."

Rachael laughed. "That's perhaps the best one-word description of him. Still, that doesn't necessarily mean that he can't be an effective CINCPAC. Many key people in history have had major flaws, including character flaws."

"I suppose so."

They sat in a comfortable, companionable silence for a while. "We have 13 days before I go out on patrol again. I'll have to check in with the relief skipper from time to time, see Admiral Onets and the squadron commander, and the usual stuff, but we'll pretty much have most of the time to ourselves. We can go on picnics, go to the beach, sleep in, work on lists of names for the baby, see some movies, and just talk."

"Sounds wonderful."

"We can also figure out what to do with our fortune once the war is over."

"The more I think about it, the more I think I'd like to stay in Hawaii. It's just choosing which island that might be difficult."

"But we have plenty of time."

"That we do. By the time the war is over, we might have a couple of kids."

"Or three."

"Don't be so pessimistic."

"I was just kidding. It'll be over by the time the second kid arrives."

"That's more like it.

It was a sunny day, but Rachael needed the sweater she was wearing to be comfortable, and Dade was wearing his dress blues. "You look really handsome in that uniform. I especially like the top ribbon." She pointed to the pale blue ribbon with five stars.

"Thanks, you look pretty good yourself."

"What have you been smiling to yourself about for the last few minutes?"

"I've been thinking that I never thought I could ever be this happy."

"With a war going on and God knows how many patrols ahead?"

"Yes. Even with all that. When we're together, like now, I'm very, very happy, and when I'm on patrol, I'm happy knowing you're waiting for me here."

Rachael smiled tenderly. "I'll always be waiting here for you, Dade."

If you enjoyed this book, I'd greatly appreciate it if you'd take a moment and write a short review on Amazon. This sequel was written in response to a number of readers who expressed an interest in one, and I thank you for your interest. As you can see, there's still a lot of war ahead until the Japanese surrender in 1945. Dade and Rachael will continue fighting the war in the Pacific in subsequent books in this five-book series.

Made in the USA
Monee, IL
07 November 2020